SHADOWS OF THE SHORT DAYS

SHADOWS OF THE SHORT DAYS

Alexander Dan Vilhjálmsson

GOLLANCZ
LONDON

First published in Great Britain in 2019 by Gollancz
an imprint of The Orion Publishing Group Ltd
Carmelite House, 50 Victoria Embankment
London EC4Y 0DZ

An Hachette UK Company

1 3 5 7 9 10 8 6 4 2

A CIP catalogue record for this book is
available from the British Library.

ISBN (Hardback) 978 1 473 22410 0
ISBN (Export Trade Paperback) 978 1 473 22411 7
ISBN (eBook) 978 1 473 22413 1

Typeset at The Spartan Press Ltd,
Lymington, Hants

Printed and bound in Great Britain by Clays Ltd,
Elcograf S.p.A.

www.orionbooks.co.uk

For Rakel

Contents

SHADOWS OF THE SHORT DAYS

The split church tower of Haraldskirkja reigns proudly over Reykjavík, a splendid monument to the holy royal lineage of Kalmar. Even on this remote northern island, the divine might of the king's bloodline manifests itself.

A Kalmar Commonwealth
Citizen's Primer to Hrímlandic

So you have found yourself on the very edge of the Commonwealth, away from familiar sights and comforting languages, stranded on a sorcerous island and surrounded by unwelcoming faces speaking a savage tongue that seems to have avoided the passing of time and ignored progress. Welcome to Hrímland, traveller.

This short primer will aim to assist the newly arrived citizen of the Kalmar Commonwealth in their attempts to make sense of this archaic tongue and the peculiar peoples that eke out a living on the edge of the known world.

Regarding Orthography & Pronunciation

Hrímlandic is an old language, believed to be largely unchanged since times of settlement approximately a millennium ago, due to the island's extreme isolation from the civilised world. Academics believe that Hrímlandic's vocabulary and pronunciation is derived from the old Nordic as well as a significant Gaelic influence. This combination, when left alone for centuries, has resulted in the language currently assaulting your ears and eyes. But do not be dissuaded, this primer will help you decipher and master this inbred linguistic beast.

Alphabet

Hrímlandic special characters that might seem wholly unfamiliar are: Æ/æ, Ð/ð, Þ/þ. Some more familiar variations of vowels are: Í/í, Ý/ý, Ú/ú, É/é. Hrímlandic also uses special diphthongs, such as *au* and *ei/ey*. An accent over the vowels does not indicate that they are stressed; the stress is always on the first syllable in Hrímlandic. They are different sounds from unaccented vowels.

Vowels

Following is a list of the Hrímlandic vowels, including an accurate phonetic transcription for the diligent students reading this, along with a few examples which attempt to approximate the sounds in question. Note that the examples from other languages are usually not completely accurate, only an indication of the pronunciation.

A a [a] is pronounced as in 'alphabet' and 'bar'.
Á á [au] as in 'found' and 'loud'.
E e [ɛ] as in 'bed' and 'head'.
I i [ɪ] as in 'inside' and 'inn'.
Í í [i] is an 'ee' sound, as in 'eerie' and 'fully'.
O o [ɔ] is pronounced as 'o' in 'bore' and 'bolt'.
Ó ó [ou] as in 'sole' and 'go'.
U u [ʏ] is an unfamiliar vowel to the Kalmar speaker, who might

have to look to foreign languages. 'Über' has a similar u-sound, also 'cul' (as in cul-de-sac).

Ú ú [u] is an 'oo' sound, as in 'zoo'.

Æ æ [ai] as in 'I', 'life' and 'bye'.

Ö ö [œ] as in 'u' from 'urgent', 'fur', 'thunder'; 'i' from 'bird'.

Au [œi] = A diphthong made from the Hrímlandic sounds for Ö and Í, so effectively the 'uh'-sound from 'thunder' combined with 'ee' from 'see'.

Ei/ey [ei] = As in 'stay'.

Th- sounds

Ð/ð is not, as many Kalmar citizens assume, a 'funny shaped o', but instead considered to be a 'funny shaped d' by Hrímlanders. It has a soft 'th' sound, as in the words 'feather' and 'that'. Ð is never found at the beginning of words.

Þ/þ is not a variety of 'p'. It has a very similar 'th' sound to 'Ð', but considerably stronger, as in 'think' and 'thorn'. It is never at the end of words.

Hr- /Hl- sounds / Voiceless sounds

The first sounds in words like 'Hrímland' and 'hljóð' are not found in many languages. They can sound rather strange and can be hard to pronounce for a foreign speaker. The spelling can indicate that these words begin with an h-sound, but the first sound is in fact an unvoiced variety of the following sound, in these words a voiceless 'r' and 'l'. These voiceless varieties could be described as a combination of 'h', which is a voiceless sound, and 'r' or 'l'. Instead of using the vocal cords, as when pronouncing the voiced varieties of these sounds, one must try to pronounce 'h' at the same time as pronouncing 'r' and 'l' in order to reach the correct pronunciation. The tongue is placed to pronounce 'r' and 'l' while 'h' is produced. These sounds are rather common in Hrímlandic pronunciation, as you can see in the glossary list. Hrímlandic also contains voiceless varieties of 'm' and 'n' which can be found in certain words, such as 'seiðmagn' and 'stiftamtmaður'.

General notes

Only a limited number of Hrímlanders have family names. Usually these are people of a higher class than others, but this is not a formal rule by any means. Most humans in Hrímland follow the ancient tradition of deriving their last name from the first name of their fathers. A woman called Bríet Bjarnhéðinsdóttir has the first name Bríet and is Bjarnhéðinsdóttir (the daughter of a man named Bjarnhéðinn). If a man is called Ingólfur Arnarsson his first name is Ingólfur and he is Arnarsson (son of Arnar). In these examples, the patronyms Arnarsson and Bjarnhéðinsdóttir are not names as such and are never used to refer to someone. As such, Hrímlanders are almost always addressed by their first names, regardless of their formal or informal station in society, and there are no polite forms of address which use the patronymic alone. Other peoples, such as the huldufólk, have adopted this naming convention.

I and Y share the same pronunciation, as do Í and Ý.

The HV- sound is pronounced as KV.

The double LL- sound gives Kalmar citizens considerable trouble. The sound is pronounced like 'dl' or 'tl', with a flattened tongue and a slight click. It is sometimes pronounced as a long L-sound in certain words.

R always has a trilled pronunciation.

If unable to type in the Hrímlandic letters, then they can be substituted as follows:

Ð/ð = D/d
Þ/þ = Th/th
Æ/æ = Ae/ae

A full glossary can be found at the end of this book.

I

Island

One of the most disturbing variants of Hrímlandic galdur, the tilberi is a vile creature of darkness. This servant will do its master's bidding, without soul or conscience to question its purpose.

Eitt

Garún removed her mask and stepped away from the wet graffiti to see clearly the whole of the hex sigil she'd painted. It was difficult breathing through the filters on the leather mask and it felt good to taste the fresh air. It was dark, the only light coming from the pale moon that sat low in the sky. She relied on insight and feeling when she painted, so the dark didn't bother her. She didn't need to see to know if the graffiti was good or when it was ready. She simply felt it, but it was a raw feeling. She wanted to be sure, so she slipped the goggles over her eyes in order to see the sorcerous seiðmagn bleeding from the paint.

Sharp geometries jutted out unexpectedly from the red and obscure graffiti, and even though the paint wasn't dry yet the seiðmagn already radiated powerfully into the environment. Exhausted from the work, Garún felt dried up after using so much delýsíð paint in such a short time. While she painted, the emotions expressed within her art were amplified by the delýsíð in the paint and cast back to her in a vicious psychedelic cycle: she was the snake that fed on itself. Now, it was complete. Garún turned down the volume of the electronic music booming in her ears and focused on letting the painting speak to her.

The graffiti was in a good location atop the store Krambúðin and with luck it would be weeks until it was discovered. All the while it would continue to bleed seiðmagn into the environment, where it would infiltrate the subconscious of those nearby. It would slowly infect their minds and sow the seeds of discord. If left undisturbed, the painting would become as a death mask over the building and its neighbourhood.

Krambúðin was a store owned by Sigurður Thorvaldsen, a merchant who ran several enterprises in the greater Reykjavík area. The one below Garún's feet had become one of the most popular colonial stores in the city since Sigurður had moved to Reykjavík and set up shop almost the same day as the occupation of the Crown began. Not for the soldiers, but for all the people from the countryside flooding to the city to work for the army. The Crown needed a large working force, especially to build the forts in Viðey and the barracks on Seltjarnarnes. Sigurður had pushed those out who threatened his business, threatening, blackmailing and maiming – but, above all, profiting. By the time occupation became colonisation and the forts of the colonial masters were built, Sigurður Thorvaldsen had become a wealthy man and Reykjavík a fully grown city.

The graffiti Garún had sprayed on the roof was an antiprosperity hex. It was intended to drive away the establishment's elite customers who prized Krambúðin's imported luxury products. Exotic spices, delicate fabrics, handmade soaps, candies and perfumes were only a small fraction of the merchandise available. Those who did not subconsciously avoid the store would become victims of the hex. Pushy customers would argue with the staff, who in turn would be unhelpful and patronising. With luck the influence would spread over the whole street as the graffiti fed on the people's negative emotions and spewed them back out. She hoped that it would be able to remain unharassed for longer than her other work, which had all been found within a few days.

She took the spray cans and the painting mask and stuffed them into her backpack along with the goggles. Before climbing down from the roof she double-checked that she'd left no empty cans behind. She slid down the fire-escape ladder in the back and turned up the volume again. It was calm and slow, the bass steady and comforting, telling her that nobody was around, nobody was watching. She ran silently through empty yards, vaulted over the fences in her path. The beat became faster the closer she got to the Hverfisgata Road and the stressed rhythm hinted that the police might not be far down the street. She weaved through alleys and backyards alongside Hverfisgata's busy road. The evening traffic had barely started to trickle downtown. Sudden breaks and booming basslines told her if someone was about to cross her path or about to look out of their window, and she reacted instinctively, ducking into cover and waiting for the threat to pass. She could never be absolutely sure that she had not been seen, and often it was hard to read the music, but after endless practice it had become almost second nature, a part of her natural reflex. She let go and let the music speak to her subconscious.

The closer she got to Hlemmur the more uneasy the music grew. Patrol automobiles were lined up in front of the police station, which was fused with the central station like a tumour grown outside a body. The beat was thick and murky, the music absolutely deafening. She turned down the volume so it was barely audible, pulled her hoodie up and tried not to think about what would happen if she was stopped for a random search.

The central station was home for those who had nowhere else to go. Hobos, junkies, a few blendingar. She made sure not to glance towards them as she felt them notice her walking past. As if they resented her for not sitting with them in the gutter. Policemen stood by the ticket booth and gates, docile but formidable. She tried to keep a low profile, but without it being suspicious. Just as would be expected from a blendingur like her.

She took the train to Starholt. Most working people had got home by now and the nightlife didn't pick up until after midnight, so the train was relatively empty. The city lights took on a blurred halo in the grimy windows.

ᚠ

No one greeted her when she came home. She missed Mæja. What was she thinking, leaving the cat with Sæmundur? He could barely take care of himself, let alone a cat. She was unsure what her intention had been, exactly. She'd wanted him to feel guilt or remorse, or anything at all, there at the end. But he had been simply too numb and now her little cat was probably starved to death underneath worm-eaten manuscripts and dirty socks. One more thing she tried not to think about.

Her studio flat was a bedroom, kitchen, working area and living room simultaneously. The sink was filled with paintbrushes and squeezed paint tubes were found on almost every surface. Half-completed paintings were scattered around in stacks leaning against the walls. The air smelled of paint, oil, acrylics and spray mixed in with a faint, sour reek of delýsíð. It was probably good that she was rid of Mæja. The cat would have been long dead from all the toxic chemicals in the air.

Garún took off her large headphones and removed the audioskull from the backpack. Sæmundur had summoned the noisefiend himself and bound it into the skull when she'd started to tag small, powerful delýsíð staves here and there. Wires stuck out of the bare headphones, an old operator's headset she had converted. She had always meant to make a casing from wood or brass, but had never got around to it. The headphones were plugged into the forehead of the audioskull. The skull had a blue shade to it, covered in runes and esoteric symbols coloured a dark red. It was both illegal and dangerous to summon demons, but Sæmundur never cared about risks. She'd got a used portable transistor radio cheap and had been listening to it on the go, carrying it around in her backpack. That's what had given him the idea. Transmundane beings were incredibly dangerous even when bound in bone, and Garún had absolutely lost it when he gave her the skull. Still, she had used it.

She took off the black clothes and emptied her backpack. She hid the clothes, along with the backpack and audioskull, under a loose board in the closet. Inside there was a hidden compartment where she put the nearly empty delýsíð spray cans. She was practically out, and she needed more. She'd gone tagging a bit too frequently these last weeks, excited for the upcoming protest they had planned. She would have to get more. The bright and unnatural colours had stained her fingers. She turned on the shower and washed her hands with strong and coarse soap before stepping in. The water smelled faintly of sulphur, a familiar and soothing feeling.

After the shower she dried off with a towel and wrapped it around her head to dry her shoulder-length hair. She stirred a raw egg into skyr and read a book while she ate. The book had come free from a nearby café; many of the coffee houses in Starholt had various kinds of free shops and trade markets. Many of the local residents were artists and it aided them in their never-ending pursuit of inspiration and materials. Almost a century had passed since the book was written, long before the occupation by the Crown. The novel was about a huldukona who wanted to become a poet, but her poems were rejected by the Hrímlanders because of who she was. Because of *what* she was. All her life was one long struggle. The book was a handmade reprint some decades old. It was singed and burned and many pages had been ripped out of it. There still remained some readable parts and Garún devoured them. She'd never found a novel about huldufólk before.

When she finished eating she wrapped the towel around herself, sat out on the balcony and rolled a cigarette. Just a bit too tight, so she had to work her lungs to inhale the livid smoke. Winter had begun smothering autumn and the evening dark was sharp and deep. The apartment buildings surrounded a playground where a few children played in an old wooden play castle that had once been multicoloured, but the paint had peeled off long ago. No one was monitoring them. Late as it was, this was a common sight. She looked over to the other balconies. Clean laundry hung out to dry on taut clothes lines everywhere, among the junk that artists and collectors had gathered: old fishing nets, rusted iron and driftwood, sheets of corrugated iron and other garbage that was a gleaming treasure in some eyes.

Garún threw the butt over the balcony and went inside. She had to get more delýsíð spray paint. Viður would hook her up. She put on a pair of old jeans and a plain black top, grabbed a moss green coat on the way out. She took her time walking to the central area of Starholt, the epicentre where the artistic types and other ideological outcasts, self-declared or not, met each night with the common goal of gossip, flattery, drink and dope in various degrees. As she got closer to the heart of it all, the neighbourhood came to life. Massive cement towers gave way to lower, friendlier houses. Electric lamps with stained glass lit up the streets, twisted modern sculptures that were a welcome change from the Crown's uniform standard issue lamps everywhere else in the city.

Gangs of náskárar sat on eaves over dark alleyways, selling drugs. They were adorned with markings of their tribe, all of them warriors with iron claws or beaks. Bright laughter moved through the crowd like an infectious cough and occasionally glasses of beer shattered. Huldufólk and humans hung together in separate groups outside bars and clubs.

The huldufólk's attitude towards her was reserved when she walked past them, all of them reflexively reaching out to see who was there. Garún barely noticed, having grown used to shutting it out long ago. Not that humans considered her an equal either – on the contrary – but some huldufólk had a vicious way of upholding what they considered the old ways, and she served as an offensive reminder to them of how far they had fallen.

She shook off these thoughts and lit another cigarette to clear her head. Those strangers didn't matter. She had found her own people. And above all, she had herself.

Tvö

Sæmundur reached out on the floor and fumbled around for the carved wooden pipe. He tapped last night's ashes out of it and stuffed it with moss, finishing the rest of what he had. Started the day with a smoke, as usual.

Sometimes he woke up and thought for a moment that she was lying next to him. Between waking and sleeping his mind and body reached out for her. The sting of waking up alone didn't seem to be fading. If anything, it had grown to reach deeper with time.

Mæja climbed on top of him and purred loudly. He petted her and somehow she managed to purr even louder. His mind wandered to Garún and he thought about what she was doing now. She had left the cat behind and it only reminded him of her. He pushed the cat off his torso.

He stretched out in the bed and smoked, scratched his balls. It was time. A big task to do today. He couldn't reschedule the hearing again.

When he finished the pipe he sat up, sniffed his clothes and found those that stank the least. It took him a long while to get dressed properly. The moss was starting to work and rippled the waters of his mind. Next to the mattress was a bass amplifier that served as a nightstand, desk and dining table. Half-empty beer bottles, an ashtray, notebooks and dirty plates were stacked on top of the amplifier. Sæmundur turned it on and lit a badly rolled cigarette. He picked up the bass from the floor and tuned it, started playing.

The room vibrated with music. He felt the way each object echoed the sound and warped it through itself, how his body fell in tune. He stretched the note, drew it deeper and the world sank into the deep with him. He sang along, preparing the galdur incantation in his mind.

He started chanting. Each syllable had its tone, which was amplified in the pounding bassline. The light faded, becoming grey and pale as it retreated slowly. The incantation grew stronger and clearer, the notes of the bass heavier, and the room appeared to bend under the pressure of sound. Dirty clothes, which lay scattered about on the floor, trembled like a wild growth and began moving in a convulsive dance around the mattress. Sæmundur sang louder and louder. He warped and stretched each sound that came from him, rode the chaos of galdur and gave it form, reined it in.

He drew these sounds inside himself, into his voice and the bass, then transmuted them and locked them into the incantation, bound them with rhythm and words of power. Everything sounded with transformation. Drenched with galdur, the rags on the floor crawled into small piles that slid together into a single mass of clothing in front of him. The melody grew stronger, the beat faster, and the dirty laundry rose up and shaped itself. Shirtsleeves and dirty socks became jutting limbs that grew erratically from the central body. Sæmundur stopped playing, handed the creature a wad of crumpled bills and commanded with a strong voice:

'Go to Rotsvelgur. Buy moss. Return.'

Immediately the thing collapsed and rolled out towards the

window. Underwear, shirts, jackets and jeans, stretched up to the window ledge and pulled themselves up. Woollen socks and hoodie sleeves grabbed the ledge and the creature rolled itself out of the window.

Sæmundur threw himself back on to the mattress. He felt as if he was coming undone from the reverberation of the world's composition.

ᚠ

Sæmundur slept while the highland moss wore off. He dozed on his mattress in a fugue and didn't come around until noon had passed and the cloth-golem returned. Rotsvelgur had put a rat's tail in the bag with the moss, a sign that this was his last chance – it was time he paid his dues. A problem for another day. Sæmundur commanded the filthy pile of clothes to go and wash themselves in the laundry room. He really should have done that yesterday, he thought. The hearing was today, after all.

He moved to the kitchen and prepared a simple breakfast. Oatmeal and a few slices of liver sausage. While he ate he scanned through a yellowed manuscript, one of the countless documents that lay scattered around the apartment. Bruise-coloured patterns and symbols decorated the page and even though Sæmundur could read the ancient scribble well, his mind couldn't stick to it.

No one could use galdur like he did. The cloth-golem made that obvious. It never occurred to anyone to make a golem any way other than with the traditional methods, which Sæmundur found preposterous. *Cowards.* All he had done was combine the foreign tradition of golem-making with a Hrímlandic svartigaldur – the thieving tilberi. To properly fuse them together one needed not only the exact esoteric language, but a new cadence, a new rhythm, which belonged to both incantations equally.

He had looked outside academia to find the methodology to combine these two incantations: music. It was very risky, yet he'd made incredible progress.

Still – it wasn't enough. Not for Sæmundur. He still couldn't comprehend the source of galdur's power or how it worked. But he was closer. He just had to risk pushing the limits a little bit further.

But he'd get nowhere without Svartiskóli.

After Sæmundur's expulsion from the university he had discovered a remarkable wellspring of ambition within himself. He'd dived head first into his independent studies, inspired by a sense of liberation from the dogma and distractions of the university's overbearing bureaucracy. He'd used all his available resources to get the manuscripts he needed for his research, or at least copies of them.

Then he'd reached a dead end and with no favours left to call in, nor allies to lean on, he'd made no progress for weeks. Admittedly, he had learned something before getting stuck, but it wasn't nearly enough. He had to get back into Svartiskóli.

Sæmundur had studied galdur at the Royal University of Reykjavík. The School of Supernatural Sciences was housed in a special building, called Svartiskóli after the Hrímlandic school of old. Svartiskóli was split into two faculties: seiður and galdur. To the public these two were basically interchangeable; sorcery was sorcery, no matter what you called it. But that was not the case within the walls of Svartiskóli.

It was once believed that seiður transcended human under-standing; that it was an unpredictable and esoteric force, which did not abide by the rules of the natural sciences. This force was found in certain places of power, where seiðskrattar drew seiðmagn from the land like water from a well and used it for supernatural works. Few such places remained in the world.

And where seiðmagn could be found in sufficient quantities, the energy source was violent and primal. Hrímland, mostly the highlands, was such a source for seiðmagn, but had been considered too dangerous and unworkable up until a few decades earlier, when Vésteinn Alrúnarson stepped forward with his theories on seiður and built the first sorcerous power plant on the forested hill of Öskjuhlíð. The esoteric rituals of seiður became supernatural science. Seiður became a force of supernature that could be understood, controlled and harnessed.

Galdur was fundamentally different; it could not be drawn from nature like seiður. Unlike its supernatural cousin, the force that powered galdur was unmeasurable and unknowable. It did not belong to this world. All you needed to use galdur was the right incantation and words of power, an uncomfortably low threshold for the dabbling kuklari – the slightest error could result in terrible consequences. If a slight warping in pronunciation or the smallest syntax error crept into the incantation then the effects were unpredictable. Many galdramenn had doomed themselves because of a simple mistake or a lack of precision. When rituals of galdur took a turn for the worse, demons tainted the bones of the unsuspecting galdramaður, sometimes resulting in their becoming possessed. The threat of the demonic was always there, even in the most innocent galdur. This fact resulted in a strict ban on experimentation and research in galdur at the university. Only studying tried and true rituals and maintaining an age-old tradition was permitted. That was the only way to be safe from the devouring outer dimensions.

Naturally, this core edict was what Sæmundur had set his sights on bringing down.

From the beginning, his questionable theories turned the whole of academia against him. He had dangerous theories on the true nature of galdur and wanted desperately to find out what really made it work through the use of the ultimate taboo – experimentation. He wanted to unspool the thread of words and incantations and get into direct contact with their primal, chaotic source.

In Svartiskóli this was considered borderline heresy by any stretch of the imagination. It bordered on treason to bring up such blatantly dangerous ideas. His fellow students nicknamed him Sæmundur óði – Sæmundur the Mad – and soon he heard even his lecturers use it. They flunked every critical essay, every thesis he put forward. Even the most menial assignments were scrutinised and rejected if he drifted ever so slightly from the established canon. They made it clear he was a deranged outcast who had no business in an institution of higher learning.

It had been several months since his expulsion. The first thing he did was demand a hearing, but when the assigned date drew closer he kept on postponing it. As much as he resented himself for it, Sæmundur couldn't help but be afraid. Afraid of rejection, afraid of feeling powerless and helpless at the mercy of the institution he both despised and loved for being the only venue for his academic ambition. But now he couldn't run away from it.

He'd finished eating and realised that he was reading through an entirely wrong manuscript. It didn't matter, it was all there. All the knowledge he'd gathered was clear and organised in his mind, all neatly lined up to back up the false, dishonest argument to reassure the committee and allow him to be readmitted.

Today Sæmundur would disown his previous theories entirely and pay lip service to the stagnant dogma the university had set itself to preaching. He'd play the well-behaved, disciplined student for them, at least for now. Begrudgingly he'd admitted it to himself: he needed them. He needed their facilities, their faculty, their library, for his research to progress further. He had to play the long game here. Convince them now to live to learn another day.

ᚠ

Sæmundur's tie was askew and his jacket was stretched tight over his broad shoulders. It turned out that the dress trousers from his Learned School graduation five years ago didn't fit him. But that didn't matter. He looked presentable enough. It was about the work, after all. The shirt was relatively unwrinkled, at least. He'd glanced in the mirror before he went out and thought he looked mostly fine. Almost respectable.

The sour glances of the hearing committee immediately smothered any meagre sense of self-worth he'd accrued from wearing his suit as soon as he walked in. The disapproving stares of all eight people in attendance told him in no uncertain terms that yes, he probably should have sent his clothes to be cleaned yesterday. The thought of the cloth-golem invoked a fierce sense of pride in him. No, to hell with them. To hell with what he wore. He was the best galdramaður to be found on Hrímland, and they knew it. No one could chant galdur like he did. This hearing would be over soon enough and he'd be able to continue his work in peace.

They didn't invite him to sit, even though there was a desk, a chair and a small cabinet nearby, apparently intended for his use. He was surprised at this – it seemed a practical test of some sort was in order. Each of them noted something down. Sæmundur took his place in front of them, trying to look serious.

'This appeal hearing is now in session with the plaintiff, Sæmundur Sigfússon, the plaintiff's head of department, Professor Almía Dröfn Thorlacius, and the appeal committee in attendance.'

The chairman of the hearing committee was Doctor Laufey Þórhallsdóttir. Sæmundur didn't know her personally, but he was glad to see her there. Laufey had a reputation of fair-mindedness and avoiding most of the politicking and power plays of academia. Next to her sat a sour-faced older woman, her jacket decorated with the golden esoteric sigils of high mastery. Professor Almía Dröfn Thorlacius. Sæmundur had butted heads with both her and her department's faculty dozens of times during his studies. She was the lecturer of galdur at Svartiskóli and was considered the supreme authority on the craft. And, he suspected, the prime reason for his expulsion. The other members were unfamiliar to him, except for Doctor Vésteinn Alrúnarson. Almost everyone in the country knew who Doctor Vésteinn was.

'Sæmundur Sigfússon, you were expelled at the end of last semester from Svartiskóli's Department of Galdur for the use of illegal thaumaturgical narcotics, disorderly conduct when attending classes, failing to meet the academic standards for your thesis after having received two semesters to rework your thesis statement, as the university's code dictates, and last but not least, inciting canonical dissent. You filed a request for an appeal on the grounds that your expulsion was not in line with the university's rules. Please elaborate on the matter and submit any evidence you might have to further your case.'

'Yes, ah, I do have some documents...'

He opened up his suitcase and started rummaging around in it. Even though he was no longer a student himself, he still sold moss to a couple of the students working at the university press. They'd sneaked in a quick print run of a dozen copies for a few grams of moss. He handed each committee member a copy.

'Here you have my expulsion defence and a new dissertation outline, rectifying the misconceptions –' he paused to emphasise the word even further – 'of the outline I initially submitted.'

He glanced at Professor Thorlacius. She was leafing through the papers and slightly smirking to herself.

Good.

'We will get to your dissertation should your expulsion be reviewed,' Doctor Laufey said in a flat tone. 'What have you submitted in order to back up the appeal against your expulsion?'

'Yes, well.' Sæmundur cleared his throat, straightened his posture a bit. 'In my report I've gathered a few points which I believe render the expulsion invalid. To begin with, the use of the highland moss was an infraction, I'll admit, but not worthy of an expulsion in and of itself. It's worthy of a stern reprimand and a log on my record, yes, but that's as far as that should go. Every year students are apprehended with thaumaturgical materials charged with either seiðmagn or galdur of various degrees of illegality, and they are not expelled until repeat offences have come to light. I've noted which segments of the university's code of conduct apply to this situation and provided excerpts in the appendix.'

His voice felt raspy and dry. He was starting to sweat. The committee leafed through his papers, uninterested, barely paying attention to him. Except for Professor Thorlacius. She stared him down with unwavering attention.

'As regarding my supposed disorderly conduct, I argue that it has a direct correlation with the third reason for expulsion. My...' The words caught in his throat like barbed wire. 'My misconceptions about galdur in theory and praxis are what led to most of the more heated confrontations in the classroom. I regret my previous behaviour. I was arrogant in my misplaced theories and overreacted to criticism. I sincerely apologise for my behaviour and believe that my new, refined dissertation will show that my mind has changed completely.'

Professor Thorlacius had been leafing through Sæmundur's

dissertation outline while he was talking, and the smirk on her face had now reached insufferable levels of smugness.

'Sæmundur, in all seriousness – your theories on galdur verged on being blatantly heretical. And now you submit before us a mind-numbingly simple thesis about the grammatical nuances of the Seven Opening Incantations. You expect us to take this seriously?'

Doctor Laufey leaned over and glared at Almía.

'Professor Thorlacius, I will thank you to speak to the student in a respectful manner, as he has seen fit to himself, and to allow his new dissertation the benefit of the doubt.'

Almía hand-waved the reprimand, squinting at Sæmundur.

For crying out loud, Sæmundur thought to himself, *she really wants to see me grovel*.

He nodded, swallowed back a snide remark.

'Well, Professor, you are correct. It is a drastic change. But my theories were dangerous and...' He struggled to finish the sentence. 'Unethical. I now fully realise that.'

'And what exactly,' Doctor Vésteinn Alrúnarson suddenly interjected, 'were those theories?'

He arched his eyebrows at Sæmundur, who found himself at a loss for words. Part of his inspiration had come from what Vésteinn had done for the modernisation of harnessing seiðmagn and using seiður. Vésteinn was over sixty years old, although he barely looked fifty, and most of his groundbreaking work had been accomplished when he was a university student himself, a few years younger than Sæmundur.

Professor Thorlacius jumped in before Sæmundur could possibly risk defending himself.

'Sæmundur has theorised that by deconstructing a series of magister-level incantations, he could start *practical*' – she spat out the word to a chorus of gasps around the table – 'and *experimental* research on the very nature of galdur itself. A canonical truth which requires no further scientific testing! By unravelling the very essence of the grammatical and acoustic elements, he thought he would gain some insight into the underlying forces that dictate galdur and achieve some imagined mastery over it.'

'I see.' Vésteinn nodded slowly. 'So, in short, a disastrous invitation to transmundane possession.'

'Exactly,' Almía added. 'As if a mere postgraduate could conduct this series of experiments, which would elude the highest master of galdur in the modern world. And when faced with valid and – dare I say, sane – critisism of this mad endeavour, he quickly burst into a rage, spouting obscenities!'

Sæmundur winced. She was exaggerating, but she wasn't that far off. He'd lost his temper several times in class, once resulting in his being dismissed from the lecture. It wasn't his fault, he reminded himself. It's hard to hold one's temper in check when people refuse to listen to sound logic.

'Sæmundur here believed that he could revolutionise the way we think about galdur. That he could reach some imaginary heart of its power and return unscathed, bearing bountiful and profound wisdom for the rest of us mere humans.' Almía scoffed. 'I've spent hours arguing with you, Sæmundur. You are an insurgent and a heretic – you offer nothing but discourse where there is none to be had. Without the canon we lose control. Without control there is nothing but unchecked chaos and ruin. Do you seriously think you are the first young, arrogant galdramaður we've had who wants to revolutionise the craft? That other misguided galdramenn before you have not tried to achieve the same lofty results you are hoping for?' She shook her head and stared him right in the eye. His gaze did not waver. He did not even blink. 'This is a charade. A farce. I know your kind. Talented, intelligent, yes – but reckless. Misguided. You will not know when to stop when the forces beyond tempt you with more power. And it will turn your bones blue and bring disastrous ruin upon us all.'

The room turned cramped from the oppressive silence that followed. After a short while, which felt like an eternity of time, Sæmundur spoke.

'Thank you for the critique, Professor Thorlacius. I do empathise with your feelings on the matter, but I reiterate my point – I am completely serious in my change of mind. My current dissertation is something I stand by one hundred per cent. I have abandoned my previous . . .' *Mad theory.* He bit his tongue. 'Unorthodox theory of the origin and nature of galdur as a thaumaturgical force. I only wish to continue studying the craft and gain a deeper understanding and mastery of it, within the limits of the established and proven canon. It is as you say, Professor Thorlacius – it is what keeps us safe from demonic possession.'

The board considered this for a while.

'Thank you, Sæmundur,' Doctor Laufey said. 'We will review your documents and call on you within the next hour. Please wait outside the meeting room.'

Sæmundur waited outside for less than half an hour before he was summoned again. The board's expressions were inscrutable – stone-faced and serious academics, the lot of them. Even Almía's face was unreadable. In the middle of the room someone had placed a pile of irregularly shaped rocks. On the desk a thigh bone had been set out, along with a ball of rough wool yarn and an instruction sheet. Sæmundur already knew what was in store.

'The board has decided to consider your request,' Doctor Laufey said, 'but feels that additional verification is in order. As such we've set up a practical test for you.'

She pointed towards the desk and shelf Sæmundur had noticed when initially entering the room, which now had a variety of components in place.

'A simple enough task for any postgrad student. Please.'

Sæmundur shuffled over to the desk and picked up the instruction sheet which had been placed there for him. The galdur's description, instructions and invocations had been clearly written out by hand, accompanied with a few galdrastafir. Those magical symbols were believed to ground the galdur and provide it with more structure, helping the galdramaður to keep his focus and control the incantation. Sæmundur had quickly found them to be a crutch – and a bad one at that.

The galdur was intended to summon a tilberi, a mindless demon created for a single task. Traditionally it was used to steal milk from cows and sheep belonging to unsuspecting neighbours, writhing around like a bloated worm, the size of a newborn. It spat out the milk after having returned to its master, who fed the abomination on their own blood. It was a complex spell – for uneducated peasants – albeit with some practical applications. Sæmundur had used it as a basis when constructing the galdur for the cloth-golem, but it was a needlessly convoluted galdur. This made the incantation as a whole that much riskier.

It was a trite, convoluted mess of a ritual. The incantation was full of needless gibberish. The sigils, the hand movements, the burning of certain alchemical mixtures – all nonsense. He'd figured that out long before. It was an insult to the craft.

He took the end of the woollen thread and tied it around the femur. He fished out a knife from within his coat and ran it across his palm. He started reciting the incantation as he wound the thread around the femur while smearing blood into both.

The words flowed through him. Language. Sound. Vibrations of his own voice, moving through him. The bone started to change shape. The blood-matted wool grew together, starting to throb and ebb as though the bone was breathing. The end of the femur twisted and deformed into a mockery of a face.

He was doing it before he realised it. The traditional incantation was ugly, uncivilised, bafflingly idiotic in its coarseness. It was almost all superstition, there was no reason behind it. Reciting it like a mindless drone, without thought or intent, felt wrong. *He knew better*. He was better than this. And he would show them. He would prove to them how far he had come and how far he could go.

He wove the elements of the cloth-golem's incantation into the galdur. The bone started to elongate and took on a pale shade of blue. Ridges rose in waves, a spine growing underneath the grey wool. The wool thickened and spun itself into a myriad of limbs, making the tilberi rise from the table on thin, spindly legs. At the end of the femur the head grew bloated and lengthened, a sharp crack divided into a mouth. Thin and razor-sharp teeth glistened in the newly formed maw. It had no eyes, but it looked around, tendrils feeling the air around it. He'd never made a tilberi such as this one. This was no single-tasked automaton. This was a complex summoning, capable of complex tasks. A ritual worthy of a master. It was the culmination of his work so far, the promise of what could be in store. He stretched out the last vowel and started to weave the galdur into a different incantation. With more sense and intelligence the tilberi could be a promising servant, if he only utilised the—

Sæmundur did not get any further. The words stopped in his throat. Professor Almía Dröfn Thorlacius was standing along with the rest of the committee, their clothes billowing in a wind unheard and unfelt. They were all speaking in unison, although he could not hear the words. He could not hear anything. Almía's face was twisted in righteous anger. Sæmundur tried to combat them, but he did not stand a chance against their unified efforts. His vision faded out and back in, rhythmically. They were unmaking his galdur. All of them, in unison. They had been prepared for this. Perhaps even wanted this. The tilberi shivered and fell as its weak limbs gave under its weight, its thin back cracked and shrunk in quick spasms. It threw back its misshapen head and roared with a cacophony of voices that sounded almost human. Its chest rose and fell with its breath. Then it burst. And the screaming stopped.

Sæmundur could hear again. He listened to the committee finish off the undoing galdur. When Professor Thorlacius finished the incantation and started her outraged tirade, he wished he was again trapped in that world of silence.

The committee exited the room, leaving Sæmundur by himself, bearing the weight of his failure on his shoulders. Only one of them lingered: Doctor Vésteinn. The man looked deep in thought.

'It was . . . interesting, what you were attempting,' Vésteinn said after a while.

Sæmundur leaned against the desk, forcing his hands to remain still. Trying to calm himself down.

'Crude, unfinished, but – inspired.' Vésteinn took out a handkerchief and polished his glasses, giving himself a moment to gather his thoughts. 'You have some potential. Don't give up on your work yet, Sæmundur,' he added quietly. 'It could lead you to some very interesting conclusions.'

Doctor Vésteinn put on his glasses and headed out, his footsteps the only sound in the room. As the door clicked shut behind him, Sæmundur slammed his fists on the desk, stifling a roar of frustration.

Þrjú

Karnivalið was one of the few places of entertainment in Reykjavík where humans and huldufólk drank together. Garún was familiar with the bouncers working the doors and slipped them a few krónur as they let her in. She'd had the cash ready in case someone unfamiliar was on shift, but decided to still slide them the money. The bouncers wouldn't hesitate in deciding who to evict the next time she throat-punched some asshole, probably human, for groping her. Hopefully.

The bar was filled with smoke and loud, drunk people, located in an antiquated house that was in no way built to house a bar of this scope. Every night Karnivalið filled up with people who called themselves artists, writers, poets, kuklarar, revolutionaries, and so on. Everyone was busy being seen and seeing others.

Garún felt as if she vaguely knew everybody in there, as if the same night was on repeat weekend after weekend and everyone knew their designated role and lines beforehand. They identified as artists, but Garún felt they were more into saying they were instead of actually working at it. They talked ten times more than they worked; every sketch was an accomplishment, every idea pure brilliance. Some of them lived together in communes, usually as squatters. It was a source of pride to live on the margins of society, of not belonging. But for them it was a self-imposed exile, a choice. Many proudly identified as part of some grass-roots organisation, as radical revolutionaries, but when the call came to take real, dangerous action, there was always a sudden change of tone.

Her friends were gathered in the same corner as usual. Or, she hoped that they were her friends. Most of them, at least. She did not know what they said about her behind her back and while she tried not to care, she sometimes couldn't help it.

Not all of them were like that, of course. But some. They were like most of the people in this bar, in Reykjavík. When it came to fighting for real change, to take action that truly meant something, they hesitated. They became afraid.

Garún glanced at the group and tried to spot if Diljá, Jón or even Hrólfur were there. Didn't look like it. She'd been avoiding most of them all summer. She really could have used Jón's presence there to get into the conversation. Garún thought it was largely due to him that the others had accepted her so quickly when she'd started hanging around the same bars as them, seeing them at the same art openings. He'd always given her space to talk, to be heard. To exist. When she'd voiced the idea of staging a demonstration in front of City Hall, he had been first to back her up. Instead of giving in to their reflexive fear, dismissing her, they'd listened. He was a poet, called himself Jón Fjarðaskáld – *poet of the fjords*. A bit tacky, but it had stuck. He wrote beautiful, subversive prose, where opposition to oppression and injustice were hidden in naturalistic metaphors. Garún wasn't much for poetry, but she thought she recognised the real deal when she read it.

Garún was the prime agitator for the demonstration. It had been her idea. Not that it mattered, but still. It made her feel as if she was doing something that truly mattered. They were going to change things. The others hadn't liked it initially, but Jón had supported her fully through the debate. He'd convinced some of them to take part. Make a difference. She'd been surprised at how even the most passive and content people had joined in. But she didn't really feel comfortable facing them right now. She had other things on her mind.

Garún tried to sneak past them unseen to the stairs that led to the upper floor. Lilja noticed her and waved, gestured for her to sit with them. A friendly sign, but Garún knew better. The looks on their faces as they noticed her told her everything she needed to know. She signalled to them that she was first going to the bar. She might as well start drinking now.

At the bar she almost had to scream at the bartender to get service. Even though Karnivalið was open to blendingar, that didn't necessarily mean that they were well treated. When she finally got her beer she was pretty sure that she paid considerably more for it than the other guests. But at least she was served.

She made her way back to the table and grabbed a free chair. At the other end of the table people were talking politics at full volume. It overwhelmed any other discussion, as so often before.

'The protest will just be the beginning,' said Jónas Theium.

He called himself a poet, a radical, and a revolutionary. He'd been adamantly against Garún's idea when she first brought it up. He and most of the people at the table were unlikely to show up, she thought. It would have to be up to Jón. Garún wasn't good at sucking up to people she hated.

'The people have the power and we need to show it! It's just a matter of gathering a crowd and marching back down to ...'

Garún stopped listening. She'd heard it a dozen times before. Others agreed with Jónas and rattled off hollow and meaningless clichés, inflating their own egos with a superficial discourse about equality and revolution. None of them had taken any part in the organising, in reaching out to people. They hadn't understood her in the slightest when she started talking about how oppressive the city walls were, how they were intended to keep the 'undesirable' non-humans out, not to protect the city from the dangers of untamed nature. The walls were a comfort to them. Just like the Crown itself. The Crown meant stability and security – who cared if a few people got hurt in the process? Did they even consider huldufólk, marbendlar and náskárar to fully be people? None of them actually wanted change. Real change was painful and demanded a bloody sacrifice that these people were not willing to make.

'Hi. Long time no see,' said Lilja overenthusiastically, as she moved over towards Garún. She tried to hide her discomfort as she felt Lilja reach out and feel her surface emotions. She wasn't really feeling sociable, but it would be incredibly rude to just block her off.

'Yeah. I've been busy.' Garún replied in turn by reaching out and feeling Lilja. *Giddiness. Contentment. Joy.* A thin trace of underlying smugness. Not good.

'You don't say? There's been talk about that,' Lilja said, and smiled.

Garún wondered what Lilja herself had felt. If she had managed to obfuscate her own deeper emotions.

'What do you mean?'

Garún's voice was lined with a cold edge, but it was contaminated by fear.

Lilja was a huldukona and reminded Garún of the huldufólk from the old tales. Too beautiful and too dangerous. Ravenous for drama and disaster. Lilja had never liked Garún, although she'd always tried to hide it.

'Oh, you know. The exhibition you've got going on is spreading like wildfire.'

Garún relaxed. 'Yeah, I guess so.'

Lilja leaned in closer, smiling in a conspiratorial tone.

'And haven't you also started tagging all over town? Every week I hear about thaumaturgical graffiti that's driving everyone crazy.'

'I have no idea what you are talking about.'

'Oh, well. Suit yourself. Dangerous to do such things.' She put up an insincere look of worry. 'You could end up at the Nine for that. Especially if you're a blendingur.'

Garún didn't reply. She didn't like the way Lilja had said that last word. It had not been meant in a nice, neutral manner. It had not been said like a regular word. She let her silence turn cold and angry. Tempered her anger into a sharp weapon. A calculated, ruthless strike.

Lilja went on, mindlessly unaware of Garún's body language. If she had reached out to her right then she would have recoiled, as if touching a burning hot stove.

'But you know me. I'm known for my discretion.'

She winked at Garún, as if they were just two friends bonding. Right.

'Hold on a minute. I'll be right back.'

Garún was stopped at the top of the stairs by a heavyset man. He was way too muscular for his height and it looked as if his suit was about to burst at the seams.

'Closed upstairs. Private party.'

His voice matched his appearance, heavy and slow. Everything about him resembled an unmovable boulder.

'Is Viður in there? Tell him it's Garún.'

The slab of a man walked up to the door with heavy steps and knocked. A skinny huldumaður opened it immediately and looked down at Garún. His nasal septum was completely eroded.

The grunt said something to the huldumaður, who sighed and told her to wait a minute. They stood there silently, the bouncer staring ahead at nothing, Garún sipping at her beer. In a few minutes the huldumaður returned and said Garún could enter. She squeezed past the bouncer, who didn't move an inch to let her through.

The top floor was thick with smoke. People lay numb and smiling on old sofas or piles of pillows, humans and huldufólk alike. On low tables were pipes and torn cigarettes, along with small piles of sorti, highland moss and white, crystalline delýsíð. A few couples were lethargically making out or perhaps copulating under thin sheets, others lay paralysed from an ecstatic high. People smoked and coughed, snorted delýsíð up their noses. Not many had their septums whole, on most of them it was burned off. The rich smell of sorti mixed with the mossy smoke had created a vile concoction, a thick and pungently sweet smoke that tore at her lungs.

Viður sat by himself in a small room that just contained two couches up against a small table. Dirty ashtrays and various kinds of pipe decorated the table, which was laid out with drugs like a buffet. Garún was unsure if he was in the process of packaging it or about to use it himself. He was lithe for a huldumaður, almost like a teenager, his hands delicate and smooth. Viður had avoided hard work his entire life – but that didn't mean he was soft. He smiled when he saw Garún in the doorway.

'Well, well. Good to see you.'

He spoke slowly and she noticed his dilated pupils. He didn't have a septum either. Snorting delýsíð had burned it away completely.

'Hello, Viður.'

She sat on the couch against him. He felt around for her emotions in the customary greeting, clumsily, sloppily, like a drunken man trying to give a handshake but turning it into a hug halfway. She in turn felt around his feelings in a curt, distanced manner. He was fucking wasted and felt like a god-damn mess.

'What the devil have you been smoking now?'

'A-hahaha-haha-ha.' His laughter was empty and erratic. 'You can't smoke a demon.'

'I know, I was just—'

'Unless of course you've got it in a bone. A femur, maybe. And you grind it into dust. And snort it.' He looked as if he was dumbfounded by what he was saying. He wrote something down. 'Actually... that's not such a stupid idea. But you can't smoke it!'

He laughed again at the thought.

'Anyway.' She tried to bring him down to the ground with her. 'I came because I need delýsíð. Liquid, same as last time.'

Viður shook his head. 'Nope. All gone!' He smiled like a naughty child.

'What do you mean *all gone*?'

'Nothing left. No liquid, no powder. Nothing. Crown found the last shipment. All gone.' He hung his head. 'Poor lads. I hope they were hanged and not sent to the Nine.'

'Damn it, Viður!' Garún stood up, agitated. 'If they trace it to you then I'm as good as dead, if I'm in luck! Why didn't you let me know earlier?'

'No, no, no, sit.' He motioned to her to quieten down. She looked at him, livid. 'Sit!' he commanded in a harsh tone.

She obeyed. She had a bitter taste in her mouth. Iron.

'Relax a little.' He dug around on the table for a pack of cigarettes. 'You are always so wound up. They can't trace it to me.' He held up a finger before Garún could interrupt. 'Because there are people at customs and the police that work for me.

Not the Crown. Me.' He lit himself a cigarette. 'Don't worry. It's all good. Sometimes they just need to hit their smuggling bust quota.'

He offered her the pack but she shook her head. He stared at her and smoked so intensely that the cigarette almost burned up all in one drag.

'You really are tense tonight,' he said, exhaling smoke slowly.

She felt him suddenly fumbling around for her hidden emotions. It was aggressive, clumsy, a vulgar intrusion of her personal psychological space. It was repulsive. She pushed him back, hard, making him recoil visibly, and shut herself off from him. He looked surprised and then actually had the nerve to smile. Fuck that rotten son of a bitch.

'Just had some trouble downstairs,' she said. He nodded slowly, as if he knew exactly what she was talking about. 'It's nothing.'

'Anything I can do? You just have to ask.'

She knew that would be a dear favour to pay back.

'It's all right. I'm fine. I just need the delýsíð.'

'I'm out, Garún, I told you.'

'You must be able to hook me up. Do you know anyone else? Someone who can be *trusted*?'

She emphasised the last word, even though she knew it wouldn't matter in the slightest to Viður.

'That you can trust, huh?'

She felt him reach out again. Just on the surface this time. But she didn't feel like letting him get close to her.

He furrowed his brow. Garún held his gaze. She tried to keep her face completely neutral. Frozen. But who knew what he could see? She might try to close herself off, but the huldufólk could possibly still pick something up. She also knew that Viður smoked highland moss regularly – a thaumaturgical plant that had a unique effect on the conscious mind. It might make him

33

more proficient with the huldufólk's innate gift. She couldn't stand it, but Sæmundur had used the moss unsparingly in his research. Or that's what he told himself it was for.

'Well,' Viður said finally, when she didn't let down her guard or reach out in turn. 'I know people who know people, who … *know people*. I still can't guarantee anything. You're not buying directly from me as usual. And the price is higher. Considerably higher.'

'Who are they? How do I reach them?'

'It's not easy. He's in the Forgotten Downtown.' He stopped her before she could say anything in protest. 'I'll give you instructions on how to get to the other side. Solid instructions.'

He started scribbling something down on a wrinkled sheet of paper. It took him a long time to write, in long careful strokes.

'Can I trust him?'

She tried to catch a glimpse of what he was writing.

He didn't look up.

'Can you trust me?'

No.

'Yes,' she lied.

'If you say so,' he said with a smile, and looked up. The smile didn't reach his dilated eyes. 'It's a big old house in Rökkurvík. You'll find a huldumaður there. Odd fellow, with long hair, looks like he's dying from hunger. Always wears the same torn leather coat. Name is Feigur. Tell him I sent you and you should be fine.'

'How do I get through to the Forgotten Downtown?'

He handed her the note. 'These are solid gates both in and out. New ones, still hidden. Don't let anyone see you cross.'

She nodded and stood up. Handed him a few banknotes without being prompted. He took them without counting.

'Thanks, Viður.'

'Any time, Garún.'

He watched her leave, never dropping his smile.

ᛏ

When Garún came downstairs Diljá had joined the others at the table. Styrhildur and Hraki were there with her. A strangely upbeat but sombre song blared from the speakers. Someone had put on a record. Diljá noticed Garún and looked concerned as she came closer and reached out for her emotions.

'Are you all right?' she asked, and respectfully dialled her emotional outreach back. Garún replied in turn, but only out of politeness. Diljá felt mellow, tired, and now, slightly anxious. 'I'm sorry,' Diljá continued, 'but you look and feel like a goddamn mess.'

Garún shook her head quickly, then nodded. She noticed Styrhildur and Hraki sitting quietly next to Diljá, trying not to look as if they were worried about Garún.

'Yeah, I'm fine. Just need another drink.'

As she moved towards the bar, Diljá placed a hand on her arm.

'Don't worry,' Diljá said. 'Let me do it. Cheaper, too,' she added, and flashed a quick, apologetic smile.

Garún returned it and went to sit down at the table. Diljá did that all the time. If something was easier for her because she was a huldukona, then she did it for Garún. If someone gave Garún shit because she was a blendingur, or just gave her shit in general, then Diljá always had her back. Always. Garún hadn't known many friends like that in her life. The most beautiful thing about it was that it wasn't exclusive to Garún. Although Diljá had taken more of a big sister approach to their relationship, she was also like this towards most people. She often helped or spotted other blendingar or huldufólk and backed them up in trouble.

She stood up to injustice, regardless of whether it was major or minor – to her they were all gravely serious.

Styrhildur and Hraki had made it into the city only a couple of years earlier. Garún was so relieved and happy that Diljá had somewhat taken them under her wing. She'd helped them find jobs in Starholt and a small apartment that the siblings rented together. Garún loved them, they were blendingar like her and she'd known them since they were kids, but she didn't want the responsibility of taking care of other people. Taking care of herself was enough.

'What's up, guys? Aren't you a bit too young to be drinking?'

'You're only a few years older than me!' Styrhildur said in a scolding tone.

Garún smirked and playfully pushed her shoulder against her. The girl smiled, but Hraki looked embarrassed. He was a few years younger than his sister. He couldn't have been more than sixteen. The three of them quickly reached out to one another. Styrhildur felt excited and happy, Hraki a bit nervous, but still, that same kind of happiness. They were living independent lives in the city, at a bar surrounded by friends. This was good. Maybe better than any of them had ever expected. It made her feel pensive. Something so normal shouldn't feel exceptional.

Diljá returned with a beer and Garún reached for her purse.

'No, no, not this again,' said Diljá, but Garún didn't let off until she'd successfully pushed the coins into Diljá's hand. 'All right, but this is the last time. One day you'll have to let me buy you a round.'

'Nobody buys anybody rounds, what are you even talking about?'

They stared at each other, flaring out scans of each other's emotions. This was a set routine between them by now. Each focused on mock feelings of stubbornness, trying to outdo the other.

36

Finally Diljá caved in, as always.

'Okay, maybe nobody really buys rounds. But still. One day I'll buy you a beer.' She grinned.

Garún shrugged. 'I don't like owing anybody anything.'

'Yeah, no shit.' Diljá took a sip of her beer. 'Lilja said you were upstairs.' She lowered her voice and leaned in. 'Is everything good?'

'Viður's out,' Garún said in a low voice, 'but he knows a guy who's selling. I'm not sure if I should trust him on this.'

'Who's the guy?'

'Nobody I've heard of. Apparently he lives in Rökkurvík – permanently.'

The nickname was a bad pun, one that had stuck. The Forgotten Downtown was cast in unending darkness, its decrepit old-style houses reminiscent of faded photographs of the city that Reykjavík once was. So it was nicknamed Rökkurvík, literally meaning 'twilight bay' – as opposed to Reykjavík's 'smoke bay'.

'Come on, Garún. The *Forgotten Downtown*?'

'I have to try.' She hesitated. 'Will you spot me when I enter and exit?'

'Of course,' Diljá replied without hesitating.

'We will help,' Styrhildur said quietly. 'With us three, you can cover a lot of ground.'

Garún was more relieved than she expected at hearing that. She wanted to say no, to tell them that they should stay out of it. But they wanted to help, to make themselves useful.

'Thanks,' she mumbled. She handed them the note Viður had handed her. 'Look over the points of entry and exit. I'll go in at a specific time. I'm not sure how long this will take, but it shouldn't be long.'

They nodded and started perusing the notes, memorising them as quickly as they could.

Then Garún recalled Lilja's remarks earlier.

'Listen,' she said to Diljá, pulling her in and a bit away from the siblings. 'You haven't told anyone about the tagging, have you?'

'No, of course not.' Diljá suddenly looked extremely worried. 'Why?'

Garún glanced around. They sat next to each other, slightly away from the others at the table, who were deep in discussion about the latest theatre review to appear in the *Tíminn* newspaper. Garún focused on Diljá and instigated a deep reach out for her feelings. She felt her initial hesitation, which quickly gave way as Diljá embraced her with open arms. Garún felt uneasiness, joy, and both fear and worry in sharp, almost hurting pangs. Whether it was because Diljá had let something slip, or because she was worried that Lilja knew something, Garún had no way of knowing. Garún felt Diljá reach out in the same way and also gave in.

They held their connection steady, holding each other by the hand, staring into each other's eyes.

'I'm worried,' said Garún, still holding the connection, 'that we have a snitch.'

'Who?' asked Diljá. 'Katrín?'

They let their connection search and probe their feelings on the matter until they reached a united conclusion.

'I agree,' Diljá continued, 'that she's a risk. But I believe she has the best interests of the cause at heart. She has her reasons.'

Garún felt a sudden upsurge of pain and regret, empathy, anger, injustice. She knew something about Katrín. But there was also trust there. A feeling of a kindred spirit, a sister.

'Hrólfur?' she ventured. 'He would hardly gossip to huldufólk.'

Diljá smiled and Garún smiled with her. Diljá's joy was her own joy.

'Well, you never know,' said Diljá.

Garún felt something surprising. A hint of warm affection. The feeling invoked a quickening of her own heartbeat. Dangerous.

Diljá sensed Garún's hesitation at the new feeling she'd inadvertently broadcast and blushed.

'It's not anything, it's just—'

'I know,' Garún said. 'Don't worry. I'm sorry I reacted that way.'

'That's all right, you don't need to apologise.'

They let their mutual understanding reinforce itself for a while. Then, Garún's mind turned to Lilja. The dark cloud in her heart passed over Diljá's face.

'Garún... Oh no,' Diljá said.

'It doesn't matter who it was. She still knows, when she shouldn't. I have to do it.'

Diljá couldn't have possibly known from their connection what Garún was thinking about, but they knew each other well. Diljá knew what Garún had in mind.

'You don't have to—'

'We can't trust her. We have to remain safe. No matter the cost. And besides' – Garún knew she didn't say this with full conviction, and that Diljá would feel it – 'she won't remember a thing.'

Diljá's sadness and anxiety washed over Garún in strong waves. She let her own feelings show, feeling them echo in her friend. *Fear. Determination. Anger. Hope.* A strong, relentless fire.

Diljá nodded. 'Okay,' she said.

Garún finished her beer in a long gulp, then got up and walked straight to Lilja. She was chatting with a few people at the other end of the table, who all fell silent as Garún came and leaned in towards her.

'Come with me to the restroom. Let's have a little talk.'

Lilja raised her eyebrows but stood up and followed Garún to the toilets. There were only two restrooms in the bar, in a narrow hallway. The line was long and coiled oddly around the tight space. Lilja was not interested in standing in line with Garún and bullshitted her way to the front of the queue, which was not a difficult task as most regulars at Karnivalið knew her. They went in together.

The lock on the door clicked. Pipes and valves stood out of the walls. The seat was loose on the toilet, which didn't look as if it had been cleaned in a very long while.

'Ooh, what fun!' Lilja laughed as she checked herself in the mirror. 'It's about time we caught up with some gossip.'

Garún leaned against the door and felt the pulse from the music and the people outside.

'Right,' she said, and pushed Lilja down on the toilet. 'We have to freshen up your make-up. Let me fix it.'

An angry grimace flared up on Lilja's face, which she tried to subdue. She reached out for Garún's emotions, which she kept closed off as tightly as she could.

'Aw. Thanks,' Lilja replied.

Garún opened her purse, took out a powder box and started painting Lilja's face.

'How did you know I was behind the delýsíð graffiti?'

'I wasn't sure. But I'm sure now.'

'Did you hear it from someone?'

'What?' Lilja stared numbly up at Garún. 'No. I ... just ... It made sense. You've always been so much ... like that.' She started to slur her words. 'Don't be scared, I ... I won't tell anyone. I was just joking earlier.' Her eyes glazed, her voice sounded far off in the distance. 'I just like to play around... and see what happens...'

Garún rubbed her make-up sponge against the powder, crushing the microscopic delýsíð crystals that were hiding there. She stroked Lilja's forehead delicately. She spoke to Lilja in a soothing voice as she painted her face.

'When we go out, you won't remember that this happened. You won't remember our conversation earlier. You won't re-member that I painted that graffiti. You will never connect me to anything illegal. You would never believe that I would do such a thing.'

Lilja nodded slowly while Garún painted over her memories.

Sæmundur slammed the door behind him and stood for a moment in his hallway, frozen with impotent rage. Then he kicked the wall, once, twice, cracking the wooden boards. He stormed into his room, kicking over his amplifier, sending the mess of ashtrays and dirty dishes on top of it crashing to the floor. He cursed. He screamed profanities, spitting with each word. He ripped off his tie and jacket, tearing them in the process. He grabbed his bass guitar and flung it across the room. It hit the wall with a thud.

They'd undone his incantation before he was even able to finish it. Startled by the horror of the unknown, or perhaps by the capable way he'd woven a new galdur from seemingly nothing, they'd resolved to unmake his work instead of allowing it to be. They had summarily destroyed it. They'd screamed at him afterwards. Threats of lawsuit, of having his tongue severed and vital digits removed. Of severing his ties to galdur completely. He was too dangerous, Professor Thorlacius had said. Foolish. Naïve. Reckless.

Worm-minded pieces of shit. Worthless, pathetic insects. They had no higher understanding of the craft they practised, and they did not even desire to seek any glimpse of it. They were content with fumbling in the dark, ignorant of the powers they messed with. They were the halfwits. They were the careless ones. How could civilisation ever progress without research? Experiments? Anything that was worth something demanded a sacrifice of equal measure. But they were too craven to make it.

But he would. They would not stand in the way of enlightenment. If they would not hand him the tools he needed to hone his craft – to gain higher understanding of the nature of galdur – then he would seize them for himself.

An idea resurfaced in his head. Something he'd given up long ago, deemed to be too dangerous, too mad. But that's what they called him now. Sæmundur the Mad. He turned over a pile of books and manuscripts in the corner. It was there somewhere.

His notes were in disarray, but they all seemed to be there. He didn't have the manuscript any more, but he recalled it clearly enough. Coarsely copied illustrations of spores, twisted roots, wide mushroom caps littered the pages, which were covered in a nearly intelligible scribble. It wasn't much. But it would do. He just needed the materials and then he would get what rightfully belonged to him.

ᚠ

He worked through the night, putting together a plan. He had an idea of how to make the gandreið mushroom non-lethal, of how to control the fungus so that it wouldn't completely take over. But still, the galdur he was working on was a bit too theoretical even for his own tastes. He was assuming too many things and if he was wrong about any part of this the results could be disastrous. Not only for others, but for himself as well.

He just needed some time to work on the formula. Structure a new kind of incantation. And when it was done it would be a masterful stroke. With an unseen hand he would swipe the most sacred texts of Svartiskóli's library for himself.

He would read the pages of *Rauðskinna* and live to tell the tale.

Then there was a knock at his door.

Garún couldn't stand art exhibitions, even less so when they were her own. For that meant she didn't have the liberty of just disappearing when she'd had enough. Gallery Gjóta was a hole-in-the-wall establishment in central downtown, known to exhibit relatively unknown artists as well as the ones more established on the scene. She'd shown up at the opening for as long as was the absolute polite minimum – she didn't want to be disrespectful towards the curator who'd brought her in all those years before – but she found it absolutely insufferable. Tightly wound, rich art snobs and pretentious hipsters all stirred together in a toxic cocktail. Diljá would usually keep her company, but she'd not been able to make it last time, and Garún had felt alone and stranded in a sea of disapproving human faces. The only other non-human there had been Bragi, a huldumaður who was one of the founders of the gallery. He'd been the one who'd brought her in when he saw her work for sale in one of the weekend flea markets in Starholt. It had been the first time someone paid her a real sum of money for her work. She wouldn't forget that.

This wasn't an opening – her exhibition had been on for a few weeks now. Apparently a few clients had asked to meet her. It was not something she really did, but in this case it was for a very expensive painting. And she needed the money for the delýsíð. Her plans for the protest depended on it. So she'd agreed to meet them.

She walked through the cramped alley into the hidden courtyard where the gallery was located. A few hipsters sat by a bench, gossiping while they smoked. They all stared at her unabashedly as she crossed the small yard and entered the gallery.

Gjóta's gallery space was bright and open, but still small enough that there wasn't a clamour when a decent crowd gathered together. Bragi stood alongside an older man and his wife, both of them looking over one of the bigger paintings in the room. It was Garún's work, something she called *Untitled Mask of the God in the Stone*, a massive, amorphous shape like something out of a cosmology book, a murky, swirling galaxy in formation. At a distance, if you relaxed your vision and focused on the work, it could almost resemble a face. Garún had laced the painting with microdosages of delýsíð. She hid the shape of the mask from the viewer, so that although it visually didn't seem to be there, it was actually hiding there in the formless void. Your brain picked up the shape of a face, a mask, in the murky painting, but your eyes couldn't see it. None of this was known to Bragi, of course, or if he suspected anything he'd at least kept quiet enough about it. It was the most expensive work Garún had ever had on display, and Bragi had asked her to come over today because the prospective buyer was apparently dropping by to view it for the third time. This time he was bringing his wife. Or more likely, his mistress.

'...one of the most exciting artists in Starholt today. A true rarity among her—'

Bragi stopped talking as he heard Garún's footsteps approach in the hall.

'Ah, speaking of the brilliant artist. Garún, pleased you could make it.'

He flashed her an encouraging smile. She'd noticed when she was walking in that several of her paintings had been marked as sold in the last weeks. She found herself beaming, but her smile froze and her heart started pounding when the man and woman turned around to greet her.

She recognised him instantly. She'd been tagging one of his stores not that long ago. Sigurður Thorvaldsen. One of the richest people in Reykjavík. He was well into middle age, impeccably dressed in a fine suit. The woman, markedly younger than him, was his wife, Anna Margrét Eydal Thorvaldsen. She was descended from finer folk than Sigurður, her mother's side of the family having bishops and celebrated composers, and more than one goði on her father's side, the Eydal family. Garún had a simple rule of thumb when it came to people with family names instead of the traditional patronyms: don't trust them. Either they belonged to the upper classes, or worse, they wanted to *be* one of them.

Her heart was pounding and her ears were buzzing.

Run. Get out. He knows.

She met his eyes, trying to remain calm. Did he know? Was this an elaborate trap? If so, the police were already waiting for her outside. No. Better to stand still. Frozen in front of a dumb, lumbering predator.

Sigurður held out his hand. Garún shook it almost reflexively and immediately regretted it. Anna Margrét looked at her coolly and offered a stiff smile, the polite gesture not reaching her eyes.

'Garún, yes? I am happy that you could take the time.'

'It's the least she could do with the price she's asking,' Anna Margrét interjected.

Bragi replied before Garún could find the words to lash out at this stuck-up woman.

'Yes, indeed! This is one of the finer pieces we've put on

display in recent years. Truly a tremendous, authentic work of the huldufólk's deity.'

'Doesn't look like much, does it?' Sigurður approached the painting and squinted at it. 'I thought their … or well, *your* god was supposed to be holding a hundred masks?'

'Adralíen-toll has myriad depictions, one of them being with an uncountable number of masks, yes. This is a more modern take on this story.'

Sigurður stared at the painting for a while. They stood in silence. Why had these people brought her over, Garún wondered. A power move? Because they were bored? She was finding it hard to believe that Sigurður had been made aware of her recent work. It shouldn't even have triggered properly – that was supposed to take days.

He sniffed and shook his head.

'I don't get it. I mean, I like it – but I don't get it.'

Sigurður looked at Garún expectantly. Anna Margrét and Bragi followed his cue. She stared at them blankly. Bragi gave her a hopeful look.

Go ahead. Sell it. Sell them the damn thing.

'It's an interpretation of the huldufólk's god,' Garún said. 'It's not traditional in that sense. There's not much to *get*. Just to … experience.'

Anna Margrét shook her head. 'Nonsense. I said so, darling. We'd be much better off with a Kjarval.' She glared at Garún. 'She's not even one of *them*.'

She almost spat out the last word.

Garún bristled. Bragi looked alarmed, but most likely only at the thought of losing the sale. Typical. She felt herself clench her fists and forced herself to loosen her hands. She'd not let them see they had got to her. Those fucking pigs.

Sigurður turned to the painting and took it in.

'Just think of having it in the dining room for the next dinner party.'

That painting could pay for five times the delýsíð she needed. It could pay her rent for the year. It could change her life, if it sold. If one person bought it, then another would surely follow. She knew how these circles were. Word got around quickly in Reykjavík, doubly so among the so-called elite. But she also knew where their money came from. She would change her life, but it wouldn't be because of the patronage of people like Thorvaldsen. It would be on her own terms.

'It's not for sale.' Garún's voice turned cold. 'It is not for the likes of *you*.'

Now it was her turn to spit out the last word with all the resentment she could muster.

Anna Margrét and Sigurður stared at her, incredulous.

'Excuse me?' he said, puffing up like a rooster. She stared him down.

'You heard me. Not for sale. It's as you said, you don't get it. It's not for people like you.'

She walked away.

Sigurður and Anna Margrét started yelling at Bragi, who started apologising profusely.

'This is a misunderstanding, surely, Garún – wait! Garún!'

He caught her in the alleyway outside the gallery.

'Garún, come on, don't fuck this up for us! We're close – come in and apologise and make this better! This is an insane amount of money, we talked about this! This will be a game changer.'

'I'm not apologising for shit, Bragi. That painting is not for sale to those assholes, got it? Now, I'll be needing the commission for the pieces already sold.'

Bragi stared at her, stunned.

'Are you fucking kidding me? You show up here, fuck up all

the hard work I've done on your behalf, and then demand to be cashed out? I'd be glad to, dear, but the payments are done on delivery of the artworks and this wreck of an exhibition is up for another month, remember?'

She gritted her teeth in frustration.

'What?' he kept on. 'Thought I'd do you a favour and pay you the advance? I'll goddamn think about it – if you come in and put this right.'

Garún considered this.

'Right. I see how it is.'

She walked away without sparing him a look back. Fuck them and their money. Her integrity was not for sale.

She hadn't been to Sæmundur's place since last spring, when it had all blown up and she'd finally recognised how toxic their relationship was. Nice as it had been, at certain moments. But in retrospect that's all it had been. Moments.

It was a raised single-storey house, with the basement floor being only half-sunken. The windows let in some light as a result, but it didn't matter in Sæmundur's case. He kept them curtained with heavy, dark drapes.

The rush from telling off the Thorvaldsens and Bragi had quickly worn off as she'd walked from downtown to the university campus. She'd probably burned whatever bridge she had built with Bragi and the gallery in the process. How the hell was she supposed to pay for the delýsíð she needed now? The works already sold at the exhibition would pay her rent for a few months when she eventually got paid, but then what? How was she going to make a living after that? Word didn't only get around fast with the money-hungry upper class – it spread like wildfire in Reykjavík's tiny art world. The gallery had already been hesitant to take in a blendingur. If she got on Bragi's bad side she'd be frozen out for good. Fucking hell. Goddamn assholes. She felt anxious, but also relieved. It had felt so good to walk away with her head held high. If that came at a price, then so what? She'd gladly pay it. She'd fought for everything her entire life. She'd made something out of nothing before. And she would do it again, if she needed to.

That still left the current problem with the delýsíð.

Shit.

But one headache at a time. She needed to call in a favour. One she had hoped she wouldn't have to ask for.

Garún knocked on Sæmundur's door, a bit harder than she intended. The whole encounter had left her a bit strung up. She saw movement out of the corner of her eye and lit up when little Mæja came trotting along the house, her tail straight up and curled at the end like a question mark, mewing in a complaining tone as Garún picked her up.

'Hi, love.' Garún pressed the cat against her, stroking her little head as she purred loudly like a broken engine. 'I've missed you, baby.'

She still regretted leaving her with Sæmundur, but at the time it had felt like the right call. There were too many noxious fumes in her apartment from the paints and the delýsíð, a cat could easily die when exposed to them. Or so she thought. At least with Sæmundur she got to go outside.

Sæmundur opened the door wearing a dark look of anger that instantly faded into shock when he saw her. This is how they had last said goodbye to each other. Garún holding Mæja at his doorstep. Except then it had been in the pouring rain.

'So,' she said after a short silence. 'Aren't you going to invite me in?'

Fjögur

Before

They'd woken up late, that day. Garún got up before Sæmundur and made breakfast. The cold spring sun lit up the small apartment through grimy windows. Mæja jumped off the kitchen cabinet, where she usually slept. The cat stretched and mewed. Already she was begging and Garún gave her a piece of dried fish. When breakfast was ready Garún got Sæmundur out of bed. He'd barely moved, even though she hadn't been especially quiet. They ate porridge and rye bread with butter at the rickety kitchen table. Mæja rubbed herself against their feet and purred loudly.

'What time is the party tonight?' Garún asked.

'It's not a party,' Sæmundur said. 'It's a social event. Everyone who's anyone at the university will be there. Donors as well.'

'Just because it's a boring party doesn't mean that it's not a party.'

Garún stirred her porridge listlessly. It was already cold and growing colder by the second. Like the sinking feeling in her stomach.

'So, what time is it?'

'I don't know. Eight? Something like that.'

'When should I be over?'

Sæmundur focused on eating.

'I'm not sure people are allowed to bring dates.'

'Okay.'

The words stuck in her throat. She wasn't used to that. Garún stood up and threw away the rest of her porridge. She felt nauseous. She didn't want to have this conversation – didn't want to believe she had to have this conversation.

'Sæmi. Are you ashamed of me?'

He stopped eating and looked at her. She forced herself to turn around and face him. His face expressed hurt and something else. Regret? It felt like an act to her. She'd seen this fake indignation too many times.

'Garún, come on. You know I'm not.'

'Then why don't you want me to go with you?'

'I do want you to come with me.'

He reached out and held her hand. Started stroking her fingers with his. He'd done that when they'd first begun sleeping together. It hurt feeling him do it now, only to misguide her. Convince her of the lie he was telling her.

'I don't want to accidentally stir up trouble by bringing a plus one when it's not expected. I want to make a good impression, that's all.'

'Which will definitely not happen if that plus one is a blendingur.' He started to object but she didn't give him the chance. 'I know how these people are. I know what they'd think if I was there. I know why you don't want to bring me. I just… I thought you'd still at least ask me to go with you.'

'Garún, love, please listen to me. I want you to be there with me. I'd feel so much better. But I've been stirring up enough shit at Svartiskóli already without adding insult to injury. It has nothing to do with who you are. Trust me on this.'

He got up and moved next to her. Held her eyes with his, stroked her hair behind her ear.

She didn't believe him. But he would never admit to this ugliness in his heart. He would never tell her the truth about this. This lie wasn't only for her. It was also for himself. Maybe if he lied to her enough times it would become true for him as well.

She wasn't willing to let this go. Not like this. He was lying to her, acting as if she was imagining things, being hostile and paranoid. She wasn't. She knew she wasn't. She would prove to herself and him that she was telling the truth. Even if it broke everything they'd built together. If it was all based on lies, it wasn't worth anything to begin with.

Humans have no real way of defending themselves against the huldufólk's emotional empathy. That natural ability was also what allowed huldufólk to barricade their emotions from an invasive reader. She'd done it instinctively when they'd first met, and he'd later admitted to her that he found it uncomfortable. This was after they'd been together for several months. Garún had been occasionally reaching out to feel Sæmundur's feelings. Usually when they were doing something nice – out walking together, talking, drinking – but what really did it for her was when they were making love. Feeling his desire, pleasure, eagerness, on top of her own – it was intoxicating. But it had been a one-way street.

She had promised not to do this any more. It made him feel kind of abused, the privacy of his emotions broken, as he had no ability to reach back. It wasn't a bridge between them, but a wedge. So she'd stopped. As integral to the huldufólk as the ability was, it wasn't everything to her. She was human as well. So they had built a human intimacy, based on whispered secrets, gentle intuition and good intentions. She told herself she didn't have to know for a fact what he was feeling all the time. It surprised her that after a while it felt as if she did anyway, and vice versa. Subtly they'd grown so close that she could tell what was on his mind depending on how his brow furrowed as he pored over his manuscripts, how he scratched his head when he was worrying over something, and likewise how he held her when she was rolling a cigarette over and over on the balcony, knowing she felt depressed and alone. It might not do enough to pull her out of the slump, but it warmed her heart. They had built a bridge between them.

Now they stood at opposite ends of a chasm. She felt as if nothing could possibly close this gap between them. If she reached out and scanned his feelings to know that he was telling the truth, then she could trust him. But in doing so she would have broken her promise to him, irreversibly shredding the tender connections they had cultivated with each other. He wouldn't be able to forgive her. And if she was right – she couldn't forgive him, either. They were at an impasse. The only way for no one to get hurt was to accept the lie. An impossible choice.

He saw her worrying, saw some glimpse of this storm of doubt and fear tearing through her. He held her shoulders, looked into her eyes.

'Garún, you know how important this is to me. I'm on my last extension for my deadlines and getting some people in the department to back me up could really help me out. Almía's really gunning for me. They're gonna kick me out if I don't get someone to help.'

'You wouldn't have to worry so much if you'd just done it steadily over the school year. If you'd just—'

He rolled his eyes, threw up his hands in exasperated defeat. 'Yes, yes, I know, Garún! I know how this-and-that would be if I had done this-and-that. But this is how things are right now. I can't do anything about that.'

He went and started to get dressed. It looked as if he had decided to leave.

'All right. You'll do what you want. As usual.' She went to the balcony and lit herself a cigarette. 'I knew you didn't care. Like you don't care about anything. You have no problem with how people treat me. It's no skin off your back. You don't even care how the Crown treats people like me – they fund your university, after all.'

'Don't say things you can't take back. I do care! I can't stand how these fucking snobs treat you, or me for that matter! They are thick-skulled, mindless drones. But I still have to go. Besides, it's not like your friends treat me any better.'

A cold feeling sank in Garún's stomach.

'Is that so? What about them? How are they *mistreating* you?'

Sæmundur struggled with buttoning his shirt as he responded.

'Well, it's just ... they think they're so much better than anyone else. These people are so smug that it makes me sick.'

'Right. And you think that's the same as me not being able to meet anybody in your department? As not being able to attend as a university student if I wanted to?' The words turned to ice as she spat them out. 'Spare me this pathetic pretence of an inferiority complex. They think you're all right.'

'No, they don't. They only tolerate me because they know I can get them moss. Without that I'm just an annoying stray that follows you everywhere.'

She smoked, contemplating. Tapped the ashes from the cigarette.

'And so what? Have you ever considered that the reason they might act strangely around you has nothing to do with you, but simply because you're with me? Then you complain about it, when I can't even meet the fucking snobs that you call your colleagues!'

'Yeah, but ... that's different.'

He shrugged, trying to make it seem nonchalant.

'Why?' She shook her head, blowing smoke. 'It's different, all right. You don't meet my friends because you don't want to. I don't have that choice, apparently. You are such a fucking hypocrite.'

'Your friends are artists! It's completely different! You know how Svartiskóli is regarding huldufólk and blendingar – the Crown runs the entire goddamn university, like you said! What can I do about that? You know I don't want to keep you a secret.'

'You say you don't want to – but you do. You're still ashamed of me.'

He was fully dressed. Her cigarette had burned up. Blue-grey smoke flowed from her mouth as she talked.

ᚠ

Garún sat for a long while on the sofa after Sæmundur had gone home, staring into empty air as she smoked and petted Mæja. She tried to paint but everything she made was flat and unexciting. She finally got up and put on her moss green coat.

The train rattled down the elevated railway. The trains in Reykjavík were tired and worn-out, second-rate carriages that the Crown imported from the mainland. She exited at Hlemmur. The station was packed. It was the height of rush hour. Two police officers stood guard at the end of the platform, lazily carrying heavy skorrifles as if they were toys. They made her sick, their faces hard and threatening.

They stopped her as she was heading from the train platform. Mæja was cuddled up to her inside her coat and they told her to stop and show them what she was hiding. It's just my cat, she explained, I'm bringing it to my friend who will be taking care of it. Do you live in the city, they had asked. She said yes. They asked for documentation. She had some. It was one of the most expensive things she had ever purchased. The huldufólk living outside the city walls in Huldufjörður were not officially documented anywhere. If they managed to move into the city they could apply for official papers of identification, but a blendingur couldn't even pass through the gates. The city's bureaucracy wouldn't make blendingar official citizens, not unless they were born in Reykjavík. Even then they would have a hard time. Diljá had been the one who had hooked her up with a forgery. She knew people.

The officers inspected her papers carefully, then her. She did not meet their eyes as they took her in from head to toe, obviously and obnoxiously eyeing her up. She felt afraid of what they might do.

'Fancy outfit,' one of them said, 'for someone like you. Where do you think you're going?'

'I'm just going to see a friend,' she replied.

The officer handed her papers to his comrade.

'Do these look fake to you?' he casually asked.

He kept his eyes fixed on Garún, looking for the slightest sign of anxiety. Her heart was racing. She wanted to run. But they had guns. One false move and they'd shoot her without hesitation. And no one would mind. Just another illegal blendingur taken care of.

'I was born here.'

Her voice sounded weaker and less confident than she'd wanted.

The other officer went thoroughly over her papers with a stern look. This was it. This was how everything would end for her.

They would ask her to come with them back to the station for questioning and she would disappear.

Then they'd handed her back the papers.

'Don't go making any trouble.'

She nodded numbly, took her papers and walked away, holding back her instinct to run as fast as she could, trying to look composed.

'Fucking whore,' one of them muttered, loud enough that it would definitely be within her earshot.

Her ears rang with seething rage, but she just walked on, her heart racing, holding the cat tight up against her chest. She started to purr and Garún started to feel a bit better. Then she almost burst into tears. But she bit back and buried the feeling, as she'd done countless times. Don't waste your energy on sorrow, she told herself. Get angry instead.

It had started to rain. A type of rain rarely seen in Hrímland, falling straight down from the sky in the calm weather. An inexhaustible spring downpour that meant to drown this rock in the ocean where it belonged. She stood outside his door, drenched, holding Mæja up close to her for comfort. She knocked.

She forced herself to smile at him when he opened the door, a startled look on his face. He was wearing his suit. It didn't fit him properly. She still thought he looked good. Afterwards, she wondered why she hadn't told him what had happened, how scared she had been, how badly she had wanted to go in and cry and hide from the world for a while. She didn't want him to accept her out of pity. She didn't want anyone to see her this vulnerable.

'Hi,' she said, stroking away the wet hair sticking to her forehead. 'I thought I'd go with you to the party.'

It was a ridiculous thing to say. But she saw the answer written on his face, clear as day. Still, she had to know for sure. She reached out and read his emotions. Not holding back, she took him by surprise and dug deep.

Surprise. Regret. Anxiety. Fear. Shame.

She felt them as clearly as if they were her own emotions welling up inside her. He was afraid to be seen with her. Afraid to be judged. To be ostracised even more. He wanted to hide her, to bury her away from his academic life. He wanted her, but not visibly by his side. And then, the hurt. The feelings of betrayal over her breaking his confidence, of her reaching out and reading him like an open book. Everything else was flooded by a wave of self-loathing as he realised what this all meant. That his true feelings had finally been laid bare.

'Here,' she said coldly and handed him the cat. He hesitated. 'Take her!' she yelled.

Speechless, he took the cat. Mæja mewed, miserable and wet from the downpour.

'What are you doing?' he asked.

'She's yours now. Maybe she'll help you find a place for someone besides yourself in your life.'

'Garún, come on. You can't just—'

She put her hand up, silencing him. They looked at each other. Without saying anything at all, they said goodbye. Sæmundur saw something in Garún's face he'd never noticed before, an unknown feeling and intention that was a mystery to him.

She stood on the threshold and looked as if she was about to say something. Then she walked away and left him holding the cat.

Fimm

Sæmundur's place was a wreck. He didn't want to let her in, but given how they'd last left things he felt he had no choice. His amplifier was upturned, shards of broken plates littered the floor, piles of books and torn manuscripts were scattered everywhere. Sheets of papers showed esoteric symbols and layouts of a building, interspersed with unreadable scribbles. He cursed as he knocked over the inkwell on the floor and spilled black ink over them.

Garún took a moment to register the complete mess.

'What ... the hell ... happened?'

'Nothing, it doesn't matter.' Sæmundur gathered up the papers, using one sheet to soak up the spill. He suddenly turned and glared at her. 'It's none of your business. What do you want?'

She put Mæja down on the floor. The cat trotted over to her bowl and started eating the pellets of cat food that had spilled over.

'Right. I've obviously caught you at a bad time. I'm here because I need a favour.'

He was about to flat out reject her, but he hesitated for a moment.

'Why?'

'You're the only person I know who knows any náskárar. And we need to get in contact with them.'

'Who the hell are "we"?'

'The Kalmar opposition. Or something – it's not like we have a name. We're staging a protest and we want the náskárar to join us. We've already got a few marbendlar on board from the riverfront at Elliðaár.'

'Right. So you want me to introduce you?'

'Yeah. You don't have to back me up or anything. Just get me a meeting with them.'

He thought about this for a while. Of all the days she could have knocked on his door, it had to be today. But it was an odd turn of fate.

'Well,' he said, 'it so happens that I was just heading out to meet a náskári this afternoon.'

She spared him a smile, then looked as if she regretted it.

'Sounds good.'

ᚠ

A sprawl of factories, warehouses and shabby-looking storefronts, Skeifan had been designed to be the market hub of Reykjavík, and its manufacturing heart. The heavy industry might be in Gufunes, with its ironworks, quarries, leather works and tanneries, but here the city's more refined industries were placed: textile and woollen mills, meat processing plants, cooper workshops, along with various stores and small markets.

Sæmundur hadn't been in any hurry to meet Rotsvelgur. He owed the náskári a considerable sum of money at this point and he was about to ask for more credit, plus introduce him to a stranger who also wanted something from him. His entire plan depended on getting the gandreið mushroom, which was a big ask. Even for someone as notorious as Rotsvelgur. Sæmundur would have liked to have asked Garún to wait, but he'd been so shocked at seeing her that he didn't have it in him. It had hurt a surprising amount to see her there on his doorstep. He hadn't admitted to himself quite how much he had missed her. How much he despised himself for being too craven to stick up for her and stand with her.

If his plan worked, he wouldn't need the approval of anyone in Svartiskóli to do his work. He would be his own master. Breaking into Svartiskóli's library had become something of a mind exercise for him in these last months. It was a cathartic exercise which soothed his nerves. Proof that despite his having burned every bridge, there was still a way forward; that he could not be stopped. Still he had never thought he would actually be desperate enough to do it.

The náskárar convened at a vacant lot in Skeifan, the cleared site of a building that had burned down a few years earlier. Currently it was used as a store yard for stacks of pallets, rusted iron rods, mounds of fishing nets and colourful buoys. There were plans to build something new there, but they had all been halted when a bureaucratic cog had broken somewhere in City Hall. Now it was common enough knowledge that the náskárar roosted there, although they wouldn't deem just anyone worthy of engaging in conversation with.

A pair of dark silhouettes took off from a rooftop far to Garún and Sæmundur's left just as they entered the store yard. Scouts. Sæmundur glanced above them. No dark shapes in the overcast sky. But náskárar had incredible eyesight and could be watching them from a good few kilometres away. He kept wiping his sweaty hands on his coat. He and Rotsvelgur went way back – but there was a limit to his patience.

The náskárar landed like falling meteorites, hitting the ground with four resounding, heavy thuds as they dropped from the sky like dead weight, their enormous wingspan slowing their descent just enough to keep them from injuring themselves. Sæmundur jumped, although he had been expecting this, but Garún just grew more alert, her posture shifting to that of a cat about to pounce or flee. He almost told her to relax, they were fine, but then thought better of it. They were probably far from fine.

The náskárar surrounded them, perched on freight containers, their rough, iron talons digging into the rusted steel as if it was soft earth. Each náskári had three legs, with a heavy set of talons on each foot. The leg in the middle was commonly called krummafótur – raven's foot. Something parents said to their child when they put their shoe on the wrong foot. Should one of the náskári choose to pick Sæmundur up in their claws and carry him aloft, there would be little he could do about it.

Right in front of them was Rotsvelgur – the hersir of Those-who-pluck-the-eyes-of-the-ram. He was large for a náskári, towering over them despite his hunched back. Menacing and cold eyes sat behind a long beak that curved a little further down than was usual. Sharp iron like hardened lava covered it – a weapon made for tearing and disembowelling. He was armoured in helskurn, a roughly cast half-plate armour that covered his torso. The story went that it was made from the armour of soldiers Rotsvelgur had killed, fused with the arcane seiður of the náskárar. His hertygi, the harness going over his shoulders and around the armour, was decorated with trophies and status symbols Sæmundur could not identify. Many seemed to be from kills of monstrosities found in the sorcerous highlands, but among them were skulls and scalps from humans and huldufólk, claws of náskárar and fins from marbendlar. The other náskárar were similarly ironed on their talons and beaks, their hertygi decorated with varied trophies. Each of them had a large horned skull of a ram dangling from their harness, splotched red with dried blood. Blóðgögl, as he suspected. Soldiers. This wasn't a polite meeting, as he had hoped.

Rotsvelgur leaped down and shambled towards them with his uneven three-legged gait. Garún and Sæmundur both reflexively took a few steps back. He was a predator, a lumbering creature of malice and iron, his breath reeking of old blood and marrow. His black feathers ruffled in the wind. It looked as if it was going to rain.

'Sæmundrr,' the náskári growled in rough, archaic Hrímlandic. 'Err þérr arriv'd to pay the skuld?'

'Hail and well met, Rotsvelgur. I received the ... er ... memo, that was included with my last purchase. So I have come to negotiate with you.'

'Negotiate, þérr say't,' spat Rotsvelgur, and he leaned in closer. It took everything Sæmundur had not to step back. He could not afford to show weakness now. 'Talking err-at paying.'

'I can't pay now. But I promise you, I just need one last thing, and then I'll pay you back. Double.'

The náskári leaned back, stretching out his back. Contemplating. Calculating. He stood on his third leg only, using his other two talons to contemplatively shuffle his claws. At his full height the corvine being stood at almost three metres.

'Who err that gestr þérr brought?'

Rotsvelgur glared suddenly at Garún, his pitch-black eye narrowing.

'This ... uh ... is—'

Garún interrupted Sæmundur before he managed to make a mess of introducing her to the leader of the most powerful tribe of náskárar in Reykjavík.

'My name is Garún. I'm a friend of Sæmundur's. I've come to talk to you about an alliance.'

Rotsvelgur tilted his head sideways, staring her down

inquisitively. So much like a raven, but still so different. This close, the dark stains of blood were visible in the coarse iron that had been fused with his beak. It reminded Garún of the wild lava fields by Huldufjörður.

'Þérr err betwixt worlds,' the náskári said after a while.

Garún's heart sank – was there no goddamn being on this fucking island that couldn't give her a break for who she was? She kept silent, waiting for Rotsvelgur to make the next move.

'Err-at bad,' he said finally, nodding slightly.

It seemed like a learned gesture – a human gesture. Garún looked towards Sæmundur, who nodded at her encouragingly. It seemed like the -at ending was a negative.

'Such err the way of skrumnir, as well. Powerful seiðr.'

She made a mental note to ask Sæmundur about that later.

'I represent a group of people who are staging a protest against the city walls that are being used to oppress the people of Reykjavík. We will be protesting Kalmar's presence in the city as well. I'm here to talk to you about a possible alliance with your tribe. We could change things if we stood united against the Crown.'

Rotsvelgur kept staring her down. She held his gaze. She felt as if she was being tested. She'd heard of how confrontational the náskárar were, how highly they valued ruthlessness, strength and cunning. This was the first time she had talked with one, however, and she was becoming alarmingly aware of how much of her information was second- or third-hand knowledge and prejudiced hyperbole.

'Ok what ask þérr of *Krxgraak'úrrtek*? At die for another's cause? Convenient. This wall err-at of relevance to us.'

She didn't understand a bit of skramsl, but even she knew what Those-who-pluck-the-eyes-of-the-ram called themselves in their own tongue.

'That's not what I'm asking at all. We will not incite violence at the protest. We only want to make ourselves heard. I know that Kalmar constantly harasses the náskárar all around the country, not just in Reykjavík. We are fighting to remove their death grip from our society.'

The náskári started pacing from side to side as she spoke. He cawed when she finished speaking, a sharp sound of disapproval.

'Kalmarr understan't only violence – respect only violence. As þeirr should. Ok þérr shall be slaughter'd by their hand. As þérr should.'

'There must be something we can work out. If we discuss this and you could hear—'

'Vér speak-at to weaklings who fight-at.'

Garún was seething, trying to calm herself down with the thought that this was at least a good first step. A dialogue had been established. She hadn't been lifted up and dropped from the sky. Politeness was mandatory when you were surrounded by armed, flying soldiers. The náskári turned away from her to face Sæmundur.

'Rotsvelgur,' Sæmundur started, 'I swear to you I will make this worth your while.'

'Ok what hav't þérr to trade what ek desir't?' asked Rotsvelgur.

Sæmundur found them weighing heavily on him again – those pitch-black raven's eyes that did not see a man standing before them, but meat and bone. He only had one thing to trade. Whether this would end peacefully or in disaster rested on this moment.

'Svartigaldur,' said Sæmundur in a grave voice.

Rotsvelgur laughed. A náskári's laugh sounded like teeth being dragged down an iron rod, smiling all the while. The story went that they did not know to laugh until humans settled Hrímland, and then the náskárar had only learned it to be able to laugh at their competing settlers. Sæmundur was uncertain if he had offended Rotsvelgur. He stood prepared, with an incantation on the tip of his tongue in case he needed it.

'Svartgaldr, say't hann, as if Gottskálk the Cruel ha't arisen.'

Rotsvelgur strutted back and forth in front of Sæmundur, his iron claws hitting the gravel with sharp, ugly sounds.

'I'm not an idiot, Rotsvelgur.' Sæmundur leaned in towards the towering náskári. He reeked of sea salt and carrion. 'I know why you've let me rack up all this debt. Why you've been dealing with me, personally, even after you became hersir of the Ram Eaters. Galdur is forbidden among the náskárar. A vile, despised art. Do me this one last favour – and I'm your ace up the sleeve.'

Rotsvelgur stopped pacing.

'Do not forget yourself, old friend.'

He spoke in slow, clear skramsl. The language of the náskárar was rough and ill-suited to the vocal cords of other species, but through the years that Sæmundur had known Rotsvelgur he'd made the effort to learn the basics of the náskárar tongue, so he could better understand him.

'You are my tool regardless of whether I help you now or not.'

'Perhaps.' Sæmundur weighed his options. 'But it's up to you whether I will be a volatile weapon or not.'

'First you do what I ask. Then I will consider your request. What is it – moss?'

'Fungus. Gandreið fungus, mushroom caps heavy with spores.'

He ignored Garún glaring at him, knowing she would have some words for him later.

Rotsvelgur tilted his head. He seemed to be intrigued by this.

'I will call upon you in the next few days. Be ready. Then you will have your cursed fungus added to your total debt.'

'Wait, Rotsvelgur—'

'Fail me on this,' the náskári interjected, speaking in a low voice thick with the promise of violence, 'and you will be fodder for our ravenous young.'

He raised his iron beak and cawed to the other náskárar. They took off at once, the force of Rotsvelgur's beating wings threatening to throw Sæmundur and Garún off balance. And then they were gone.

'Sæmi,' Garún said in the quiet industrial yard, 'what the hell are you up to?'

He ignored her question. The gravel ground against his boots with every step.

Sex

Before

Ever since Garún could remember, her mother had dragged her to church. It had been a weekly event that broke up the monotony of her early childhood, as Hulda had insisted that her daughter never skip Mass. Not even if she was sick. Garún didn't go outside much and so the trips to the church were some of Garún's earliest memories.

She hated and loved it. Going outside was frightening but wonderful. Sitting in the church was dreadful yet beautiful. That was life in Huldufjörður for many people.

Garún's grandmother would babysit her when Hulda went to work or to the grocer's. Garún didn't like being left alone with her strict grandmother. Her name was Snædís and she looked as if her name suited her well – a cold, pale goddess of snow. Most of their time was spent in silence. Her grandmother would knit while Garún played with her shells and bones. Garún's grandmother taught her that they were animals and that she could play at keeping them as a farmer. She hadn't ever seen real cows or sheep, but she knew what horses were because they pulled carts filled with linens and fish, and she knew what dogs looked like because there was one in a yard on the way to church and he always barked at her when they passed by.

Her days were spent staring out of the window, where the neighbourhood kids would see her as they passed and shout obscenities at her. When they went too far and threw stones, Snædís would storm out and drive them away, screaming even fouler words at them, sometimes swiping at the kids with a broom if the mood struck her. Garún was often afraid and embarrassed, but she also felt warm seeing her harsh, distant grandmother standing up for her. Garún knew that she was different and that her grandmother didn't like it, even though Snædís pretended not to mind. But she still stood up for Garún. They were still family.

Sometimes Garún was home by herself when the kids came along and she would hide under her bed until they gave up and left. She was always terrified that they'd break in and beat her up. A few times they went too far and broke a window, for which Garún was scolded and sometimes beaten when her grandmother came back home. If her mother came home first, she would find her in her hiding place and hold her tight for a long time. She showed how afraid she was in front of Garún. Her mother cried later, when she thought Garún was asleep.

When Garún's mother had first taken her to church the reverend had tried to eject both mother and daughter. Garún couldn't remember it, since she was just an infant, but her mother repeated this story every time Garún kept dragging her feet when she was getting ready for church. As soon as they entered the deacon had fetched the reverend in a panic. The priest came partially dressed, with only his cassock on and the collar not properly attached. Her mother had heard people whispering disapprovingly, but she didn't care. She'd come with her newly born daughter and wanted her to be baptised. She deserved to learn the history and customs of her people. The priest did not agree with her on that and said that Garún did not belong to the old world – she belonged to this world. She was tainted by it and should be cast out.

'And you?' Hulda had asked, shaking with anger. 'Were you born in the old world? Do you not belong to this world? What makes you any different from my baby girl?'

Two adult men started to escort her firmly out, taking care not to use force to injure a woman holding a newborn, but still not giving way.

People just watched them throw us out, Hulda always said. The hurt of the betrayal had not softened with the years. It had made her harder. The next week they came again, but this time she brought every single blendingur in town who wanted to attend. There were around ten of them, mostly kids or young people who lived in the halfway house old Fjóla ran. Fjóla and Hulda teamed up to tear into the priest, the deacon and the people who sat by while kids were denied basic decency.

'These are your children,' they said. 'It takes a village. And by shutting your doors to them you might as well leave them out in the freezing cold.'

A quiet fell over them. A chilling reminder of the methods used by Hrímlanders in the past, both human and huldufólk. There was too little food on this barren island and oftentimes too many mouths to feed. Livestock fell sick and died, or were mutated horribly by the sorcerous land they fed upon, long winters and cold summers rendered crops useless. Infant mortality was more common back then, so why waste the resources in bringing up yet another child when there were too many working mouths to feed already? Many of whom were as likely to die from disease or hunger, anyway. Back then, blendingar had frequently not even been given the benefit of the doubt.

And in reminding them of that unspoken, buried past, the two women conjured up a deep and hurtful shame, especially in the older members of the congregation, some of whom had lived through the last days of those long, dark times. Perhaps some had even carried out those bleak, cold sentences of death on crying infants. The lava fields were said to be riddled with the spirits of children dead from exposure – called útburðir in Hrímlandic. But such angry spirits would be the least of the dangers found lurking out there in the sorcerous, jagged terrain.

The people joined Hulda and Fjóla in their protest. Let the children in, they said. Let them be baptised and hear the holy word. Let them know the history and downfall of their people. They had to know their past so it could not be repeated.

It felt like the worst kind of winter storm, Garún's mother had said, when the huldufólk reached out to each other back and forth, giving in to feedback loops upon feedback loops, trying to reach a consensus. Trying to understand and empathise.

They could attend Mass, the reverend finally agreed when the overwhelming feeling of the congregation had settled, as long as they stood at the back. Blendingar were not to be seated.

This, too, would change in time. But one step at a time was what Garún's mother used to say. A phrase Garún started to loathe as she got older. She wanted to take leaps and bounds, not baby steps. She wanted to run, to soar.

The church in Hamar was a tall rock at the centre of town, as great and imposing as the grandest cathedrals built by humanfolk. Or that's what the huldufólk said. Garún had never seen such a building. She wondered what kind of buildings her father's people had. What was on the other side of the towering city walls. The houses in the village were humble shacks made from driftwood and rusted corrugated iron, the buildings neatly placed between the undisturbed lava rocks. Foundations were laid by packing turf and rocks, in the traditional house style. There were no roads in Huldufjörður, only winding paths that connected the village in an intricate web. Some houses were painted, and people often pooled their money together and bought cheap paint imported from the city. They picked bright, vibrant colours: dandelion yellow, crimson, sky blues. Some huldufólk were better off than others, but you couldn't really tell from their homes. The times of abundant riches, overflowing decorations and vanity had passed, but they still wanted their village to be beautiful. This world could never replace the one that they had lost, but they still wanted to make it theirs. To make it glamorous in a different manner. They were all stuck together, barely surviving by the fractured remains of their ruined world, far away from Reykjavík's city walls, as close to the sorcerous energies of the seiður-infused lava fields as they could possibly be while still remaining safe.

Garún quickly grew to despise going to Mass. Not only was it difficult to walk with her mother through town with people staring at her, she was also afraid that the children leering outside her house would catch up with them. And the Mass itself was more often than not a hateful sermon of the downfall of the huldufólk, their pride and hubris and lust for entertainment at the cost of the suffering of other, lesser races.

Sometimes she saw the other children on the street, the blendingar hiding behind tubs of fish or stacks of pallets. They stared at her and she stared at them. These were Fjóla's kids, the strays she'd taken in. Hulda told Garún that they had just been left on her doorstep through the years. Orphans from the city. Maybe if Fjóla hadn't been there, they would have been carried out into the wilderness and left there. Garún couldn't believe that someone would do that to an infant. It broke her heart every time to think about it.

She often asked her mother about her father. Who he was. Why he never visited. If he was dead. If he knew she existed. Her mother didn't respond. The only answer she got was being told to keep quiet and not to be insolent, and that was that. When she asked her grandmother, she was told not to reopen old wounds.

On just one occasion had Garún managed to get something out of her mother, when she came home drunk one night. Garún was eleven. She didn't know why she felt compelled to ask at that moment. She had reached out to Hulda, and found a profound sense of tenderness and sadness. Alcohol usually made her mother harder, not softer. The feeling was so new and overwhelming that Garún flinched.

'Liljurós,' her mother had responded in a slurred voice, perhaps too drunk to have noticed Garún reaching out to her. 'He called himself Liljurós.'

Then she went to bed and fell asleep.

Garún kept the name deep inside her, like a fragile treasure. She didn't even dare to whisper it out loud, even though she was by herself and no one could hear her. It was too delicate, too precious, to risk it.

Later in life she would better know what feeling it was that her mother had felt that night, usually buried too deep within her for anyone to find a trace of it. It was grief.

Garún began trying to get out of attending church. At first she tried crying, but that didn't work as her grandmother took to silencing her quickly with a slap. Worse would be coming if she kept on, Snædís had told her.

'You are too old to cry and I'm not about to let you spoil

73

all the hard work your mother has done on your behalf. Be thankful.'

And that was the end of that.

It was a general rule of Garún's childhood that she grew up too fast – or was made to grow up too fast. They lived in a rickety shack in Huldufjörður. It was a small village and gossip spread fast. Garún's mother was not about to let it be known that her daughter didn't go to church, after all the trouble they had gone through. She had a responsibility, Hulda had said. To make things better for the ones that would follow. Snædís never went to church.

'The old world is gone,' she would say every time Hulda invited her along with them. 'I'm not about to spend my Seiðday grovelling by its ruins.'

The world of the huldufólk had ended quickly and violently. There were many stories about how it had happened. Thaumaturgical wars, ecological catastrophes, divine punishment. How it happened wasn't that important, only that it had happened. In the end, every story reached the same conclusion. They all blamed the arrogance and depraved urges of the huldufólk, the privileged, corrupt world they had made for themselves. Their world had been one based on limitless desire, beauty and greed. For centuries the huldufólk had used gateways into other worlds to lure people in and feed upon their memories. Their supernatural charisma, allegedly heightened by the thaumaturgy of their own reality, coupled with their other-worldly display of riches, could lure in any kind of creature. The huldufólk made them into pawns in their cruel games. They stole away children, elders, teenagers, human and non-human alike. Supposedly their reach had encompassed countless realities. The feasts could last for months, where groups of extravagantly dressed ladies and lords would feed upon the succulent minds of their captives until nothing remained. Delicious morsels of fear and suffering, tender love and compassion – everything tasted exquisite to their refined palates. Revenge was practically impossible, no one could utilise the gateways except the huldufólk themselves. Their weapons and sorcery assured their absolute dominance. They were beautiful and cruel, and the other worlds were created only for their amusement.

Until the foundations of their reality shook and shattered and the huldufólk fled in terror-stricken panic into any other dimension they could. Their fate elsewhere was unknown. Maybe there was still an empire in another dimension where the huldufólk ruled over their inferiors, as if nothing had happened, but if that was the case then no one could verify it. When the huldufólk fled into this world they were not met with mercy and were actively hunted down. Their centuries of cruelty, along with the folklore spun about them, gave the humans more than enough justification to pay them back in kind. In remote Hrímland, they had found a foothold, where the land was almost unpopulated and toxic from seiðmagn. Here they could try to endure. News of huldufólk abroad was rare; travellers of their own kind existed, but they were few and far between – unverified rumours brought on passing ships. They were scattered to the wind, still, after centuries.

The apocalypse shut almost every single portal into the huldufólk's dimension. There was no going back. But what remained were ruins like the church in Hamar and abnormal oddities like the Forgotten Downtown. When an entire reality collapses, others feel its aftershock. Cracks start to appear, which widen into gaps with time and erosion.

To Garún, the church in Hamar was like a god lording it over the town, a protective vættur of the land that was only challenged by the city walls in the distance. After all, the huldufólk were Hrímlanders, and just like all Hrímlanders they had to live by a mountain. The church was their mountain. Huldufjörður's people streamed into the rock on every Seiðday. The lava rock was tall and angular, jagged and coarse, almost like a stalagmite. To all appearances it seemed like a regular part of the volcanic landscape, barring its unusual size. But as you walked inside, another world came into view.

Glory was the word that came to her mind every time she entered. *Divine glory.* The ceiling was high, much higher than the rock's height indicated. Tall windows reached up, many of them broken but some still intact, their stained glass covered in fine cracks. Broken statues lined the walls, one between every pair of windows. No matter what the weather was outside, golden light and a warm summer breeze always came through the windows. The stone pews were made of lustrous marble. They were carved from the same material as the floor and the entire inside of the church. It was all one seamless marble stone, which looked as if it had been shaped with seiður or galdur, not physically carved. The stained glass and statues depicted events and creatures that had been forgotten hundreds of years ago. But it didn't matter. They were all masks of the one god.

The altarpiece itself depicted Adralíen-toll in all its glory. The one god was made from countless hands, each of them holding a mask of a vættur, a god, a demon, a monster. In the centre was a white, expressionless mask. Disconcerting light shone through its eyes. This mask was the only consistent one among the countless others, which were never the same any two Masses in a row. Sometimes it swapped out the mask in the centre during Mass, but no one ever saw it moving. At one moment the blank mask would be there, but then something realigned itself in the blink of an eye and Adralíen-toll would be holding up the mask of Drókumljár, the god of galdur and disease. In a moment the altarpiece could change again, so the hand would now be holding the mask of Týrrkt, the three-tongued betrayer. Neither the priest nor anyone else had the explanation or the knowledge of how the altarpiece worked. It was an ancient piece of art, one of the few intact remains of the world that had been.

Garún usually spent her time at Mass gazing out of the window. She sat by herself at the back as soon as she was old enough. Her mother sat with Fjóla and the other children. With time they had been given the privilege of sitting down, not that she considered this to be anything resembling a kindness. It simply made them easier to ignore if they weren't standing. Garún had seen through the priest's façade. He too was just a mask, hiding his true face.

The church was enormous and as a result, even when everyone in the village was in attendance, was only half full at best. The priest's voice sounded clearly through the church, reverberating in the nearly empty chamber. The acoustics carried his voice so he always sounded as if he was standing right behind Garún. Every Mass the reverend talked about the sins of the huldufólk and their fall from grace, their arrogance and unnatural greed that caused Adralíen-toll's heart to be filled with contempt, making him place the mask of the Destroyer Who Creates the Vortex upon his face, shaking the foundations of the world until they collapsed. He spoke of how they had to repent for the sins of their past, for the millennia of lust and cruelty, and only then could each and every one of them earn their place in the embrace of the one god, becoming a mask in his hand that the god might one day place upon his face and thus grant them eternal life. Everyone could hope. But it was a hope tainted with self-reproach.

Garún learned to ignore the reverend's preachings, let the vile

77

hate disappear into the background so he was nothing more than the ocean roaring in the distance. So she spent her trips to church mostly doing what she did at home: looking out into a distant world and daydreaming.

Behind the cracked glass she simultaneously saw the weathered hovels of Huldufjörður, and something else. If she let her mind wander she sometimes saw very clearly into the world that had been, which still let its sun shine into the church. Every time she saw a different place. A ruined city made from singing glass, slowly being taken over by an exotic nature. A boiling, black sky filled with colours she had never seen before, where living lightning bolted through. Vast forests of rotten trees and impossibly shaped mountains in the distance, split down the middle. Over it all, a brighter and redder sun, more cruel than the one she knew. Hungrier. But all these visions were like the glass in the window, broken and incomplete. Vanished splendour. Garún wanted nothing more than to shatter the window and jump through, flee into a broken world where she might be able to live her life in peace, unharassed. But she knew that if she did so she'd only land on the hard ground outside the rock, still in Hrímland, still in Huldufjörður. That world was gone and would never be revealed to them again.

'She has to go out,' Hulda had said while stirring the pots. 'She's a child, she should be playing outside. This isn't healthy for her.'

Garún was sitting at the top of the stairs, trying not to breathe. The entire house had creaked like an ancient mansion from the day that it was built and she was not about to alert her mother and her grandmother to her eavesdropping.

'She might get hurt. They might do something to her.'

Her grandmother's voice was thick with stubbornness. And something else. A tone Garún was not used to hearing Snædís use. Worry.

'Keeping her locked inside will do her even greater harm.' The sound of utensils, knives in the drawer. Hulda was likely about to cut the rye bread. 'Things have changed – are changing. Even the reverend knows it and has stopped trying to fight it. I won't bring my daughter up to be afraid because of who she is.'

'What she is,' Snædís said.

The gentle sounds of cooking stopped. The pot was bubbling.

'She is not a thing. All right? I won't have you talking like that, Mamma. Not in my house.'

A murmur of agreement. The cooking resumed. The knife tapped the board as it cut through the tough brown bread. But it was sweet and delicious with lots of butter. Garún hoped her growling stomach wouldn't alert them.

'When I'm looking over her we abide by my rules,' Snædís said in a definitive tone.

'No, Mamma. She is my daughter. She deserves a better world. And we're making it for her. But I can't—' A sound. Her mother swallowing a lump in her throat. 'I can't do it if you're in our way as well. Not with everything else stacked against us. Against her.'

Quiet.

Snædís got up, started helping Hulda with the cooking. They started setting plates.

'I know, elskan, I know.' Her voice was soft now. Gentle. 'I'm not against you, I just … I don't want to see her get hurt. There is so much hurt in the world, out there.'

'I know, Mamma. But we will make it better for her. And she will make it better for others.'

Garún scurried away from the top of the stairs as her mother walked out into the kitchen doorway and called out to her.

'Garún! Dinner!'

ᚠ

She couldn't remember how old she had been. Six? Eight? Too old to be going out properly for the first time by herself. Too old to play with other children for the first time, that's all she recalled. The feeling of inadequacy and anxiety. Her heart was racing as Snædís called to her the next morning, after her mother had gone out to work at preparing the salt fish.

'Garún, get down and dressed! You're going out to play. No sense in keeping you inside in weather like this.'

It was early summer. The sun was shining, not all through the night but still close. The days were long. Before she went out, almost running from all the excitement, her grandmother gripped her arm, hard.

'Promise me, Garún,' she said in a grave tone. 'Do not play outside the village. Do not play in the lava fields – do you hear me?'

Garún nodded. Her grandmother squinted her eyes and quickly reached out for her feelings. This got her a light tap on the head.

'I said, do you hear me?'

'Yes, Amma,' she said meekly.

They reached out to one another. Found an understanding. She felt her grandmother's worry. It felt as if it had a hundred sources, too many entangled roots to be able to tell them apart.

'Good.'

She went outside. For the first time by herself. The first thing she did was to run towards the shore. On the bay, small fishing boats were being rowed out on the glittering sea. She played in the rocky shoreline and found new, weird creatures she'd never seen before. A starfish, countless shells, limp, ugly flowers that smelled and piles of seaweed like the hair of a vættur, or maybe a marbendill. She had heard about them but never seen them. She watched over the sea, looking for movements from unfamiliar creatures, but saw none. The waves were mesmeric. They made the most wonderful, calming sound as they dragged the countless pebbles down with each small crash.

'Hæ!'

Voices behind her. Giggling and shouting. A group of children were approaching her. For a moment, she was afraid that it would be the kids who threw stones at her house. But it was another group of kids. The blendingar from church and some of the other kids from the town. She didn't know that the huldufólk children could play with the blendingar.

'Hæ.'

Garún approached the girl who had called out. She was older than Garún, almost a head taller. She was a blendingur like Garún. She smiled.

'My name is Fæðey,' she said and beamed. 'What's your name?'

'Garún.'

The gaggle of children caught up with her and they started playing in the sand, running around, asking her questions. *Where do you live? Why don't you ever go outside? Can you read? Do you have any brothers or sisters?* Garún was overwhelmed by the sudden attention. She didn't know where to begin.

Fæðey grabbed hold of two younger children, only toddlers, really.

'These are my siblings.' The two children looked up to Garún with snotty noses and big, questioning eyes. 'Styrhildur, my sister, and Hraki, my brother. He's the youngest.'

'Am not!' he shouted, and he raised his fist as if he was about to hit Fæðey.

'No!' Styrhildur interposed herself between him and their sister. 'No hitting!'

'Sorry, they are a handful.' Fæðey said, smirking at Garún. As if she knew how this was. How it was to have younger siblings. Garún felt so jealous of them. How easy and natural their bond was. 'Go out and find the biggest starfish you can find!'

The kids immediately ran off, each claiming they would be the one to find the biggest starfish ever. She turned back to Garún.

'Have you ever played Fallen Stick?'

Garún was hiding behind a cluster of rusted barrels, half-sunken into the grassy earth. In the distance she saw Harmdís standing by the stick, leaning up against the wall of one of the abandoned houses, scanning the surrounding landscape in search of the other children in hiding.

Suddenly, Fjalar, one of the other kids, jumped up from the mounds of tussocks where he had been hiding and sprinted towards the stick.

But Harmdís was faster. She immediately saw him and started towards the stick, reaching it way before he was even close.

'Fallen Stick for Fjalar, one-two-three!'

Fjalar stopped running and threw his hands up in frustration. He joined the group of other children who had also been spotted and struck out by Harmdís. They were sitting idly in the grass, waiting to see if someone could outwit her. There couldn't be that many left. Maybe only herself and a couple of others.

Suddenly she saw Fæðey on her left, in the shack behind where Harmdís was standing. She couldn't spot Fæðey from that angle, but Fæðey could see Garún where she was crouching.

She stared at her meaningfully – had probably been trying to catch her attention for a while. She mouthed something that Garún couldn't figure out. She pointed to Garún, then towards Harmdís, then nodded affirmatively. Garún thought she understood. She nodded back.

Fæðey ran behind the house and started banging on the corrugated iron. Making it sound as if she was trying to climb on it or something similar. Harmdís heard the sound and ran towards it – she had to see who it was before she could run back to the stick, touch it, and strike the player out.

Garún didn't think – she ran. She didn't bother keeping low or sneaking around; this was a matter of speed. Harmdís didn't notice that she was making a run for it until Garún was very close, but still, Harmdís was taller and stronger. Garún ran faster than she had ever done in her life. Her heart was beating so fast it felt as if it wasn't beating at all. She was like the wind.

'Fallen Stick for everyone!' Garún shouted with the last breath of air in her lungs.

Her hand reached the stick just before Harmdís got to her. She threw the stick in the air, sending it flying off into the heath. All the captured kids jumped up from where they had been sitting, cheering and shouting cries of victory. Fæðey came around the corner of the shack and beamed at her. The plan had worked – they had done it. Together. They had won.

She had set them all free.

Sjö

Sæmundur didn't like where this was going. A messenger had arrived for him the very next day, a tall, scarred blóðgagl that had landed in his goddamn yard for all to see.

'Skeifan. Dusk,' it said, and took off before Sæmundur could get a question in.

He still didn't know what exactly Rotsvelgur wanted from him. But it had to be svartigaldur. Some really bad shit, if it was something he or his tribe couldn't or wouldn't do. Sæmundur honestly had a hard time piecing together just what that might be. The náskárar were outlaws by choice, the laws and structure of the ground-dwelling species of no concern to them. An eagle did not follow the rules of the field mouse.

With a distracted mind he started gathering up a few helpful things: some scrolls; a few small, tattered journals; bones. He could really use a smoke, but he had to conserve it. He had been feeling down ever since he and Garún went their own ways last night. They'd walked back to the train station together, and he had waited for her to ask about the mushrooms. She hadn't. Instead she had told him that he'd better be careful, whatever the hell he was doing. Then she'd asked him if he would go to the protest they were planning.

'I don't think so,' he'd said, shuffling his feet. 'I don't know if I can make it.'

'Right.'

Garún's face had not betrayed any kind of emotion she was feeling. Or he was too stupid and self-absorbed to notice what that might be. Yeah, probably the latter, he thought to himself.

Her train arrived first. She had started walking away, but had then turned around. His heart leaped. Maybe she was going to suggest that they should meet for a drink. Or something. That they could be friends. That she wanted to forgive him. Anything.

'What is a skrumnir?' she had said.

'What?'

'Rotsvelgur mentioned it. A skrumnir – familiar with it?'

'Uhh ... I think it's kind of like a seiðskratti. But a náskári. They're born different, somehow, can do seiður intuitively. I'm not sure. Why?'

She thought about this for a second.

'No matter. Thanks.'

And that was that.

He'd spent considerable time feeling sorry for himself after she had dumped him. He'd been a selfish coward and promised himself that he would do better. But, in truth, what disturbed him more than his letting her down was the fact that the social event in Svartiskóli hadn't really resulted in anything beneficial for him. He had made no allies. He had still been an outcast. And then they had kicked him out. He'd let Garún down with nothing to show for it. That, he felt, was what had been truly unforgivable of him.

Fucking halfwits.

Whatever was about to happen to Svartiskóli would be on them. They drove him to this. They left him no choice, and he would not back away from his right, his destiny. He would wield galdur like an unparalleled master. They would be forced to acknowledge him as their superior. And then he would make things right with Garún again.

Rotsvelgur was waiting for him in the store yard. He was alone.

'Sæmundrr. The day of reckoning has come,' the náskári said in skramsl.

'Yeah. I would have appreciated some information beforehand on what kind of galdur you want. I can't just show up and do whatever, you know. I have to prepare.'

'No excuses,' Rotsvelgur continued in a low voice. 'You will do as I request – or pay.'

'All right, relax. What do you want me to do?' He felt sick asking this question. 'And do you have the fungus?'

The náskári shambled up against him, leaning in close.

'Do not make demands before you have upheld your end of the bargain. My demand is simple: weave a galdur of fear and awe the like of which has never before been seen. A galdur of protection and dominance. Make them fear me.' He spoke with malicious hunger. 'Make them cower. Make my soaring shadow blot out the sun.'

ᚠ

The meetings were held in the stockroom of a grocer's in Starholt. Diljá's uncle owned the place and sometimes attended their meetings. He was the one who distributed their periodical, *Black Wings*, outside Reykjavík. He wasn't in tonight. This meeting had been planned for weeks now, with endless debate and discussion leading up to this point.

They were gathered in between stacks of crates, sitting on top of barrels and boxes. There was better attendance than usual, which was a good thing, Garún tried to tell herself. It meant people were interested, that they wanted to actively change something. But it also made her worry that they were going to derail the discussion or hijack the protest somehow. Jónas Theium was there with his usual gang of followers. Lilja was with them. Garún wondered if she remembered anything from their last encounter, when she had painted over her memories. If Lilja did, then she made sure to hide it.

Diljá greeted Garún with a hug and a kiss on the cheek. They reached out to each other and Garún felt Diljá's nerves and hope all piled up together in a bittersweet feeling that probably mimicked her own. Hrólfur came up and nodded in greeting to her, which she returned. The two of them had been talking by themselves when Garún had come in, in the corner by the coffee pot and mugs. Garún often wondered if there was something between them. Hrólfur seemed a bit too stuck-up for Diljá. He wore cheap but smart suits and sharp-looking glasses that complemented his features. He worked as a secretary or something for the city, a cogwheel in its bureaucracy. It was through him that they got most of their intel on how the city government worked with the Crown and how they came into occasional conflict.

'More people than the last few meetings,' Hrólfur said. 'Looks like it'll be a proper demonstration at least.'

'Yeah. I hope so. It's important we stay on track.'

'It will be great, Garún.' Diljá placed a supportive hand on her upper arm. 'We're all here because we believe it's the right thing to do. We're going to make a difference.'

'Not if we don't get this meeting started,' said Hrólfur, and he checked his watch. 'Where are Katrín and Jón?'

'Katrín couldn't make it,' said Diljá with an apologetic smile.

Garún was annoyed to hear this, but not surprised. She would have put money on Katrín bailing at the last minute. Why would a rich human girl like that risk everything? Writing articles would always be good enough for those people. That way they felt better and never actually had to get their hands dirty.

It had been almost two years since Katrín joined their group. Until then it had been the three of them: Hrólfur, Diljá and Garún. They had founded *Black Wings*. Hrólfur and Diljá had done the layout; Garún mostly put up protest posters, stencilling words and symbols of resistance around the city. She also worked on the printing press when a new issue was due – they all did. Except Katrín, that is. She claimed to have a busy schedule and couldn't let herself go missing for hours at a time. Understandable enough, but still Garún was frustrated at her even though she always pulled her weight. Her monetary contributions covered a huge part of the paper and ink they needed.

It was hard to get good articles for the magazine. People were scared of being caught and didn't want to risk drawing the Commonwealth's attention. The journalists who had insisted on continuing to write damning pieces in the newspapers had quickly found themselves out of a job, their credit rating shot, any prospects of finding proper work basically turned to ash in their hands.

The periodical was printed in secret in a small space above a metalworkers' workshop in the industrial district in Höfði. Hrólfur was responsible for renting out the space, and the craftsmen working the floor below had made it their business to not know exactly what the tenants above were up to. It was easier for everyone that way.

Initially, Garún had written a few articles for the magazine, some of which were well received. She mostly focused on the racism in Hrímland, which was stoked and reinforced by Kalmar's xenophobic policies of segregation and human-first regulations. At first, she had felt good seeing her words in print, knowing they would get all around the city and beyond. She felt as if they were accomplishing something. She wrote under a pseudonym, like everyone else, but word spread around their tight-knit inner circle. People respected her. They listened. They became aware of the adversity she faced and agreed that rooting it out was a huge part of why they had to rise up against the Crown.

This feeling of well-being soon faded. Months turned into years and nothing changed. It was as if they did nothing except print repeats of the same old articles, the same phrases, just with new writers penning them. People could talk and talk, but it didn't matter if no one with any real power was listening. It didn't matter if no real action was taken. Garún knew well that people had to be forced to listen to uncomfortable or undesirable things. The knee must follow the abdomen, as the saying went. You had to follow through, no half measures. Hrímlanders had been writing about the Crown for decades, first in public, then in secret, and it never came to anything except giving people some temporary outlet so they could keep on accepting the status quo. That was good enough for most people – too many people. They had to be shown that things could change.

It had been a while since Garún had made her way to the printing press at Höfði. She didn't bother much with the magazine any more.

Jón came in like a storm, carrying a bundle of papers, trailing coat and scarf. A cliché of the Reykjavík poet if there ever was one, with a beard impeccably trimmed in an unkempt style and hair made up as if he had overslept. Although he derived his poetical last name from the fjords, Garún suspected he had been born and raised in the city. Perhaps his family came from the countryside. Or not. He was a poet, after all. There was no harm in a little exaggeration.

'Jón! You're late!' said Garún in a mock-outraged tone.

'No! You're early!' He pointed to his watch, then moved it away before Garún could read it. 'How is that, can't artists tell the time?'

'Just as well as you poets can rhyme,' she replied in turn.

Jón's laughter was sincere and loud and infected her with its warmth. She found herself smiling.

'All right, everyone, sorry I'm late!' Jón waved to the crowd and started shuffling through his papers. 'You could have started without me, but I guess I'm now... uh... leading this meeting or something. I don't know. Why don't we get right to it?' He found the paper he was looking for, folded it, and flashed a smile to the gathering. 'Same rules as before. One person has the floor at a time, raise your hand if you want to speak, raise your fists in support with the speaker – no cheering or shouts of hear, hear. All right? All right.'

He cleared his throat. In a few words he'd gathered the un-wavering attention of everyone there. They'd gone over this again and again in previous meetings, but there were some faces in the crowd that hadn't shown up for a while. This was their last meet-up before the protest. They had to be on the same page.

'The Kalmar Commonwealth has been here for more than five decades. They've built army bases, fortresses – that flying mon-strosity – and the Reykjavík city walls. We were all brought up to believe that Kalmar's work is to the benefit of all its citizens. But that's just it. Non-humans are second-class citizens, at best.'

People silently raised their fists in agreement.

'The city walls are said to protect us from both an invading army and the creatures roaming the wild highlands. Creatures corrupted with seiðmagn, the wandering tröll and malicious vættir. But since they've gone up no wars have ever reached our shores except briefly, fifty years ago, and no creatures have ever wandered towards the city. That is because the walls are not to keep us safe – but to control us and eliminate non-humans from the city.'

Jón looked over to Diljá, who had raised her hand. He pointed to her and sat down as Diljá got up and spoke.

'Count Trampe founded the Directorate of Immigration along with the Hrímlandic authorities. As a stiftamtmaður he didn't technically need to involve local government, but Trampe knew that the institution would be that much stronger with Hrímlandic interests partially involved. The person who first led the institution and made most of its policies is currently the police commissioner in Reykjavík, one Ragnar Kofoed-Hansen. Trampe sent that son of a bitch to Kalmar in his younger days, where he was trained by their secret police in ruthless, fascist tactics they've long since perfected. Ragnar returned home an expert on police brutality, racial segregation and spying. He's done a fucking good job of implementing it with the city walls in the last few decades. The Directorate's people guard the gates and hinder free passage, escorted by armed police officers. Every single non-human must carry a variety of documents of identification and intent of travel. If they are found lacking, they are kicked outside the gates, or jailed. It doesn't matter if you're travelling from inside the city, they still arrest you. Huldufólk and marbendlar are constantly harassed going in and out. Blendingar hardly ever receive proper documents of identification, even when born in the city, which traps them on either side. People with authentic documents have even had them confiscated – that includes humans. Especially if they are known to have inconvenient political opinions. Remember, it's no rumour that Kofoed-Hansen founded an intelligence agency within the Directorate. It's a fact, just not one that's ever been reported by the so-called free press.'

She fell quiet for a moment and glanced nervously at Garún, who nodded encouragingly to her. They'd talked about this so many times. There were many humans in the crowd. They needed to hear this.

'Garún hasn't been able to visit her mother and grandmother in Huldufjörður since she came to Reykjavík six years ago. She's being held prisoner in her own city. Being caught smuggling means you're fined, if you're human – it means the Nine if you're not. Marbendlar rely almost solely on the rivers from Lake Elliðavatn, which pass through a customs checkpoint in the wall. They are strictly regulated and fined when the slightest errors occur. Last week, Kryik'traak, a friend of ours, was travelling by land from the Coral Spires of Þingvallavatn. He found himself held in custody for four days because he was missing a stamp on his merchant's permit for the journey – meaning he had neglected to bribe someone. He was transporting precious pearls and crafts from the spiral city and had it all confiscated. He faces financial ruin because of this.'

Two hands were raised in the back. Garún recognised them: Styrhildur and Hraki. They stood up, blushing when everyone turned to look back at them, looking for a moment like the children Garún had known growing up. They'd smuggled themselves into the city a few years after her. They looked like teenagers, so self-conscious that it was almost painful to look at them.

'When we came into the city,' said Styrhildur in a faint voice, 'we didn't have any money to bribe the guards with. We didn't know any traders or farmers going in. We had no documents, nothing proving who we were or where we came from. No one would help us.'

Her voice was quiet. Barely more than a whisper. A deep calm had settled over the room, as people held on to her every word. People were unconsciously holding their breath.

'I felt like nothing. Less than nothing. Then Garún and Diljá found us. Kind people helped us get through, so we could live in the city. Have a chance to learn something. Become something. Meet people. Read. See works of art.' She looked down at her feet, flashing a faint smile. 'It was everything to me. I don't want anyone to ever feel like that again.'

In the back, Jónas stood up and spoke out of turn.

'And what will a protest at City Hall do to fix this? We should march down to the gates, make them open them for us! Do a fucking real protest, some real activism! Just holding up signs won't—'

'Jónas!'

Hrólfur's voice boomed over the assembly. He didn't say much during meetings, but he made himself of great use by usually being the one who made sure that some manner of order was upheld.

'Respect the meeting!'

A cluster of raised fists shot up in agreement, including from Garún and Diljá. Jónas sat back down, mumbling some form of apology.

Styrhildur looked a little lost after the interruption. Garún raised her hand and got the word from her. She and her brother sat back down, relieved.

'The city is in charge of traffic through the gates. Kalmar's army mans its battlements, finances its upkeep – but when it comes to actually getting through the gates, the city, acting as the Directorate, has the final word. The mandatory check for identification, intent of travel, taxes – all of this is issued and controlled by the city. Everyone knows that the Commonwealth are the ones holding the reins, sure, and everything the city is doing is in line with Count Trampe's agenda for Hrímland. Kalmar has the city and parliament in its pocket.'

She took a moment to look over the crowd. Read their faces. She saw the fire reflected in their eyes. Some of them were burning with ardour, with revolutionary will to change everything. There was anger and fear and doubt – but also hope.

'But we have to decide to start somewhere. We just have to find the right place to push them. The right way to rally people and get them to realise that things don't have to be like this. We are too few in number for a protest at Lögrétta – a protest outside parliament in Austurvöllur has to have a big crowd to have an effect. Charging through the city gates will just get us shot, or worse – arrested and sent to the Nine.' She set her jaw and caught Jónas' gaze directly. 'At least the ones of us who aren't human.'

He stared at her, defiant. She hoped he felt some semblance of shame over how much of a fool he was acting.

'We're not idiots, Jónas. You're not the only person in the room with at least half a brain – try applying part of it to some empathy or logic.' Some laugher to this, a fluttering of raised fists from smiling faces. 'We've thought this through. There are armed guards at the gates, easily by the dozen if an alarm goes out. If we put pressure on City Hall, then it might get something moving. We know there are plenty of people from all over the city who aren't happy with the state of things. Including people in the government. We just have to push them into doing something decent and standing up for the people. To have the courage to fight for change that will benefit everyone – not only humans.'

As she said this the gathering raised their fists and some who couldn't hold back yelled out their support. She let herself smile. They were behind her. Most of them, at least. This could actually happen. She still needed to get the delýsíð, but she'd take care of that. They agreed with her. They believed in her.

Still...

Still, she couldn't let herself relax. She had meant everything she'd said, but regardless she had a hard time actually believing much of what she was saying. Reform was not really a part of Garún's politics. It was better than nothing, sure, but to her it felt like ladling water from a sinking ship. It was just enough to stay afloat, but it didn't address the real root of the problem. It wasn't drastic enough to make a difference. She could not find it in herself to truly believe it could make radical and authentic changes in her lifetime. But it had worked for her mother, when she was a child, so – she had to give it a try. Sometimes a little change can mean a world of difference. She knew that. She wanted that.

She was just tired of endlessly settling for scraps. She wanted the real thing. That day would come. This was only the spark. She would ignite the fire in their eyes. She raised her fist and started chanting, joyful fury gathering in her as others joined in.

No more Crown! No more Crown! Hrímland out of Kalmar, no more Crown!

ᛦ

Sæmundur was losing control of the galdur. He was struggling to rein in the forces flowing through him from outside this world. Something was wrong. Through his muttering of forbidden words and weaving of language and sound he had opened a metaphysical rift, one he was struggling to contain.

What Rotsvelgur had asked for was not impossible, but there was no established ritual that would permanently provide him with the protection and the aura of awe and fear he wanted. A temporary enchantment could be manifested, although with significant risk of a demon infesting the bones of either the galdramaður or its target, but it could be done. But a permanent

95

galdur, that was still not manifested in the bones or flesh of its target... That would require some thinking out of the box.

Creating the audioskull for Garún had been an intriguing task for Sæmundur. He had been obsessed with the connection of music to galdur, how the actual intonation and shift in key affected the incantations themselves, and the noisefiend had been a kind of by-product of his research. He'd acquired a skull from one of the doctoral students in galdur in exchange for some highland moss and bound the demon into it. The galdur he used to make it was almost entirely a new creation. The demon was simple-minded, and so not a great risk, creating music from the proximity of danger to the person carrying it.

What Rotsvelgur needed was a similar kind of demon. One monitoring its surroundings, letting its wielder know of danger looming unseen around the corner. But it also needed to gener-ate a kind of aura of fear and power. Its purpose was complex, but it still would have to be without the sentience of a tilberi or a golem due to its extended existence. A demonic servant was usually banished again within twenty-four hours, or after their task had been done, whatever it was. As long as it was busy at work the galdur had a higher chance of safely working. Idle hands were the devil's plaything. This kind of demon would not have a task to keep itself busy with. It only had to watch and wait. Idleness was a dangerous thing for a malevolent sentience.

With every step he took to wrest control of the unearthly energy he was drawing on, the more he felt his grip of the galdur loosen. Nothing reacted in the way he wanted it to. Something else was taking over the reins, and the more he resisted the stronger the pull of the current became, drawing him towards the whirling centre of the abyss he was being forced into.

Sæmundur started chanting a galdur of binding. It was too early for it – the demon was not fully manifested and he had only an idea of how its power would manifest – but he had no other option. It was either that or risk a full-blown possession. Slowly, he felt the galdur come to a close. He held on to the rituals of the binding like a drowning man on to a rope. He was seething with anger over his own incompetence. This was all from his own lack of understanding. He was stumbling around blindly, finding obstacles where he expected clear paths and unblocked ways where he expected a closed door. He hated that feeling and the fact that he seemed to be unable to get over it. This was not something he could adjust to. He was at his limit and he knew it.

Rotsvelgur was watching Sæmundur from a distance, perched on top of a construction crane. Should the ritual go awry the hersir had no intention of being caught in the crossfire, or blamed for this mishap. He'd said he would stand on a lookout, but Sæmundur was not convinced the náskári would have his back if the worst came to the worst.

With aching lethargy, the binding incantation started to take hold. The demon would be bound into human ribs, welded into Rotsvelgur's helskurn. Slowly the bones started taking on a faint shade of blue. The breastplate was made by the náskárar, roughly moulded out of iron with their seiður. It was coarse and uneven, covered in ugly, sharp edges. As if it had been found out in the lava fields, a relic cast in an eruption centuries ago. It was easy enough to move the iron apart with galdur to make grooves for the ribs on the inside of the armour. After the galdur was finished Sæmundur would seal them in, making Rotsvelgur's galdur imperceptible. The only way to catch it would be to use the sorcerous glass of the seiðskrattar's masks, something in- credibly rare and unlikely to be used by náskárar.

Sæmundur keeled over as he felt a cloying, aching pull at the core of his heart. The connection he had made, the pathway he had opened within himself to the outer forces, resisted his will. They would not relinquish their hold on this world, now that they were in. They would not let go of him so easily.

He had felt this pull before. But never like this. His lips trembled as he spat out words of protection, of exorcism. With trembling hands he dug into the gravel and the earth beneath it, sketching out galdrastafir and runes of power. He knew that these symbols were only instruments to focus his mind. He knew that the true power came from the incantation, the galdur itself. The very force with which he was struggling. But in that moment, he didn't care. He felt small. Weak. Powerless. He would have kissed a holy symbol of the sovereign kings if he thought it would help him.

And then, it ended. The malevolent force, which just a minute before had felt all-encompassing and all-powerful, faded into nothingness. He was crouched on his hands and knees, sweating as if he had been running for days, grovelling before a presence no longer in his presence. Before him, the ribs were laid out in the armour shell, coloured a deep, ocean blue. Whether or not the demon had been manifested as Sæmundur intended, he had no way of knowing. He sure as hell had no interest in casting further galdur to find out. Whatever this was, it would have to do for Rotsvelgur.

The náskári landed on iron talons in front of Sæmundur.

'Is it done?' he growled. 'Was the fell ritual effective?'

Sæmundur wiped his face with his sleeve.

'See for yourself.'

He pointed towards the bones. With slow, cautious movements, Rotsvelgur leaned in and inspected the armour and bones, tilting his head to the side like a raven.

'Good,' Rotsvelgur said. 'Seal the bones up. Hide them.'

'And my end of the deal?'

Sæmundur was not about to finish the job until he knew he had what he wanted.

Rotsvelgur removed a leather pouch from his belt. It had been firmly sealed with wax.

'Do not open it in my presence.'

'How will I know if it's the real thing?'

Rotsvelgur stood silent, his feathers ruffling in the wind.

'All right, I suppose you've never let me down so far.'

Sæmundur took the pouch and hid it inside his coat. Even with the demon-infested bones in front of him, he still felt that he carried a greater force of malevolent destruction in that pouch. He started speaking to the iron and made it seal the bones within.

This ritual had almost cost him his life. But soon that would all be behind him. Soon he would gain true understanding. No matter the price.

Átta

Garún looked up towards Haraldskirkja. The split church tower loomed over the city. The stars were out in multitudes, the faint shimmer of the aurora moved lethargically in the east like streaks of oil on water. Electronic skylights lit the church up from below, bathing the twin spires in an amber light so it stood like a beacon in the dark, with a foundation reminiscent of rows of basalt columns. To Garún it had always looked like a carcass split halfway down the middle, as in the violent old sagas, the forked crevice between the towers a jagged wound.

Haraldskirkja's bell tower rang. It was a quarter to midnight. She shuffled her feet and tried to rub herself warm through the leather jacket. She was standing at the end of Skólavörðustígur, leaning up against a concrete garden wall on the side of the road where she wouldn't be noticed. Bare branches hung over her head, the autumn leaves already gone. The colours hadn't bothered to stay. Fucking Hrímland. The autumn barely lasted a week, it was just summer and then winter. Although calling it summer sometimes felt like a stretch. There was no good weather to be had, no matter the time of year. Or that's what it felt like. Everlasting night or ceaseless day. Both exhausting and thrilling in their different ways. Yet, Garún felt a sense of elation. She preferred the long shadows of winter, the nights stretching into late morning and falling again in the afternoon. It made for better cover when tagging.

Garún killed time by rolling a cigarette. She preferred hand-rolled over the manufactured factory crap that the colonial stores sold. Tobacco was supposed to have character, a soul. The cigarette was ready and she licked the paper carefully, making sure the tobacco didn't come loose. Lit it. Six minutes. The cigarette was rolled too tight, just like she preferred it. Smoking wasn't worth it if you didn't have to work for each drag.

There weren't many people around and no one spared her a second glance. Trains rattled past on elevated tracks behind the church at regular intervals. In the distance they sounded like old toy trains. The electronic music buzzing in her headset was muted, calm, the audioskull hidden in her backpack. Everything was still. On a corner in the distance she saw a woman standing in the shadows by a couple of bare trees. Diljá. Styrhildur and Hraki remained out of sight, ready to warn her of any sign of trouble.

It was a calculated risk to sneak into the Forgotten Downtown. This wasn't like shoplifting from the store. If you were caught at the grocer's you only risked losing a finger, maybe a hand. If you were caught going in or out of the Forgotten Downtown you would vanish. There were a handful of people that she knew of who she suspected the police had caught. It was still just guesswork. They could have escaped or moved, perhaps they were hiding in Huldufjörður or out in the country. Maybe they'd made it to the mainland. There was no way of knowing for sure. But Garún was pretty sure that no one could vanish so completely and unexpectedly without the *assistance* of the Crown.

Two minutes.

She threw away the stub and walked determinedly to the statue in the centre of the square, right in front of the church.

She glanced around. The great square was empty, not a soul in sight. The majestic buildings of the háborg, the city's acropolis, were dark and silent. The neoclassical buildings lining the square felt to Garún like a different kind of wall, a fortified citadel in the heart of the city that watched her from all directions. A prison within a prison. She felt trapped.

The statue was a powerful piece of art, a bronze sculpture of Hrafna-Flóki. He carried an axe in one hand and from the other a raven was taking flight. The king had brought it as a gift for the Hrímlanders and built it on top of the cairn that was there before. Before the statue was built and the square properly paved, the cairn had stood neglected for quite some time, years of negligence and laziness diminishing it to a pile of rubble. Times had changed during the intervening decades. Reykjavík wasn't a small town by the shore any more. It was a city.

It was no coincidence that the gate was there. There was power in this place, an energy that Garún felt, but could not name. If the heart of the city was somewhere to be found, it was here. As Garún walked up to the statue she wondered if something had been there before the students built the cairn. Perhaps a monument had always been erected here, since Reykjavík was founded. Perhaps predating it.

The clock struck midnight. Garún started walking anticlockwise around the statue. She counted the steps carefully and made sure to complete the first lap on the fourth stroke, the second one on the eighth. On the twelfth stroke she stopped in front of the statue and faced it, striking its concrete foundation with a flat palm.

As soon as her hand touched the rough rock her feet were swept from underneath her. The sky fell into itself, forming a black sun. A sharp, freezing wind tore into Garún, trying to drag her up into the roaring abyss. Above her was no longer the starlit darkness of cold autumn nights, but something else. Something behind the darkness. Something that was waiting.

All this happened in an instant, the moment between two beats of a heart. Garún collapsed. She was shivering and her vision vibrated. It only grew worse if she shut her eyes. She gave herself a few minutes to recover slightly before looking up.

She was in Reykjavík, but at the same time she wasn't in Reykjavík. There was no church behind her, no buildings in sight. No moon or stars or clouds in the sky. At her feet was an irregular pile of rocks where the statue had stood just a moment before. They looked ancient. The city centre, where the streets were lit up by electric lamps, was now dark and vacant. A broad dirt road led down the hill on the same spot as Skólavörðustígur was in Reykjavík. It was always foggy here, and in the distance lonely hrævareldar lit the streets. The electronic music had transformed as soon as she passed through. A vague threat was hiding in the tune and the beat became irregular and paranoid. Static surged in the background.

The Forgotten Downtown. What Reykjavík once was, or could have been. A dream from another world. Rökkurvík.

Garún walked down the hill of Skólavörðuholt. Unlike Reykjavík, here the houses were low and simply constructed, with large, wide gaps between them. The corrugated iron was rusted, the shell-sand panelling had cracked and crumbled. Trees spread their leafless branches over gardens overgrown and filled with rubbish. The trees were all dead, but still standing.

The Forgotten Downtown was like a faded photograph, blurred and vague. A disappearing memory. Its existence was not officially acknowledged, but it was irrefutably still a part of the city. Some research into the place had taken place when the Crown had just come to Hrímland with foreign technologies and knowledge, but it had very quickly been stopped and all traffic in between strictly forbidden. There was not a soul who knew for sure where the Forgotten Downtown was: if it was in another country, another planet or another dimension. Some thought it to be a part of the ruins of the hulduheimar, or a side effect of that apocalypse, but there was no way of determining it.

Here Lækjargata was a muddy track alongside the stream running from a marshland lake. The stream looked filthy and it ran deceptively deep in the ditch, separating the central city into two parts. Garún crossed the brook using a makeshift plank bridge.

She followed the instructions of Viður's rough map down a path that she called Tryggvagata in her head, but there were no streets marked here. She walked briskly past the bar Gómorra and tried to lie low. There were not many people about and those that were passed each other with hunched shoulders, avoiding one another, their mere presence here a severe taboo. The music in her headphones picked up when she passed it, alerting her to possible danger, but Garún knew the beat and knew that she'd be safe as long as she didn't stick around.

She recognised some of the derelict houses as they had an identical twin in Reykjavík. These were only phantoms of their counterparts in the real Ránargata. There was not a single unbroken window and every door had been nailed shut. These were the dwellings of shadows. Blue-tinted hrævareldar floated aimlessly down the streets, their eerie flames sputtering in the air, the only street lighting to be found in this dark and sombre place. Garún was careful not to look directly at one, in fear of being led to her doom.

Finally she came to the place that Viður had described. It was a two-storey house, with a deteriorated shell-sand finish. The windows were dark and she couldn't spot any movement inside. It looked as if the house had been abandoned for decades.

She went through the overgrown garden on a paved pathway that was cracked and ruined. It led her behind the house to the basement. Two dead trees slanted precariously over the yard, which was filled with rubbish. A rusted tricycle lay upside down, the thick grass slowly engulfing it. She wondered if children had ever lived here, or if this was just a phantom of the past like everything else. A thing from nowhere, made of nothing and used by no one.

Garún stepped carefully down the crumbled stone stairway and knocked on the cellar door. There was no light inside, but the glass in the door was unbroken. There was no response. Nothing moved inside. She knocked again. She had turned back and was heading up the stairs when someone opened the door.

ᚠ

An intensely focused eye measured her through the crack in the doorway. They both stood completely still, measuring each other up. Garún didn't like the sound of the music buzzing in her headphones and slid them off her ears.

'Feigur?'

No response. The eye didn't even blink.

'Viður sent me. I need … Well, I need delýsíð.'

The crack widened, the person inside moved away. Garún hesitated, gathering courage before she went in. The door clicked shut behind her.

The foyer was shut off from the rest of the house by black sheets hanging in the doorway. Feigur went through them without speaking to her. She followed him into the living room.

Windows were boarded up, curtained or simply painted black. There was hardly any furniture in the living room. The yellowed walls were bare and on the floor was a filthy mattress, the rest of it covered with empty bottles and junk. Torn rags and piles of garbage were in the corners of the room. A low coffee table sat in the middle, covered with full ashtrays, dirty plates and scratched vinyl records. There was no record player in sight. A pungent stench of decomposed food permeated the air. Feigur sat on the mattress by the table and stared at Garún. She pushed a few bottles out of the way with her foot and sat on the floor opposite him.

The huldumaður was gaunt and withered, his pale skin stretched over his skull like canvas. His long hair was thin and the beard unkempt and wispy, as if it was glued on. He was wearing a torn leather coat that barely hung on his frame. They remained silent for a while. He stared and said nothing. Finally, she couldn't take it any longer.

'Viður said you were selling delýsíð.' He didn't respond. 'I need some. Liquid, not powder.'

Feigur sat still for a long while before he replied.

'Are you Garún?'

'Uh. Yes, that's right.'

She was a bit taken aback by his knowing her name. Viður must have contacted him somehow.

'I've got delýsíð. Liquid. Undiluted. Pure. But it doesn't come cheap.'

His voice was brittle and cracked like branches snapping underfoot.

Pure delýsíð. She'd never got close to anything like it before. Usually it was weak and thinned out. This meant she would have to approach the chemical in a completely different manner. She could mix it into the paint as usual, or use it instead of linseed oil on a painting, or spray a clear finish over a graffiti after it was done. She might as well skip using colours altogether and paint with a clear finish. The effects could be completely different. Maybe stronger, maybe more subversive. Her heart raced.

'All right.' She forced her voice to keep calm. 'How much?'

'Ten millilitres go for five thousand. Fifty you can get for twenty, seventy-five would be—'

She stopped him, holding up her hand. These were preposterous amounts.

'You've got nothing mixed, nothing cheaper?'

'No.'

'Why not? You could just thin it down, right?'

No response. Right.

'Do you accept any trades?' she ventured.

'That depends on what you have to offer.'

She started listing paintings, jewellery, but he shook his head. 'No, not objects. Memories.'

A shiver ran down her back. He was one of them. She should have been able to tell: the noisefiend screaming at her through the audioskull that this was not safe in the slightest.

The huldumaður sitting opposite her collected memories. Or rather, he fed upon them. Consumed them like little morsels. The experience was said to be an unfiltered ecstasy, incredibly clear and sensual. He was obviously an addict. It was probably the only thing keeping his body going. Without memories to feed on, he would soon become nothing but dust and a worn leather coat.

The delýsíð was integral to their plans. Without it the protest could fall short. She had to come through.

'What kind of memories?'

She immediately regretted asking. She was not sure if this was something she really wanted to know.

'Childhood memories. Sweet. Painful. Rare.'

'In return for what?'

'If it's good – one hundred millilitres. Otherwise… perhaps a minimum of fifty.'

'How do I know if you will like it?'

'There's no way of knowing until after the fact.'

He tilted his head and she felt him reaching out, feeling for her emotions. It felt disgusting, invasive. She endured it for a while, then blocked him off.

'Hmm. Seventy-five minimum. Hundred max. Deal?'

She felt nauseous.

'Deal.'

Stealing memories was something that huldufólk had done in great excess, centuries ago when the gateways into hulduheimar still existed. When they were a shining empire, wealthy and powerful. They arrived like beautiful demons and robbed people of who they were. Garún felt sick at the thought of playing a part in that dark inheritance. This was deeply wrong. But she didn't have a choice.

Feigur stood up and went for a moment into a back room. After a while he came back with two small soda bottles made from glass, sealed with ceramic stoppers. In them was a clear liquid. One was just above half-empty, the other had only a bottom fill. He put the bottles on the table. Garún flicked the ceramic plug off one of them and smelled the contents carefully from a distance, making sure not to breathe too heavily. She felt dizzy. It was without a doubt delýsíð. Very pure. She'd never seen anything like it.

Without saying another word she lay down on the mattress. Garún had heard enough horror stories to know how this happened.

'Can you choose what memory you take?'

'Sort of. Sometimes.'

Feigur sat next to her, almost as rigid and tense from excitement as she was from dread. He leaned in and she felt an odd, sour odour emitting from him.

'Will I know what you take?' she asked with his grim face looming over her.

'No,' he responded.

'Good,' she managed to mutter before everything went dark.

ᛄ

Feigur slammed the door behind her. Garún stood shivering outside the cellar door. The lock clicked. She stared uncomprehendingly at the bottle of delýsíð in her hand. It was full to the brim. One hundred and fifty millilitres. She placed the bottle in her backpack, as if in a trance.

She went up the stairs and out into the backyard – the same way she'd come, but she didn't quite remember what she was going to do next. It took her a while to recall how to get back. She checked Viður's instructions on the crumpled note, just to be sure. She found herself staring at the rusty tricycle covered in wild grass and scattered sticks. Fallen branches from the dead trees littered the ground. It reminded her of something, but she didn't know what.

Garún put on the headphones and started walking. She just wanted to get the hell away from that place. The music calmed something inside her and she walked aimlessly through the streets of the Forgotten Downtown, not caring what the tiny demon trapped in the skull was trying to tell her, just glad that someone was looking out for her, telling her to take care. It made her feel as if she wasn't completely alone.

She was walking in circles. No, that couldn't be. Garún stopped, looked around. She was at the same spot, almost in front of Feigur's house again. She'd gone too far, crossed the boundaries in her thoughtlessness. Near the borders of Rökkurvík the streets circled in on themselves, deceiving and turning careless walkers around endlessly. No matter how far you walked you would never get anywhere. There was nothing outside of the Forgotten Downtown.

Garún felt sick and claustrophobic, as though she were a prisoner in a maze. She wanted out.

A blue hrævareldur floated nearby. Before she could stop herself she looked right into it. Her feet led her towards its warm and inviting flame. It floated further away and she followed. It knew where she was going. The fire would lead her home to safety.

Garún managed to stop herself with her toes just off the edge. Below her, black waves beat against the concrete harbour. The hrævareldur floated above the water, just out of reach. The sea was deathly cold. From the faint light cast by the hrævareldur something could be seen moving in the deep – something pale and massive under the surface. Tremors shook her body. This had been too close.

It was an arduous task to find the place described in Viður's instructions. The house was weathered, even though there was no weather or sunlight in the Forgotten Downtown. There was no floor inside, wooden scraps and rusted debris covered the earthen foundation. The doorways were empty. Scraps of wallpaper hung on the walls. A rough, concrete staircase led to the upper floor.

Upstairs was bare concrete, open doorways, windows boarded shut. It was even colder here than downstairs. Only one room set itself apart. Iron pipes jutted out from the floor, thick and solid, in place for a bathroom, most likely. Someone had sprayed a galdrastafur on the middle of the wall. Garún sensed it before she saw it and realised she'd been heading towards it subconsciously from the moment she stepped inside the ruined building.

The sigil was an arcane shape, an esoteric form that spoke directly to the subconscious. The spray shimmered wetly, as if it had only been painted an hour ago. Its shape was of long arms stretching out in a curved, overlapping circle from the centre of the stave. A vortex, a black hole that devoured everything. Garún placed her palm on the centre of the galdrastafur.

The world crashed into her, and Garún felt as if her breath had been punched out of her lungs. Immediately the music exploded in her years.

The police.

$$\mathsf{Y}$$

She found herself inside a bathroom stall. Her hand rested on cold tiles, scribbled with illegible tags and lewd messages. The guiding symbol was not there. Loud dance music overwhelmed the deafening warning from her headphones. The noisefiend was going berserk. The police were close, accompanied by something worse. There was danger everywhere.

Garún barged out of the booth, still wobbly from the physical trauma that came with the shift in reality. The cramped bathroom was filled with men, reeking of alcohol, cigarettes and sweat. They laughed and cheered when she limped out of the stall, obviously thinking that she was with someone in there, and wasted by the look of it.

'Well, well, a blendingur! You've still to do one of those, Jói,' said a man dressed in a suit, pissing into a urinal.

'Jemmgh,' Jói slurred, and tried not to piss too much on the floor.

'How much do you charge, love? Or do you come free?'

'Where – am I?' Garún finally managed to grunt. It was hard to breathe.

'Haha! The whore doesn't even know where she is!'

A middle-aged man came up next to Garún and leaned in. He stank of cigars and brennivín.

'What's a half-breed like you doing here? Go and whore yourself somewhere else!'

He tried to grab her, but Garún pushed him back as hard as he could. She spat in his face as he stumbled backwards and fell.

'Go fuck yourself, you fucking pig!'

She shoved her way past the men and out.

The club was packed to the doors. Modern spotlights cast multicoloured light over the crowd and tried its hardest to turn a regular living-room floor into a dance floor. Garún looked around, bewildered. She didn't recognise this place. Downtown clubs didn't usually let huldufólk in, much less blendingar. She still knew that this wasn't the same house she'd come from in the Forgotten Downtown. She'd shifted somewhere else. She made her way to a window and looked outside. She wasn't on Hverfisgata, she was on Laugavegur. She wanted to vomit. This felt wrong. She didn't know you could leap this far between places.

The noisefiend screamed in her headphones. People stared at her and even though she couldn't hear what they were shouting she knew it wasn't good. She had to get out before things got worse.

Then she saw them. They were not in uniform and almost indistinguishable from the rest of the crowd. But to her they were like jesters at a funeral. The police scanned the crowd for a face that didn't belong. A safe gate, right. That idiot Viður. And she was a bigger idiot for trusting him.

One of the police guarded the door while the other two made their way through the dance floor. Garún kept low and retreated towards the stairway leading to the upper floor.

She looked back just before she was out of sight. That was when her eyes accidentally met one of them. Their gazes locked. He knew. Some drunkard stumbling down the stairs knocked into her and broke the deadlock. She dashed up the stairs as fast as she could, leaving behind a trail of outraged people with splashes of beer on their expensive shirts and dresses.

Upstairs, people sat on worn couches by tables sticky from spilled beer, smoking and drinking. She rushed past looking for an exit, a balcony, anything. The windows were of a decent size and she managed to tear one open. She reached into her backpack and fetched her last can of delýsíð paint. The humans stared on, bewildered, as she sprayed an arcane symbol on the middle of the floor before hoisting herself out of the window. Drunken men tried to grab Garún but were too late – she was out.

Instantly a violent fight broke out in every corner on the upper floor. A couple who were flirting a moment before were now tearing each other's hair out; co-workers were trading punches; girlfriends were scratching each other bloody. The suit-wearing officer appeared in the window, his face dark red with rage as he screamed at people to control themselves. It was not a good sign that he could restrain himself. Wild-eyed, he scanned for her and saw her making her way across the roof.

'Stop!' he screamed.

He was punched in the face before he could do anything else.

The roof was small and steep, too high to be able to jump down from. She moved down the roof until she reached the top of a garage. The officer had somehow managed to escape the clutches of the frenzied guests and was now out the window. Garún lowered herself down but instinctively let go when a resounding crack broke out between the houses. She hit the concrete, hard. Drunken people let out horrified screams in the distance and Garún realised he was armed.

She jumped to her feet and sprinted as fast as she could.

Another bang echoed and she could feel the bullet as it flew past her ear.

Garún ran until she could taste blood. She took a sharp turn into an alleyway between houses. She tried to quieten her breathing and listen for the officer's footsteps, but it was almost impossible. When she no longer felt as if she was inhaling dozens of razor blades, she risked checking if she had been pursued.

Electric lamps illuminated the sombre night. Trees spread their bare claws towards the sky. A cat sneaked noiselessly across the street. Everything was still. Garún let herself slowly sink, her back against the wall. She noticed the graffiti all around her, the esoteric messages left by teenagers, gangs and kuklarar. She breathed a sigh of relief. Had Viður known that the exit was compromised? Did he betray her, making sure that she'd be ambushed on her way back?

A clammy hand gripped her throat, so quick and unexpected that her head was knocked against the wall. Her vision darkened. It was him. Blond, oil-slicked hair and a cruel look on his face. The audioskull hadn't warned her until she'd felt his fingers around her throat. This was no regular police officer. He was using seiður to hide his presence. Garún cursed and spat. She tried to struggle, but he was immovable, his hand like an iron ring around her throat.

'I could smell your stench all the way out to Grandi,' he said. His nostrils flared. 'Delýsíð. So you're the one who's been busy all over Reykjavík? And you're crossing over to Rökkurvík?' His laugh was hollow. 'How did you possibly think that you could…'

He leaned in closer, focusing. He sniffed her. The whites of his eyes became slightly illuminated.

'Is that a demon I smell?'

He looked down, towards the audioskull.

She kneed him in the groin as hard as she possibly could. He didn't move. She could just as well have kicked a wall.

'You really are one stupid bitch.' He started to smile, slowly. 'You have no idea what kind of shit you've got yourself into.'

He grabbed her by the hair and banged her head hard against the wall, once, twice. He tugged at her hair, forcing her to look at him. Warm blood ran down to her neck.

'You are now under arrest. You'll be coming with me down to the Nine, for a private interview. If you co-operate, we might be merciful. Your execution will be expedited. You—'

There was a movement from the edge of her vision and then dark blood spattered Garún's face as something bashed the officer in the head. She twisted herself out of his grip. Another hit to the body lying on the ground, with a sickening crack, then another.

Styrhildur stood over the body on the ground, a bloody crowbar in her hand. Hraki and Diljá came running, putting their arms around Garún, helping her up. Her legs were weak, giving in with every shaky step. Everything was a blur: the man, bleeding on the street; running through the dark alleys; the sounds of footsteps fading in the distance; the crazed music of the noisefiend in her headphones.

Sirens in the distance.

Níu

Sæmundur stood by the sink. The tap dripped at a steady pace. He was stuck in a loop, going around and around on a problem, always arriving at the same result, no matter what different approaches he tried. There were no other ways, no other solutions. *Rauðskinna* had the answers he wanted, it was as simple as that.

He was faced with only two real choices: give up and admit defeat, or seek the answers he needed.

Simpletons. Sheep. Ants.

They had forced his hand. They had left him no choice. Nobody would call Sæmundur 'mad' again. They would witness what it meant to be truly *learned*.

He went to the cabinets and pulled out the ingredients he had prepared. After lighting the stove he started warming up the leftover stock from the night before. He lifted the lid of the pot and smelled its contents, stirring it. It was a thin kind of soup, just slightly thicker than water, with herbs and powders that would protect his digestive system from what was to come.

Sæmundur fetched a ceramic jug from the cupboard. He filled another pot with water and lit the stove. While the water rose to a boil he put on thick cloth gloves, took a handful of dried mushrooms from the jug, deathly pale in colour, and put them in a coffee press. The gloves went in the bin. When bubbles started forming in the water he poured it into the press. A potent stench of mud rose from the broth and the water became brown and murky, as if it had been fetched from the marsh. Sæmundur picked up the manuscript he'd been reading and gave it another read, tried to chisel it into his mind. He didn't dare mumble it out loud to practise.

He pressed the mushrooms and poured the brown liquid into the broth on the stove. He lifted the pot and held it up so the foul steam would rise to his face.

For a brief moment he was assailed by doubt. It wasn't too late to stop. He didn't have to go through with this. For that short moment he allowed himself to feel that doubt; he let the weight of the decision he stood in front of to fully settle in. Either because of his certainty or his foolishness, the doubt could not sway him. He wasn't sure if this obsession came from a place of weakness or strength. It was too late to stop now. He had started down this path a long time ago.

He started to chant in a low, steady voice. He pulled out a large clump of dried highland moss from the bag the cloth-golem had brought and ground it over the now bubbling broth on the stove. Communicating with and controlling the fungus would require some seiður mixed with the galdur he was about to weave. The moss sizzled and dissolved immediately. He felt his body resonate with the galdur he was chanting. The foul-smelling mushroom broth was ready.

If he didn't go through with this, he was just a waste. A waste of talent, intellect, emotions, meat, bone, life. He told himself this, over and over again.

Sæmundur took a large swig of the broth, forcing himself to chug until he almost threw up. He focused on drawing in the seiðmagn from the moss and fungus, weaving it into the galdur connecting his own body to the gandreið fungus. When the bowl was empty he tossed it in the sink and put on his coat. It was a grey woollen coat, large and bulky like Sæmundur himself, all the buttons torn off and the ends worn. Mæja rubbed against his legs when he was putting on his shoes. He felt nauseous. He pushed her away, surly, but somewhere in his groggy mind he realised that she was probably very hungry. Who cares, that was not his problem right now. He didn't have much time.

A dim afternoon gloom covered the city. Light had started to fade, it would be dark soon. Sæmundur walked hurriedly towards the University's main building. Electric lamps flickered with amber light, turning on one after the other, as they prepared for the coming darkness.

The university was less than fifteen minutes' walk from Sæmundur's apartment. The main building was a huge, grey concrete mass, planted where the land rose to its highest. A curved road led up to the main building, as if it was a noble manor rather than an official government building. Along the road were ragged tracks and a small tram platform in front of the main entrance. The tram was just a few minutes from arriving when Sæmundur came along. It was a considerable distance to Svartiskóli from the main campus and its surrounding university facilities. A few students were waiting at the platform.

The mushrooms were starting to kick in, but with the power of the incantation and the amplifying effect of the moss he could contain the effects. He tried to remain inconspicuous as he kept his distance from the others waiting. The tram rattled up to the platform and stopped.

He didn't recognise anyone on board, but their suppressed glares indicated that he was not a total stranger to at least some of them. He didn't care if he was looked down upon for using and selling moss to students, or if they thought he looked like a vagrant. Dealing moss was probably more of an advantage, since it could be hard to get to a reliable source of seiðmagn besides what the university supplied. What did incense him with a shameful rage was when he was looked down upon for his *delusional ideas*. For *foolishness*. When they called him *Sæmundur the Mad*.

The tram jolted down the small incline, past the great, flat university grounds where geese sat in the dwindling autumn light. The route went on with regular stops in the student apartments in Vatnsmýrin, right towards the looming hill of Öskjuhlíð where Svartiskóli loitered by the edge of the forested hill, crowned by the thaumaturgical power plant in Perlan. It was a behemoth of dark steel, its glass dome illuminated from within with eerie, pulsating lights.

Svartiskóli was newer and more fortress-like than the other university buildings, as if it was purposefully designed to dominate the more traditional main building. Sæmundur saw ripples move over the school's pitch-black walls and pseudopods stretch out from it. He forced his eyes shut, rubbed them and didn't look towards the school again. Svartiskóli had been constructed from the same obsidian pillars that were mined to make the apartment towers in the nouveau riche district of Skuggahverfið. Obsidian was especially useful as an insulation against seiðmagn and so it was by necessity that almost the entire school was made from it. Every edge, corner or ledge was razor sharp. Wounds caused by obsidian cuts would not heal without the assistance of a seiðskratti or a galdramaður. Even then a thaumaturgical infection could still flare up, which could have grotesque consequences. In those cases it would usually have been preferable to die from exsanguination.

The tram stopped and everyone departed, aside from the few students of seiður who were heading up towards Perlan. A considerable number of people stood waiting at Svartiskóli's tram platform, it being Fárday and classes generally over. Sæmundur tried to be inconspicuous but knew it probably just made him look all the more questionable. A thick haze of paranoia was settling over his mind as the mushroom broth in his body dissipated into his blood, his flesh. Everything felt off kilter.

The gigantic birch wood doors of the main entrance were open wide and students flowed outside. The doors had been grown by the head seiðskrattar of the university, rumour had it that they were fused with a potent seiður of protection. Sæmundur felt he could see bloated eyes in every crack of the knotty natural wood. Large and deep pupils, all pointing directly at him. He jumped when the eyes all blinked simultaneously, and he almost lost his composure. A mumbled word of protection subdued the hallucinations somewhat. He moved away from the main entrance and followed the smooth obsidian wall until he came to a side entrance, a short flight of concrete stairs leading down to a heavy iron door. Before he knocked he put on a pair of leather gloves. He only managed to get one knock in before the door opened with a jerk.

'You're late. Do you have the moss?'

Kári glared at him through the crack in the door.

'It's not my fault you didn't assume that I'd be late as usual. Aren't you going to let me in?'

Sæmundur made a show of looking around nervously, even though he knew there wasn't another person in sight, to encourage Kári's neurosis. It actually wasn't that hard to fake paranoia when the entire sky was boiling and undulating. Whispering.

Kári grimaced. 'Sæmundur, come on. You know I can't.'

'Oh, all right, I'll just sell you the illegal narcotics infused with seiður right here in the open, for all to see.'

'Quiet!' Kári hissed at him. 'Are you out of your damn mind?' Sæmundur could hear Kári grinding his teeth from frustration. 'All right, get in.'

The door opened enough for Sæmundur to slip in. Gangly and pale, his chin as weak as his handshake, Kári was a stereotypical student of Svartiskóli. But this weakness was only an illusion. Given a few years he could reshape the world. If he had the constitution and ability needed to survive his studies and graduate as a powerful seiðskratti.

Kári was one of the many students that Sæmundur regularly sold highland moss to at a grossly inflated price. Most students at Svartiskóli weren't exactly able to hold their own in Reykjavík's underworld and the demand for moss was always high. Many of them came from wealthy families as well, like Kári. Occasionally Sæmundur would offer moss in return for access to manuscripts, essays and scientific articles that were not available to the general public. Moss gave users a hit of seiðmagn beyond what they could summon alone, which could be the difference between a student passing or failing. The risk was considerable, it being an illegal narcotic after all, but there was hardly an exceptional student to be found who didn't find *some* method of empowering their seiður.

Sæmundur had got the gram of moss for two hundred krónur straight from Rotsvelgur, and sold it for four hundred or more. Kári's family was from old money in Reykjavík, or so Sæmundur believed, and he was a very regular customer. Sæmundur always charged him more than others. When he never complained, Sæmundur started raising the price regularly, claiming that the Crown's security around the city gates was more rigid than before. No objections came from Kári, not a peep. This was why Sæmundur felt terrible having to jeopardise their relationship, potentially sacrificing the golden calf who'd kept him going for months. But it would all pay off in the end.

Kári pulled a fat leather wallet from his back pocket and started counting the money.

'What was it, three grams for fifteen hundred, right?'

'Yeah, adds up.'

Kári looked at him worriedly with the stack of bills in his hands.

'Are you all right? You seem odd. Odder than usual.' He squinted his eyes behind the thick glasses. 'Look at the state of you. Your pupils are all—'

Sæmundur punched him in the jaw and followed up with a headbutt. Kári lay dazed on the floor, blood spilling from his mouth and nose. Sæmundur grabbed his head with both hands, muttering words of galdur over him as he flailed around weakly, before finally succumbing to deep, restful sleep. With luck he wouldn't remember having met Sæmundur at all.

He was standing in a small concrete room, part of the maintenance network in the basement. Hissing pipes covered the ceiling. The walls breathed, slick with sweat – no, moisture. Sæmundur pinched his eyes shut. He had to get his shit under control. He moved into the next room, along a maintenance corridor, stumbling around until he found a metal staircase leading into Svartiskóli proper. He climbed on weak knees, feeling as if the stairs pulsated up and down in sync with the breathing of the walls. Everything moved. Everything was alive. Discordant notes echoed in the distance, a maddening cacophony of flutes. The dizzying mushroom high had sunk its claws deep into Sæmundur, holding him in the palm of its hand. The hissing of the pipes became louder, whispering, the sound echoing in his mind. He was in the belly of the beast. It knew he was there, inside it. He didn't see the eyes staring at him, but knew they were all around him. Hidden, invisible.

He was afraid. Because they had always been there.

ᚤ

From the outside Svartiskóli was a monumental building, a pitch-black and windowless fortress that more resembled a dwelling from another world than anything designed by human minds. Inside everything was more familiar and down to earth. Institutional hallways, lit up by high-tech and power-demanding fluorescent lighting, stretched onwards like a maze, every turn too perpendicular, every plain door too identical to the other. Sæmundur knew from experience that this mundane front said nothing of its contents. A closed door could lead to the laboratory of a biological seiðskratti, filled with unnatural mutants, stitched-together ghouls, trees that bore organs instead of fruit – or it could just be a regular lecture hall, with half-sleeping students trying to jot down the notes from a lecturer speaking in a monotonous drone. Every room was marked with only its own, unique cipher. It was nobody's concern what was in each room unless they had business there.

He knew where he was going, even though he had only been there once. On the day of his expulsion, she had wanted to deliver the news to him personally. She'd wanted to see him squirm in private. And he had made a point of memorising her office cipher.

At Professor Thorlacius' door he knocked curtly, twice, then let himself in. He was surprised at the lack of security, especially as there didn't appear to be any wards in place, either. The complacent arrogance of it.

Tall bookshelves lined the walls, filled with neat rows of leather-bound books. A sofa and two chairs, upholstered with the finest imported materials, were on his left, and Almía's desk stood at the end of the office. It was a massive thing, grown out of the floor in the same manner as Svartiskóli's massive front doors, a huge, malformed trunk of gnarled birch, shaped with seiður into a desk, its surface flat and polished to a lustrous sheen. The shelves behind the desk were stacked with curios, bones, some lightly tainted with faded blue, tattered manuscripts in glass cases, pale things in jars of formaldehyde that twitched or swirled lethargically, arcane galdrastafir etched into obsidian plates. Treasures and tools of a high master of galdur, the galdramaður sitting in front of him behind her desk. Professor Almía Dröfn Thorlacius glanced up from a pile of documents at her desk, not seeming the slightest bit surprised to see Sæmundur shambling into her office.

'Sæmundur,' she said in an exasperated voice. 'By all means, invite yourself in. You are no longer a student of Svartiskóli. What do you think you're doing here?' She dipped her pen in the inkwell and scribbled something down, then stamped the document. 'If this is regarding your expulsion, then I assure you there's nothing further to discuss. You've dug your own grave, Sæmundur. Do not come begging to me, expecting me to help you out of it.'

'No, Professor,' Sæmundur said in a strained voice. The books were overflowing with words; forbidden, cursed mutterings poured into his mind. He had difficulty hearing what Almía was saying as the whispers intensified. 'I have not come here to beg.'

He reached the end of her desk. She looked up to him with an annoyed glare. Sæmundur felt inside his coat for the right leather pouch. It took him a while. He felt odd, ill but somehow well, his hands as rigid as crab's claws.

'Wait a minute,' she said, as she watched him fidgeting around for the right pouch. She flashed a loathsome smirk as she took in his overall condition. 'Sæmundur – oh, Sæmundur. Did you seriously show up here intoxicated?'

Sæmundur stuck his gloved hand into the pouch and pulled out a handful of fine dust. Before Professor Thorlacius could go on, he leaned over her desk towards her, holding out his hand with a flat palm, and blew the dust right into her shocked face as the whispers in the room reached a violent crescendo.

'What the hell!' Almía shouted.

Sæmundur leaped backwards, partly because he feared Almía might lash out with galdur, but mostly because he was absolutely terrified of the mushroom spores that covered her. He ripped off his gloves and tossed them away. Almía stood up, dusting herself off, coughing uncontrollably.

'This is the ... the last time that I ... that I ... What the fuck is this?'

Her breathing was becoming ragged. The cough became more intense and rough. Almía stopped dusting herself off and looked at Sæmundur, into his dilated pupils.

'Oh, no. You didn't. Even you wouldn't—'

'Almía, I'm sorry. I just ... I just had no choice.'

Almía started chanting a powerful galdur, her hands trembling weakly as she tried to reach for an obsidian dagger on her shelf, but the cough tore deep into her lungs, not allowing her a chance to speak clearly. None of that registered to Sæmundur. He stared dumbfounded at the glowing creature that blossomed inside her chest and started spreading. He knew he wasn't hallucinating. In front of his eyes the mushroom spores spread through Almía's lungs. She'd stopped chanting to focus on being able to breathe. Sæmundur saw the lethal roots of the fungus, of which he'd just drunk moments before, move through Almía's body like oil through clean water.

She collapsed on her knees, heaving, trying to soundlessly

breathe like a fish on dry land. The black-glowing infestation reached Almía's spine and coiled tightly around it, spreading up and down. A piercing headache hit Sæmundur and he grabbed his head, feeling as if he was splitting open from the inside. Almía mimicked him and for a moment they moved like marionettes controlled by the same hand. Their agony was completely in sync, and then the fungus reached Almía's brain and everything went instantly still.

Gandreið can be cast in several different ways. Sæmundur knew the major theories about the phenomenon and its various manifestations. No method was as exact and precise as this one, but it was considered the vilest svartigaldur, despicable even by the measures of those who practised such heinous acts. No amount of reading could have prepared Sæmundur for the paralysing horror that crippled him as his consciousness was split in twain. He gagged, threw up into his mouth and forced himself to swallow it back, which just made him want to throw up all the more. He couldn't lose the shroom broth from his body. Everything would fall apart if he did. Almía sat limply on her knees and mimicked Sæmundur perfectly, hands clasped over her mouth. The sight made him despise himself afresh.

When Sæmundur was sure he wouldn't throw up, he sat down with his head in his hands. Almía did the same, her face numb, her eyes like glass marbles. He moaned hopelessly and jumped when she moaned as well.

The gandreið fungi was one of the most lethal organisms found in Hrímland. It lived wild on the highlands, spreading either by growing clusters of toadstools in nature or inside a host. The fungus killed the host and controlled it, drove it mercilessly in order to spread spores as much as possible until the body broke down and couldn't move any further. The corpse would then become fertile ground for a new colony of toadstools.

Reining in control and trying to comprehend what he was seeing was more difficult than he had ever expected. The visions that assailed him were not meant for human comprehension, or for any other sentient creature on this earth. The simultaneous perception of his conscious reality alongside the conscious reality of Almía's corpse was an experience of a completely alien nature. Everything was wrong. Himself most of all. He had been assimilated into the grotesque nightmare world of the mushroom.

ᛁ

He stood up, almost collapsed with dizziness, sat back down. Almía did the same in an almost mocking mimicry. There wasn't much time. He had to get this under control.

Sæmundur stood up and stared straight into Almía's face. Almía mimicked him, her facial features slack. She mirrored Sæmundur's movements, but not in an accurate manner. There was something unnatural about her movements. They were sluggish and rough. Delayed. Almía seemed off even when standing still. She wasn't breathing. When Sæmundur raised his right hand, she raised her right hand. It was like standing in front of an enchanted mirror. Little by little he managed to get Almía to move somewhat convincingly, but he couldn't get the hang of moving only her body, not his own as well. Finally Sæmundur got down on the floor while forcing her to keep standing upright and tried to control her like that. It felt incredibly odd to walk while lying on the floor, but with a little bit of practice Almía's movements became approximately normal.

Getting a human look on her face proved to be even harder. The hallucinations were coming in strongly now, crashing over him, and Sæmundur felt as if her nose and mouth were melting off and that her eyes kept shifting in colour – which, for all he knew, was as likely as anything else. Recorded knowledge of practical gandreið using the fungus was very limited. In the end Almía seemed normal enough, at least by Sæmundur's reckoning, but he knew well that in this state he had no right to be the judge of that.

Opening the door was more difficult than he'd expected. Almía handled like a stiff wooden puppet. Sæmundur finally realised that by closing his eyes he could ignore his own self and almost feel that he was only controlling one body. Eventually Almía grabbed the door handle with an odd, stiff gesture. Sæmundur made her reach into the folds of her robes and pull out her pocket watch. It was a golden antique, and had no doubt been in her family's possession for generations. This whole endeavour had only taken him around twenty minutes. Kári would be out for a while. There was still time. Sæmundur took great care in putting the watch back in its pocket. The gesture could have almost seemed natural from a distance.

Sæmundur walked Almía through the halls towards the library. Everything was quiet; he didn't meet anyone on his way. Finally, he came to the only door that was different from the others, a double door made from a heavy and dark wood, a miniature version of the door at the main entrance. He hesitated and gathered his courage for a moment before he made Almía open it, sticking his own hand up into the empty air as if to open the void.

It took him a while to get used to the gloom in the library's reception, after having been in the unrelenting fluorescent lighting. The room was a short corridor, at the end of which was a wide service desk that went from wall to wall. Behind the desk was a quite ordinary office door with a matt glass window. Stacks of books and manuscripts covered the desk so that the librarian behind it was hardly noticeable.

The service desk was the toll gate between the library and the outer world. The librarian of Svartiskóli alone decided who went in and for what reason. Her rule over her domain was absolute in every regard. Most students found it very uncomfortable to meet her for the first time. Compared to the dreary surroundings and Svartiskóli's reputation, most expected a wizened hag, a gaunt ghoulish person, or even a limping hunchback. A freakish outcast that was in accordance with the oppressing sense of foreboding that dominated everything, that came with the stories of every library visit told to freshmen and outsiders. Sæmundur, walking as Almía up to the desk, was greeted by a warm, elderly lady with half-moon spectacles and her hair in a tidy knot. The glasses were delicate and golden, hanging from a fine pearl necklace. A beautiful pin accented her neat, grey suit, which she wore over a spring-yellow cardigan. The pin depicted an open book with a flaming quill, the symbol of the thaumaturgical order to which she belonged.

Her name was Edda. Like the halls of Svartiskóli, she was uncannily mundane, so amicable that it was disturbing, especially in contrast with the library itself that lurked beyond the door. Her smile was warm and her manner calm and caring. Despite that, nobody could stand her – and everyone feared her.

'Can I help you, dear?' Her voice was soft and kind.

Sæmundur was wholly unfamiliar with the terms on which the librarian and the head lecturer of galdur spoke. He tried to dig around in her memories, but found himself reeling from the disorienting cacophony that threatened to overwhelm him. Only noise.

'Edda, this is a matter of urgency,' he ventured, in a similarly harsh tone that Almía had taken with him before. 'I'm here to enter the inner sanctum.'

The librarian leafed through a large logbook that lay open in front of her and searched it carefully.

'I can't see that you are signed up today, Professor Thorlacius, and neither tomorrow nor the next day. Is it possible that you forgot to apply for access?'

He tried to smile at her, but felt like an ape in a zoo baring his teeth.

'Enough of the act, Edda. Not today. You will find that I can be a considerable thorn in your side, if I decide you're worth the effort.'

'Is that so?' Neither Edda's face nor voice implied anything but helpfulness. 'For what work was this regarding?'

'*Rauðskinna.*'

Sæmundur made Almía put as much weight behind the word as possible. It didn't cut it. He could just as well have asked to be seated on the king's throne.

'Impossible. Simply impossible. Such an application would never have been lost or misplaced, and besides, it is simply unthinkable that permission for a viewing has been acquired without my knowing.'

'I am aware of the seriousness of the matter, please spare me your little lecture. As I said, this is a matter of considerable urgency. I will remind you that I am head lecturer of galdur at this university.'

'And I will remind you who the librarian of this facility is. No one, do you hear me, *no one* can show up here and expect to leaf through the inner sanctum manuscripts as if they were today's issue of *Þjóðviljinn!*'

Her face became red as she spoke, with spots flaring up on her throat.

'Let me through, Edda,' Sæmundur said in Almía's gravest voice, 'or I will let myself through.'

The librarian stared at her, stunned for a moment. Then an eerie calm descended upon her.

'Almía,' she said in sincere disappointment, 'what has got into you?'

Sæmundur was starting to panic. This was not what he had expected. How did Professor Thorlacius herself not have ready access to the inner sanctum? Had he overestimated her power at the university? Or underestimated the paranoia and security surrounding the closed library department?

'I cannot find any permission for this kind of access, nor even the application for it, and so I simply cannot let you pass. Almía, please, this is pure folly. And furthermore, this must be reported!'

Edda pinched her lips together and spat out the last word as if it were toxic. One by one his options were being taken off the table. She'd cornered him. So there was only one thing left to do.

He relinquished control over Almía.

Sæmundur was thrown back into his body, suddenly not aware of Almía any more. The mushroom high was unexpectedly potent now that his consciousness was only inhabiting his own flesh. Everything was crooked and wrong, the background filled with inexhaustible noise, and the feeling that he was now experiencing the world for what it truly was had become even stronger than before. As if he were closer to some kind of truth. Time passed oddly. It was hard for him to gauge for how long he'd left Almía out of control. He mumbled a word and—

—his hands were around her throat, his maw wide open, the jaw dislocated, his face right up against hers and when he released his

*grip on her neck and she drew in a quick breath, a cloud of spores
erupted from him—*

Sæmundur cried out and left the professor behind, let the
merciless, wild fungus do what was in its nature.

ᛉ

The spores took control of Edda with frightening speed, just like
with Professor Thorlacius. The shock of splitting his perception
of reality and self into three parts was even greater than before,
even though he kind of knew what to expect. Sæmundur got
Almía to crawl under the librarian's desk and remain there.
While he manoeuvred her body, Edda sometimes moved in
the same grotesque, stuttering jerks as Almía and Sæmundur
himself. It was almost more than he could manage to be simultaneously in control of three bodies. Almía's corpse had been
transformed into a walking horror. Toadstools erupted from her
open mouth and every ragged breath now spewed out spores,
her lungs having blossomed into fertile mushrooms. Sæmundur
looked at the librarian with Almía's eyes. His brain could hardly
manage to process the three perspectives at the same time. She
looked terrible. Her hair was now a mess and her glasses were
bent; her neck was red and bruised after Almía's iron-grip
stranglehold. He managed to straighten the glasses, but the
hair became even more ragged after he made a mess of fixing it
with jittery motions, so he left it as it was. He hid her injuries
by throwing a shawl around her neck. It didn't do much but it
would have to do.

He opened the door to the library and entered an enormous
vault. Tall and dusty bookshelves reached up into the dark,
powerful monuments of knowledge. Only the bibliognosts knew
how many volumes the library held. The only source of lighting
was from torches and candelabra on baroque fittings, but no

smoke came from their flames. The air was dry and dead, like in a freshly opened tomb.

The head bibliognost greeted Edda as soon as the door shut behind her. He was dressed in a plain, torn robe which had probably been in use for two or three generations. Hanging from his belt was a large tome on a chain, locked with iron hinges. He was small and scrawny, his hair thin and miserable. They were all pale and weak, as if they weren't fed enough or never saw the light of day. Rumour had it the latter was true, at least.

'Edda,' the bibliognost said worriedly, 'are you all right?'

'No,' said Sæmundur in her ragged voice, 'I wouldn't say that. I have received a request from the head lecturer of galdur. Professor Thorlacius has requested a page copy from *Rauðskinna*.'

The little blood that was in the bibliognost's face drained.

'Why am I hearing of this only now?' he hissed in a low voice. 'Why on earth does she wish to see *Rauðskinna*?'

Sæmundur dug desperately around in the woman's memory, searching for a name connected to the face. It was confusing and messy, like tearing up mouldy boxes in an old basement and tossing their contents on the ground.

Árni.

His name was Árni.

'The application has been reviewed and approved by the head lecturers as well as the rector. This is not a regular, official request by any means, do you understand? Now tell me, Árni – are you going to escort me to *Rauðskinna* or must I make a fool of you by going there by myself?'

Officially Edda was 'just' the librarian, but she wielded considerable authority within its walls and received as much reverent respect from her colleagues and student body as the most esteemed professors and scientists at the university. The rector was in charge of Svartiskóli – Edda was in charge of the library.

Those were the top ranks of Svartiskóli's academia. Sæmundur made Edda give Árni a friendly smile. The librarian had been uncanny when she was still alive. Whatever it now looked like to Árni, then it did the job. A bit startled, he gestured for her to follow.

Árni led her along aisles between the bookcases. Svartiskóli's library was massive, a sprawling maze spreading both on the surface and underground. Parts of it predated the modern building, no one knowing who built it or why, only hushed rumours circulating about its original builders. On their way they came across other bibliognosts carrying out their work: filing books, looking for certain volumes, escorting other guests to their allotted destination. Each and every one of them had a tome hanging from a chain on their belt. The books were of various sizes and shapes, but none was as great and heavy as the tome Árni carried. They were all locked. Their path led them past a row of reading tables with small oil lamps, where students sat busy reading while the bibliognosts patrolled from table to table. Sæmundur grew nervous seeing all these people and was glad he had locked the reception area. Hopefully it would be enough.

After threading the maze of the library for a good while, they finally came to the vault. An enormous round iron door shut off the inner sanctum. It was a rare event that anyone was let through. Two guards stood at the heavy door, tall and muscular so they filled out their torn, ill-fitting robes. They didn't have any books attached to them and were dressed in some sort of leather armour over the thin rags. Their thick leather gloves had iron knuckles fused to them. They reminded Sæmundur of club bouncers. An odd thing to find in a library. The thought made him smile, but he stopped himself when he realised that the librarian must be smiling as well.

On the door were two large valves that the guards turned

until something clicked. A low hiss came from the mechanisms in the door. Two small iron discs turned and revealed a pair of keyholes. Each guard pulled off a glove, one from the right hand and the other from the left. Their index fingers had been removed at the joint and replaced by intricately made bronze keys. They turned the keys in the locks simultaneously. The door rumbled while its internal gears turned and clicked and moved. Gusts of steam blew out from the edges of the doorway and the massive iron door slowly started rolling to the side, sliding into a slot in the wall.

Another bibliognost was waiting behind the door and he bowed gently to Edda without speaking, taking over the visitor escort duty from Árni. Black wounds remained where his eyes had formerly been. The only visible source of light in the inner sanctum was from an old lantern he was carrying. He also had a book chained to him, but unlike the others this tome was very small and ancient, made from a dark leather and almost falling apart at the seams. They went on down the narrow corridor, into the darkness. Behind them the machinery shut the door, entombing them inside. An immense sense of claustrophobia overtook Sæmundur until he realised that he wasn't really trapped in there. Edda's body was.

The light from the lantern was incredibly weak. First Sæmundur thought that the reason must be supernatural, that the latent power of the books was twisting the laws of nature, but he soon realised that the reason was because the entire corridor was made from pitch-black obsidian, which reflected almost no light at all. They went past closed doors, every one of them a different shape. One was a regular suburban door, the paint peeled and the wood rotten and soft; another was made from roughly cut logs; the next of rusted steel with a porthole, its glass cracked. Sæmundur wasn't sure how many doors they

passed, it was too dark. Besides, he couldn't be staring at everything around him – it would be suspicious if Edda behaved as if
she'd never been in there before. He couldn't be sure how much
the bibliognost could truly see.

They walked straight ahead, moving step by step deeper into
the abyssal heart of the library. Sæmundur had no sense for how
long they kept going in the crushing darkness. Time slipped
from the mind's grasp like sand between fingers. Eventually they
reached the end of the vault. It had only a single door.

It didn't fit into its frame, which was too angular and well
made for a botched piece of work like that. Uneven boards
made from driftwood had been put together, bent and pale,
making a door that wouldn't even suit a poor peasant's cottage.
There was no lock or keyhole on this door, unlike the others.
The bibliognost stopped and gestured to Edda to go inside.
Sæmundur hesitated but couldn't manage to say anything. The
air was too heavy here to carry words. He opened the door with
a gentle creak, which echoed overwhelmingly in the silent void.
Inside he faced an endless midnight. The bibliognost rummaged
around in his pockets, pulled out a small candlestick and lit it.
Sæmundur understood. This was the time he was allotted.

He crossed the threshold.

Tíu

They beat their drums as if the world was ending. A relentless rhythm, constantly on the verge of cascading into noise and cacophony, a frenzied beat giving their voices structure as they cried out as one for justice and freedom, demanding the basic decency of equal rights. There was excitement and a sense of joy in the air. For a moment Garún relaxed and let her guard down. Smiling. Happy. Carefree. She felt as if things would change. She truly believed it, in that moment. There were more people attending than she had expected. For a moment the sun was blotted out as Loftkastalinn floated across the sky in the distance, the noise from its engines so loud that they had to raise their voices considerably. Biplanes buzzed around the floating fortress like wasps protecting their hive.

Today was Óðday, the sixteenth of Harpa. It was fifty years since the naval fleet of the Crown had docked at Reykjavík. It was a defensive measure, they said, to protect the lives and interests of Hrímlanders against the war raging on the continent. The war ended, but the Crown stayed. And with them came development and the walls.

No more gates! Tear down the walls!

The hidden delýsíð laced on their placards bled out raw emotions that seeped into the parched crowd, saturating them with powerful feelings of solidarity, unity, outrage over the injustices of the world and the suffering the walls had brought upon them. Not that they needed the encouragement, as Garún had feared, ever the cynical, borderline pessimist, but the added sorcerous effect made them move and feel as one.

So when the police showed up in force with shields and batons charged with seiður, positioning themselves around the square and in front of City Hall, blocking it off, the crowd grew only bolder, stronger in their conviction, more determined not to be cowed into complacent silence. City Hall was a blocky, fortress-like building, lurking by the city pond. It had only been finished a few years earlier, its striking architecture a popular topic of debate among the citizens of Reykjavík, as with any other new building. Passers-by were stopping at a safe distance to watch the demonstration. Jón came up to Garún as she was shouting words of protest, a megaphone in his hand, pointing out to her a group of people, two of them carrying unwieldy wooden boxes.

'Journalists,' he said. 'And they brought cameras.' He smiled. The cameramen set their boxes down and started unpacking the cameras. 'We're making history, Garún!'

He brought the megaphone to his lips and led a new chant. An old, familiar chant, not uttered for years. Decades.

'Free Hrímland! Free Hrímland!'

He handed Garún the megaphone, joining her in the rest of the chant.

'Hrímland out of Kalmar, no more Crown!'

The crowd joined in, the drumbeats growing in strength and power. The rows of police officers tightened. After a few rounds of the chant, Jón started his speech.

He spoke with conviction and fire. He spoke of a better world. One where the plentiful resources found here could be used to make a better society. An equal society. A society where there was a place for every race, every person as they were. A place where people could be free. Where walls were not a tool of imprisonment and oppression. Where seiðmagn was not harvested for military use, but for the improvement of society. The thaumaturgical power plant in Perlan was a symbol of Kalmar's failure to the Hrímlandic people. Instead of a shining beacon of hope and healing, it was enslaved to the monstrous military fortress they had built. The seiðmagn could be used to power seiðskrattar working in hospitals, healing diseases, or greenhouses, growing new and wondrous produce for the people. The walls were an even greater failure, a structure built for protection instead used for oppression. For segregation of the Hrímlandic people and violence against the citizens the Crown allegedly swore to protect.

They cheered, beating on drums, applauding, shouting. The flash of cameras went off, once, twice, just out of sight.

No more gates! Tear down the walls!

Free Hrímland! Free Hrímland! Hrímland out of Kalmar, no more Crown!

Garún patted Jón on the back, congratulating him for a job well done. He had voiced their common thoughts, which Garún had grown so tired of hearing. But now, she felt as if she was hearing them for the first time. Now they meant something, outside the bubble of their secretive meetings. She saw movement up in the windows of City Hall – curtains being moved, shadows stirring in offices.

Styrhildur sidled up, leaning in towards Garún and nudging her playfully.

'It's happening. Just like old times.'

'What do you mean?'

Styrhildur smiled awkwardly. 'Like when we were kids, playing Fallen Stick, and you'd move in and save us all.'

Garún furrowed her brow. 'What on earth are you talking about?'

The smile faded on Styrhildur's lips. Someone started chanting anew, and Garún joined in, raising her fist and cheering, unaware of Styrhildur's numb expression next to her, barely holding it together.

Jón handed the megaphone to Jónas Theium, who was leafing through a worn notebook. He had been adamant about wanting to speak, to 'recite powerful, revolutionary poetry'. Garún was of the mind to tell him to shut up and listen to something beside the sound of his own voice for once, but people had raised their fists in support and she'd let it go. Let the pretentious bastard play out his little role. At least he'd shown up, despite having been so opposed to the protest. Garún guessed he just saw it as a platform to further himself. Whatever. Let him have his little moment.

A crackle from the police lines. Somewhere at the back, a person was speaking into a megaphone system.

'This is an illegal protest. Disperse and vacate the premises immediately.'

The drums kept on banging, the chants fired up again, doubled in force. The tinny voice on the megaphone repeated itself.

'This is an illegal protest. Disperse and vacate the premises immediately.'

Garún looked around. She saw people who looked a bit unsure, afraid of the police force that had surrounded them. But they still went on. She found Diljá in the crowd and joined her, seeing the same fierce determination reflected in her that she felt burning in her own heart. Sometimes that fire burned so much it hurt. Today she could let it burn brightly. Today she could find it an outlet.

'The weight of suffering breaks the worker's back,' Jónas Theium started, enunciating into the megaphone in a theatrical voice, 'as the dawn's rays strive to reach him, still eluding—'

Theium didn't get much further in his recital as thunder echoed through the square. One of the burning blue-white shots burst through the air crackling with a violent, unnatural energy. Streaks of chained almost-lightning shot over the crowd, following the volley of blasts. People screamed and cowered, Diljá grabbed Garún by the arm and reached out to her and the other huldufólk. A wave of empathy washed over the crowd, agitated feelings of fear, worry and outrage feeding back on each other, as the huldufólk and blendingar checked if anyone was injured. Nobody seemed to have been hit. Warning shots. Then Garún saw the firing squad, a line of the Crown's soldiers that had just stepped out from behind the line of policemen, stepping behind them to reload as another line stepped forward, crouched, aimed their skorrifles at the protestors.

People were screaming obscenities at the soldiers and police, telling them that this was a legal protest, that they should fuck off, that only a tyrannical government would shoot at its own citizens. Another flash from the cameras. People weren't running. They stood their ground. Garún shrugged Diljá's hand away and took off her backpack. She'd been prepared for this. With a chilling realisation, she felt that part of her had been hoping for this. She poured out the pack's contents. The stones were weighty in her hand, but not too heavy. Styrhildur and Hraki had emptied their backpacks as well and people were grabbing the stones. Garún felt Diljá's disapproving feelings on the matter as she reached out to the group for consensus, but she ignored it.

The first stone went flying through the air, crashing into the police lines. Styrhildur followed its trail intently. Hraki threw his stone after his sister's and the crowd followed, letting loose a rain of stones beating down on the rows of officers and soldiers behind them. They raised their riot shields and held fast. Garún saw a few of them go down, their faces bloodied.

Then they fired.

The skorrifles whirred and flared with a blooming whiteness, crackling energy surging through them, around them, finding tender flesh and warm blood. Where the thaumaturgic shot found purchase the energy latched on to the wound like hooks, coiling around it and burrowing into its victim, exploding in a blossoming gore as bone and muscle and stringy tendon burst out in a twisted, cancerous growth.

A handful of protestors ran off from the crowd. They were chased by police, hit with thaumaturgic batons, collapsing in violent seizures and throwing up as they were arrested. A few escaped their grasp. Most stood their ground. Why weren't they running? If they all made a run for it, they had a good chance of making it. The police hadn't blocked them off.

The delýsíð. The seiður emanating from it was keeping them unified, determined to an unnatural degree. Subduing their survival instinct. Garún felt it herself. She didn't want to run. She felt as if they could win. As if facing this slaughter could somehow be a victory to their cause.

'Garún,' Diljá said, reaching out to her, finding no connection, looking at her pleadingly. 'The signs are messing with people.' She looked around at the angry crowd, stones in their arms. 'We have to take them down. People are going to get hurt.'

She nodded and rummaged through her pockets, found her red-tinted googles. She put them on.

The world was almost unrecognisable. People looked like weathered statues. The sky was flat and grey, all of her surroundings distant and artificial. Seiðmagn was the only thing that stood out in this bland world.

Their signs flared like violent rashes, hyper-coloured, pulsating sickeningly with an unnatural turmoil. The seiðmagn bled out from the signs and over the crowd, which drank from it, becoming tainted by its aura. It held them all under its spell. She had to unmake it.

There was more movement behind the line of soldiers, who were busy reloading their thaumaturgic skorrifles. A thick, heavy cloud of murky, sorcerous energy, potent and almost caustic in nature, blurring one's vision just to look directly at it. A cloud pregnant with malevolence and the promise of violence. She slid off the goggles and saw it. Heavy red robes marked with esoteric runes. She caught only a glimpse of the bone-white mask, its long beak-like nose, crimson lenses identical to the ones in her own goggles.

Garún's heart plummeted. She wanted to throw up. It was here. It could see their delýsíð signs, clear as day, luminous with seiðmagn. It was watching them. A predator in hiding.

With trembling hands she reached deep into her nearly empty backpack and found the can of spray paint hiding in there. She rushed to the centre of the crowd, where they had dragged the wounded, their wounds a grotesque growth of sharp, twisted bone and deformed flesh.

Jón came to her as she was spraying on the ground. His hands were covered in blood.

'Garún, what are you doing?'

'It's here – it's watching us. We have to run, we have to make a break for it.'

She painted a circle within a circle. An eye. She struck over it with two parallel diagonal lines. She wasn't sure what she was basing this on. Some half-remembered sigil. It didn't matter.

Anything that could possibly work to counteract the protest signs. To her it screamed fear, suffering, blindness. *Run.*

Some form of realisation dawned on Jón.

'What did you do?'

He looked up at the signs of protest, still held aloft, took in the drumbeat, still sounding out, the foundation upon which the ongoing protest shouts were based upon. He saw people picking up more sharp stones and throwing them at rigid lines of cold, hard uniforms.

'What did you do to us?'

She finished the sign and grabbed the megaphone from Jón's hand.

'Seiðskratti!' she screamed with all her might. 'They have a seiðskratti!'

A flash of lightning. Thunder, in the distance – but she could feel it resounding through her. Jón was staring at her. His left eye twitched, rolled lazily to the side. Then his head burst in a coral structure, a sickening crystalline flower made from bone growing like frost on a window before her very eyes. In an instant he was gone and this malformed thing was standing there instead.

He dropped to the ground, dead. The blood-red growth kept blooming. People were screaming. Another flash, but not from the firing squad. Cameras. There were more of them now.

'Run!' she shouted.

Diljá was looking at her, filled with horror as people around them lay dying, screaming, their bodies twisted and broken.

'Grab the wounded!' Diljá shouted. 'Run for it!'

The spell was undone. People woke up from the trance, fear in their eyes. Two marbendlar picked up a wounded huldukona and a human man, carrying them easily, but moving slowly. People shielded them by throwing stones, holding up signs. The police moved in to make arrests now that they were broken up. They beat down the outliers with brutal force, the batons collapsing a woman instantly. The man she had been supporting fell down, the gnarled bone-branch growing out of his leg breaking with a sickening snap. He was not spared from the beating, sending him into a seizure. Blood welled from their mouths and spattered the street.

Garún picked up a wounded man, his shoulder deformed into an asymmetrical aquatic flower, and dragged him as fast as she could. Behind the enemy lines she saw that pale mask, still as emotionless as before, but now it looked almost livid. It was watching her. It saw what she did. Her knees gave out and she almost vomited. She was going to die. They were going to arrest them all and execute them one by one.

Then, hands underneath her arms, pulling her up. Styrhildur. Hraki and Diljá pulled up the man she had been dragging. They ran, stumbling. There was smoke in the air, tears welling up in her eyes. They ran forward, but the police were closing in on them.

They landed with a heavy thud, crushing the officers beneath them in an instant, using the momentum to lunge forward, eviscerating even more on their coarse, jagged beaks. Náskárar. They jumped forward with their powerful feet, using their wingspan to elevate even higher, then dived down again, crushing and gutting those unfortunate enough to find themselves within range. Garún looked up and saw a squadron of them diving into the firing squad, their wings beating as they tore into the soldiers in a wild spray of blood and gore. She saw a man, clad in a soldier's uniform, holding in his guts as they poured out.

She felt the surge before she saw it. An unnatural wound in reality. A forceful unmaking about to be unleashed. She turned and ran. Behind her, a wild torrent of sorcerous energy was unleashed as a náskári tearing into the soldiers burst in a blinding flash. The air smelled of static electricity and fresh blood. She sprinted as hard as she could, her feet steady now from fear, helping Diljá to carry the injured man. She risked a look behind her.

The air crackled around the seiðskratti in spasms. Around it was a wasteland of death, a crater of deformed bodies. It turned its white-beaked mask towards her and watched as she ran.

Ellefu

Sæmundur flung open the apartment door and slammed it shut behind him. His heart was pounding in his chest as if it wanted to burst out. He felt the inside pocket of his coat again and was relieved when he felt the thick skin page was still there. It hadn't been a hallucination.

He looked out of the window to see if anyone was outside, if he had been followed. The bare trees shivered in the autumn wind. He pulled down the curtains. He was drenched in cold sweat and shivering uncontrollably. The mushroom high was still potent, turning his mind sluggish and murky.

When Sæmundur had made Edda return to the library's lobby he found Almía where he had left her, hidden underneath the librarian's desk. The fungus had spread out of her throat, all over her face and down the neckline. Her head had been transformed into a colony of mushrooms. The air around them was visibly thick with spores already.

This wasn't supposed to happen. The infection wasn't supposed to take hold so quickly. It had become too powerful for him to be able to put a stop to it. The fungus had slipped his control and would now work to spread its deathly spores to as many people as it could. He had lost control somewhere, without realising it. The galdur had perhaps been incomplete. It had buried itself

147

deep inside them. They were worse than dead now and soon others would share their fate.

He left Almía there and made Edda stumble back to him, as fast as she could. His control over her walking corpse had dwindled rapidly. He felt how she could no longer breathe because of the growth spreading in her lungs.

Fortunately she was not spotted shambling from the library like a rigid corpse. Eventually Sæmundur lost control and Edda collapsed outside Almía's office. He had dragged her in, tearing the page from her stiff, gnarled hand, and run away, delirious with fear. The hallucinations had become intensely disturbing and all illusion of control had evaporated. It was only a matter of time before the galdur would completely fade away and the fungus would bring Almía and Edda back to life, under its own power and unchained will. He shuddered at the thought. The fungus-infested corpses would shamble around and spew spore-clouds, attacking every living creature that came into range.

He'd thrown up, somewhere out in the marshland surrounding Svartiskóli. He wanted to scream, to cry. None of this was supposed to have happened. This was not what he had intended.

He told himself, over and over again: this was the only way forward. He had been cornered, forced into this position. There was always a sacrifice. He knew this. That was the essence of studying and practising galdur. What was the price you were willing to pay? That was the only real question a galdramaður faced.

But he had been unaware of the true cost he had just paid. They were dead. Other people could be killed. The infestation could spread out into the city. Hundreds of people might die.

Sæmundur fished the patch of skin out of his pocket as delicately as he could, his hands shaking uncontrollably. He collapsed down from weak legs on the mattress in the middle of the floor and spread out the manuscript page.

The skin was ancient and the blood-brown writing faint. A circular symbol occupied most of the page, a spiral swallowing itself. A black hole. A vortex. Oddly shaped galdrastafir and words were located around and inside the symbol. Between them were drawn straight lines, forming a weird symbol over the spiral itself. It was a circle of invocation. Cramped handwriting filled the rest of the page – instructions for the use and purpose of the galdur, alongside incantations. Fresher handwriting was in the margin, written in different hands throughout the ages. He'd tried to take a copy of the manuscript but Edda's hands were too stiff for such a delicate task at that point.

Sæmundur devoured the text in the weak lamplight. He inspected the circle of invocation thoroughly and identified a few symbols of galdur, but he didn't recognise most of them.

Suddenly he sat up and folded the page hurriedly. The spiral had started to turn, without his noticing it, and he could hear a low scratching in the back of his head. As soon as he looked up from the symbol and folded the page the scratching stopped.

He didn't fully comprehend the ritual. Some of the words of power were like nothing he'd seen before, although he understood enough to recognise that he stood on the deranged precipice of galdur and pure insanity. Any serious ritual of galdur was time-consuming, but this one demanded only a handful of raw materials, all of which he had ready. The actual invocation, the central nervous system of the ritual, was esoteric and complex, but not impossible for him to manage. Sæmundur contemplated the folded skin and considered if he'd torn the wrong page from *Rauðskinna*. Whether this was a trap set by Gottskálkur the Cruel.

Sæmundur sighed and lay back on the mattress. There was

no guarantee that this ritual would help him understand the nature of galdur, but he needed assistance. Blindly researching the causality of galdur would be as reasonable as sending a man into a darkened dynamite factory with a box of matches. He needed *outside* assistance.

Mæja started mewing at her bowl for food. He didn't have anything for the cat, so he ignored her. She purred and butted her head against his feet, occasionally giving an inquisitive mew if he stirred, but eventually she gave up and started to groom herself. He reached for the pipe on the floor. Found the pouch that the cloth-golem had fetched for him and stuffed the pipe with moss. Sæmundur gave it a good whiff, taking a moment to enjoy the fragrance. Real stuff, probably from Snæfellsjökull glacier. Nothing like the crap they picked from the lava fields just out of Huldufjörður. He sat up, lit the long pipe, and smoked.

The smoke moved around him like an eel in the depths. He had burned every bridge behind him. Kári would wake up soon. He'd spoken a galdur of forgetfulness and amnesia over him, but who knew how much he retained? There was no way but forward. What was done was done. He could ponder the consequences later, sober. When he had fully grasped what this ritual offered. Only then could he weigh up the cost of it.

He'd fucked up so many things. First his relationship with Garún. Then the expulsion from Svartiskóli. He'd lost control over the moss smoking a long time ago. Probably that had been the first thing to go. His debt with Rotsvelgur was spiralling out of control. He'd be lucky to get out of that with only a limb or so missing. He suddenly remembered that he had a concert coming up soon. He had completely forgotten. He doubted he would live or evade arrest for that long. He laughed weakly to himself. Why, of all things, was he feeling anxious about the concert now? The most insignificant problem facing him.

He finished the pipe and dropped it on the floor. It was getting dark outside, the season making darkness reach further and further into the day. The only light came from his oil lamp. The shadows were like ink around the lamplight when the moss hit him hard, like a blast of sound crashing over him. The high merged oddly with the dregs of the mushroom trip. He could hear the scratching again, but now it was as if something was trying to claw its way inside, break through the floor, walls, roof. He knew he was hallucinating, but not in the sense that he was imagining it. He was sensing things too clearly.

There was no sense in procrastinating. It could possibly be his only chance. He was ready.

The page was next to him, folded. It looked as if it was absorbing the darkness around it, swallowing it hungrily and growing fatter, more bloated. He picked up the page, saturated with darkness, and felt how his fingers went numb – as if it was leeching the life out of him. Carefully he unfolded the page and spread it out on the floor. He pored over the page thoroughly. Again and again he traced the spiral in his mind, etching its form into his memory. It wasn't enough that the invocation circle was made perfectly; it also had to exist within Sæmundur in the same perfect form, creating an unbreakable barrier both within and without. When he felt it was complete he had the feeling that he had sometimes been unconsciously closing his eyes, while still seeing the symbols and letters in front of him, floating in the dark. But he was so stoned that he couldn't be sure.

He wandered around the dim apartment until he finally found the antique jewellery box, and fetched a stick of chalk from it. Underneath dirty trousers and socks he found an old dagger that was starting to rust. He kicked the clothes and the junk cluttering his room into the corner and made enough floor space free for the ceremony.

The spiral was simple enough, although it was elliptical in shape, which was unusual. Despite that, he didn't find it hard to draw it with the chalk. It was as if his hands already knew what they were doing. As if he'd done this before, in another time, another place. Over the spiral Sæmundur drew perfectly straight lines that intersected in key locations, the sharp corners located inside or outside the spiral. The lines made up a chaotic-looking star, which at a glance looked like a toddler's drawing, but a closer look showed that it was made with a certain elusive order in mind. An alien purpose. Sæmundur drew with extreme precision the galdrastafir on their designated spots within the spiral. The ritual circle was complete. It just had to be sealed off and the ritual could commence.

He compared the circle with the drawing on the page. Everything matched, it seemed like. Blissful waves of pleasure buzzed through his body and he rocked slightly on his feet. The moss was preparing him. Syncing him to the rhythm, the beat of the incantation to come. He read Gottskálk's instructions again:

Rísta skal þennan karakter og skal hann eigi sólu líta. Vek blóð úr vinstri hönd og dreif um stafinn frá ystu mörkum að innstu með offrið í miðju. Gakk þrisvar rangsælis og les þessa særingu. Consummatum est.

Carve this character and shall it not see the sun. Draw blood from the left hand and spread from the outer limits to the innermost with the offering centred. Walk three times widdershins and read this invocation. Consummatum est.

Flesh. Bones would not suffice for this galdur. No, it had to be flesh as well. But Sæmundur didn't know if it should be dead or alive, or if that even mattered. If the demon possessed dead flesh, could it spark back to life? Or was the entity more like a parasite that needed a healthy host to live? His thoughts zeroed back in to Edda and Almía in Svartiskóli. It felt as if a claw was squeezing his heart, robbing him of his breath. Murderer. He was a murderer.

No, no. Not this, not now.

Sæmundur rummaged through the piles of manuscripts while trying to recall everything he knew about transmundane beings, especially those that were called demons. The first one he had trapped was in a skull for Garún. As soon as the entity was bound to the skull the bone had taken on a blueish hue. At the time, he had been trying to trace the source of the power that fed galdur and made it manifest. Why did it alone attract transmundanes, and not seiður? It was dangerous to open yourself to other realities. Something else might bleed through with whatever you were calling. Every single galdramaður was always at risk of becoming prey to unseen forces. Sæmundur wondered if his bones had started to turn a faint blue without him knowing. If he was unknowingly infected with them already.

There was no time to go to a butcher's and get a piece of meat or a carcass. Everything could fall apart around him at any moment. Anything should suffice – a half-butchered ram or the head off an old workhorse. He could go out and look for a stray animal. Sæmundur looked at his own hands and considered whether the being could manifest in one of them should he chop it off. Unlikely.

Why was he considering this? Bad vibes, bad vibes. The scratching intensified. He sat on the mattress, rubbed his temples. The moss was leading him down a dark path.

He could let the entity manifest in his own body. It wasn't so hard to believe that Gottskálk had done exactly that, back when he lived. Invited the devil into his own head, offered him his own bones, his own flesh. Gottskálk was an inhuman bastard, by all accounts, and likely to match the devil in feats of ill temper and evil. If anyone could contain a demon in his own bones – tame the beast and use it for his own desires – then it was the Reverend Gottskálk 'the Cruel' Nikulásson. But not Sæmundur. He knew himself too well. Too capricious, too weak. One day, perhaps. But not now. He had to find something else.

Mæja pranced back to him and gave him a miserable mew. She looked as if she had lost weight. Sæmundur petted her and tufts of fur came loose with each stroke. Poor Mæja. This wasn't a cat's life. She didn't ask for much. Water, perhaps the occasional drop of milk, and something to eat. Almost anything. And a warm place to snuggle. But she hardly got even that. He was pathetic. Not being able to care for a single, tiny cat.

An idea struck Sæmundur's mind and he stopped petting the cat. In the thick, drugged fog of his mind he felt as if a black candle had been lit, a black conflagration, a black sun. He became distant. Cold. Frozen. Mæja kept butting her head against him and purring.

He couldn't. What would Garún say?

Nothing.

She would never find out. He looked at the cat and the elliptical chalk circle.

'Kitty-cat. Are you hungry, Mæja, dear? Come, let's eat. Come.'

He cleared the junk off the amplifier and lined up the tallow candles on top of it. The only light came from their weak flames, yet it appeared vigorous in the oppressive darkness. The spiral

seemed to move in the flickering light. Sæmundur had tied
Mæja's limbs together with string and the cat lay mewing in
the centre of the circle. She cried out ceaselessly and her hoarse
cries merged with the scratching in the wall. He felt nauseous.
The slow realisation of what he had done and was about to
do threatened to overwhelm him. Make him freeze. He shut
himself off from the horror of it.

The candle lights were many and spread out, multiplying
Sæmundur's shadow. The flames gleamed and the shadows
danced on the walls. He began the ritual.

First he closed the circle. He put down branches of birch at
the edge of the spiral while mumbling an incantation. The birch
branches slid from his hand, falling to the floor like heavy iron
rods. When the circle of invocation had been sealed, he started
walking widdershins around it while chanting thrice the eleven
forbidden names, summoning the forces that were simultaneously the bridge and the barrier between worlds.

It was as if the room was in free fall into the depths of the
earth. Gravity felt vague, fleeting. The walls seemed to slide past
at extreme speed, as if in an elevator, but still they were not
moving. The scratching intensified and the floorboards groaned.
The moss sent electric waves through his body. Sæmundur heard
a murmur rise within his head and beyond the wall simultaneously, but he paid it no heed. The gates were open.

Mæja had stopped mewing. She was stiff, the hairs on her
back standing up. She didn't fight, didn't try to escape. The cat
just stared at Sæmundur. Stared and kept quiet. He looked away.

He took his place in the same spot where he'd started, the
candles at his back. The shadows danced over the invocation
circle in front of him, playing in the dizzying spiral, which was
now turning lethargically, but turning nonetheless.

Fear paralysed Sæmundur when he realised that he couldn't

recall the key incantation, the summoning itself. He completely froze. Yet, before he knew it he was spouting the incantation without hesitation, even though he could never recall the next word before he spoke it out loud.

He felt the sound of the world surrounding him. He drew it in, closer, weaving it around him. Noise from factories, vehicles, animals and people. People talking, laughing, walking, singing, fucking, screaming, whispering. Sound from dust settling, wood rotting, water running, flames that burn. Sound from worms crawling, flowers dying, trees growing, mountains being weathered down, grain by grain. He heard the deafening rumble of clouds moving across the sky, the crackle from the embers of the sun, the clamour of the stars and the overwhelming, never-ending tone of everything that is.

The pressure built up and everything trembled. Cracks splintered across the walls until the darkness surrounding him grew so deep and thick that he could no longer see them. The pitch darkness smothered the candlelight, and his shadows grew darker and stronger. Intense, incomprehensible words of longing came from beyond the walls. Sæmundur had to summon every ounce of strength he had not to run away and tear away the boards, welcoming that which was knocking on the window of his soul, begging to be let in.

Mæja screeched loud and long. A primal, panicked scream. Sæmundur had finished the invocation without realising it. The cat convulsed in agony, twisting and fighting in its desperation to escape, but the knots were too strong and the twine cut deep into her. She hissed uncontrollably and suddenly Sæmundur understood why. The shadows slid together, flooding into Mæja like oil down a drain.

Something cracked within the cat. Mæja screeched even louder. The candles flickered. Sæmundur's hair and beard moved in a wind from nowhere, even though he felt no breeze on his face. His shadow had vanished. It was if he wasn't standing there in the light at all. The cat twitched and squirmed involuntarily. Sæmundur heard her bones break and saw them moving underneath the fur, as if something was trying to hatch. Her back arched, swelling, and a spatter of blood erupted over the floor when the stretched-out skin finally gave. Mæja had stopped screeching. Instead only deep, dying gurgles came from her.

Pitch-black chitin, shining with blood and ichor, pushed itself out of the cat's carcass. Steam rose from the slimy body. The creature straightened itself and the corpse cracked open, like a hatchling breaking through a shell. A small, horned head appeared and the creature opened its eyes for the first time. They were a silver void. A long and hairless tail appeared, its end shaped like an arrowhead. The earthly remains of Mæja were nothing but skin and a few bones at the creature's feet. It was as if she had been skinned.

The being turned and looked up at Sæmundur. Countless rows of tiny, sharp teeth shone in its predatory smile. The creature took a deep and ceremonial bow, speaking in a low voice.

'*Master, what is your command?*'

II

Dusk

Uncommon on the mainland, the royal seiðskrattar might initially have a threatening presence, but do not fear! An honest citizen of Kalmar has nothing to fear from these sorcerous servants of the Crown.

Tólf

Her apartment was a mess. Drawers hung open, cabinets had been raided, clothes were scattered on the floor. Garún had managed to stuff everything she needed into her backpack. It was astonishing how few of her possessions were truly necessary and how easily she could leave them behind. She only had a hard time deciding to leave her painting supplies, not because they were valuable, but because she wanted to paint. But taking anything would mean leaving behind something she could possibly need. She told herself she was coming back. But she wasn't sure.

The secret compartment had been emptied out and securely hidden. There was only one thing left to do. She went into the bathroom, shut the door, knocked twice and went back out. Without looking behind her, she closed the door shut behind her back. She stepped back into the bathroom, while simultaneously opening the door again behind her back. An uncomfortable shiver passed through her. She'd entered the strongroom.

At first she'd kept the delýsíð paints there, but she used them too much and didn't like entering the room too often. It might not have been a smart move, but it made her feel safer. This place was unnatural. The shelves were empty and laden with dust. The only item in the strongroom was a blue-tinted jawbone, sitting on one of the shelves. Garún lifted it up, touching it only with her fingertips. She stuck it in the back of her waistband. It radiated an unnatural chill.

She headed down from Starholt, kept to side streets and roads with less traffic. The audioskull emitted soothing electronic tones. It was a long walk all the way downtown, but it was way too risky to take the train. The cold night wind kept the streets mostly empty. Winter was in the air.

Occasionally the music flared and Garún hid herself as automobiles passed her, most likely unmarked police autos, or police officers walking their evening route. She wanted to fetch Mæja, but knew it was foolish. There was no time. She headed down by Elliðaár, smelled the scent of salt and seaweed from the marbendlar's dwellings in the river. She avoided Hverfisgata, but moved alongside it by Skútuvogur and Vatnagarðar, then by the shoreline. She stopped by the sea wall and looked over the city. The brooding, obsidian towers of Skuggahverfið loomed over the low clusters of buildings. The protected dwellings of the rich and powerful, the only ones who could afford a view over the walls. Above it all, Haraldskirkja towered in the distance, with the buildings of the háborg around it like fortifications. The electric lamps were faint and scattered. The city pretended to sleep.

An exaggerated laugh echoed through the downtown streets. She heard yelling occasionally, no way to tell if they were celebrating or enraged. Fárday night was about to turn to dawn and those who remained downtown had become seriously intoxicated. A drunken couple clumsily groped each other by a crumbling concrete wall. A group of teenagers lounged under the gigantic high seat pillars on Ingólfstorg Square. Nobody paid Garún any mind.

Garún was let in before she could knock on the door to Hrólfur's apartment. They were waiting for her inside. Once they were certain Garún wasn't followed, they let themselves breathe easy for a moment.

Diljá was standing by the window, her blonde hair framing a deadly serious look on her face. She didn't reach out, which told Garún everything she needed to know about the seemingly calm situation. Things were in uproar. Katrín sat on a worn chair by her side and smoked. Her hands were too calm, her prim posture too straight, the ivory cigarette holder between her fingers held like a weapon. It was clear as day that she didn't want to be there. It seemed as if they had been arguing just before Garún entered. Hrólfur was sitting by a dining table, along with Styrhildur and Hraki, the three of them looking defeated. She exchanged cursory feelings with them, validating her reading of the room. She felt their support. Next to the skinny, middle-aged man the siblings looked as if they were just kids. And Garún supposed that they still were, to some extent. They all looked exhausted.

'What did you do, Garún?' said Katrín, before any of them had a chance to greet each other.

'Well, aren't you being direct? For once in your life.' Garún dropped her backpack on the floor, taking a seat next to Styrhildur. 'It doesn't suit a lady to ignore pleasantries.'

'Don't...'

Katrín was about to follow up with something more, something Garún suspected would actually be honest.

'Cut the shit, Garún,' she continued in a strained voice. 'What the fuck did you do? Did you really put delýsíð on the signs and banners?'

Garún glanced over to Diljá. She shrugged in response. Garún tried to read her. What had she said, exactly?

'It's your fault those people are dead,' said Katrín quietly.

In the silence that followed, her words could just as well have been shouted in rage.

'I didn't see you at the protest, Katrín,' Garún said through gritted teeth. 'Big words for someone who didn't have the guts to actually fight for change.'

'You know I couldn't be there.'

Her voice betrayed a hurt Garún found exhilarating to hear.

'Garún', said Hrólfur, 'is she right? Did you lace the signs with delýsíð?'

She sat silent for a moment.

'Yeah,' she said finally, 'I did.'

'Why?'

He sounded as if he was asking with sincerity. As if he was trying to understand. So she dignified him with a sincere response.

'Because people need solidarity. A unified front will make us stronger.'

'Why couldn't you trust them to do that of their own accord?' Katrín asked. 'These people showed up because they cared. Because they wanted to make a change. Why wasn't that enough?'

'You said you would cut back on the delýsíð tagging in the city,' said Hrólfur. 'But now I'm hearing that you've been at it so much you had to go and get more. And that the police almost caught you. Do you think they're stupid, Garún? Do you think they can't put two and two together? You're the reason they had that seiðskratti on standby. You're the reason they brought in soldiers with skorrifles. They shot them because of you. Because of what you did.'

'I've seen what happens to people when they face the Crown,' Garún said, forcing herself to remain calm. 'They get scared. They think they can't win. They've got weapons. They've got numbers. Their officers and soldiers are fucked up with all kinds of seiður, heightening their senses. We have to use everything at our disposal to create an advantage.'

He shook his head. 'This isn't the way. You might as well have been drugging them.'

'She was not!' Styrhildur said. 'It's not a drug, not when it's used like this. It made us stronger!'

Hraki nodded his agreement. 'I felt it. It made us united.'

'They would have run away sooner,' said Diljá.

She had known and approved of Garún's plan. Garún tried not to show how hurt she was at Diljá turning on her now. She wasn't sure she was managing it.

'Delýsíð isn't mind control,' Garún said. 'All I did was give them an extra ounce of courage.'

'And that got them killed,' interjected Katrín. 'That's on you.'

Garún jumped to her feet, pushing Styrhildur as she moved to hold her back, so the girl fell on the floor. She rushed up to Katrín, smacked the cigarette holder out of her dainty hand, grabbed her collar and pushed her against the wall, pushing her face up to hers.

'Listen up, you privileged, condescending bitch, I wasn't the one who pulled the trigger! I wasn't the one who shot them in the fucking head! They were my friends, too!'

She dropped her hold on Katrín, suddenly aware of the overwhelming tension and judgement in the room. Styrhildur and Hraki were on edge like wildcats about to kick into fight or flight.

'Don't you ever put that on me,' Garún continued. 'Do you hear me? They pulled the triggers. They killed them. The people you invite to your home with a smile, the people who put fucking bread in the mouths of your family. That fancy wine you drink at society events is watered down with their blood, do you hear me?'

It started to rain outside. For a while the only sound in the room was of raindrops spattering on windowpanes. Katrín took a seat and lit herself another cigarette.

It was Diljá who broke the silence.

'You told me you were leaving.'

Garún took a deep breath. 'Yeah. Listen – what's done is done. The seiðskratti noticed me. It was staring at me, intently. The officer who caught me the other day might have briefed them on the delýsíð. I don't know. But I'm not going to wait around for them to break down my apartment door and claim me. They saw my face. They'll find out who I am. So I'll be staying in Rökkurvík for now.'

'Garún, no, please, the Forgotten Downtown is ...' Styrhildur bit her lip, thought better of finishing her thought. 'People don't move there. They disappear.'

'What portal will you be using?' asked Diljá.

'The same as before. I just have to take the chance. It will only be temporary.'

'Yeah, right,' said Styrhildur. 'How many people do you think have told themselves that before?'

Garún shook her head. 'I know. But I still advise you to do the same. Things aren't safe right now.'

'We can't,' said Hrólfur. 'At least not me. We're about to go to print with news of the protest. I don't think the newspapers will cover this in a beneficial light. We have to retain some control over the discussion. If we let them paint this as some unruly riot we might as well give up.'

'You could go to Huldufjörður,' said Hraki. 'We know people who smuggle. It's tough, but possible.'

'I'm not risking going through the city gates. Not after that. Besides, I want to stay in the city. I want to keep fighting.'

Katrín looked at her in disbelief. 'You can't be serious? You're going to keep on using the delýsíð? After all that?'

Garún stared her down. 'I'll do whatever it takes to fight the Crown. For some of us, the belief in the cause goes beyond writing articles.'

'It's not only up to you, Garún!' said Katrín. 'We decided in unison not to take drastic action, but you – you chose to completely ignore it by painting delýsíð all around town! And then this, with the signs.' She shook her head, looking dismissively away as she took a drag of her cigarette. 'You might not give a fuck about yourself, but you're risking our lives by doing this.'

Garún was gathering her thoughts when Katrín visibly calmed herself and continued, her voice quiet and firm.

'But the harm is done. We've got no choice, I guess. Might as well go all in now.' She flashed Garún a meaningful look. 'We'll stay on high alert.'

Garún got up to leave. Styrhildur and Hraki got up with her, but she gestured for them to sit down. In a quick flurry they felt out for each other's feelings. They quickly reached a conclusion of unity and resilience.

'We'll visit you in a few days,' Styrhildur said, and Garún nodded.

Hrólfur walked Garún to the door and placed a hand on her shoulder.

'You're not the only one who wants change.' He gestured towards the others. 'We all do. But we have to be patient and wait. The timing has to be right.'

He gave her a crooked smile.

Garún wanted to believe him. It would be a comforting thought, to imagine that all she had to do was wait.

'The time for revolution won't come by itself, Hrólfur. We have to create it.'

Then she went out into the rain.

ᛣ

The sound of rainfall was deafening. The air inside was humid and heavy. Sæmundur wanted nothing more than to open the window and let the fresh air in, to feel the cold spray of rain on his face. Bury his fingers in the wet earth.

For a long time they stared each other down, Sæmundur and the demon. It never stopped smiling and never blinked.

'Master,' the creature repeated, 'what is your command?'

Sæmundur kept looking at the imp and Mæja's shredded skin, discarded on the floor. It surprised him how devoid of feeling he was. About Mæja's fate, about the spore-induced killing. No lump in his throat, no regret. Nothing.

'What is your name?' he said, after a long silence.

'I have countless names, master. Which one would you choose?'

'Your own.'

The demon laughed. 'Your knowledge of my kin is lacking. Pseudonyms and falsehoods are all I have, none of them my own making, all of them given to me.'

'And by what name did Gottskálk call you?'

'That one called me Kölski.' The imp took a deep bow. 'And what should I call the master?'

Sæmundur was not about to fall for that. He'd rather die than give a demon his true name.

'You shall never hear my name when anyone speaks it. Grákufl you shall call me and never remember any other name.'

'As you wish.'

One of the tallow candles crackled. Grákufl – grey robe. Not the best name, but it would have to do.

'What is your command?' the demon repeated.

'Step outside of this circle.'

Kölski's smile wavered for a split second.

'Master, you know that very well to be impossible for me.'

'Do as I command,' said Sæmundur with a heavy air of authority.

The demon immediately walked towards the edge of the circle on the floor. As its foot was about to cross the boundary it was as if Sæmundur's eye twitched. Kölski flickered, his vision vibrated, and suddenly the demon was again in the middle of the circle.

Sæmundur nodded, satisfied. The ritual had succeeded, to some extent at least, but the outcome was vastly different from what he had expected. This tiny imp, this gremlin, was not the noble and all-powerful transmundane being he had envisioned would be summoned from the forbidden pages of *Rauðskinna*.

'I assure you, master, that I am the one you seek,' Kölski said suddenly, as if Sæmundur had just voiced his concerns. 'The one who can give you the answers you so deeply desire. All your life you have been met only by locked doors, crawling in the dark in search of truth. Only for a fleeting moment you have seen shadowy figures on the cavern wall, distorted falsehoods and illusions. Others will be satisfied with that, but you want more. You want to cast away your chains, you want to witness the one, true source. You walk the narrow but straight path, but you have reached a hindrance on the road. An insurmountable hindrance.' The demon's smile widened. 'Until now. I assure you, I am the one you seek. I am the gate on your path, I am the key to the lock of your mind, I am the road upon which you walk.'

Sæmundur's heartbeat buzzed in his ears. The demon had read him like an open book, whispered to him all that he most deeply wanted to be true. He knew better than to trust the imp. But he had come this far. He had to try.

'Very well, Kölski. Show me what lies beyond the threshold.'

'As the master commands.'

Kölski melted down into the floor, slid down into a shadowy form that stretched the ink-black void, casting itself upon the wall. Unnatural lights came from beyond the heavy curtains. Outside, thunder could be heard, so rare in Hrímland, and even stranger sounds merged with the cacophony of the storm.

Þrettán

The world was different now. Sæmundur felt like a mountain-top overlooking a village, its denizens small, fragile and uniform. If he cleared his throat, they'd be killed by a rockslide; if he shivered, an avalanche would wipe them out. He saw the strings that held people upright and he understood that with only a few vowels he could pluck them and make each person dance to a tune he chose. What had once been hidden behind a closed door in his mind, something only hinted at when he used galdur, was now everywhere around him. Behind buildings, windows, his own flesh, the sky itself, was something else, something that was simultaneously everywhere and nowhere, always remaining just beyond sight. Something he could almost see in the corner of his eye, but not comprehend. Not yet.

He spent his days with Kölski. He sat opposite the demon on the floor, his eyes shut, reaching out into the abyss. He practised new incantations Kölski had taught him, and with the demon's close instruction he tried altering them and distorting their sounds. The results were remarkable. With a small amount of practice he managed to make the cloth-golem, which had before been a barely sentient pile of clothes, unravel and weave itself into a new being that spoke, thought and was capable of making independent decisions. He made branches grow out of the floorboards and bear fruit. When he ate these yellow-blue appleberries an overwhelming high infused with seiðmagn hit him. The world lay open before him.

Despite these small miracles, which would have caused his colleagues and professors to gasp in terror and admiration, he wasn't satisfied. Too often he hit some kind of wall, some restriction, that kept him from progressing further. He better understood the connection between sound and galdur, how these two could be fused into one, but that understanding was not complete. What he sensed all around him was still unseen, beyond his senses. It wasn't enough. He tried to demand answers from Kölski.

'You – *are*,' it replied. 'This world – *is*. We are not. We have always been, and never will be.'

'So you come from beyond, like the huldufólk?'

'No. The huldufólk came from another world. Not us. We are there, but also here, but in truth we are nowhere. We are in between, behind. Seiður is *here*. Not galdur. It is nowhere, as I am.'

'Show me more.'

'That is impossible, master. Already you have gained more power and understanding of the higher order than I have ever seen a mortal man accomplish.'

The demon flashed an oily smile.

Too often he'd been told that something was impossible. *Foolish. Heresy. Mad.*

'This was a command, Kölski, not a request.'

The demon sighed, but its smile did not waver.

'As the master commands.'

172

Kölski tried, but it wasn't enough. The demon could teach him new galdur, new words of power and methods of distorting sounds, but he never achieved results comparable with that initial revelation. That leap into blinding enlightenment. Sæmundur tried to push through his own limitations, but he always ended up losing control. When he kept pushing, the galdur would twist in his hands and leave him exposed and vulnerable to the beyond, to possession and disaster. Despite being significantly more powerful, and with an understanding that was in some sense profound, he was still as trapped as before. He still found something holding him back.

'It is a common delusion of your kind to view the world in a structured framework of order and laws,' Kölski said after another failed galdur. 'What is keeping you back is your very world view. Something I cannot change.'

'What do you mean?'

'You try and try to understand the nature of galdur, to comprehend the nature of a thing which does not exist. It is an impossible task.' For a moment Kölski's smile was replaced by a look of utter contempt, which vanished just as quickly as it had appeared. 'You are thinking on the terms of your reality about something that exists without it. You can't help but to think in a causal context, where the same cause always yields the same results. That is not the nature of galdur. Galdur is untamed chaos. Yes, what you are doing is harnessing the untamable and bringing it under your will – but that is only temporary, and only a minor fraction of the true power that lies in galdur. With all due respect, master, no mere mortal creature can reach the source of galdur unharmed or unchanged, let alone be able to understand or wield its true primal form. I can hardly explain to you why it is an impossible task – the concept itself is incomprehensible to causal beings. There are no reasons – do you see?'

'So how are creatures of your kind capable of doing so, if not through understanding? You are teaching me these spells and rituals, opening my mind to new vistas of reality – how is that not making me better control and understand galdur?'

The demon laughed. 'Still, you misunderstand. Always trying to understand, or misunderstand. We do not understand galdur. That is impossible – as I said. We do not use galdur. We *are* galdur. It's only here that we break out in a formed, logical image, because those are the demands your fracture of a world places upon us. You are still so filled with the delusions of reality. You probably still believe that the ritual you performed had exorcised me from whatever dimension I dwell in, that one moment I had been a demon cackling in hell, the next being born on your living-room floor. Master.'

The imp added the last word hastily, its tone having grown increasingly harsh as it spoke.

Sæmundur hesitated. What Kölski described was more or less what he had thought, it was one of the fundamental theories about transmundane beings.

'Was that not the case?'

'No, master. Why do you believe that careless and inferior galdramenn risk that so-called demons possess their bones, so they turn blue and their minds are driven to madness? Do you think that there are demons and vættir outside this world, malevolent sentiences waiting for a foolish kuklari to accident-ally open the gates to the in-between, so they can charge in and cause chaos and terror in this world? Do you think that is the reason these entities exist? To destroy and corrupt this world?'

He didn't know how to reply to the imp. He'd never doubted this truth, which had been repeated to him from his very first day of school. Kölski's patience wore out.

'When you summoned me,' it said gruffly, 'it was not a

being from another world that cracked out of the poor cat you sacrificed, no – it was the ritual itself. When kuklarar mess up their incantations or push their limits so hard that the galdur escapes their weak grasp, it is the galdur itself that settles into their bones, takes form, not some demon from whatever hell you have imagined.' The demon scowled. 'That is why you will *never* completely understand galdur,' it spat out. 'Because it does not belong to this *cage* that you call a world.'

Sæmundur found himself unable to speak. The demon's speech had suddenly taken on an angry, almost hateful tone. For a moment he felt as if Kölski would have attacked him, if he had been able to, and he found himself shaken by the dreadful feeling.

Kölski's toothy grin returned quickly.

'So you see, master,' the demon continued, 'that you cannot complete the task you've set yourself. You certainly have a unique aptitude for galdur, for a human being, and trust me when I tell you that. You have reached further than any other man who has studied the ancient poetry, as they call it. But you've reached your limit. No mortal was meant to go further.'

Sæmundur tore open the kitchen window and sucked in fresh air. The air inside had become thick and stale. He felt sick. Kölski was waiting out of sight in the darkened living room, silent and patient, trapped in the protective circle. Suddenly Sæmundur could feel his own hunger and thirst along with a deep exhaustion. His lips were parched. He drank lukewarm water from the tap until he felt nauseous. There was nothing to eat. He didn't know how many days it had been since he'd eaten. Had he slept at all? His experiments with Kölski had melted into one continuous fever dream.

He couldn't stay there any more. He needed to be among people, talking, drinking. Maybe even laugh for a change. A wave of anxiety crashed over him as he thought about Svartiskóli and the library, the fungus that had without a doubt reanimated the bodies by itself after he left it to its own devices. He retched over the sink and threw up the water he'd just gulped down.

Svartiskóli had to be in quarantine by now. Students or staff might have been infected. Perhaps the fungus had spread over to the main downtown area. Was the entire city infected at this point? His vision darkened, his knees grew weak. He splashed water on his face and wet his hair and beard. The risk had been clear to him – or so he'd thought at the time. What the real price of forbidden knowledge was. Some people would have been hurt, sure. But they weren't supposed to die. Not like this. Did the brain retain consciousness after the mushroom took over? Were they watching, trapped inside their own bodies, as they stumbled around as unrecognisable monstrosities? Did they feel the spores spewing from the freshly grown fungus caps?

All that pain, the horror he had invoked. He had taken those lives. And for what? He still found himself restrained. They would come for him, sooner or later. They'd crack his galdur on Kári and discover whatever he could remember. Yet, even so, Sæmundur didn't fear the Crown. As soon as they realised what he had learned – that he was reading and working galdur from *Rauðskinna* without losing his mind completely – he would become an asset to them. Not that he wanted to. They would enslave him if they could. Trap his mind and body in sorcerous bindings and shackles. Turn him into just another cog in their machine of empire.

He threw the front door open, one hand halfway into his coat. This line of thinking was making him sick. He knew Kölski was right. He wouldn't find any answers in a book. He needed a change of scenery. A cold gust of wind came blowing in, carrying with it a potent stench of rot. On the doorstep was a pile of dead rats, all of them tied together by their tails. White maggots squirmed on their black fur.

Rotsvelgur.

Fucking Rotsvelgur. Apparently he wasn't happy with the galdur Sæmundur had woven for him. He didn't know exactly what this rat king meant, but it was clearly a serious summons. He couldn't think about this now. The náskári would have to wait. He had to get out, clear his mind. Eat something. He threw the rats in his neighbour's trash and walked briskly towards downtown.

The sky was clear, the fading winter sun cast diluted, thin light over the city. Sæmundur found even the weak sunlight almost too much to bear. Steam rose from his mouth as he breathed. In his pockets he found a worn pair of fingerless gloves which he put on, so his hands wouldn't shake too much rolling a cigarette or two. A leafy-brown slop covered the streets, mixed with grimy slush.

He walked down Aragata towards Gottskálksgata, heading to the central area. Reykjavík was in full view, a small city on a small hill trying to stretch beyond its reach. Haraldskirkja's split church tower ruled over the háborg, the acropolis in turn lording it over the city itself. From here the city looked beautiful and dormant. He looked to the south, towards the thaumaturgical power plant, Perlan, where Loftkastalinn floated lazily above its shining dome. Thick cables descended from the fortress, connecting it to Perlan. Loftkastalinn was the first of its kind, a technological colossus that defied the laws of nature. However, its use of seiðmagn wasn't quite efficient enough yet, meaning the fortress had to charge its engines every couple of days in order to remain aloft. The Kalmar Commonwealth had grand plans when it came to utilising seiðmagn for military purposes. Sæmundur could just hear the roar of the thaumaturgical machines keeping the behemoth afloat, even at such a distance. Over his head a squadron of biplanes soared towards the floating fortress.

He walked around Reykjavík's more affluent streets. He took in the upscale houses on Tjarnargata, sombre and respectable, decorated with delicate carvings made by skilled hands. Gnarled trees reached over the shell-sanded garden walls. There was not a spot of rust to be seen, the wood in the window frames white and shiny, the double-glazed windows clear of blooming frost-work. He kept walking. He didn't know where. It didn't matter.

Deep in his pockets he managed to find a few krónur, which he used to buy hot dogs at Bæjarins beztu. It was dark, the wind colder and sharper as soon as the sun went below the horizon. The central area was deserted. Those who were outside walked briskly and with determined steps, wrapped in warm clothing like mummies. Armed police officers and volunteer militia crossed Sæmundur's path frequently, which nearly sent him running at first. They paid him no mind. Reykjavík was still there in one piece, more or less. Security had obviously been increased, the whole place felt on edge. But apparently they weren't looking for him. Yet.

Sæmundur wandered up Laugavegur. The walk left him un-usually weary, drained his energy completely. He told himself it was because of a lack of nutrition and rest, but he knew that wasn't the only reason. He went down Barónsstígur and headed towards the Baron's Cowshed. The Baron's was an old building, poorly maintained for years now, and it showed. It was one of the oldest bars in the city, the original cowshed having been there long before the Crown showed up and modernised everything.

All the tables were occupied inside the dark, windowless space, which was illuminated by fish-oil lamps and tallow candles, some of them so haphazardly placed that it was a wonder the place hadn't burned down ages ago. The smell of stale beer and sweat hung in the air, but faintly in the background the stench of farm animals still lingered.

Sæmundur sat at the bar and ordered a stout. The soft foam of the beer drenched his moustache when he took the first sip. He felt better immediately. He went through piles of old newspapers and enjoyed listening to people talk. There was something healthy and vigorous about these sounds, the polar opposite of his workings with Kölski. He smiled to himself. A woman laughed, a man ordered a beer and joked with the bartender, someone did an impression with a funny voice, people clinked their glasses together in celebration. The chatter merged into a single sound, as if one voice spoke ceaselessly. He looked up from his newspaper and felt as if there were threads streaming out of people instead of words, long threads that wound up on themselves and wrapped around above them and Sæmundur knew that with a couple of words, one incantation, he could pluck them and make them—

Someone touched his shoulder and Sæmundur came back to himself. He'd been lying over the bar table, hands over his head. He'd been mumbling, perhaps moaning – he wasn't sure. Leifur, an old schoolmate of his, was looking worriedly at him.

'Sæmi. You all right?'

'Hmm? Yes. Yes, yes, I just ... uh ... I was thinking.'

'All right, man, sure,' Leifur said condescendingly. 'Maybe you just need a little bit of fresh air,' he added.

'Yeah,' Sæmundur said. 'Fresh air.'

He couldn't stand the tone – not from this stuck-up asshole. They'd attended the Learned School together. Leifur had frequently purchased moss from him when he was a first and second year studying seiður. The additional seiðmagn had given him the edge he needed to excel in his exams. He was now on the fast track to take on an apprenticeship in Perlan under Doctor Vésteinn Alrúnarson. He had a chance to become a leading academic in the field. A pioneer. Or, he could become a living weapon of the Crown, a royal seiðskratti. Power and prestige were laid out before him in neat, clear lines.

Leifur sat back down at his table, where his friends were waiting expectedly. They didn't try to hide their smirks and stares. He recognised some of them. Second- and third-year students of seiður. As soon as Leifur sat down the others leaned in and started asking. He didn't have to listen in, he knew what they were saying.

It's him, isn't it? That guy who was expelled. Sæmundur óði – Sæmundur the Mad. He does look like a mess. It's true what people were saying. His name obviously suits him. Sæmundur the Mad!

Leifur had everything. Sæmundur had nothing but blood on his hands.

He couldn't stay here. None of this had any significance – Leifur, their mockery, it was all just noise. The world had changed in the room with Kölski. He couldn't act as if it hadn't. He downed his beer and prepared to leave. Then he glanced at the headlines of the newspapers he had been leafing through.

ILLEGAL PROTEST TURNS VIOLENT

The article painted a dark picture of unruly and violent anarchists who had staged an illegal protest outside City Hall, threatening civilians and resorting to violence when asked to vacate the premises. The confrontation escalated into a bloodbath when náskárar had attacked the police, murdering several officers in cold blood, forcing them to retaliate with open fire and tactical use of seiður to disperse the mob. The authorities were offering a significant cash reward for any leads resulting in arrests of the dissidents.

Accompanying the article was a grainy picture of a crowd, their protest signs askew and in disarray as they were hastily retreating from armoured police officers, seizure-truncheons up in the air, sparking with seiðmagn. In the background he saw a line of crouching riflemen, bracing heavy skorrifles up against their shoulders, and there in the back, almost hidden in the black-and-white grainy photo, a pale inhuman face. The mask of a royal seiðskratti.

He scanned the crowd, his heart racing. People were carrying others, who looked as if they couldn't stand. The people who had been shot. He looked for her, there in the mass. He couldn't find her. The crowd was a mess of people, only the occasional tail of a marbendill separating individuals from each other.

She might be dead. They could have killed her. Or arrested her. She could be imprisoned in the dark of the Nine as he was sitting there, drinking beer and feeling sorry for himself. He'd let her down so many times. She could already be lost to him, for ever. He had to get back to Kölski. He had to know she was all right. He had to find her.

'Hey, Sæmi!' Leifur shouted after Sæmundur as he was heading out. There was something about his tone of voice. 'Did you hear about Svartiskóli?'

A cold shiver ran under Sæmunder's skin. He slowly turned towards Leifur, sitting with his friends.

'No,' he said in a quiet voice. 'What about Svartiskóli?'

He felt his face getting warm. They knew. They knew it was him.

'It's crazy, man,' Leifur continued slowly, swirling his glass of beer like it was wine. Stirring up the foam. 'The entire campus has been shut down, placed in quarantine. People are still held in there. We should be in class now, you know? They say it's because of an accident with seiðmagn, some botched experiment – but I heard there's a plague outbreak. And apparently someone broke into the library's inner sanctum.'

Sæmundur tried to read the faces of Leifur and his companions. There was not a hint of suspicion. Just the mocking disdain.

'The library? How? That's impossible.'

'Yeah, that's what everyone's saying. But something happened, everything's on high alert down there.'

'What ...' He cleared his throat, tried to look nonchalant. 'Who on earth would think to break into Svartiskóli?'

'You tell me, buddy. It's simply *mad*,' Leifur said and laughed with his friends. Sæmundur kept quiet and stared them down. Their laughter quickly dissipated.

'They're saying it was a terrorist group,' Leifur said in a serious tone, pleased to find himself the centre of attention. This was his night. 'Some kind of revolutionaries. Definitely the same group that has been painting the thaumaturgical graffiti all over town. Fucking bottom feeders. Those psychopaths apparently used some form of seiður at the riot they planned, I heard their signs and banners were laced with seiðmagn. I just hope the Crown can get their hands on those idiots before they do any more harm. It's because of this sort of garbage that desperate measures had to be taken at City Hall. They act like goddamn savages and make others suffer for their actions. They're planning something big, you can count on it.' Leifur nodded wisely and took a sip of his beer. 'They must have stolen something extremely dangerous from the library.'

'Right,' Sæmundur said. 'All right, Leifur. See you around.'

He headed out and heard the snickering and mocking remarks

as soon as he turned his back on them. He was glad. To them, nothing was as preposterous as him doing the heist. Sæmundur the Mad? The drug addict and lunatic? To them he was just a burnout who wouldn't amount to anything. They wouldn't be saying that, in the end. He'd silence these fools. He just had to take the next step. He had started down a winding path he didn't fully understand yet. Kölski would guide him.

His heart was pounding as he left the bar. They were blaming Garún's group for his heist. He was furious at himself. He couldn't do anything right. He'd first betrayed her by being ashamed of her. Then again by sacrificing Mæja. He was doing a fantastic job proving her right, that he was selfish and egocentric. He'd sacrificed lives in his search for power. Now he'd sacrificed her as well. He wanted to disappear. Become nothing. But that wouldn't do. He had to find Garún and make things right.

Trailing behind him, consistently keeping Sæmundur at such a distance that he was always just a step from being out of sight, was a man so wholly unremarkable that he could have passed his own mother without a second glance. He adjusted his hat and followed in the galdramaður's wake. If anyone had noticed him it would have been an uncomfortable, if forgettable, moment, as the man in question didn't look like anyone at all.

Fjórtán

Garún was a Hrímlander. She was used to the everlasting darkness of winter. But in the Forgotten Downtown, time ground to a halt. There was no way to tell if it was night or day. At first Garún had made an effort, but as time wore on the boundaries quickly became more abstract and she stopped caring. There was only candlelight and the dangerous glow of the hrævareldar. She'd give anything for a glimpse of sunlight.

She wanted to get out after the first night. The thought of being truly forgotten here stirred a real fear within her. She sat on the bed and lit a tallow candle to see her watch. There were no electric lamps here and no moon in the sky to illuminate the dark. Seven thirty. She'd slept for almost twelve hours.

Her room was a wreck. Old furniture, that no one had ever built or purchased, had been broken into scraps and splinters of wood. Squatters had stayed here before, leaving behind ruined mattresses and broken junk. Time stood still. She kept the bare necessities ready in her backpack, in case she needed to move. This was not a place she intended to settle into. She had to get out, go somewhere else. The air in the apartment was suffocating, the reality waiting outside like a bad dream. Reality had failed her. Now only nightmares remained.

At first Garún spent her time wandering around the Forgotten

Downtown, but she quickly gave that up. She had nowhere to go and the streets weren't safe. The empty windows looked as if they were hiding something. The hrævareldar were stalking her. She found them appearing unusually frequently in her way, so she had to regularly divert her path to avoid them. It felt as if they were tracking her.

Her fingers itched to paint. She had nothing better to do than drink, so she spent her time at Gómorra. The place was empty and depressing. Dejected drunkards and addicts stared down into half-empty glasses of beer. An old record player played old-fashioned songs about romance in the countryside and that most beautiful island in the north. The warped records and ageing record player lent the sound a hollow tone, making the cheerful songs sound sombre. Gómorra was the only place of entertainment in the Forgotten Downtown, located in a house that seemed to have been converted from old fishermen's huts. Around the neighbourhood were many buildings related to the fishing industry, even though they'd never been used for that purpose. They were useless; after all, no one rowed out into the unnaturally calm sea.

She ignored everyone and everyone ignored her. A silent agreement had been established. It was only here, on the edges of the real, that she could live a life where she was free to be herself. There were no glares here, no people to bribe just to be treated like everybody else, nobody looked at her twice, let alone gave her any kind of shit. Whether it was apathy or open-mindedness wasn't a concern to Garún. It was the only nice thing about this forsaken place. It made her remember that things could be different – *would* be different.

That night the record player was thankfully off at Gómorra. On the stage a band played a lethargic funereal jazz. The band members were clad in black from head to toe, wearing black hoods over their heads. They took turns drumming, playing the trumpet, accordion, keyboards, violin, even shaking heavy chains. They were so identical to one another because of their clothing that you could not keep track of them as they switched instruments. Garún slumped over the table, trying to listen to the music. Her beer tasted stale and sour. She was starting to lose even her appetite for drinking.

A slurring vagrant spouting obscenities was more often than not the only person actively holding a conversation at the bar. Without fail the man would always introduce himself to Garún as Jón-not-reverend-Jón. Every night he told a different tragic story from his own life. From the sound of it, Jón-not-reverend-Jón seemed to have packed more suffering and hardship into each year of his life than the average person could possibly manage. Looking at his weathered cheeks and tattered clothes, it was easy to believe him.

If Garún somehow drew his attention then he usually started cursing her for being a blendingur, talking about how her inter-dimensional presence made him exceptionally uncomfortable, which she found hilarious coming from a hobo reeking of piss. After that he usually diverted into ranting about various other races – náskárar, marbendlar, huldufólk. If it wasn't human, it couldn't be trusted. Garún didn't know why she indulged him. Possibly because it was better than the silence. It was too quiet here. When Jón-not-reverend-Jón wore himself out, she moved in with her response. It was almost sad watching him losing his grip on his vile world view. It was just a front – something for him to latch on to, to hate. It felt good to break down his pathetic rants. It fed the fire burning within her. It gave her some kind of twisted hope. If Jón-not-reverend-Jón, a broken wreck of a human being, filled with nothing but moonshine and resentment, could be changed, then, well – maybe – there was hope for the rest of the Hrímlanders as well.

After his usual epistle of hate, the bum ranted about how life had mistreated him and kept him down, that nobody had ever shown him a shred of kindness, which is why he had to drink so much. She kept quiet while he gushed out his life's sorrows, and bit her tongue while he ranted yet again about the deceitfulness of huldufólk and the unnatural violation that was the blendingur. It reminded her of when she was a child and went to church with her mother, where she had to sit under sermons that condemned her in a new way every week. She'd endured worse.

All her life she'd heard the same story. That she was unnatural. That she carried the worst of both worlds. That she shouldn't exist. The Forgotten Downtown had drained her strength. The fire burning in her heart now felt too much like a bloody cavity. A tender, sore wound. She avoided thinking about Jón Fjarðaskáld. If the funeral was over yet. She had seen what the newspapers were saying about him and the protest. The Crown painted him as a degenerate, a man of violence and an alcoholic. The rest of them were called degenerates and delinquents, rioters without a purpose beyond that of violence. The Commonwealth had taken him and others away from this world and now she was hiding here in the dark, hidden from sight on the blurred edge of reality. It made her feel trapped. It made her sick.

When she spoke to Jón-not-reverend-Jón she pretended she was talking to the late poet. As if this Jón was just a misguided friend who needed some help and perspective. It felt hollow. But even that was better than nothing.

'Why do you think you can't get any work in the city, Jón?' she asked him. 'Because the huldufólk are taking the available jobs?'

He nodded in agreement and was about to interject, but she didn't give him an opening.

'Think – who is the biggest employer in Reykjavík? The Crown. Kalmar has been building almost non-stop for the last couple of decades and they only hire humans. Do you know why? Because it's according to the law. Hiring non-citizens, people with no official status within the government system – which are mostly blendingar, marbendlar, náskárar and a lot of huldufólk – is illegal. So what's left behind?'

She noticed other people glancing at their conversation. She wasn't sure if it was an interest of ill-intent or not. People had lost all hope here. Maybe she could spark something in them. Kick these outcasts out of their apathetic slump and get them to do something.

'Humans. Kalmar only hires humans. When you blame the huldufólk for your troubles you're putting ammunition into the hands of your oppressors, Jón-not-reverend-Jón. You're giving them the fuel they need to keep their empire running.'

This shut him up for some time. She was certain not a word had seeped into his thick, groggy skull, but maybe she had reached someone else there. Rökkurvík was not a place where you would find allies of Kalmar. And she needed all the backup she could possibly find. She ordered another beer. She was half-way through it when Jón-not-reverend-Jón started mumbling again.

'It's not for an honest man such as myself to work these days,' he said in a self-pitying tone. 'What little I manage to scrounge together is stolen by scum like you, and if not you, the fucking huldufólk. And if you manage to keep the rabble away, the Crown takes every ten krónur you manage to acquire, as greedy as huldukóngar in their hidden palaces, if not worse!

But if I peddle my wares here, their filthy claws can't reach into my pocket. That's where I get them.'

She looked up. 'What do you mean?'

He didn't reply to her, turning to his empty glass.

'Ah, so now you're listening? You thieving bitch. You're all the same. Forget it, it's not a place for an aberrant such as yourself.'

'Where do you sell your junk? Is there a market here?'

The vagrant ignored her, trying to catch the bartender's attention. She grabbed him by the shoulder and forced him to turn to her.

'Look at me when I'm talking to you.' Without taking her eyes from him, she stuck a dagger she kept in the inside pocket of her coat up against his side. 'I've had enough of your bullshit. Where do you sell your stolen loot, you miserable wretch? Where?'

He looked around for help. No one spared him a glance, not even the bartender, who stood calmly at the other end of the bar, pretending not to notice anything. The band kept on playing their melancholic eulogy.

'All right, all right! Control yourself,' he spat out. 'If you can, you half-breed bitch!'

She pushed the dagger up against him, puncturing his speckled coat, possibly breaking his skin. He yelped.

All right! Kolaportið!' he whimpered through a clenched jaw. 'Put away the blade and I'll tell you how you can get there.'

The dagger didn't move until he'd talked. She downed the rest of her sour beer and headed straight outside.

After saying goodbye to Leifur at the Baron's Cowshed, Sæmundur had headed straight back home. He knew of a galdur which could be used to track down Garún, but he couldn't risk leaving Kölski behind. He'd strongly felt the demon's absence.

The more time that passed away from the demon's presence, the weaker he felt. When he opened the door to his apartment he was out of breath and trembling, stars flickering at the edge of his vision. Inside, Kölski waited, just as Sæmundur had left him, silent as the grave.

'What ... have you done ... to me?' Sæmundur groaned.

'Nothing, master,' Kölski said with a sharp smile. 'Nothing you didn't do to yourself.'

Sæmundur collapsed on his mattress. He immediately felt better, now that he was back in the company of the demon.

'What do you mean?'

'When you dragged me into this ... *world*' – it spat out the last word like a curse – 'you did so with two sacrifices.' Kölski held out its black, chitinous claws. 'The flesh.' It opened its right claw. 'And the spirit,' it added and opened the left.

Sæmundur stared into the demon's silver eyes for a while before he realised what it meant. The shadow.

'Shadow has no essence, it has no material component, no frequency. You can't use a shadow, it's ...'

He thought about the ritual, how shadows had danced on the walls like living darkness. How they had been drawn in by the demon. He reached for a tallow candle that was on top of the amplifier and lit it. He held up a hand against the flame, tried to cast a shadow on the wall, floor, something. Nothing happened.

'Impossible.'

'Darkness is everywhere. You just need light to see it. Every man casts a shadow if they stand in front of the light. Like fire burns and suns shine, people are radiant with darkness. That is the essence of life.'

Sæmundur collapsed like a marionette with its strings cut.

'Absurd. That doesn't make a shred of sense.'

Kölski's laughter was like a cold wind over bleached bone.

'Do not despair, master! Gottskálk considered this to be a good sign, by exorcising a demon he was ridding himself of evil's influence. "A man without shadow is pure of heart," he said. You should rejoice!'

Everything has a price. It had been one of his earliest lessons, but he'd never taken it seriously. Galdur meant being powerful, not powerless. All these words, these incantations, they were his weapons. How could they turn on him like that? How could he have unwittingly sacrificed a part of himself?

No.

He stood up. No, this sort of thinking would not do. He knew what the risks were when he decided he had to read *Rauðskinna*, no matter what. No price was too dear for him. This was the nature of ascending – transformation. After only a few weeks he'd reached a higher understanding and control than any galdramaður who had ever studied at Svartiskóli. All the taboos and prohibitions that he'd been taught were irrelevant. He had to see them for what they were – falsehoods and hindrances placed either from misunderstanding and fear or as a way for those in power to keep it from the reach of others. He was beyond them now. He had started to gain a true understanding of galdur.

That was when he noticed the corpses, hidden away in the dark corners of the room. Twisted bodies, entwined together, seeping blood from skin as if it was porous. It took him a moment, staring at them frozen in disbelief, to recognise their uniforms as those of the military.

He resisted the urge to stumble backwards and flee from the room. Instead he turned to Kölski, speaking slowly, but clearly.

'What ... the ... fuck?'

'Ah, yes. The visitors.' Kölski moved to the edge of the circle, tilting its head as it considered the warped bodies. 'I thought it would be best to take neat care of them, master. They came in as soon as you left. Snooping around.'

'You did that?'

Kölski performed a neat, flourished bow.

'Yes, master. I will not let lesser beings compromise your domain. Soldiers of Kalmar, their broken spirits told me before I sent them off. They have been hiding for some time now, waiting for the opportune moment to strike.'

Sæmundur threw up on the floor. He was glad he had something to vomit. He felt disgusted. Sick. How had he not spotted the soldiers?

It was some time before he found the strength to speak again.

'Are there others waiting outside now?'

The demon shut its eyes. The walls creaked as the darkness inside grew thicker.

'Yes, master. They are shrouded by feeble illusions. Seiður, it feels like. A person who has been stalking you. Their leader.'

Stupid. Stupid, stupid, stupid.

He should have performed a galdur of hiding. Something. But he'd just stumbled around like an idiot.

'I can't stay here. We have to go.'

'Very well, master.'

'You can't remain as you are. If you're seen among people there will be hell to pay. You'll have to be disguised somehow. Can you turn yourself into a fly or some creature?'

'I'm afraid not, master. If only it were that simple. But with a simple word of command I can retreat back into the form of your shadow. Would that suit you?'

'It will do.'

'You can temporarily bind me back into the shadow-form with an archaic incantation. It is fairly simple in structure, but to keep the galdur strong you will have to constantly reinforce it. It will be draining. You will also need a different name from the one you now use to call me. Kólumkilli is one of my ancient names – one of hidden power and patience. That name is laden with the power of deception and illusion. I will teach you how to sing your shadow back into existence.'

It took him a long time to pronounce the name properly and incorporate it into the chant. There was something about the pronunciation that he had a hard time with. When Sæmundur spoke the galdur, the protective circle broke and the demon faded back into a flickering shadow.

Garún had walked past the building countless times, the windows broken and nailed shut here like everywhere else. When she looked inside there was nothing to see except scraps of wood and rusted iron, remains of large industrial machines. It was a dead place, abandoned, although she was certain that nobody had ever worked there. The only door was rusted shut. It turned out to be quite easy for her to break in through one of the windows. Silently she made her way between the machinery. The floor was covered with broken glass and scrap: screws, bolts, faded electrical wires with worn-out ends. No one had ever used these things. No one had made them or left them behind. Still they were here. Why? She pushed these thoughts away.

At the end of the factory floor was a dusty break room. Dirty mugs were in the sink and yellowed notebooks lay open as if someone had just stepped away decades earlier. Nothing was written in them. Rows of pale green steel lockers were at the end of the room. The paint was mostly peeled off and had fallen in flakes on the floor around them. Garún crammed herself into the third locker from the left and closed it.

The musty air was heavier in there. The faint light trickling through the vents on the door faded. She heard nothing except her own breathing. Then she was there. She could smell it before she could see it.

One moment she was inside a locker, trapped with the stale darkness, the next she stumbled around a corner and found herself in the middle of a market.

Oil lamps cast a yellow light on booths lining crooked, twisting paths. It was crowded, making her feel as if she was actually in Reykjavík proper. The market was in a large building, probably a warehouse, but the windows had been bricked over. Nobody paid her any mind, despite her being the only blendingur in sight. It smelled of old books, stockfish and dusty heirlooms, lost trinkets and family baubles that nobody wanted any more. People who might have seemed quite normal in Reykjavík became undesirables in Kolaportið, odd and fetid; here new clothes were as worn-out rags. Gaunt paupers tried to pawn an odd mismatch of junk and knick-knacks, stern marbendlar offered lumpfish, shark and other peculiar creatures from the deep. Kuklarar sold illegal, home-made magical solutions and sorcerous artefacts, eccentric collectors displayed stamps, books and collectibles. Hunched náskárar patrolled from booth to booth in their odd, three-legged walk. They carried no decorations, but were fully armed with leaden skrumnisiron, fused to their beaks and claws. They stood a head taller than everyone else, who made sure not to get in their way. Garún realised that they were korpar, warriors without clan or honour. Two walked past her, their iron talons hitting the floor like swords dragged over stone. Everything was for sale but nothing was priced, and a shiver crawled down Garún's spine as she considered that perhaps some wanted something besides krónur for their wares. Just like Feigur.

She wandered aimlessly around the market. Beside the occult

items and a few illegal books, she did not find much that aroused her interest. She bought a used oil painting set cheap and a few ragged brushes with it. At another booth she bought old and torn sheets. She knew that she was being fleeced for these common items because she was a blendingur. Haggling was no use – the prices were as set in stone as in the finest colonial store. But at least she got to shop. Here, among the dregs of society, she belonged. More or less. Garún had very little money left, only a few krónur. She thought it more important to paint than to eat, however. Before she headed out she bought herself a long, sharp knife in a sheath for two krónur, discarding her old, dull dagger which was more useful for threatening rather than an actual confrontation. It was a soldier's knife and she got it cheap. Being found in possession of stolen loot from the royal army was not desirable.

Kolaportið had only one door. A golem made from white-washed driftwood stood guard and let people out, sometimes in groups, sometimes one at a time. The eyes of the golem were conches; inside each was a drooping growth similar to a sea anemone. Garún stood in line until it gestured to her to approach. As soon as the door shut behind her she found herself outside the factory, the steel door rusted shut behind her. She waited for a while before going home, but she saw no one else come out or go in.

When she got back home she hung one of the sheets up on the wall. The oil paints were in various conditions, but by stirring them up a bit most of them were usable. She put thick blotches of colour on the sheet and spread them with strong brushstrokes. The sheet wasn't taut enough and sagged, but that just demanded a different approach from painting on a canvas.

Once she'd made decent progress with the painting she filled a dropper with delýsíð and put two drops in the linseed oil. The effects were much stronger and sharper than she'd experienced before, and she found the reflections of her own emotions even more honest than before. Purer.

When the painting was finished she could barely manage to look at it. It was a dark brown, chaotic mess with coils in crimson and white, a forming galaxy. Conflicting emotions collided with each other and confused her, supercharged by the delýsíð.

Useless. She tore down the sheet and tossed it into the corner. The feeling emanating from it was faint but still lingering, like shards of a broken mirror covering the floor. She strung up another sheet.

She put more drops of delýsíð into the paint. Her head felt groggy. This time she painted a much simpler image. A crude dragon with nine heads, a crown sitting on each one. She put a skull in one of the dragon's talons, a dagger in the other one. Garún didn't spare any attention to detail, intentionally making the painting coarse and ugly. She poured a lifetime of hate and resentment into the painting. Every moment she had felt powerless or small or afraid. She let the feelings she'd grown so accustomed to suppressing rise to the surface, bringing them to an unbearable, scathing boil. She let herself hate until it became exhausting. On the stomach of the dragon she wrote *J IX* in large letters. The initials and insignia of King Jörundur, the ninth of his name – the ruler of Kalmar. It was a bit too direct, but she didn't care. Ambiguity and propaganda mixed like oil and water.

As the painting dried its initial effects became stronger. Garún forced herself to stand in front of the painting, exposing herself to the torrent of emotions that threatened to overpower her with each minute that passed. Her fists whitened and her nails dug into her palms. Streams of sweat crawled down her back.

She felt her heart beating faster and faster and her face getting scorching hot. Her jaw clenched shut, teeth grinding, the hatred radiating from the painting about to tear her apart. Her own hatred, multiplied tenfold.

She spent her time painting. It was almost impossible to tell how long she spent on each painting. The only measurement was when she got tired or hungry, but even those sensations quickly became insignificant. Sleep, eat, paint, sleep. She had no idea how often she went through this cycle each twenty-four hours.

She kept the sheet with the nine-headed dragon under her mattress. Each night was a sweat-covered struggle and she woke up with half-coagulated clots of blood in her nose. The emotional radiation from the delýsíð painting seeped into her mind, keeping her anger flaring hot. She would not let this place drain her of her anger, turn her into an apathetic zombie. She would never give up the fight. As she woke, she could never remember the nightmares, but they gnawed at her subconscious every waking moment.

Her hatred multiplied each time she rested, so she had to let it out. When she felt sociable enough, she went to Gómorra. Jón-not-reverend-Jón kept his distance after their last inter-action. To her surprise she found other people approaching her. Outcasts with sunken eyes and strained faces, who looked at her hungrily for hope and direction. One way or another they had been pushed to the edge of society by the powers that be. A middle-class woman who had fallen in love with a soldier. Her family had sent her to Kleppur, the insane asylum, from which she had escaped before her scheduled lobotomy and hysterectomy. A man who had written a column for one of the newspapers and summarily found himself unemployable. A couple who had refused to hide that they were dating – her being human and him a huldumaður. There were also drunks and addicts, having succumbed to their addictions before or after they found themselves here. It didn't matter to Garún. She told them about the protest, about the people who had died fighting to make things better. She told them about their network of cells, spread around and outside the city, fighting for a free and equal Hrímland. Garún gave them a few wrinkled copies of *Black Wings* that she'd found in the recesses of her backpack, and they devoured each word. At first they hesitated, but the huldufólk of the group reached out to her and she opened herself to them, ignoring the intrusive feeling of having someone reach deep into your emotional core, and after that they trusted her. Talking to them and thinking about the masked band that had been playing earlier, an idea started to take shape. This could become a new frontier. A rallying point.

When she couldn't stand the company of others she walked restlessly on the streets of the Forgotten Downtown, which were empty more often than not. Without fully realising it she had started searching for a way out of the labyrinth, but Rökkurvík's streets always led her back to where she started. The audioskull's music was faint and incomprehensible, useless most of the time, but in certain places she could hear a weak noise, a static similar to when she had crossed over at Haraldskirkja. The sound was stronger or weaker in certain places. Garún hunted down the static until it reached a climax. By intuition she pushed a loose brick that looked out of place and found herself pulled over into Reykjavík in an instant, standing on the roof of a building in the central area. She was completely blinded for a few good minutes. It was daylight. She hadn't seen the sun for such a long time. It took her a while to figure out how to get back, but when she walked backwards three times around the chimney she suddenly stepped back over into the midnight of the Forgotten Downtown. She started to hunt down other portals.

Few of these seemed to be in use. Most likely they were naturally formed cracks bridging the gap between worlds, accidental fractures in reality. Sometimes she couldn't find exactly the correct method, or the right place, but more often than not she found a way to cross in both directions. She designed a delýsíð symbol intended to keep people away from the place where it was painted. She tagged useful portals on both sides with thinned-out, clear delýsíð spray.

She'd only meant to map these hidden gates and find out where they brought her, but she found that she couldn't stop there. With a can of paint in her hand, Garún started spraying powerful and militant staves all over Reykjavík, a few militant lines that in unison screamed out *anger, discord, revolution.*

Fimmtán

She was shrouded by the early morning darkness, tagging a symbol in clear delýsíð in an alley off Hverfisgata. Through the thaumaturgic goggles the graffiti looked vibrant and alive, writhing with raw, sorcerous energy. In Reykjavík seiðmagn was everywhere, as naturally a part of the city as clouds were a part of the sky. In some places it would shatter into forms, like esoteric symbols, frozen lightning charged with incomprehensible secrets. This was especially true if seiðskrattar had recently done their dark work in the vicinity. The fractured traces lasted for days. The thaumaturgic power plant in Perlan emitted heavy, huge currents, unnatural aurorae thick with power and sorcery.

Garún focused her will and made the seiðmagn in the delýsíð form in the shape of her intent. *Dissent. Discord. Uprising.* The noisefiend was buzzing steadily on, emitting rhythmic music, not exactly calming, but stable enough. Danger was just around the corner, police and soldiers patrolling the streets in greater numbers than she'd ever seen before. But she was hidden here. For now.

A man cleared his throat behind her. She spun around, spray can raised like a weapon, not knowing if it would even help her at all, but ready to fight for her life by any means necessary. Someone was there without her knowing. She was being ambushed.

She turned around and saw a man made out of darkness, glowing with unsettling colours unlike any she had ever seen before. She'd never seen transmundane influence truly mani-fested in the real world, only faint shadows of their real power, like the audioskull and the jawbone. Still, she recognised their influence when she saw it. This was a demon. She shouted in surprise, holding out the delýsíð can like a pistol, one hand held behind her back. Reaching for the blue bone tucked away. Her last resort. This would be her last stand. She was going to die.

'Garún, relax, it's me. Please, it's just me.'

Sæmundur. Big, clumsy Sæmundur with his wild man's beard. The words stuck in her throat and her mind went blank.

Sæmundur?

She slid off the goggles and saw him standing in the dark alley, hands held up in a soothing gesture, his body where the man-shaped darkness had stood a second before. He had been possessed, she thought. He'd lost control and doomed himself. With a heavy heart she realised that she had been waiting for this for quite some time. A doom as unstoppable and irreversible as the sunrise.

Then, she realised: no. Possessed bones would glow in an unnatural blue seen through the thaumaturgical goggles. Sæmundur had been untouched. It was the darkness itself that had been shining. The shadows surrounding him radiated a mad-dening, other-wordly light, casting him in an abyssal silhouette.

'Sæmundur – what the hell? Are you trying to give me a heart attack?' She relaxed a bit, then tensed up again. 'Wait – how did you sneak up on me without the audioskull hearing you?'

She lowered her arm and let out a breath that made her knees weak with the crash of adrenaline that followed.

He breathed out a sigh of relief.

'Sorry, I didn't mean to scare you. I've been trying to find you, but every time I got close your signature just vanished.' He hesitated awkwardly. 'I figured the noisefiend was somehow being triggered by my presence. So I... uh... masked my approach.'

Now that she had somewhat relaxed, she realised with a shock what a terrible state he was in. She barely recognised him. Dark shadows underneath faded and glassy eyes, his skin pale as a ghost and stretched over his bones. He was like a scarecrow emptied of its straw. Sæmundur had always been tall and big. Now he was like a walking coat hanger.

'The noisefiend only picks up hostile intent,' she said warily. 'Isn't that what you said?'

'Well, I mean, it's not pinpoint accurate. It can pick up a lot of variables. And I guess something triggered a signal that made you think it was best to get moving.'

She nodded. The audioskull had saved her skin several times now. The city was crawling with police and military patrols. Sometimes they were escorted by a seiðskratti. They were trying to hunt her down. Or maybe it had just been Sæmundur trying to find her.

'How did you get past the noisefiend? Can other people do that? And what do you want?'

'I just want to talk, Garún. It's... ah... well... Things are getting a bit complicated. I don't think that other galdramenn could mute the noisefiend. They'd have to know exactly what they're dealing with and they'd have to wield considerable power and understanding. I just blanketed the demon's entire perception, so it wouldn't know I was coming. I couldn't pinpoint only myself, you see.'

'Turn it off.'

'What? Garún, don't worry about that now, just listen. I—'

'I said turn it off! Now!'

She was yelling at him now, holding one headphone speaker up to her ear. Only calm, soothing tones were emitted by the audioskull. Sæmundur sighed and mumbled a single word of power. The air around him twitched, or perhaps it was just her eyes. Immediately the music flared up violently, screaming *danger, run, surrounded, fear, run, now.*

'Something's wrong. We have to—'

A hollow, tinny voice interrupted her from the back of the alley.

'Do not make any sudden movements. Turn around – slowly – and raise your hands in the air.'

Sæmundur turned around and Garún saw behind him a line of soldiers blocking off their exit. In front of them was a sharply dressed man holding a megaphone. Her heart sank. It was him. The officer who had almost arrested her the other day.

His face twisted in a victorious grin. He recognised her as well. He looked pleasantly surprised, as if some suspicion had been confirmed. She realised that he had not been expecting her at all. They had been trailing Sæmundur.

'You fucking idiot,' she hissed as she slowly raised her hands. 'You've led them here.'

'Garún, relax,' he said in a deep, calm voice. There was nothing comforting about his tone. 'Everything's going to be fine.'

'Sæmundur Sigfússon' – the man cracked a predatory smile – 'you are under arrest for double homicide, illegitimate and immoral use of sorcerous materials, breaking and entering, robbery of forbidden texts, summoning a malevolent transmundane entity and conspiracy to commit an act of terrorism against the Commonwealth of Kalmar and its peoples. Raise your hands, hold out your fingers, and don't move. Co-operate and no one need get hurt, Sæmundur.'

'Homicide?' She stared at him incredulously. 'What the fuck did you do?'

The soldiers advanced carefully down the street, their rifles raised and readied. The officer was in front of them.

'Can you see it, Garún?' he said to her quietly. 'The seiðmagn he's drawing in? I can almost see it. It's like a whirlwind of smog, except...'

He trailed off. Garún didn't know what to say. Her heart was beating so fast she thought she would collapse. Whatever had happened to him, apparently the extent of the transformation was unknown to even him.

'Don't come any closer,' Sæmundur said to the officer. 'I mean it.'

'Should you start muttering an incantation, or do any other activities that might be considered an act of svartigaldur, then we will be forced to shoot to kill. Do you understand me? This is the end of the line. Reach up your hands, Sæmundur, so we can see them. Should you reach for any fetishes or artefacts we will fire. Do you understand?'

Sæmundur raised his hands.

'You don't have to do this. I don't want to harm you.'

The officer nodded. 'I understand. Whatever you stole worked, didn't it? That's of great interest to us, Sæmundur. Listen, we only want to talk. All right? My name is Þráinn Meinholt. Are you co-operating with this terrorist? We can overlook that as well, we only want information. All right? Should you be unco-operative, then, well... Then you will force our hand.'

'That's not going to happen.'

'That's right.'

A gap opened in the soldiers' ranks. A small, robed figure stepped through. A galdramaður, highly indoctrinated according to the sigils on their robes. A black veil covered their face. A large femur, faintly azure in colour, was grasped in their skeletal hand, tightly wound around the hand and lower arm with string and barbed wire.

Shit, shit, shit.

Garún took a step back. The soldiers visibly jumped at her movement. She was lucky she wasn't shot right there and then, she guessed. They were all on edge. The portal to Rökkurvík was just behind her, but it would take time to activate it. She'd have to pull a brick out of the wall and insert it the other way around. She'd be lying on the street, bleeding, before she could find the right brick.

'You chose this,' Sæmundur said to Þráinn. 'Remember that.'

The galdramaður looked up at the officer, who gave a curt nod. The galdramaður started muttering an incantation, holding the bone with both hands as if trying to strangle it. Garún felt her body lock up, suddenly and violently, as if rigor mortis was instantly setting in to her living body. Sæmundur became similarly rigid, his back too straight.

'Good, Sæmundur.'

Þráinn gestured to the soldiers, who approached with handcuffs and straps that were intended to go over the head of a rogue galdramaður, blocking off their senses completely.

'Don't make them suffer,' Sæmundur said.

The soldiers pushed him to his knees and cuffed him. He looked subdued, almost as if he was talking to himself, lapsing into some kind of trance. At that moment he didn't look human to her.

The winter darkness didn't yet take up most of the day, but by now it reached deep into the morning. A wind ran through the alleyway and Garún involuntarily shivered. Suddenly everything felt colder, darker, when the opposite should be happening. The sun was supposed to start its short crawl over the horizon shortly. The darkness grew thicker, closer, pressing up against her. It was almost as if it was moving. Whispering, just out of her range of hearing. She looked up as the soldiers pushed her down and pulled her arms behind her back to be cuffed. The stars were vanishing from the night sky.

The soldiers' movements became lethargic. They stopped moving. The galdramaður ceased their chanting, falling silent, slack-jawed. The darkness pushed up against them. Garún could almost see it. Like liquid smoke. Something out of a dream.

Garún was able to move again. She watched as Þráinn retreated, staring at Sæmundur as if he couldn't believe what he was seeing.

'What is this? How are you doing this?'

Þráinn looked around wildly, as if he could hear some kind of sound and was searching for its origin. Numbly, Garún reached for her goggles and slid them over her eyes.

She immediately pulled them back down. A blinding display of wild colours roared around her, barely unseen, almost audible. She was standing in the middle of a violent storm, brimming with a malevolent joy as it acted out its purpose. As it obeyed its master.

Moving as one, Þráinn, the soldiers and the galdramaður fell to their knees and bent forward, as if in prayer, prostrating themselves before Sæmundur. They were whimpering. She could barely make out the words. It sounded as if they were pleading for mercy. Þráinn forced up his head, staring at her intently, his face frozen in a wretched grimace, his eyes and mouth leaking writhing tendrils of pitch-black darkness. The handcuffs undid themselves around Sæmundur's hands, falling to the cobblestones with a loud, jarring crash. This made Garún snap out of it, as if she herself had been entranced. She rushed towards the brick in the wall, too afraid to look back, too afraid to see what the sentient darkness was doing to these men. She pulled out the brick, turned it, and found herself back in the Forgotten Downtown as she pushed it back in. Just before she stepped through she heard sickening cracks of bones breaking and choked sounds of retching.

She let out a breath. It seemed to echo through the unnatural stillness of Rökkurvík.

'I'm sorry you had to see that,' Sæmundur said.

She yelled, turning to face him behind her, afraid of what she might see there in the unrelenting dark of Rökkurvík. But he was just standing there, as he had been before the shadows surrounding him became alive, gaunt and dejected.

'I'm also sorry that I led them to you. I was being reckless. But we should be fine now. I doubt they'll bother us again.'

'How did you follow me? *How did you cross over?*'

They were standing behind two decrepit houses in Rökkurvík. She was yelling at him, her hands trembling.

'What the fuck was that? What did I see in the darkness with you, Sæmundur?' she said, her voice almost cracking. 'What did you do?'

He looked up and met her eyes, and the hopelessness that had come over him temporarily gave way to something else. A gleam in his eyes of something suppressed for so long, but now, at last, come to the surface. Some kind of pride. Some type of hunger.

'You don't have to be afraid.' He smiled. She found herself unable to return it. 'I'm here to help.'

Sextán

Before

Garún was fifteen years old when she left home. She didn't run, she just walked away. She had lost count of the number of times she had threatened to leave, or when she'd stormed out only to sneak back in the next day, wet and cold after sleeping in a crevice in the lava just outside the village, constantly terrified that she'd get too close to the wild seiðmagn, where the rocks would come to life and suffocate her. Or worse.

Still, that would have been a better fate than to be forced to spend one more minute in the presence of her mother. That's how she felt at the time, at least. Her anger kept her warm during the cold night, but just as that fire was quick to flare up, it quickly faded as well. So she learned to stoke the embers of her anger, to keep it alive and burning.

It had happened late the previous summer, when the children had been out picking glowberries. In a place with so few luxuries, a few delicious berries at the end of summer were a unique treat. Garún had spent the summer working salt fish, spreading out the fish on a green field to dry it out in the sun. Getting a day off to go berry picking and keeping an eye on the children made her feel like a kid again. As if they were back playing Fallen

Stick together. Fæðey came with her, despite her being older and having got a job at the laundry. Already her hands looked redder and her attitude was more grown-up. Garún suspected she had started drinking and felt a bit hurt that she might have been left out.

The boundary of relative safety in the lava fields was fluid and constantly shifting. Through years of experimenting the villagers had learned which areas were more stable, although they remained impractical for building upon or otherwise being utilised. It was there, among the moss-grown stones, the sharp, black lava rocks, that the children picked glowberries. They tasted sweet, even better when cooked into a jam. The faint luminescence of the berries stained their lips a faint blue, which would glow in the dark for a short while. The sun had started setting late at night, as autumn was just around the corner. So the kids made a game out of sneaking a few glowberries to bed and staying up late, eating the berries and laughing at the ghostly sights of their stained faces, glowing azure.

Fæðey had always been the bravest. Ever since they were little. She stood up for herself. Fought for what was right. Spoke back to adults if she thought them unfair. Once, Garún saw a merchant slap her across the face for being rude. Her lip bled but still she didn't cry or lose her composure. She calmly spat on his polished boots. Fæðey had always taken care of them. Garún, Styrhildur, Hraki – all of them were like family to each other.

That day, Fæðey had gone further out than the other kids. She said she wasn't afraid of the lava. She wanted more berries. She was going to make jam lasting through the winter, so they could have sweet jam on bread, freshly baked in the hot springs. Their faces, she said, would be glowing until the sun was shining through the summer night once again.

A few days later, Fæðey's hand started to itch. She figured

it must be the work, all the chemicals and almost scalding hot water. They thought nothing of it. Then her neck and body started to itch, turning an inflamed red. Fæðey didn't tell anyone about that until she showed Garún the flowers that had grown on her arm. Initially they were small, but they soon bloomed and grew bigger, the skin becoming tough and knotted. Like bark.

She was kicked out of her home. Made to live in the street. Garún demanded that they take her in, but neither Hulda nor Snædís wanted Fæðey in their house. Garún begged her mother to show her childhood friend some kindness. But she didn't budge.

Garún sneaked out to feed her. She bought ointment from the healer, but it did nothing to alleviate Fæðey's pain. Her body stiffened up in only a few days, making her unable to move her deformed limbs.

Then one early morning Garún found her standing out in the middle of the street. She stood in front of an abandoned shack she had been sleeping in, feet rooted in the earth. Beautiful flowers bloomed on her arms. The hair on her head had vanished, replaced by a thick, luxuriant crown of wild flowers. None of them were alike, each a previously unseen type of blossom. She couldn't speak or move. But Garún saw her eyes still moving. She was crying.

When the people in the village saw what had happened, they chopped her down with an axe and burned her. Blood did not flow from the stumps where they cut her down. Only tree sap. All the while, she remained frozen and silent. But she still screamed in the fire.

Garún started to despise the village with all her heart after Fæðey died. Its ugly little houses, twisting roads, the small-minded people and their pathetic little politics and gossip. As if all these insignificant, mundane things mattered when the fucking walls towered over them and kept them apart from the country they were living in. She'd heard of the seiðskrattar and the galdramenn, powerful users of seiður and galdur who might have been able to save Fæðey. If only they'd had the chance. Of course, none of this would have happened if they could just live inside the city walls like everyone else. Not trapped out here, in their hovels, alongside the lethal nature encroaching upon them day and night. She didn't understand how the people could stand it.

She also suspected the villagers didn't mind that Fæðey was gone. She had started being labelled as troublesome. Every time a new blendingur was born, she'd interject herself in the naming ceremony at the church and protest as the naming council gave the blendingar their names. It was an ancient tradition, believed to be a relic of the old world, although some weren't so sure of that. Blendingar traditionally got their names from a separate pool of options. They were odd names, cursed names, given to what had once been considered cursed children. Quite a few people in the village resented that as well, and took Fæðey's side when she protested. Parents should get to choose their child's name themselves, not some town committee, and blendingar should have the same kind of name as anyone else. The committee and the village elders refused to give in, and to Garún's surprise a lot of people stood with them on that. It was tradition. A part of their culture they needed to respect and hold on to. Deciding your own name was for humans.

Garún considered changing her name, just to spite them. She was part human, after all. Why not? But she decided against it. Her name had become a badge of honour. She liked it, despite its connotations of being somehow distant from god. Her name was a corruption of the name Guðrún, meaning god-rune. The 'Ga' in Garún was a mangled pronunciation of the word for 'god'. She liked that, it turned out. She denied all gods, as well as all authority. It suited her. She'd set an example and show them how far a person with a 'cursed' name could go. She'd turn it into a source of pride for others like her.

Every day Hulda worked hard, washing linens from Reykjavík in the hot pools. Most of it was dirty laundry from the city hospital, but sometimes big imported automobiles, trucks with stencilled symbols, would show up and dump a huge order to be done the same day. Later Garún learned those trucks came from the Kalmar military base. Hulda slaved away for meagre aurar on the hour, working for a hospital that would never admit her should she fall ill or injure herself, and an army that would not protect her, but instead kept her out here. It made Garún furious. When Garún confronted her mother about this, she didn't have much to say. Sitting by the kitchen table, her hands reddened from the chemicals and hot water, smoking a cigarette before going to bed at midnight only to get up in five hours' time. She used simple charms, channelling seiðmagn with kukl, to help her ease her tiredness and worn-out body. Garún learned from her how to manipulate seiðmagn.

'That's just how things are, elskan,' Hulda had said wearily. 'There are some fights you can win by yourself. This isn't one of them.'

'Mamma, that's bullshit. What if you had said that when I was born? You fought for me. For us. You didn't just accept things the way they were.'

She shook her head, blowing smoke through her nostrils.

'Huldufjörður is different. We've had to change a lot, you know. For better or for worse. We've always been good at adapting.' She tapped her cigarette on the ashtray. 'This was the next step in the right direction. People wanted to change, I just pushed us along.'

Garún had had this discussion with her mother countless times and couldn't stand to repeat it again. Instead, she reached out to her mother. Opened herself. Hulda hesitated, then reached out as well. Garún felt that cloying presence, the soft and tender love Hulda had for her daughter, the weariness of toiling away for scraps, the deep-rooted resolve and defeat she had cemented within herself regarding her own situation. Garún didn't know what her mother felt, but she tried to bring her feelings to the surface as calmly and purely as she possibly could. To show her how much she cared, how they could change everything for the better, if they only worked together. She tried to pass to her some of the flames that burned within her own heart.

'You'll only get hurt,' Hulda said after a while, and closed her off. And that was the end of that.

Garún didn't know what had brought her mother to this point. And if she was being honest with herself, maybe she didn't really care all that much for the reasons why. She found it pathetic. Hulda had committed a cardinal sin, at least to Garún. She had let the fire within her go out. Garún pitied her. She was determined to never become like that. She would never give up hope, never stop fighting.

When Garún left home there had been no argument, no screaming, no doors being slammed. She took everything she owned and went out just before dawn to the gravel road that led to the city's southern gate. She'd been saving up a runaway fund ever since she could remember. Every single aur, every króna she managed to acquire, went into this fund. When she was a child she'd dreamed of travelling abroad, where people didn't hate blendingar like herself and cities didn't have walls to keep people out. That dream was quickly turned to ash when her mother told her that the huldufólk had been persecuted almost everywhere in the world, except in Hrímland, after their world collapsed and they fled into this one. But there were still rumours of huldufólk living abroad. Maybe not every place was like this. She decided to scale back her daydreaming and put her feet on the ground. Instead of fantasising about foreign lands, she decided to start by getting out of Huldufjörður, in through the city walls. The rest she could figure out later.

The sun bloodied the sky and the wagons started appearing one after the other. Every day farmers headed into the city with what it needed to thrive. The earth was not as toxic with seiðmagn in Reykjavík's surroundings when compared to most other places in Hrímland, but the closer to the mountains or the further from the sea you went, the more potent it became. The wagons carried crates of bottled milk, barrels of salted meat, livestock, barley, eggs, leather, wool, furs, sand, gravel – whatever was needed. She hailed them and offered them everything she had in return for smuggling her through the gate. Those who didn't stop, she followed. It wasn't exactly illegal for huldufólk or blendingar to live in Reykjavík, but the guards would stop every non-human party that tried to get through without having the proper papers or identification. The huldufólk were meant to stay down in the fjord and the marbendlar in the lakes.

She was refused again and again. No one wanted to risk angering the guards. The best case scenario was that they'd be fined and Garún tossed out. Worst case scenario, they'd be imprisoned and Garún sent to the Nine. To her, that was a more desirable fate than be forced to waste her life trying to survive in Huldufjörður. She didn't give up. All her possessions didn't amount to much, but were still a small fortune to those farmers, most of whom went so frequently through that no one saw a reason to look through their cargo: 176 krónur in total.

The sixth one she stopped didn't have a horse towing his wagon, but a well-horned reindeer buck. She'd never seen such a beautiful beast. He looked odd with a bridle in his mouth, but he carried his fetters like royal raiment. As if he'd voluntarily chosen to work himself to death for some peasant.

'What the hell do you want, girl? Get off the road or my buck will ride you down.'

'I have to get through the wall. I can pay.'

The farmer stared her down for a long while. His gaze was heavy and suspicious.

'To beg the aid of others is submission to an independent man,' he finally said.

'I am no man, but I am independent,' she answered, defiant.

The farmer snorted. 'Does not seem so to me, standing like a dependant of the county begging for scraps.'

She felt her face turning warm.

'Very well. I am not fully independent. So far. But no person is an island and now I need help. So are you going to help me or not?'

'Maybe you think that independence can be found on the other side of that wall? The skuggabaldur is more free, sitting in my cage.'

A filthy, blonde head jutted up from the carriage.

'Hi,' the child said in a bright voice.

'Down, and shut up!' the farmer spat at the girl.

The girl retreated from the farmer's harsh tone, as if she feared he was going to strike her. When he didn't seem likely to do so she studied Garún carefully with inquisitive eyes.

'You're like me!' the girl suddenly realised.

As soon as the girl said it Garún couldn't understand how she could have missed it. Those unique features, those eyes from another reality which looked ever so alluring, but still so humanly crude, the human and hulda merged together. But more than anything else, the presence, the feeling which surrounded her, the disturbance that follows two dimensional realities intertwining. To Garún the child looked overwhelmingly comforting. Like home – a form of home, at least. Garún wanted to take hold of the girl and never let go.

The farmer gave the girl a frustrated look, and she slowly sank back down. When he felt sure that she'd stay out of sight he turned back to Garún.

'What's your name, girl?' he asked.

'Garún,' she managed to get out.

'Well, Garún, you say you desire independence and I can tell you that you will not find it in there, where men eke out a living like rats and mice in one great throng, stuck in a trap they do not understand nor perceive, but call it home nonetheless. I am, however, willing to offer you a different option than a life spent under the heels of other men and that is true freedom and true independence, as unquestionable as the sun and the sky, the mountains and the stubbornness of the Hrímlandic sheep. The best part is that you won't have to pay a single króna for it.'

'What do you mean?'

'I own a fur farm and I need workers. It's not big but I own it myself, absolutely free of debt. I can offer you food and a place to live, along with a salary. No vistarband, even though you are homeless and a godforsaken blendingur. Our arrangement would not be the government's concern. You wouldn't have to handle the beasts yourself, hateful bastards that they are, at least not while they live and bite and fight. But you'd have to clean the cages, feed them, work the skins and flay the carcasses. It would still remain primarily my responsibility, after all. I'd leave you the housework. What do you say?'

The thought of a job, of money, gave her such a quick and overwhelming sense of hope that she almost jumped into the wagon, accepting immediately. But something held her back.

This wasn't part of her plan. He'd also mentioned the vistarband, something she was only vaguely aware of. Out in the country, people had to register with the state for work at a recognised workplace. People could be bound to employers for years, indentured to them and completely dependent on being held in good standing. If the farmer was abusive, or stole from you, or something else – who would people believe? An impoverished farm labourer, new in the county? Or a land-owning farmer with a fine reputation? She didn't know if being inside or outside the vistarband would be better for her situation. She was willing to risk being illegal in the city, less so out in the isolated countryside.

'What's the name of your farm? And what kind of animals do you breed?'

'I breed skuggabaldur, a beast almost as unfriendly and hostile as the Hrímlandic weather, but all the more controllable as long as you keep them in their cages. The furs get more valuable as the years go by, it seems that the mesdames can't get enough of fur coats in their bottomless wardrobes. But the farm, you would likely not have heard of it, being a runaway from Huldufjörður. It had such an ominous name, like everything else on this godforsaken island, because of some nonsense or other about ghosts or some similar inane superstition, so I renamed the farm as Ægisá and that name suits it much better than the one it had before.'

She hadn't told him anything of being from Huldufjörður and she minded that he was right about her without asking, no matter how easy it was to figure out.

'If it's all the same to you I'd prefer getting to Reykjavík, but I thank you for your offer.'

'So you'd rather chose fetters than freedom, no matter what

I have to say. A sheep's stubbornness is as nothing compared with a—'

'Compared with what?' she yelled at him, accidentally losing control of herself for a moment.

She'd just about had enough of this man. Her fists were clenched. She didn't care, she saw nothing but red. No one, let alone some hillbilly peasant, was going to stand in her way or talk down to her like that.

He stared. Tried to break her, force her to look away. She gave no quarter. He was a mountain, single-minded and unyielding, but she was the wind, a light breeze that could turn to a storm in an instant, that slowly but surely eroded everything to nothing.

'Compared to nothing, I suppose,' the farmer finally said. He considered for a while. 'Very well. You'll lie under the furs and not move a muscle. But I won't take a króna from you for what I only do for love of my Sóla, who suffered the same cursed misfortune as you to be born deformed.'

Garún gritted her teeth in an effort to hold her tongue. She'd heard worse. She could suffer through this. This was the chance she had been waiting for. The money would be useful in Reykjavík.

A brown waxed tarp covered the wagon. Underneath were stacks of black pelts. The girl was lying in a small gap between two stacks.

'Come! You can lie down here.'

She lifted up the tarp and Garún lay down in the crevice.

'Lie down as flat as you can.' The farmer started to move heavy piles of furs over her feet. 'I'll even it out so nothing looks amiss.'

He covered her up to her chest, and she felt as if she was being buried alive. The coarse furs were filthy, and stank.

'Turn your head to the side, like that, so you can breathe.

And not a single sound, or you'll end up on the gallows. Do you hear me?'

She nodded. Then he placed a reeking pile of fur over her and everything turned black.

The wagon shook forward in the dark. All sounds were muted and distant. Garún lay there awkwardly under the weight and couldn't move at all. Her joints ached. She felt like a corpse buried under a hill, disturbed by children playing after years and years.

The smell of the furs filled her senses, mixed with the stench of dried blood and old meat. She didn't believe that this man could sell these wretched tatters, which were hardly better than any carcass you could find up on the heath, dead since last winter.

The shaking stopped as the wagon halted. Were they inside the walls? Or had the guards stopped him to search the wagon?

Someone stepped up on to the back of the wagon and tore off the tarp. Before she had time to react the skins were yanked off and she was blinded by light.

The farmer stood over her and she sat up. The girl peeked, smiling, from the gap she'd been hiding in. At first Garún thought it was the city wall towering over her, somehow all around, but then she realised they were houses. Buildings larger than she'd ever seen, solidly and beautifully built, with many floors. They were in a small alley, which was not a trampled muddy path but paved with stones. She jumped down from the wagon.

'Thanks.' She didn't know what else to say. The farmer mumbled something in return. 'Do you know how to get to Starholt?'

'Down here to the right, then onwards until you get to Hverfisgata. Then right again and onwards east towards the apartment buildings. Hverfisgata leads all around the city, heavy with traffic, but if I were you I'd lie low. People are not as friendly as I am towards the likes of you.'

It can't be worse than in Huldufjörður, she thought to herself, but kept quiet.

'Goodbye. Thanks again.'

She turned around and started to walk away, but the girl chased after her and ran in front of her.

'Come live with us at Bægi– I mean Ægisá. I'm lonely.'

'Sóllilja!' the farmer shouted. 'Not this cursed damn nonsense and hysteria!'

'I can't. I'm sorry, but I'm going to live in Reykjavík now.'

The little girl nodded, her face downcast. Then she added, 'Are you my sister?'

The girl's words wounded her deeper than she knew was possible. She swallowed the lump in her throat, forced her eyes not to well up with tears. Were they sisters? Why not? How could she be sure? She knew nothing of her father, except that he'd called himself Liljurós. It could just as well be that man. Sóllilja. Liljurós. It would at least explain where her stubbornness came from.

'I'm not your sister. But I'll tell you something. Let's swear ourselves into blood sisterhood with each other and we'll never stand alone. No matter what happens, we'll always have each other. Deal?'

The girl nodded in triumph as she took Garún's outstretched hand.

'Deal,' she said, smiling from ear to ear.

She never saw the farmer from Ægisá or his daughter again.

Sautján

Garún had contacted Diljá a few days earlier. She had trained a select number of people in using extremely diluted delýsíð spray and had to talk to the others about it. Their efforts had already made their mark on the city. She met Diljá late in the night, at an illegal bar in a cellar in the Hlíðar neighbourhood. She had to bribe the thuggish bouncer to get in, and the landi for sale was seriously overpriced – for her, that is. Diljá and, to her surprise, Katrín were waiting for her. Katrín looked pale and tired, with dark circles under her eyes. It wasn't like her to venture outside her comfort zone, let alone take any real risks. She must be really pissed off to interject herself into this. Or afraid of what Garún might do on her own.

The bar was dimly lit with flickering tallow candles, dripping off counters and tabletops in cascades of wax, forming over the years like glacial icicles. Garún and Diljá were the only non-humans in there. It made her uncomfortable. Depressing and dangerous as the Forgotten Downtown might be, at least it was a safe place to talk.

'They've shut down Thorvaldsen's,' Diljá said as Garún sat down with her expensive tumbler of landi. The moonshine was clear, obviously quality stuff, but still smelled almost like turpentine. 'A group of huldufólk were refused entry, and the

221

human clients apparently took their side. The heated argument exploded and they just started looting the place. Police shut it down yesterday.'

Garún couldn't help but grin. The graffiti was working.

'Unfortunate. But now you see it works.'

'Perhaps,' Katrín said in a low voice, 'but you're not going to start an uprising by hypnotising people.'

Garún scowled. 'It doesn't hypnotise them, Katrín. It only pulls away their blinkers to the injustice all around them and helps them find the courage to do something about it. People need to know they can make a difference.'

'I'm not interested in a few riots. I'm interested in making a real change.' She placed a folded-up newspaper on the table. 'Have you seen this?'

She picked up the paper. It was *Ísafold*, a known mouthpiece for the Citizens' Party, of which Katrín's father, Valtýr Melsteð, was an affluent member. *Ísafold* was conservative, human-centric and known for avoiding controversy. The Citizens' Party was slightly opposed to Kalmar, wanting more autonomy, the same as the other big four parties, except the royalists. It still played by the rules, which were stacked in Count Trampe's favour, making for a fairly toothless political force against the stiftamtmaður, the Crown's royal authority manifest in Hrímland.

The front page featured a big picture of the City Hall protest showing people running, and others on the ground bleeding out, being dragged by their comrades. Garún recognised herself in the image. She was dragging a wounded man, a malevolent growth sprouting clearly from his body. A flower made from flesh and bone. The headline read in large, bold letters:

Trampe's Execution of Kalmar's Citizens

She turned the page to the main article. Another picture of the protest, showing the seiðskratti. And a portrait of Jón. It stung to see that.

'There are goðar in Lögrétta who have been pushing against the Crown for decades,' Katrín said in an excited, hushed voice. 'But the parliament can only do so much. They see what's going on, and they don't like it. The Crown has betrayed them every step of the way. Kalmar built Perlan to harvest the seiðmagn in Öskjuhlíð, which they said was to power the city and improve our lives. Then they build this godforsaken death fortress and drain Perlan of its power to make it fly. Did you know that the forest in Öskjuhlíð is dying?' She shook her head. 'We have to stop them. Lögrétta has passed bill after bill to get more autonomy, to get local control over Perlan, which is blocked by Trampe before it even reaches the king. Lögrétta wants autonomy from the Commonwealth, from the stiftamtmaður. Home rule. One day, independence. Some of the goðar have seen what we're doing, and they're on our side.'

Garún glanced over the article. It painted, in no uncertain terms, Trampe as the perpetrator of outright murder of his own citizens and Kalmar as an oppressive force on the country. It was also partly a eulogy for Jón and his life as a poet and political ideologist fighting for a better world. She turned the page. Next up was a large double-page article about Perlan and the flying fortress. It was vehemently anti-war and anti-Kalmar.

'It's almost as if this is ripped straight out of *Black Wings*,' Garún said. '*Ísafold* has never printed anything like this.'

Katrín smirked. 'That's because it is. Most of this is from the piece I wrote after the protest. We spread it all over Reykjavík. With Kryik'traak's help we also got it to Huldufjörður and the marbendlar's coral cities in the great lakes. Someone at the newspaper got hold of it, I think. The thing is that they're taking a stand with us.'

Garún shook her head. 'They'll go to the Nine for this. The person who wrote this, their editor. They'll shut down the newspaper.'

'Maybe if it was regular people doing the publishing. But these are powerful people, Garún. They're close to people in power, real power. The journalist who wrote this, he's married to Sheriff Skúli's cousin. Trampe can't just arrest them like that.'

'Right.'

She got the gist, clear enough. *They're people like me, not people like you.*

'And you think this will actually do anything?' Garún asked. 'Besides get people arrested?'

'It will get the humans talking,' Diljá said. 'We need to reach the regular people. The people who think everything's fine just as it is. This is how we get them listening.'

Garún gave her a careful look. It sounded as if she believed it. This should have been something that made Garún ecstatic. Powerful forces were aligning with their cause. The people were waking up to the everyday injustice all around them. And part of her wanted to rejoice, to celebrate. But she took in Katrín's elegant dress – its expensive fabric, the brooch pinned to her chest, the dainty jewelled necklace around her neck – and understood what they meant: I am above you. I am wealthy. I am one of *them*. And *we* will now change things.

Garún thought of her mother. Of the years she'd spent pushing for change. How step by step she'd changed their small village, broken the taboos of the past. This was what she'd been fighting for. Then why did she feel so hollow?

'That's great to hear.' Garún forced a smile. 'Skál.'

'Skál!'

They all toasted and downed their drinks. The moonshine was awful. Diljá didn't bat an eyelid, but Katrín turned so pale she almost seemed translucent.

'So, all right. What now?'

'Well,' Diljá said, 'what have you been working on in Rökkurvík? Have you been tagging more?'

She sounded concerned. Katrín maintained a neutral façade, but Garún knew she must be seething. To her, the delýsíð was taking civil unrest too far. People didn't trust illegal seiður, let alone galdur. Wealthy people, that is. But those with less often had to make things work using whatever methods they had. No matter how dangerous. Garún felt a painful pang as she thought of her mother.

Garún hesitated. She thought of the protest. Of how upset Katrín and the others had been. Of Jón lying in his blood, his body transformed by a violent death. She steeled herself. Thorvaldsen's was shut down. That might not be much, but it was something.

'I've got a small group of people in the Forgotten Downtown,' she said carefully, gauging their reactions. 'Styrhildur's mostly leading them. I've taught them how to make a few basic delýsíð symbols. Graffiti that empowers dissent, empathy and courage. Similar to the symbol I made at Thorvaldsen's store.'

Garún had showed the group a few well-placed portals in and out of Reykjavík. The would-be insurgents were long-time dwellers in Rökkurvík, by the Forgotten Downtown's standards at least. A few of them had been there for a couple of years. Each was there escaping something; each had given up in some manner. But now they burned with drive and urgency.

Katrín was shaking her head in disbelief, but Diljá's interest was piqued.

'How do you have enough delýsíð? What places are they targeting?'

'It's extremely diluted. Not nearly as potent as what I'm using. So only a few milligrams go a really long way. There's a handful of them, so they can watch out for each other. They've been hitting heavy concentrations of traffic. Large road intersections, train stations. Stuff like that.'

Katrín huffed. 'This will only lead to the Crown mobilising more seiðskrattar in the city. Seiðskrattar which will get these people killed!' She got up. 'I'm going to the bathroom.'

They watched her walk away before continuing their conversation.

'How?' Diljá asked. 'How are you mobilising out of Rökkurvík?'

Garún reached into her pocket for her pouch of tobacco.

'I can find new portals. Cracks in reality.'

She rooted around in her coat for the cigarette papers.

'How?'

There was something about the gleam in her eye that made Garún uncomfortable. Why was she so interested? Diljá had known everything about her movements the night that Viður betrayed her. Had that been her doing? She felt Diljá reach out for her, looking for some clarity as to her suddenly hesitant manner. Garún acted nonchalant as she rolled a cigarette, keeping her defences up. Diljá tried to hide the slight hurt in her eyes at the rejection.

'I have a method. That's all.' She struck a match and lit the cigarette. 'There are plenty of portals through. Many more than the ones I've shared with the taggers. Which means that we don't have to always rely on the same ways back and forth.' She blew out smoke. 'Which, as I'm sure you remember, has proven to be quite dangerous.'

Diljá still persisted. 'You've been working on something else, haven't you? You said Styrhildur was managing the group.'

Garún nodded, unsure of how much she should say. She had been working on a new type of symbol, an eye-shaped rune made from clear delýsíð. It connected to a central symbol, elaborate graffiti she'd painted in the room where she squatted in Rökkurvík. It allowed her to remotely perceive things through the eye-runes, although what she could see of their surroundings was very haphazard and her control rudimentary. It was often hard to pinpoint where the graffiti was located. Finding good spots to tag was also another challenge. Scouting places where they could perceive something useful, but still not be immediately spotted by a passing seiðskratti, was a problem. When the connection worked, however, it was like standing there in the flesh.

'I'm mostly just dealing with the group,' she said. 'Not all of them can get the hang of using delýsíð.'

Which was true enough. Not everyone had a natural affinity for channelling seiðmagn, no matter how slight a trace, and they didn't have time to refine that instinct.

Katrín returned with a round of drinks. Normally Garún would protest – who the hell buys people entire rounds? Fucking show-off. But she was as good as broke, and Katrín was flush. Let her pay for it.

'You should tell those journalists to get into hiding.' Garún downed the drink Katrín had just handed her. 'I can find a place for them in the Forgotten Downtown.'

'I just told you – it will be fine. They know people, most of them are married to or are related to a goði in Lögrétta. Like I said, one of them is married to Sheriff Skúli's cousin, for crying out loud.'

'Trampe will be coming for them. He won't stand for this. They should go to ground before it's too late.'

Katrín shrugged. Diljá remained silent.

'What have you been up to?' She changed the subject.

Katrín reached into her purse and pulled out a couple of new copies of *Black Wings*. A striking cover in black and red, showing silhouettes of two humanoids and a marbendill raising their fists in unison, above and behind them a silhouette of a flying náskári with spread wings and three claws outstretched. In the background a coarse yellow outline of Perlan could be seen. The headline read in stark white letters:

UNITED WE STAND! RISE UP AND FIGHT!

It was a bit more daring than their usual fare. Hrólfur had apparently found an illustrator worth his salt.

'Hrólfur did it himself,' Diljá said, almost as if she was reaching out and reading her thoughts.

'I never knew he had it in him,' said Garún. 'Are these out yet?'

'Freshly printed last night,' said Katrín proudly.

'These will go out tomorrow,' Diljá continued. 'I've secured distribution around the city, especially in Starholt and central Reykjavík. The marbendlar will smuggle copies out to Huldufjörður and the coral cities. It's unprecedented. People want to hear real, uncensored news, read real, unfiltered opinions.' She smiled. 'People are finally listening.'

'Wait, sorry, just a second. Do you think we could add in a small leaflet?'

Her brow furrowed. 'For what?'

'Listen. I wanted to meet up because I've been thinking about something. And now, seeing Jón's picture in *Ísafold*... Well, it makes me doubly sure that it's something we have to do. We need to rally people. Get them into one place and get them talking. More than what we've been doing lately. We need to make a stand.'

'Where are you going with this?'

'We need to remember who we've lost, and why. We need to keep their memory alive. We're going to have a memorial concert in Rökkurvík. For those who died in the City Hall protest. And we're going to use that as a stepping stone to stage a massive protest.'

She reached for Diljá's drink and threw it back.

'We're going to overthrow the government.'

Átján

The empty beer bottle shattered on the pavement. Everything was quiet, the streets empty. The last beer bottle foamed when Garún opened it. She drank the foam, sucked the warm beer off her hands. That six-pack had evaporated fast. She'd have to go back into Gómorra to get more. The thought of tonight's concert made her sick with anxiety. She'd rather jam her hand in a náskári's beak than have to go through with this. The alcohol's numbness flowed over her, as if she was stepping into a hot bath.

Styrhildur had reported to her early the morning before. Not that the concept of morning made any difference in this place. It required a surprising effort on her part to keep up with Reykjavík's time. Styrhildur told her that a group of taggers had been arrested. They'd grown cocky. They had been tagging Hlemmur train station, mere metres away from the massive police headquarters. Hlemmur station's decrepitude was an anomaly in Reykjavík. The station was one of the busiest travel hubs in the city, and the one where hobos most frequently spent their time drinking or sleeping. It was almost as if the police station being so close placed the station in a blind spot.

Maybe that's what the group had thought: they'll never think to look right under their noses. Although the occasional tagger might get away with scribbling, and the police might turn a blind eye to human vagrants – emphasis on human – that didn't mean that they'd stood a reasonable chance of pulling this off.

Rumours about the arrest all conflicted with one another. Some said that bystanders had gone berserk, which led the police to the taggers. Some said that a seiðskratti had set them ablaze, the police arresting the survivors. But the most reliable rumour that Styrhildur had heard was that a gang of young people had been quietly arrested in the early morning, under the judgemental glares of the day's first commuters.

They were in the Nine now. And eventually, they would talk. They'd already moved houses, but that wouldn't be enough. They'd be coming for them. Maybe they would raid the concert tonight. Perhaps they already knew, if they'd got their hands on *Black Wings*.

She wanted to throw up.

To add on top of this was Sæmundur. Fucking Sæmundur. He'd told her everything and explained nothing. He'd stolen something from Svartiskóli. He'd summoned it. Now the Crown was after him and seemed to think he belonged to their little revolutionary cell. Garún couldn't decide if that was a good or a bad thing. What she knew was that those soldiers had been killed in a horrific way – another thing that left her conflicted; they had intended to take her to the Nine – and that Sæmundur refused to tell her how or why or what had exactly happened. He wielded galdur differently now. That was all he said. And that he wanted to help.

So she had let him. Maybe losing those soldiers to that horror would give the Crown some pause. Maybe Sæmundur was unknowingly saving their skin tonight. Or he was dooming them all with this suicidal meddling in svartigaldur.

She downed the rest of the beer and threw the bottle. It broke with a satisfying crash. Tonight she was alive and she thirsted. Thirsted for life and wine. Come what may.

ᚠ

Faded lights lit the tables where people sat and chain-smoked between talking over each other. A small group of people had gathered in front of the stage. They looked young and insecure. Human college kids who wanted to brag about sneaking into Gómorra in Rökkurvík. She was surprised by how much she resented them for seeming happier and more carefree than she had ever been. When she was their age she'd already been working for a living for years in Reykjavík.

On one table sat a group of huldufólk, all dressed in clothes that looked like old heirlooms from the vanished world. In reality the clothes were new and incredibly expensive. They were smoking imported pre-rolled cigarettes, talking and laughing with more fervour than anyone else. Diljá, Styrhildur and Hraki were sitting with them and they waved to Garún as she spotted them. Diljá was dressed in a beautiful sequined dress that Garún had never seen her wear before, Styrhildur was in a similar, but more practically cut dress, and Hraki was in a suit that seemed authentically antique. She knew the kids didn't have a lot of money. Diljá must have helped them out. To Garún this kind of almost formal wear wasn't really something she thought one should wear to a memorial concert and revolutionary rally. It seemed vain and out of place. But to them it was a statement, a source of pride. The vanity of the old world was something Garún was brought up to consider a disgrace, a symptom of the hubris that had led them to ruin. It also reminded her of going to church, when people wore their best to Mass. The image stirred up bad memories she'd rather leave behind.

The rest were the regular patrons of Gómorra on any given day. People who had no other place to go. In one corner a man was lying in a puddle of beer, blackout drunk. Her people stood out. They carried themselves differently. They stood up straight, had a determined look in their eyes. She wondered if this difference was perceptible by the people from Reykjavík. Most likely the people of Rökkurvík all looked the same to them.

It wasn't surprising that no náskárar or marbendlar showed up. The náskárar would never venture to this cursed place, where they'd lose the advantage given to them by flight. There were no open skies here, nowhere to fly to. Garún had no idea what would await them up in the flat, dark sky. The marbendlar didn't want anything to do with Rökkurvík, for some unknown reason. When Garún asked Diljá about it, she'd said that Kryik'traak had only shaken his head in a human gesture and said that it was forbidden.

The first job Garún had got in Reykjavík had been as a porter at the river-docks in Elliðaárdalur, moving cargo for the marbendlar. They had always remained a mystery to her for the couple of years she worked there, but this revelation of a secretive taboo was a familiar feeling to her. So it went, in the Coral Spires. It was a completely different world. She hoped she could visit, one day. She had been so unnerved by the marbendlar the first time she saw them. They looked like monsters to her. But then she'd found out that they didn't differentiate her from the huldufólk and humans. To them, all these bipedal land-dwellers looked the same. It had been a tremendous weight off her shoulders. Something she'd grown so accustomed to carrying that she'd stopped feeling it weighing her down. Throwing that weight off had felt like flying.

Diljá excused herself from the crowd of huldufólk and came

over to Garún, smiling widely to her. She looked glamorous in her dress.

'Hi, Garún! All by yourself in the corner, as usual, I see. Would you like to join us?'

She glanced over at the group. She considered her own worn jacket, the paint-spotted trousers.

'No, I'm fine. Thanks, though.'

'Just thought I'd ask.'

Diljá tentatively reached out, and Garún reached back. She felt excitement, hopefulness – Diljá's sincere desire for Garún to join them. She relaxed. She let the other woman through, let her feel the waves of her anxiety, loneliness, old memories washing over her.

'I wanted to give you this.' Diljá reached into her purse and pulled out a bracelet. 'My mother made this the other day, and I thought of you.'

It was handmade, a fine tangle of interwoven silver circles that held between them tiny gleaming jewels. Like sparkling frost on winter branches. It looked so light and delicate that it had to have been crafted with the aid of some kind of seiður. In the middle was the symbol of Láternýð, the Mountain Built from Sunlight, a mask of friendship, hope, solidarity. Diljá grabbed Garún's hand and put it on her wrist.

'For luck,' she said.

Garún could only nod her thanks. She felt overwhelmed. Like she wanted to cry out in joy, or cry in earnest from how deeply this had touched her, but she didn't know how. She didn't know what to say. And with their connection still open, the two of them still reaching out to each other, she didn't really need to. Diljá hugged her briefly before returning to her table.

Some noise-band started to play. Screams and rhythmic distortion washed over Garún and she found herself enjoying it. The singer was tattooed from head to toe. She got herself a beer. Then another one. The songs were all incredibly short, really only a few riffs stitched together that allowed the audience to lose themselves in a chaotic pit out on the dance floor. They smashed into each other, pushed and hit and banged their heads, but as soon as someone dropped to the floor they were picked up immediately by the others. In between songs the singer ranted about Kalmar, the police, the military and warmongering, their brothers and sisters killed and imprisoned after the protest.

Garún stood and watched. A part of her wanted to jump in and join the unruly crowd as another song blasted off. Would they help her get back up if she was pushed down to the floor? Would she be able to stop hitting once she started? She didn't want to know the answers to these questions. She absent-mindedly touched the bracelet on her wrist. It made her feel warm.

The crowd throbbed and someone bumped into her, pushing her so she spilled half her beer. She turned around, ready to sound off, her defences already up and ready to fight whatever shit this bastard would try to shovel over her for doing nothing but being in his way.

'I'm sorry,' he said, before she could get a word in. 'I didn't mean to, I'm sorry, Garún, I'll get you another one.'

Sæmundur looked even worse than the last time she'd seen him. His eyes were sunken. His skin was sagging slightly. He was just as big and tall as before, but Garún got the impression that there wasn't much keeping this tattered coat of his hanging upright. Something was missing.

This entire scene of bumping into her reminded her of how they had first met. It had happened almost exactly like this. The memory came flooding over her and she felt ill.

'Hi,' she finally said. 'Don't worry about it. So you got the band to play?'

'Yeah. We're next up.'

They went quiet. Looked uncomfortably at each other. They didn't know how to bridge the rift that had appeared between them. It had felt stupid to ask him to play the concert. But she had been too afraid to ask him for anything else. She had no idea of what he was capable of. He'd said he wanted to help, that they could cancel some previously arranged gig and play here instead.

'Everything worked out?' he asked. 'The planning and so on.'

'Yes.'

'Good. Listen, you said some náskárar had shown up at the last protest?'

'Yeah. Rotsvelgur's tribe. Or ... Well, I assume it was his people.'

'I think so too. I'll have to check on Rotsvelgur soon. We have some business to attend to. I can talk to him, if you want. Get their full support.'

'I should go with you.'

She had meant it as a means to show support, but it was clear by the look on his face that Sæmundur had gleaned her real intention. She didn't trust that he wouldn't botch the task.

'It'll be fine. Don't worry. You stay safe.'

'I will.'

She didn't know what to say. It felt like no matter what question she asked, she wouldn't get any real answers.

'How's Mæja?'

Something moved over his face. Something dark and unclear.

'She ... She's fine. She goes out a lot. Still purrs as loudly as ever.'

'Good.' She forced herself to smile. 'I miss her, you know.'

'I know.'

The band finished up to rowdy applause. Diljá and Hrólfur got up on stage and took the microphone. They were about to give the speech about the people who had fallen in the fight against the Commonwealth, the oppression they were facing, the dangers of harnessing the dormant power in Öskjuhlíð for war and destruction.

'Sæmundur ...' Garún started, but he stopped her.

'I have to get backstage and set up. Don't leave, watch us play. It's going to be ... It's going to be different.'

She nodded.

He was about to break. All his willpower went into holding Kölski back. He kept mumbling incantations and words of power, low enough that others couldn't hear what he was saying. He had to support himself so he could stand. Kölski was not resisting, wasn't trying to break out, but Sæmundur couldn't contain him much longer.

Every hour that passed was harder than the last. It had come to the point where Sæmundur had to constantly recite the incantation to prevent Kölski from breaking out of his shadow-bound form. He hadn't slept. His lessons with Kölski had been intense, and partly unleashing control of the demon bound in shadow had placed a great strain upon him. It sickened him how willing Kölski was to serve him. How easily he had dispatched those soldiers. Pliant and humble, a misleading smile that waited for the next instruction. He'd thought of bailing on the concert, which seemed so insignificant in the greater context of things, but after having Garún witness that he couldn't just abandon her.

Everything had changed. So much of what he knew about galdur was based on false pretences, ancient misinterpretations and misunderstandings that had become even more convoluted with time and warped everything. After only the initial few hours with Kölski, that much had been made clear.

He felt like a child being let behind the scenes after a play. He saw the ropes and switches, trapdoors and mirrors, and slowly he was realising this was all a trick. An illusion. But at the same time he better understood the greater context, the obfuscated meaning. How the illusion worked. How you could make a new trick out of an old one. How you could mix two together to make up something never seen before. And just as a child would, he had to try pulling the strings. See the puppets dance. He wanted to share this perspective on reality with others. He had to know if he could somehow impart this gnosis. The concert was the perfect opportunity.

Backstage he greeted the other members of the band. They hadn't seen each other for a very long time. They looked at him as if he was a wreck living on the streets. Which, he supposed, he kind of was. He couldn't go back to his apartment, that much was certain. They didn't have much to talk about. They had nothing in common outside of the music, which Sæmundur had ignored since being kicked out of Svartiskóli. He was waiting for them to kick him out of the band, since he didn't show up for rehearsals. But these were his old friends from the Learned School and it seemed that they didn't have it in them to kick him out of the band, just as he hadn't had it in himself to leave. It had been dangerous for them to get in and out of the Forgotten Downtown, especially when carrying instruments and other equipment. But it was exciting. A band that had the guts to play in the Forgotten Downtown was worth something. It was unheard of on this scale.

The room buzzed with excitement as Sæmundur and his band set up the stage. He was worried about his shaking hands. He felt light-headed, as if he could pass out. He mumbled an incantation and felt himself stabilise – his shadow solidify. Sæmundur had sometimes experimented with mixing some galdur into the music before. That's why he had joined the band. He had wanted to better understand how the two were connected, but he'd never managed it well enough without risking absolutely losing control. At best he'd managed to make the audience feel slightly intoxicated. His experiments had helped him develop the musically infused galdur ritual of raising the cloth-golem. But before Kölski, Sæmundur hadn't realised how to properly summon the galdur that was inherently a part of music. The untamed, raw and elusive power hidden behind the notes, making up the foundation of a traditional ritual of galdur. Galdur demanded a disciplined control, a clearly designated space, a purposeful ceremony. There was no room for improvisation, unlike in music.

But that was before his eyes had been opened. He saw things for what they were now. Or close enough, at least. Sæmundur had seen the smoke machines and false floors. A small gap had opened in his mind and through it something leaked that transformed everything it touched.

Guitar feedback cut its way through the crowd. The others finished setting up and looked at Sæmundur. He nodded. With a heavy tone he let go and started to play.

Garún had never particularly liked the music they played, but she understood why they had their regular crowd. You could forget yourself in their music. She took a sip of her beer, started to rock from side to side. Everything seemed clearer than before. Simpler. More distant.

The crowd cheered as they started playing. It looked as if they were familiar with it. It was their most well-known song.

A slow, murky riff that started out calm, but became steadily heavier until the song completely lost it at the very end. She liked it. Not something she'd listen to by herself, but a good song nonetheless.

The intro was slow and heavy, the drums like the heartbeat of a dying old man. But something was off. Something was missing. Sound reverberated through her, vibrated to the bone, set off an ecstatic feeling that spread through her body.

The melody became stronger, louder. The song rose like a wave, broke and prepared to come crashing down with all its accumulated power. It was then that she finally noticed what was missing.

Sæmundur was about to start singing. He was bathed in red light. She couldn't see his shadow cast behind him.

The crashing sound wave hit her.

Everything vanished except her and the stage. The lights shimmered up into the empty firmament. From their tendrils stars were created, brightly shining suns powered by the heavy, cataclysmic metal. She felt her skeleton vibrate with each change in chord so that her vision shook, like a large church bell being struck with a great iron hammer.

The sound broke upon her like waves in a storm. Her body was set alight with sound. In the flickering, celestial lights she saw the shapes of other figures, rigid and grey statues that moved lethargically. Numbing waves of ecstasy came crashing down on her again and again, first manifesting as goosebumps over her hypersensitive skin, then becoming more intimate, deeper, digging down into the bone marrow and spreading through her body. She felt herself getting warm, her heart beating faster and faster, the crashing sound filling her head and flowing down into her chest, her stomach, between her legs. She was beating in rhythm to the song.

The dance floor was a crystal-strewn wasteland. She realised that she was stroking herself. Every touch was like a droplet into still waters, a mountain crashing into the ocean. In the distance she saw vague forms, writhing in a bizarre dance. Sæmundur sang, but his voice was carried to her before the sound itself and echoed in her head until the tone became unbreakable. The thick bass strings vibrated from his striking them and split the world in half.

It came to her in an instant. She saw the world for what it was: a glorious, thinly veiled illusion of suffering and hope. And there, towering over it all, a titan made out of newly erupted stone, a chained god that had wound the strings of all creation around its hands. It was growing greater, rising in splendour, a sunrise of enlightenment about to be revealed to her in merciless, unforgiving light. The titan looked down upon her.

The Stone Giant.

Then, before she could truly perceive its true nature, the entire vision vanished as quickly as it had appeared, her feet giving way as the illusion that is the world collapsed and everything cascaded down into the cold and patient abyss.

Light. Dark. Screaming. Whispering.

She was shaking when she came back to herself, soaked in sweat. Her entire body ached and her voice was gone, but she didn't remember screaming. The concert was over and the band had vanished from the stage. The other concertgoers were as worn out as she was, completely exhausted and satisfied, a strange, communal look in their eyes. She was dying of thirst.

Everything was a haze. Every face looked like another,

nameless worms that thought themselves to be sentient. Walking dreams. She searched for and found him.

Sæmundur said something and she responded. They laughed. He was changed, too. She now saw through the heavy darkness that had shrouded him. He was still there, himself, hidden behind those layers of anxiety and fear and arrogance. A small glimmer at the bottom of an ancient lake. She felt the strings of his fate beating in sync with her own rhythm and knew that he felt the same. They kissed, deeply and intimately.

They tore the clothes off each other and collapsed on her bed so it groaned, hot and sweaty, consumed with an intense desire. Garún felt him against her, hard and excited, and the eagerness built up until they merged with each other. Sounds, moans, gasps, blasphemies uttered in the dark. Flesh against flesh, warm and lush and ravenous.

She woke up in the gloom. It didn't matter now if it was night or day. The bed sheets were soaked with sweat and she felt a dried wetness between her legs. He was lying next to her, pretending to sleep, and she thought of the last time they tried to sleep together. She thought of herself, standing in the rain, holding a cat. The darkness that surrounded him.

'Leave,' she whispered in the darkness. 'Leave.'

Nítján

Before

When Sæmundur was two years old his mother died in child-birth. He and his siblings were split up into foster care all around the country. Or so he was told. He couldn't remember either his mother or his siblings. His father he'd never heard mentioned, but he spent a large part of his childhood waiting for him. The only vague memory he had of his mother was that she used to sing lullabies to him. Still today he felt a regret he could neither explain nor fully understand if he heard some of the old Hrímlandic songs. Perhaps it was a false memory. Perhaps what really filled him with sadness was the thought of the childhood he could have had.

Sæmundur was eleven winters old when he put his first draugur to rest. He had been herding sheep for the farmer in Hofteigur when a great, thick fog descended upon the heath. The land faded like a photograph left too long in the sun and he felt that he faded along with it. It was the middle of the day, but the fog was so thick it was as if the sky had darkened. That was when he encountered the haugbúi.

In the fog he came upon a small mound he didn't recognise. A young girl sat on top of it. He knew she had been waiting for him. She was beautiful, but just as grey and faded as the dead grass on top of the mound. He wasn't surprised by this, even though everything was green all around. He knew that this was the infamous Hóla-Skotta, who had led shepherds and travellers to their deaths since the earliest times of settlement, when she had been drowned for cannibalism and buried up on the heath.

'Come here, shepherd-boy,' she called to him in a sweet voice. 'Up here I can see where the flock of Hofteigur's old farmer has gone.'

'Although lambs are easily herded for the slaughter, it takes more than that to entice me,' Sæmundur answered.

She laughed. 'So you say, but still your ear is tagged with my name.'

Sæmundur felt something hot drip on his shoulder. He wanted to turn away and run as fast as he could, but before he knew it he was standing on the mound in front of Hóla-Skotta. He saw how her black pupils burned and smelled the stench coming off her, a heavy smell of earth, bone and rotten blood. He was brought into her arms and she stroked his cheek, pushed him in to her bloated bosom. She was cold and the stench of rot was overpowering, but in it was an underlying, sickening sweetness that fascinated him. He'd never been so close to a girl before. The cold fog cut to the bone and Sæmundur wanted nothing more than to vanish into the ashen mound with the draugur.

'Wait.' His mind felt heavy and groggy, making it difficult to talk. It was as if the fog had gathered in his mind. 'I know of another mound, closer to the village, where people walk every week on their way to church. If I moved your bones then you could eat the fattest meat the region has to offer instead of making do with starving shepherds.'

'Why should I risk that when I've got you here? So tender and soft?'

He twitched away from her fingers stroking through his hair. 'Everyone knows where your burial mound is. You must rarely eat.'

The draugur thought for a while. With every minute that passed Sæmundur started doubting himself. What could be better than to let her touch him, to feel her teeth break through skin and tear flesh? What a sweet release that would be, to bleed into her mouth, to let her drain him of his life's essence, to fade away into nothingness in her soft, tender embrace.

The haugbúi agreed just as Sæmundur was about to give in and beg her to devour him, let him into the dark behind her eyes. She released him and immediately he started to frantically dig at his feet with his bare hands.

It took him all day to dig her up. The sun had started to set and it was likely that soon people would start looking for him. Sæmundur dug until he'd torn off most of his nails. Eventually he found Hóla-Skotta's bones. He gathered them carefully and made sure to get each and every single piece.

When they were all gathered up he shattered the femurs so Hóla-Skotta fell down, crippled. With his dagger he carved a stave of drowning upon the skull and smudged his blood over the symbol, making Hóla-Skotta cough up water until she drowned again. He then took the bone fragments and cast them into the boiling hot springs of Heiðarstaðahverir, the bottomless deeps of which were said to reach down to the eternal inferno itself.

When Sæmundur came back to Hofteigur, the farmer asked where he had been and he spoke plainly of it. The farmer was so terrified of the boy's knowledge that he dared not keep him on as a farmhand and sent him straight to Reverend Hrafnkell, who was also the most learned man in the county.

Reverend Hrafnkell treated Sæmundur better than the farmer in Hofteigur. For a long while Sæmundur imagined that Hrafnkell was his father, but he knew well that it was nonsense. He still found it comforting to imagine. The priest asked Sæmundur about Hóla-Skotta, after verifying that the haugbúi was indeed placed to eternal rest, and how he had learned to draw galdrastafir. Sæmundur knew it was very bad to know galdur without being allowed. He convinced the priest that the farmer hadn't taught him, which was true. The farmer used staves and minor incantations of galdur to fish well or bring in bountiful hay for the winter, as every man in the county did, some minor occult meddling that usually never worked. But Sæmundur had studied those symbols and seen what had worked in them and what didn't, although he couldn't explain why, and so he had made up the stave of drowning on the spot by turning a defence against drowning into its opposite.

The priest had never heard anything like it, and it was a mercy that Sæmundur had ended up with a man who was such a tolerant scholar. He strictly forbade Sæmundur from ever doing such a thing again and told him vile stories of demons and possession, men who had lost their minds and flesh to inhuman beings who only wanted to destroy and deform. Most others would have charged the boy to the magistrate, but Hrafnkell saw in him a talent that was meant to be nurtured, disciplined and controlled. He taught Sæmundur to write, read, recite a few relatively innocent incantations and words of power. It was the first time Sæmundur felt that his life meant something. This is what he had been born to do. This was his destiny.

Sæmundur enjoyed his time with the priest, but resented the weekly church visits. Kneeling in front of the king's idol, singing hymns and praying to the distant throne – it was all something he found unnatural and idiotic. The mountains outside invoked in him a much greater sense of reverence than the supposedly divine king of Kalmar. Remaining after the Mass and watching the local big shots of the county gossip and plot was terribly dull. He never mentioned this to the priest. After all, Hrafnkell was faithful and kept true to the doctrine he preached, even though he was more tolerant than most other priests.

After a few years of strict preparation and studies, Sæmundur started his tutelage in the Learned School in Reykjavík, where he made friends for the first time in his life. It was a joyful experience, but simultaneously a painful one. In the remote reaches of the north there were few peers his age, and he rarely met them. Reverend Hrafnkell wrote to him regularly and sent him money when needed, which Sæmundur managed to spend wisely for the first few years, out of fear and respect for his benefactor.

At first he liked the Learned School, the studies were demanding and opened new worlds of knowledge and skill to him. It didn't last long, however. Soon he butted heads with his teachers and was sent to the rector's office more than once for arguing with them during classes and refusing to do the tasks laid out for him. His new-found associates grew distant and he spent more time alone in the library than in their company.

Soon he started to drink, more out of boredom than anything else, and waited for the chance to get out of school and away from Hrímland, which he had started to despise with all his heart. Hrímlanders were nothing but a bunch of peasants and petty fishermen who thought too much of themselves, all of them as thick-headed as the next. Soon after that he started to smoke highland moss and experiment with seiðmagn, which was when he met a young blóðgagl that called itself Rotsvelgur. When he graduated at eighteen, almost all of his funds were spent in drinking and nonsense, but even though he barely had enough for ink or coal he managed to remain at the top of his class.

It was decided that the Royal University in Hafnía would be the best preparation he could receive for ongoing studies at Svartiskóli, which Sæmundur had aimed for ever since Reverend Hrafnkell told him stories of his years of study there. The priest said goodbye to the young man at the docks at Grandi, himself having become aged as the child turned into a man. It was the last time they saw each other, as he died shortly after Sæmundur left. Since he had no children, he had bequeathed his wealth to Sæmundur, who had squandered that money in as rapid a manner as only a Hrímlandic student abroad could.

Sæmundur had never properly thanked him. He never returned north, where the priest lay buried. It was futile. He had no home.

Tuttugu

Garún woke with a start, the dregs of the nightmare still looming over her. It had been a few days since the concert. She slept
with the delýsíð sheet under her. It radiated anger, leaking into
her dreams. She told herself it was to keep her on edge, but she
knew that wasn't the entire reason for it. Someone was pounding
at the door. She reached for the pale blue jawbone underneath
her pillow.

'Who's there?' she asked.

'Hrólfur,' was the response.

'And Diljá. Let us in, please.'

Diljá sounded as if she was on the verge of tears. It could be a
trap. But why would the Crown waste time playing games when
they could easily charge in and overpower her? Garún held the
jawbone behind her back, readied like a dagger, and sneaked
towards the door. She opened it a small crack. Through it she
saw Diljá and Hrólfur, standing alone in the dark hallway. They
looked terrible. Their clothes were roughed up, their eyes wild
like those of a cornered animal.

'Wait,' Garún said.

She shut the door again and tore the sheet infused with seiðmagn off the bed. It reeked of feverish sweat. She stuffed it in a
hole in the floor in one of the corners of the room. Immediately

it was more bearable to stay inside the room, but you could still feel faint hints of its effects. She was about to open the door, but hesitated. She had no idea why they were really here, or if they could really be trusted. Garún hid the jawbone in her belt and opened the door hesitantly.

Hrólfur and Diljá slunk inside as soon as she opened. They were like mice, sneaking along the walls. Hrólfur headed towards the boarded window and tried to peek outside.

'What happened? Where's Katrín?' Garún asked.

Diljá suddenly started to cry. Hrólfur turned from the window, his face mortified.

'They came tonight.' A long time passed before he continued. 'They've connected us to *Black Wings*. I'm not sure what happened to Katrín.' He looked towards Diljá, as if expecting her to continue, but she only sobbed. 'We'd just finished distributing the new magazine. We ran out of ink so we went home early. They blockaded the entire Melar neighbourhood. Soldiers and police outside my apartment, interrogating the neighbours. I saw two seiðskrattar enter. They didn't see me, so I ran. Met Diljá heading back towards Höfði. They'd also been at her place. We'd both hoped they didn't know where the printing press was located. But the entire workshop was up in flames.'

'But you?' asked Garún. 'Did they see you?'

Diljá had gathered herself. She sat motionless, frozen. A statue of grief.

'No,' she replied. 'I was at Starholt, walking home, when Urður stopped me. She used to babysit me when I was a kid. She said that there was a raid in my street and I knew they'd taken all of them.'

Early on they had agreed to keep their private lives separate. The less they knew, the less harm they could do to one another if one of them was captured. But still details had seeped through. Garún knew that Hrólfur lived by himself and was a low-ranking scribe or accountant in some department of the city. She was unsure if he had something to lose or not. Diljá had a large family and lived with them in Starholt, like many of the huldufólk did. She had a lot of younger siblings. But Garún didn't feel any sorrow or compassion. Just hatred for the Crown.

'What about Katrín? Why isn't she here with you?'

Garún's tone was a bit harsher than she'd intended. Katrín's absence was unsettling, to say the least.

'There's no reason to think they're on to her as well,' Hrólfur said, annoyed. 'She never goes to the press, not even to send in an article. She considers funding most of the costs her entire contribution to the printing work.'

'She still might have headed the same way you did. She lives downtown, right?'

'Yes. On Tjarnargata by the pond.'

'I hope she's okay,' Diljá said. 'At least her family is going to be okay. They wouldn't dare take them.'

'Don't be so sure,' Hrólfur said. 'She might be a Melsteð, but that doesn't matter to them. If they find out Katrín is a part of this, then they will pay. Treason is treason.'

Garún didn't like this. She'd never fully trusted Katrín.

'Just now there are only two options – either Katrín is a traitor or she's a prisoner of the Crown.'

'You can't know that!' Diljá said, shocked. 'She might have escaped.'

'Then why isn't she here?' Garún started pacing the room. She hated this feeling of losing control. 'You all had the hidden emergency portals into Rökkurvík. Everyone knew the plan in case of the worst. Regroup in the Forgotten Downtown.'

Garún always thought Katrín was naïve, a view reinforced when she couldn't believe that the Crown would move against the journalists at *Ísafold*. Still, deep down, she admired her determination to fight against her own privilege.

'All right, let's assume she might have escaped – but how long can she remain in hiding in Reykjavík? I seriously doubt she knows someone that can get her into the Forgotten Downtown. If they haven't captured her already, it's only a matter of time. We need to know what the situation is.'

'What do you suggest?' Hrólfur asked.

'We can't stay here. We need to get out of Rökkurvík. Regardless of whether Katrín betrayed us or is their prisoner, they probably have figured out that we are hiding here. If she's out there we need to find her as soon as possible, or at least figure out what's happened to her. I'll head into Reykjavík and find out what's happened while you find another place to hide here. Then we have to move. Diljá, did you talk to Kryik'traak?'

'Yeah,' she said quietly. 'Yeah, they were willing to set us up with a safe house.'

They nodded. It was settled. Garún was surprised how incredibly relieved she was. Relieved that she wasn't the one who had to kick them off the edge, out of the false security of comfort – that the Crown was the one to do it for her. It was a horrible thing to think, to be glad that their relatives and friends were now at the mercy of the Crown. But that was how the pigs operated and had for years. It was a bittersweet feeling to not feel so alone. She wasn't the only one in exile any more.

Hrólfur and Diljá went to a storage unit down by the docks. Garún had scoped it out as a possible place to hide, at least for a while. The storage was an old fisherman's workshop, filled with torn nets and fishing gear. There was no hint of the smell of fish, and as a result there was something uncomfortable about being there. As if it was a stage, not a genuine place.

By hanging by her fingertips from a broken window and letting go, she fell into Reykjavík, in a backyard just by Haraldskirkja. It was dark, which made it hard to tell what time it was. The short days of winter darkness now ruled in Hrímland. The city was covered in grimy slush. She turned up the electronic music. The noisefiend spoke to her like an old friend. A nerve-racking beat played under shady electronic music, winding and building up so that she kept expecting the music to break like a wave, but it didn't happen. This was a new variation of a familiar theme. Danger was around every corner, the smallest mistake could blow her cover. She picked up a steel-grey spray can and sprayed a symbol on the back of her jacket with the clear paint. Putting on the jacket was repulsive, as if she'd put on a bloody human skin, but she suffered through it. The symbol was a type of huliðshjálmur, for disguise or invisibility, and would make her less conspicuous. She put on the red-tinted goggles and headed towards the pond.

Garún scanned the streams of residual seiðmagn, looking for the passage of seiðskrattar. She listened intently to the obtuse messages of the noisefiend and searched for the telltale traces of seiðmagn they left behind, like waves in the wake of a ship. The huliðshjálmur would not work on them, but quite the opposite – it would make her glow like a beacon from the seiðmagn. She saw many traces of their presence, but none of them recent. Soldiers walked down Hverfisgata in pairs. Police officers were common enough downtown, even armed ones, but the army usually kept to their forts on the peninsula and Viðey. Garún was a natural at lying low when she needed to, something she'd had to learn early on as a blendingur in the city. The soldiers didn't notice her as she walked past them, her head downcast.

The huliðshjálmur had just dried and she felt better having it on, but it still felt repulsive. The difference was the same as between fresh and coagulated blood – each was disgusting in its own way.

Step by step the pond drew closer. She stopped outside a stately house and peeked through the kitchen window. The family inside was sitting down at the table, but paid her no mind, despite her being in clear sight. Inside the clock struck seven. Something made her linger. After a few weeks in the Forgotten Downtown this sight was so unfamiliar and unnatural. Like an overly stylised advertisement in the newspaper. She thought of dinners with her mother and grandmother. Now it seemed like a dream.

Katrín's home was further down the street. The greatest and wealthiest families of Hrímlanders lived here, in exorbitant estates by the pond, and Katrín belonged to one of the more powerful ones. She was a Melsteð, an old and deep-rooted family that claimed many Hrímlandic people of prestige and power as their own. Mostly politicians and priests, but there were some known poets in between. Garún had never been able to trust her completely. Katrín belonged to the establishment, she had nothing to lose. She was the most active of the group in writing articles, where she used a male pseudonym. She was well educated and made some powerful points, Garún couldn't deny that, but she'd never taken Katrín's revolutionary spirit seriously. At best she attributed it to being the whim of a rich daddy's girl – but now she feared that Katrín's betrayal could be greater than she'd thought possible.

Of all the houses on the street, Katrín's family home was the only one with its lights off. Garún lithely moved over the fence and sneaked into the yard. There was not a person to be seen. She went behind the house and found a basement door, a servants' entrance. She tagged a stave of discord on the door's window. Fine streaks cracked through the glass, which shattered soundlessly into fine dust. She let herself in.

Inside she was met with an overbearing silence. Garún moved into the kitchen. The cupboards were open and empty. Broken china littered the floor, cracking under her feet despite her best efforts. She sneaked upstairs into the lobby. The house was ransacked. Expensive sofas had been overturned, with ugly new gashes in the expensive upholstery. Paintings had been pulled off the walls, some of them cut. A portrait of a young lady, her face bearing more than a passing resemblance to Katrín, had been ripped from top to bottom. Shards of porcelain and glass were scattered on the floor. The wallpaper was half-torn off in places. Cracks in the plastered walls were visible.

The upper floor was the same. The bedrooms were ruined. Floorboards had been torn up, every drawer had been pulled out, the furniture shattered. Garún tried to identify which room belonged to Katrín, but her parents clearly had only had daughters, as the three bedrooms aside from the master bedroom all obviously belonged to girls. The master bedroom was covered in down and feathers. The mattress and bedding were shredded. The feathers almost covered a large coagulated pool of blood in the middle of the floor. A sticky set of footprints was at the edge of the blood.

The audioskull's music changed with a jolt; the bass dropped and a panicked rhythm started playing. Garún slid behind the open bedroom door. She looked through the crack between the door and the frame. Two police officers moved slowly up the stairs. Of course the house was still being monitored. She silently cursed herself – how had she missed them? There was too much background threat in the music.

They were young, both of them. Probably inexperienced. One was trying to grow a respectable moustache, which was still nothing but feeble down on his upper lip. They'd find her. The huliðshjálmur wasn't strong enough for this. The one with the moustache nodded towards the other and headed towards the master bedroom. They were armed with heavy skorrifles with bayonets attached.

Slowly, silently, she pulled out the can of delýsíð. The officer moved into the bedroom with his rifle readied. They knew she was there. They had probably been waiting for her. When he'd entered and was just about to turn back, she leaped out and sprayed him right in his face.

Abstract delýsíð painting was something that had fascinated Garún a lot. She'd worked with delýsíð for a long time in her artwork, but she'd always relied on forms and certain colours to shape the effects of the delýsíð in a clearer way. She'd never used both clear and formless delýsíð, never tried to get the psychosomatic effects she wanted without using any kind of art as the framework. Now she focused with all her power to shape an illusion out of nothing but her raw will. To paint a picture in the man's mind of his fellow officer as a monster, so that he would see his partner as Garún did. As a danger and a threat. She tried to connect all of this to the fear of the terrorist and traitor he'd come here to capture, but it was too much for a hack job like this one and she felt control slip from her hands.

He screamed and tried to rub the spray out of his eyes. Immediately his partner came running down the hallway and aimed his skorrifle. Garún dodged from the doorway, pointed to the hall and screamed at the officer.

'There she is! There she is!'

The delýsíð-blinded officer stopped rubbing his eyes and looked towards his partner. Garún flinched when she saw what she'd done to the man. His eyelids had been burned away, shrivelled to nothing, and dark purple fluids streamed from the corners of his eyes. His eyes were rigid and bloodshot, the dilated pupils like bottomless pits. In their centres were burning white dots. A quivering smile appeared on his lips. He aimed his weapon towards his friend.

'Þorgeir, don't—'

The gunshot silenced him. Garún waited until she heard the body hit the floor. Before the blinded police officer could rid himself of the hastily made seiður, Garún pulled up her knife and stuck it in deep under his chin. The blade disappeared into the soft flesh and she felt the point crack through cartilage. The officer gurgled and his body became rigid. She saw the glint of steel behind his teeth, where the dagger came up through his tongue and into the roof of his mouth. Blood came gushing over her hands, a waterfall streaming from his mouth and the wound, and she pulled the knife out. He collapsed, shaking, choking on his own blood. Then he stopped moving.

Garún searched the bodies before she got out. She took two more knives in addition to the one she had, and a token of protection one of them carried around his neck. The necklace was a small skull moulded into some kind of metal, decorated with runes and symbols. Yellow rat's teeth jutted out of the awkwardly shaped lump of metal. On the skull's forehead was the seal of the king, meaning that this artefact was consecrated by a royal seiðskratti. Could this have blocked the noisefiend? Garún was unsure what the item's purpose was, so she crushed it under her heel. She felt as if she heard a scream in the distance, but it had to be her imagination.

She managed to get out unseen, as far as she knew. Were they monitoring the house to capture Katrín, or her accomplices? If she'd betrayed them, why had the house been turned upside down? What were they searching for? The pool of blood on the floor. Footprints smudged with blood. Feathers everywhere. The feathers had been spread after the blood had been spilled. They had been lying on top of it, white and untouched like ships on a red sea. Someone had been injured before they tore through the place. If Katrín had betrayed them, the Crown was already in the Forgotten Downtown. If not, Katrín would eventually break and tell them about the emergency portals.

If Katrín was in hiding, she needed Garún's help. Why hadn't they discussed this? Garún didn't know where she should be searching.

She tried to place herself in Katrín's footsteps. How likely was it that Katrín had gone to her friends? Most likely all of them were of a similar class and background as she was. Wealthy humans who had never done an honest day's work in their lives. Possibly old schoolmates from the Learned School. It was very unlikely that any of her friends would give her shelter with the Crown on her heels. Maybe someone would. Garún knew so little about her life. She had assumed too much.

Black Wings had been struggling a couple of years earlier. People weren't reading it, so there were few who were willing to take the risk of distributing it. Then Diljá heard of a columnist who had an article for them. It was a man, known for his severe and unreserved tone of voice, who had written a few bold pieces for *Ísafold*, but not controversial enough to cause any real trouble. Diljá let it be heard that *Black Wings* was interested and eventually they had managed to set up a meeting behind an abandoned factory on Gufunes.

Hrólfur didn't want to go at all. He didn't trust this fellow, but Diljá wanted new blood for the magazine. Garún agreed with her on that front. She was desperate for direct action, direct attacks on the Crown, but the others were unwilling to risk it.

Not yet, they said repeatedly. When the time was right. As far as Garún was concerned, there wasn't a wrong time to defy the Commonwealth.

She went with Diljá to the meeting and waited all day in the abandoned basement room of the factory, where they had a good view of the meeting spot. When the time was approaching three in the morning, a woman came walking along, not a man. She was in a dress cut in the latest fashions, a silken shawl over her shoulders, obviously imported. Garún wanted to ditch, certain it was a trap, but Diljá went out by herself to meet the woman.

For a long time Katrín only met Diljá to deliver articles and shorter pieces. She continued using the same male pseudonym. Garún and Hrólfur kept their distance, unwilling to trust her with too much knowledge about how they operated for the longest time.

Then one day Diljá came with a piece from Katrín that was different. It was so long that it would take up almost the entire magazine. The article listed in the utmost detail how the Crown intended to take over the thaumaturgical energy source in Öskjuhlíð and use it exclusively for military purposes.

Valtýr Melsteð, Katrín's father, had held a seat as goði in Lögrétta for decades. He regularly held unofficial meetings at their home, where old and new party members alike would meet to discuss policies and other plans. Nobody minded if Katrín was sitting in the adjacent living room while the meeting took place; the same went for her mother and sisters. She was a part of the family, one of them. She was a member of the party, after all. Besides, she was *just a woman*. What could one vapid girl really understand? What could she do?

Katrín's father had met his party members to discuss the possible profits the state could receive from the full militarisation of Perlan. This was an unofficial meeting, to gauge the political situation, as this was likely to be opposed by many other goðar in Lögrétta. Katrín had found it easy to eavesdrop by knitting just outside the living room.

The power plant was owned by Innréttingarnar, a state-founded company established shortly after Hrímland joined Kalmar. It focused on promoting and investing in local enterprise. The woollen mills in Eimvogur and the shipyard in Gufunes were only a fraction of the company's operations. Several decades earlier, when Vésteinn Alrúnarson had put forth his theories about the mechanical utilisation of seiður without need for a seiðskratti, the company had seen an opportunity and quickly started planning a thaumaturgical power plant in Öskjuhlíð. To this date, it remained their most remarkable and successful venture.

Technically the company was owned and run by the Hrímlandic state, which meant that Kalmar pumped funds into Innréttingarnar. Building up infrastructure and industries in their colonies would only serve to benefit them. On paper it was the king himself who was the head of the venture, but in actuality the head of the Kalmar colonial authority, Count Trampe, was the one secretly holding the reins – and the stiftamtmaður's grip was tight. The board ran the company independently, but everything needed to be approved by Trampe. Most of the profits went to the Commonwealth, who trickled money back into the company as they saw fit. Trampe had been elated at the success of Perlan and quickly set his military engineers to work on creating a machine that could harness the sorcerous power. So, Loftkastalinn had risen to the skies.

Perlan did a number of great things for Reykjavík. It provided the city with electricity, heat, even limited fuel creation for ships and automobiles. There had been grand plans to use the marvel to further improve the lives of Hrímlandic citizens, but they were put to a halt when Kalmar figured out how to engineer the skorrifles and seizure-bludgeons, the weapons and engines of the flying fortress. Now, Trampe was intending to completely take over Perlan's operational power, denying the people the benefits of the power plant.

The board of Hið Hrímlenska Hlutafélag, the company designated as the owners of Innréttingarnar, was composed mostly of powerful human Hrímlanders. Making up a majority of the board were Katrín's father and his fellow members of the Citizens' Party. The party supposedly stood for home rule, but they were consistently ambivalent towards the Commonwealth when it suited their own needs. Now, they wanted Kalmar to dance to their tune.

Sheriff Skúli, the chairman of the company and the party leader, was the instigator of the meeting that took place in Katrín's home that night. Losing the power plant's capabilities completely to Kalmar's military ventures would deal a devastating blow to Hrímlandic society – but it could do wonders for their own personal profits. The way they saw it, their financial gains benefited the people of Hrímland much more than heat and electricity. The problem was persuading Trampe to offer them a good enough deal. Skúli had suggested that the Crown would lease Perlan's power exclusively for a century – ensuring a generous military cash flow to the shareholders' pockets. Kalmar had been churning on a slow burn of warfare for decades now; there were always new wars to be fought. The shareholders had just nabbed themselves a golden goose.

Or so they believed. Trampe denied the deal. He was confident in his ability to slowly take Innréttingarnar over completely and attribute all of Perlan's energy output to war. He held all the cards.

The press exploded with the news, leading Trampe to issue a temporary law censoring all publications. But it was too late. Resentment towards Kalmar spiked. The politicians in the Citizens' Party tried to save their political careers by denying the allegations of trying to profit by selling a national energy resource to the military, but confirmed that Trampe was moving to completely militarise Perlan. Trampe put out the fires before they got out of hand by claiming that the Crown had no intentions of so condemning Reykjavík, and further solidified it by swearing that all deals regarding Perlan were off the table indefinitely. To Garún's immense disappointment, the people decided to let the whole matter go without any major repercussions. But the resentment towards both governments still remained, and the Crown's intention of fully weaponising Perlan was stopped.

For now.

It would only be a matter of time until another plan to weaponise Perlan would surface. That didn't change the fact that Katrín had put everything on the line to stand up to the powers that be and send them a message that enough was enough. Perlan was supposed to belong to the people, not capitalist leeches and the military lackeys of the Commonwealth. Katrín had betrayed her own father for the cause. That had been good enough for Garún. Or so she'd thought at the time.

The audioskull improvised brooding tones as Garún moved through the city. She had the feeling she couldn't keep wandering for much longer on the streets of Reykjavík, looking for Katrín. If she hadn't been arrested she could be anywhere. Perhaps in Sæbúavogur or Elliðabær, maybe Starholt. Garún couldn't risk going there. The Forgotten Downtown was only connected to Reykjavík's city centre, not the other neighbourhoods. Going out of the central area meant losing her method of escape.

She started looking for the unique static of the audioskull and let it lead her back towards a crossing to the Forgotten Downtown.

ᚠ

Garún was heading towards the fishermen's workshops when she suddenly stopped. Unfamiliar tones sounded in her headphones, rapid staccato notes that she hadn't heard before. This hadn't happened before, the noisefiend didn't work in Rökkurvík as it did in Reykjavík. The music sounded faint, distant. At first she thought she was imagining it. The electronic music swung up and down the scales in sync with a frantic heartbeat rhythm. The streets were empty. She waited, apprehensive, but nothing happened. As she started walking again the new sound stopped. It was a warning, but different than usual. She felt that the alarm wasn't exactly aimed at her. It was more like a call for help. She turned around and listened. The music started again and led her towards the backwater.

Unlike its twin in Reykjavík, which was almost completely man-made at this point, with clouded, grey water, the situation was quite different in the Forgotten Downtown. A muddy mire stretched over a large area, all the way up to the edges of the dirt tracks that more or less lay parallel to the streets of Reykjavík. Maybe this is what the pond had originally looked like, some centuries ago. In the middle of the mire was the backwater, a murky and stagnant lake. Hrævareldar floated lazily over the dark waters. Garún avoided looking straight at them, but some part of her wanted nothing more than to stare into their seductive lights. In the pale gloom cast by the enthralling lights she saw a person in the mire, trudging her way towards the lake like a zombie. It was a woman, covered in mud and her skirts torn, her dark hair dishevelled.

It was Katrín.

Garún called her name as loudly she dared, but it accomplished nothing. In front of Katrín a swarm of hrævareldar floated and Garún felt as if she heard voices in the distance, cheerful and alluring, calling her to them. Without being aware of it, she had taken off her headphones so she could better hear them. She put them back on and held them tight, so nothing but the pounding music could reach her ears. Katrín was close to the ditch and stumbled in the mud. The hrævareldar swarmed around them, circling like carrion birds around a carcass, always closing in. Garún closed her eyes and blindly walked into the mire.

She listened for the tune that would lead her towards Katrín. It was drowned by the warning alarms caused by the hrævareldar and the mire itself, but she could still faintly detect it. Garún knew how to listen for the hrævareldar and avoid them, as she was dead set on never falling for their lethal charm again. The mud gripped her feet tightly, making it a great effort to pull herself out of the muck and take another step closer. Slowly she made her way forward, hoping that the noisefiend would lead her from the fires and towards Katrín. The pale glow of the hrævareldar flashed through her shut eyelids. Her instinct was always to open her eyes, to see and recognise the danger, but she steeled her resolve and held her eyes shut, taking another step, contrary to what her instincts of self-preservation told her to do.

The water reached above her knees. Her thighs hurt from the effort of wading through the mud and she had no idea where she was. Had the hrævareldar already got to Katrín? If she opened her eyes, would she see a motionless body floating in the ditch? Or would she be all alone in the mire with the hrævareldar, Katrín spirited away?

When the putrid water had reached her waist, Garún's

fingertips came across something. Something coarse, wet, covered in mud. She groped blindly in front of her and got a grip on Katrín. Katrín resisted, tried weakly to heed the call of the hrævareldar. Garún pulled her in and placed both her hands firmly in front of her eyes. Katrín struggled, tried to fight her way out of the grip, but Garún held on for her life. She was faintly aware of a series of flashes and despite the music she could hear cold and deep voices rising from the darkness.

Katrín suddenly threw herself backwards, making Garún lose her grip and fall back. Garún intended to leap back up and grab hold of Katrín before she could escape, but stumbled when a blood-curdling scream came from Katrín. Garún was so startled that for a moment pure reflex took over. She opened her eyes.

A moon-white creature rose from the pitch-black water, its skin waxen and its flesh sagging. The hrævareldar swarmed around it, like carrion flies around a rotten corpse. The creature's maw was lined with jagged teeth, its jaw jutting unnaturally far out. Limbs erupted from its body like broken branches, more than a dozen gaunt appendages that reached towards them, clawing forward on the marshland, trying to get a hold on the muddy bottom. Katrín stood, frozen, staring into the beast's terrible mouth. Garún felt its rancid stench on her, like an open mass grave. Its eyes, bloated orbs on twisted stalks, turned towards Garún and she felt as if she was all alone up against the bottomless abyss.

She frantically got out her can of delýsíð and the dagger she had at her belt, sprayed the knife's blade and threw it with all her might at the abomination's head. The knife slid without resistance into the creature's flesh and it let out a terrible wail that cut through bone and marrow. The creature's appendages flailed and tore out the dagger. Yellow pus burst from the wound. Its eyestalks flailed in agony, like a nest of maggots. One eyeball turned dark with coagulated blood, bloating like a terrible fruit about to burst. The hrævareldar flared and scattered as the creature retreated into the dark waters of the ditch. As soon as it vanished from sight Katrín collapsed into the mire.

That's when the sun rose.

A red sun lit up the empty sky. It flickered intensely, an eye burned into the pitch-black night. Then it multiplied and scattered, spreading out to cover the abyssal Rökkurvík sky. That was no sun. Those were flares. They moved with an unknown purpose, bathing the world in crimson light.

The Crown was here.

Garún threw Katrín over her shoulders and started running.

Tuttugu og eitt

The flares spread across the sky. Red, agitated lights, like a swarm of wasps. Þráinn Meinholt watched them move with great satisfaction. His eyes in the sky.

'We have full visual,' Magister Gapaldur hissed through their beaked mask, their voice muffled and distorted. 'Coverage stands at optimal capacity. The hrævareldar will not pose a threat as long as the lights shine.'

Þráinn gave his affirmation with a grunt and turned to Officer Lárus, the person designated as his law-enforcement liaison during this operation. Lárus was older than him by a good decade, a beat cop who had risen slowly but surely through the ranks to inspector. Lárus found himself working with the Directorate often, much to his chagrin. Þráinn requested him due to his renowned thick-headedness and tendency for unchecked brutality, features that usually posed an inconvenience in everyday law enforcement, but in cases such as these they were transmuted into refined and desirable qualities.

'Inspector, have your men all moved through the portal?'

'The last squad should come through any moment.'

'Good. Assemble them as soon as they've stopped retching. We're moving out.'

'All right.'

'I remind you that Commissioner Kofoed-Hansen expects this to be executed flawlessly and efficiently. Make sure your men understand that.'

'Will do. Sir,' he added.

Þráinn was used to the reluctance of the police and military in accepting his authority during joint operations. That didn't mean he tolerated it – on the contrary, he took exception to blatant disregard of the chain of command. Dealing with the rank and file grunts was routine enough, and he'd had time to put Lárus in his place, but working with not one but two seiðskrattar was a different beast entirely. The royal seiðskrattar were technically classified as high-ranking military officers, although they operated in a separate branch. This meant that the seiðskrattar did not fall under his authority, although Þráinn was in command of the operation. The seiðskrattar were asked to comply with his commands, but if they so felt they could safely overrule or defy him. The two seiðskrattar were Count Trampe's frequent advisors. Having both of them here meant that the stiftamtmaður intended to see that this operation went off without a hitch.

They'd set up a perimeter by a lone, decrepit house in an open mud field. The house had already been secured as a safe house by their undercover agents in Rökkurvík, and was now acting as their base of operations. Þráinn walked through the wet mud, idly wondering how the earth managed to be this wet when it never rained here. Magister Ginfaxi stood by the portal, channelling violent streams of seiðmagn through themselves to manipulate the portal they had opened in the middle of the field. Obsidian pillars jutted out of the ground in a rough circle, their bent, coarse shapes looking like malevolent fingers bursting through earth. The air was thick with vibrant currents of seiðmagn, making Þráinn's stomach turn and his hair stand on end. A group of armed police officers appeared in the middle of the circle, moving through the flickering wound in reality. The rift was not clearly visible, being freshly made and still bleeding, so to speak, but with time and the efforts of the seiðskrattar it would solidify. The police officers jogged to the edge of the circle and collapsed as soon as they were out, most of them retching and throwing up. Lárus barked at his subordinates, telling them to fall in line. Þráinn approached the seiðskratti, the force of their channelling changing tone as the last officers went successfully through.

'Are the other gateways sealed yet?' Þráinn asked the seiðskratti.

The seiðskratti lowered their hands, causing an ebb in the flow of seiðmagn around them.

'You were briefed about the extradimensional nature of this place, Agent Meinholt,' Magister Ginfaxi hissed, their voice sounding almost serpentine. Through red-tinted glass Þráinn could see the hints of feverish eyes, gleaming with fervour and wild sorcery. 'First the portal must be anchored. When it does so, it will cause the other gateways to seal shut over time. Like coagulating blood.'

Þráinn bristled. 'I recall the briefing just fine, Magister,' he said in a stern voice. 'What I am telling you is that I want them shut – now.'

The seiðskratti stared at him stoically, the long white mask lending them a skeletal semblance. Magister Ginfaxi slowly clasped their white-gloved hands in front of them. Þráinn tried to hide his discomfort. He couldn't discern anything about this son of a bitch.

'Perhaps you need another seiðskratti, Agent Meinholt,' Ginfaxi said in a measured, flat tone. 'One more capable of following your brilliant plan.'

The portal started flickering, wavering in and out of existence. 'Don't waste time playing games. I just want it done, Magister.' Magister Ginfaxi nodded slowly, almost bowing.

'Of course, *sir*.' They spat out the last word like a curse. The portal sputtered out for a moment, then reappeared. 'Please rest assured that this humble servant of the Crown is using their meagre abilities to their best to serve your noble plan. Should that not be adequate, well... Then we will retreat and request that Count Trampe find a suitable substitute.'

'No, listen... All right. Just get it done. As quickly as possible.'

'Very well. We will continue the work. It will proceed according to the plan laid out in the briefing – with your blessing, that is.'

Þráinn nodded. He could almost hear the smile in that abomination's voice. He marched over to the formation of officers and the seiðskratti turned again towards the portal, the seiðmagn flaring up with a muted thunder as the gate again solidified, the thaumaturgical energy around the gate tightening, making his stomach turn with inexplicable vertigo.

The police officers stood at the ready in tight formations, skorrifles in hand, the front line with their shields raised, armed with thaumaturgic batons. The riot gear lent them the appearance of inhuman golems rather than human flesh and blood. Þráinn grinned. This he understood. Feet on the ground, weapons in hand.

'All right,' he said, activating a small charm on him that caused his voice to boom as if he were speaking into a megaphone. 'This interdimensional anomalous zone is now under the official jurisdiction of the Directorate of Immigration. Any and all denizens of this area are now considered in violation of the borders of the Commonwealth of Kalmar. Any persons encountered are classified as international criminals and can be assumed to have non-citizen status.'

Inspector Lárus stepped forward.

'For the thick-skulled of you out there,' he bellowed loudly, 'this means that there is no paperwork when you gun them down – keep that in mind!'

Þráinn nodded before continuing.

'This is a clear-cut operation. Comb every street, break down every door, arrest any persons found and shoot any who resist with extreme prejudice. I want to turn this godforsaken place back into a ghost town within twenty-four hours. This is also a manhunt – one rogue galdramaður, likely having manifested an Omega-class transmundane infestation in his corporeal form, and one half-breed terrorist, known to use a form of liquid delýsíð. Do not take off your mask under any circumstance. It might not necessarily save your life, but the filter should hold off the seiðmagn for long enough that you can put her down. Both of these individuals are high priority. Apprehend or neutralise them at any cost. Any questions?'

He glared at the lines of constables. His own little army.

'Move out!'

The police officers moved quickly and silently, weapons raised, spreading out over Rökkurvík. Þráinn approached Magister Gapaldur, who was standing by.

'We need to find the galdramaður and the half-breed. Fast.'

'She was at the protest,' they said. 'The one who has so creatively utilised the delýsíð.'

Þráinn nodded. 'The galdramaður is our priority. We need to make sure enough of him survives for questioning.'

The seiðskratti tilted their head, leaning towards Þráinn. It made him uncomfortable, the movement almost predatory in nature. He tensed up, reminding himself that the protective charms he carried would shield him from the seiðskratti. He had submitted a highly classified report about his encounter with Sæmundur. Þráinn had only survived it due to the sorcerous reinforcements made to his body as part of his training. The Directorate's galdramenn had cleared him of any lingering transmundane influence, but he still felt uneasy knowing that the two seiðskrattar had been given access to the report.

'That might prove to be impossible,' the seiðskratti said in a low voice. 'If the report you submitted is correct, he is quite formidable. But we will see.'

Þráinn seethed with anger, but kept his mouth shut. Magister Gapaldur raised their hands and turned to the sky. A stream of crimson tendrils flowed from their fingertips into the air.

'If they are here we will find them soon enough.'

Plumes of smoke rose into the sky, shaded red by the swarming flares. The house was now properly ablaze, joining several others in the area. It had served as a bar, likely a meeting point for members of the resistance. The local denizens from this and nearby streets were lined up on the muddy road, on their knees, hands cuffed behind their backs. Three corpses were lying in the mud by the fire, patrons of the bar who had resisted arrest. One of them had been a hobo who stank to high heaven, a rambling psychopath. He had hardly resisted, only started shouting when the police charged in, but that had been enough. It looked like they would be cleansing the city of all kinds of filth tonight.

Þráinn walked down the line and took in the faces of the handcuffed people in front of him. Humans and huldufólk, male and female. They looked thin and haggard. Worn out. Likely drug addicts, most of them. Lárus handed him a backpack. It was filled with spray cans.

'Confiscated this from these two.' He pointed to a woman and a man who had been separated from the rest of the captives. 'Magister Gapaldur has confirmed faint traces of delýsíð.'

Þráinn smirked. They must have fetched their stash before trying to get out. Amateurs. He took a closer look at them. The man's face looked familiar. It was clear that the two cared for each other. Small, stolen glances, reassuring looks flashed in perceived secret. They were making this too easy.

Þráinn squatted next to the couple.

'Where are they?' His voice was quiet, the lack of threat in his tone all the more dangerous. 'You know who I'm looking for. I'm warning you – I won't be asking again.'

They kept staring intently down into the mud, as if they couldn't hear him.

He stood up and waved over the seiðskratti. Magister Gapaldur approached slowly, probably not thrilled about being called over like a dog. Whatever. The freak needed a proper reminder of whom they served. But that would come later.

'Magister.'

He pointed to the woman, nodded to Lárus. Lárus moved in and took off her handcuffs, cuffing her hands again in the front. Experience had shown it to be a more suitable physical arrangement.

'Please, commence your work.'

This wasn't the first time they had done this. It was a tired routine at this point, mostly performed deep within the dungeons of the Nine. Regular torture was ineffectual and risked killing or maiming the victim in an irreversible manner. This was a much neater method, mostly effective due to the psychological effects.

Suddenly Þráinn remembered where he had seen the man.

He wasn't a Hrímlander, he was a wanted Kalmar soldier who had deserted his post. For this girl, it looked like.

'You,' he said, and kicked the man hard in the side. He shouted from the pain and Þráinn thought he might have cracked a rib. It was still hard to gauge his strength since the thaumaturgical infusion. 'Look up. This is for you, soldier.'

The man looked up, his face set with unmitigated hatred. The seiðskratti stretched out their arms, fingers splayed – then they moved. And the woman started to scream.

Her body twitched. She bent even deeper, her face almost to the mud, then threw herself back, arching her back with sickening sounds of cracking and breaking as bones and bristle reconfigured themselves into new forms. Her teeth fell out of her mouth like unchewed food, leaving her toothless and drooling. Her left shoulder shook and her coat tore as an ivory horn broke through the fabric, her arm in turn becoming longer, more muscular. One by one her fingers broke backwards and were folded into her hand, which became calloused and misshapen, looking almost like a hoof. The handcuffs dug deep into the new, bloated flesh. The shoulder-horn kept on growing, making her left shoulder obscenely large, causing her to lose the autonomy of her neck as the mutations of her own body started to devour her. Her vocal cords started changing, becoming almost animalic. New teeth grew in her mouth, a grotesque mismatch of fangs and large, blunt molars, filling her mouth even as her jaw and skull elongated and twisted.

The man had been screaming for them to stop, that he would tell them everything, since the moment the woman had keeled over in pain. Þráinn knew that obtaining a certain visual effect right at the beginning was more efficient when it came to extracting information. It all served to better establish the real premise of this dialogue. Taking a dramatic first step made any theoretical following steps all the more horrifying to the imagination. He held up a hand and Magister Gapaldur stopped their work, with some noticeable reluctance.

Þráinn kneeled down again next to the man and fished a cigarette case out of his jacket. He struck a match and lit it.

'You know what's waiting for you. You are a deserter and a traitor to the Crown. But her – she might still live. Likely she has family to take her back in. It doesn't have to end like this.'

He held up a hand to stop the man from talking. He smoked, leisurely. Established control. The couple silently wept, waiting for him to give his permission. Like good mutts, he thought, trained for serving the empire.

'Now,' he said and blew out smoke. 'Speak.'

They were gone when the police broke down the doors and searched the house. They had marked the place with hidden delýsíð signs, diverting the officers from investigating it. They had just stormed right past it during the raid. It was a miserable hovel, filled with filthy mattresses and broken furniture. Already police officers were tearing up what little was in there, looking for hidden compartments in the floor and walls.

Lárus came running, Þráinn and Magister Gapaldur waiting for him on the upper floor in a ruined drawing room, facing a massive graffiti work encompassing the entire wall. It was a mess of a sigil, drawn in black paint. Streaks of red spray paint criss-crossed it, still glistening wet and leaking down the wall. The sorcerous radiation from the painting was nauseating, a mess of conflicting intent.

'Magister Gapaldur, what are we looking at?'

'Whatever it is, they've ruined it,' Lárus butted in. Þráinn turned around, taking a good moment to hold his gaze. 'The place is deserted, sir, I'll... uh... I'll go and manage the search downstairs.'

'That would be a suitable use of your skill set, Inspector.'

Þráinn turned to the seiðskratti and tried to decipher their disposition. The seiðskratti was staring at the graffiti, almost longingly, turning their head and taking it all in with a lethargic fascination.

'It's... wonderful,' they said in a soft whisper. 'Brutal, inefficient, barely functional – but still laden with overwhelming power. I've never seen anything like it.'

'What is it?'

'We are uncertain. The sabotage has obfuscated its purpose.'

'So it's ruined?'

That fucking blendingur. The bitch had been one step ahead of them, somehow.

Magister Gapaldur approached the graffiti, touching the wet paint with a gloved finger.

'No, not exactly. Only... obfuscated. Their sabotage was not as thorough as they would have liked.' The seiðskratti touched the forehead of their white mask, drawing a crimson symbol on themselves with the wet paint. 'Whatever this was, it was a key. A key to something greater.' They touched the graffiti with a flat palm, gasping slightly at the flow of seiðmagn, audibly resonating through the room. 'We will repair it. And we will unlock whatever secrets it held.'

'See that you do.'

Something cracked under Þráinn's feet as he was about to exit the room. A seashell, it looked like. He picked up a dark string, on which a menagerie of broken conches and shells had been threaded in elaborate patterns. The design was typical of the marbendlar, although he wasn't familiar enough with their culture to know from where exactly it came. A centrepiece was missing, a delicate woven cradle where it should sit snugly. He investigated the floorboards closely and sniffed the air. A faint scent of salt and glass.

He placed the ruined necklace in his pocket and smiled.

Tuttugu og tvö

They crossed over in a panic, using the first portal Garún could track down with the audioskull. Diljá and Hrólfur had grabbed what meagre supplies they had and carried Katrín, still unconscious, between them.

The city streets spread out before them like a hostile maze, but Garún was unquestionably relieved to see the moon and stars back above her in the sky, not that bottomless void. Seeing the red flares had filled her with a crushing feeling of dread mixed in with relief. She realised she had been waiting for this for quite some time now. They were drained after staying in the Forgotten Downtown, but there was no time to rest. Garún led them out of the city centre using the audioskull and the noisefiend as their guide. She had picked up a few roadblocks using the delýsíð network. They followed side streets along Hverfisgata, heading towards Miklatún, where the road split into Miklabraut, which ran straight towards the eastern gate. It was easy to move unseen through Hlíðar, the quiet neighbourhood home to well-off humans, respectable families working honest jobs. Or, at least, so it seemed on the surface. Only a handful of police officers came their way, walking their evening beat, and they sneaked past them with ease.

In the distance they heard sirens and a spattering of gunfire. They stopped and listened. The audioskull sounded calm.

'They're rounding up the people who escaped from Rökkurvík,' Hrólfur said after a while.

'Do you think your people made it out?' Diljá asked Garún.

'I don't know. We had established escape portals. But...'

But who knew if any of them were trustworthy, she wanted to say. Who knew if any of them had sold them out, like Viður had done to her.

'But they might not have had the time,' she settled for instead.

They headed south, making sure to keep off the beaten path by going through empty residential streets. Murky lamps fuelled by fish oil lit their way, their lights faded and soft compared to the bright yellow electric lights on Hverfisgata. Garún cursed all this lighting, which made it harder for her to travel unseen, but she was secretly glad of it. The Forgotten Downtown was too empty – too dark. The memory of the pale blue lights of the hrævareldar haunted her.

They heard Fossbúagil before they saw it. They were walking along the new and dignified streets of Fossvogur. The occasional lamp lit up the paved road and whitewashed terraced houses. As they went around a corner the road faded into a flat heath, which itself quickly ended in a sheer drop. The canyon of Fossbúagil was long and wide, roughly circular, as if a titan had stepped down into the middle of the city.

The moon was out and in its light they could see over to the rocks on the other side. Residential houses lined the edge of the canyon precariously, the dark water shimmering at the bottom. Frayed ropes and broken ladders hung from the edge down to the deep lagoon, and steep paths hugged the cliff side down to the clear water. For years this had been one of the most beloved swimming spots for the people of the city, until the vættir in the waterfall began to stir and children started disappearing. No one knew why the vættir had reappeared so suddenly. The knowledge of how to pacify them with sacrificial blót was long since forgotten. The last ruling stiftamtmaður had royal seiðskrattar 'exorcise' the vættir inhabiting the waters, and for a moment everything seemed to be in order. But when an entire school class vanished on a spring field trip it was decided to strictly forbid any swimming in the canyon lagoon. That didn't stop teenagers from sneaking in for skinny-dipping under the pale moon, and occasionally the papers would print articles about children claimed by the vættir in the waterfall.

Garún was uncomfortable out in the open, but the darkness would give them some cover. They walked along the canyon's edge towards the waterfall. Diljá stumbled more than once in the mossy heath, but Hrólfur always helped her get up immediately. Katrín occasionally groaned to herself, almost regaining consciousness. She was shaking, and reeked of sour sweat and sickness.

The river of Fossvogsá branched out from the great and strong currents of the rivers in Elliðaárdalur, flowing straight into the canyon. The waterfall ran down the cliff in a terraced slope, looking like great steps intended for ancient giants. Large nets were stretched across the river above the waterfall, catching most of the junk that floated downstream. The marbendlar had exclusive access to water traffic in Reykjavík, thanks to a centuries-old covenant, or else the canyon's lagoon would likely have turned into a toxic dumping pit long ago.

They headed upriver from the waterfall until they came to the pier. Kryik'traak was waiting for them, seemingly alone. The charm he had given to Diljá had apparently worked. She had broken the pendant of the shell necklace when Garún had barged in, carrying Katrín over her shoulders. Garún had been unaware she'd planned for this last resort and was secretly impressed with Diljá's resourcefulness. But it also made her consider what else she might be hiding.

Garún always found it strange to be around marbendlar, despite having worked alongside them when she first came to Reykjavík. Their faces, reminiscent of wolf-fish, looked cold and emotionless to her. She couldn't stand her own inability to look past their appearance and what seemed to her like peculiar manners. She hated that about herself. She should be better than that. She told herself that she just had to spend more time around them, but marbendlar, like náskárar, did not much care for the company of humans and huldufólk. Still, she wanted Reykjavík to belong to them just as much as herself. Despite that, a stupid, ugly part of her thought they looked alien. The worst part is that the marbendlar never cared that she was a blendingur. It could be that they were the group of people most tolerant towards her in Reykjavík, and this is how she repaid them.

'I've been waiting,' said Kryik'traak.

His scales were grey and coarse, covered in black-and-white spots down his sides. Fins jutted out down his back, arms and tail, decorated with rings of green-tinted copper and silver. He was a bit over Garún's height, tall for a marbendill.

'What happened?'

'The Crown raided Rökkurvík,' said Diljá, and gently put Katrín down with Hrólfur. 'We need to hide.'

Kryik'traak nodded, mimicking the human motion in an exaggerated manner.

'The Coral Spires stand with you. Riots recently by the river gates. Shooting.' He stared at Katrín. 'Shot? Injured?'

'We're not sure,' said Garún when the others hesitated to reply. 'She's sick from something.'

'We have remedies. Come.'

He led them down the pier, where a barge was waiting for them. It was loaded with barrels of herring and reeking seafood, along with a few crates and sacks. Thick ropes tied to the helmsman's seat in the prow went down into the dark water, the bridle of the nykur below the surface. Kryik'traak led them to a couple of open barrels.

'Here. Until we reach Elliðaárdalur.'

'You are kidding,' said Hrólfur. 'I'm not going to fit in there.'

'We don't have time for this,' Garún said harshly, and climbed into a barrel.

Kryik'traak and Hrólfur gently lifted Katrín into a barrel. Diljá and Hrólfur followed suit.

'Only two nails. Can break out if you need to. All right?'

They each nodded in agreement. The barrel reeked, but was otherwise clean enough. Garún sat on the bottom with her knees up to her chest. She already felt the blood draining from her legs. She didn't look forward to the trip. Kryik'traak placed the lid on the barrel and everything went black. The barrel shook from the impact as he hammered two nails into the lid. She listened as he did the same to the others. Then, heavy thuds as he moved cargo around them, hiding them. She felt the rhythm of the water, how the river moved around the barge. A sudden movement. They were on their way.

The barge moved effortlessly against the current at a steady pace. She shut her eyes and leaned her head forwards on her knees. Imagined she had vanished, was lost. That there was nothing outside but darkness and bottomless waters. That she would wake up in a new place. Somewhere safe and warm, where the sun shone throughout the year. She imagined that she had jumped through the broken church windows in Hamar.

She woke up when Kryik'traak knocked on her barrel just

before he jammed a crowbar in to tear it open. The sky had turned faintly pale, hinting at a far-off late morning sunrise. She took his hands and he helped her get out. She could hardly stand for the painful needles jabbing her numb limbs, but Kryik'traak handed her the crowbar and told her to help her partners out. Time was of the essence.

Garún tore open the rest of the barrels and helped the others get out. Katrín was semi-conscious, so weak and out of it that Hrólfur still had to support her. They were by the rivers of Elliðaár, just south of the Elliðabær neighbourhood. The river was deep here, its currents strong. Kryik'traak had tethered the barge to one of the many poles sticking out of the river. Pale buildings made of coral lined the riverbank, coarse tangles of buildings and twisted spires that reached deep down to the bottom. Marbendlar used seiður to grow and shape this unique type of coral, which thrived in salt water and fresh water alike. In a matter of days an entire city could be grown, given enough access to seiðmagn in the area. The noise from the hydroelectric plant could be heard in the distance upriver. The sun wasn't visible, but the skies were getting lighter. Soon enough the river would be filled with barges heading to Sæmannahöfn or up against the stream towards the locks of the old hydroelectric dam, the river gates and Elliðavatn.

Kryik'traak had been busy fishing something out of a vat and turned to them, holding a jellyfish in his hands. It was upside down, transparent mouth-tendrils dangling limply from its colourful core like a grotesque flower. From the middle a long, tube-shaped stalk stuck out.

'Put them on.'

He handed the jellyfish to Garún. It was so slippery that she almost lost her grip on it.

'What do you mean?'

'Like this.'

Hrólfur lifted a jellyfish to his face. He put the stalk into his mouth and the jellyfish latched on to his head. His face was distorted behind the gelatinous coelenterate. He threw himself into the river. Diljá moved the jellyfish slowly to her face, biting carefully around the stalk. Immediately the jellyfish attached itself to her face. She clawed at the creature, but it wouldn't relent, she started struggling as if she was choking. Kryik'traak pushed her so she fell into the water. He placed the jellyfish on Katrín, who struggled weakly as he carried her into the water in his arms.

The jellyfish was so slimy and foul-smelling that Garún could hardly bring herself to hold it, let alone put it on her face. She held her breath, forcing herself to stop thinking about what she was doing, and placed the jellyfish on like a mask.

The jellyfish emitted a brief electric shock when it attached itself to Garún. Her face became numb and she couldn't feel the stalk in her mouth any more. She was unable to breathe, but she had been expecting that. She was only able to see very faded outlines, only differences in brightness and vague colours, but when she jumped into the freezing water she was able to see as clearly as up on the surface. The bone-coloured coral structures created a sort of aquatic avenue, its bottom laid with slimy brown algae. The buildings were crooked and twisted, the windows open and empty, like primordial huts made at the dawn of civilisation. She tried to breathe but found herself unable to, choking for a few panicked moments before she realised she had to relax and let the jellyfish breathe for her. Hrólfur and Diljá were waiting for her across the street. Kryik'traak was just ahead, swimming towards an empty doorway, still holding Katrín. The marbendill, so awkward and slow on land, was an entirely different being in the water. Agile and sharp, moving like a bird of prey in the sky. They followed him as he swam into the building.

It was pitch black inside. The water was freezing and absolutely still. The cold was almost paralysing and Garún wondered how much longer they would be able to stand it. Kryik'traak's silhouette moved into a hallway, which was lit by strange, faintly luminous plants growing from the walls. Kryik'traak tore one off by the roots and it flared up, glowing like a torch. The plant looked like a hybrid of two oceanic creatures. At its roots glowed something that seemed like a sea urchin, while a kind of sea anemone grew from its top, streaked with glowing stripes and patterns. Garún tore one plant for herself and immediately it glowed brighter with that unsettling light. Kryik'traak led them onwards through a monotonous maze of coral hallways.

After some while, when Garún was really starting to worry about the cold, a lukewarm stream of water suddenly came rushing over her. They went around the corner and found themselves out of the coral labyrinth. The glow from the plants illuminated rough stone walls. The tunnels were mostly natural, but it was clear they'd been widely chiselled and shaped. Green algae covered almost everything, moving gently in the stream like grass in a gentle wind. The luminous plants grew in the tunnels at regular intervals.

Kryik'traak led them to a tunnel with a strong opposite current, against which he swam effortlessly, but they had to drag themselves forwards using a slimy rope threaded between iron loops that had been nailed into the walls. Soon enough the luminous plant he carried was the only visible light in the darkness, as Garún had to leave hers behind to pull herself forward. The rope was slippery and difficult to get a grip on, but they still moved faster than if they'd walked along the slippery bottom or tried to swim. Their heavy clothes impeded them, making the process that much harder.

Finally they surfaced in a small cave. The same pale light reflected on shining lava rocks, uneven and sharp. Garún pulled herself up on the bank. The only way in or out was the small pool they'd come out of. As soon as she surfaced she was again unable to breathe and the jellyfish clouded her sight. She pulled and scratched at it, but stopped when she felt the webbed hand of Kryik'traak on her shoulder. He did something and the jellyfish slid off her. As feeling rapidly returned to her face, she felt the mouthpiece retract, drawing in a slimy tendril that had crawled deep down her throat. The feeling was repulsive. Garún collapsed on her knees, vomiting and coughing. A blueish mucus came out of her stomach and lungs. She breathed in the stale air and the effort tore at her lungs. She was exhausted but forced herself to get up. Behind her came Hrólfur and Diljá. Kryik'traak had placed Katrín on the floor. She was trembling uncontrollably, lying limp on her side, throwing up. Diljá kneeled and saw to her.

Kryik'traak picked up the jellyfish and put them in a small puddle of water, which filled a naturally formed bowl in the rock. There were many of those in the cave, most of them host to the glowing anemones, which were the only source of light, just as in the tunnels. Crates and barrels were stacked at the end of the cave, which seemed to be a lava bubble, deep underground. Among the supplies were blankets, clothes and supplies in waterproof leather sacks. Garún couldn't remember what the route was to the exit, how many turns or paths leading up or down they'd taken. She'd never find her way back on her own.

'Take care of the jellyfish. Or else you're stuck,' said Kryik'traak. 'Don't tear up the lights. Won't last long and grow back slowly.'

'Is there any other way out?' she asked.

'Tunnel's the only way.'

'There's not a chance I'll find my way back. What about you?' she asked the others. One by one they shook their heads.

'I'll come, with food and more. You'll learn the way. There is a system. Don't worry.'

Garún went quickly over the supplies. Rye flatbread and steam-cooked rye bread, a bit of smoked meat, dried fish, whey-pickled sour meats, fresh water in tins. Not too much, but enough for several days. She noticed a couple of chamber pots in the stack.

'How do we empty the chamber pots?'

'Ah.' Kryik'traak seemed a bit awkward. 'Don't empty in the pool. Rather a corner.'

They were hardly better off here than in the Forgotten Downtown. But it was only temporary.

'All right. It will do. Thank you for your help.'

The marbendill nodded sombrely. 'I have faith in you. I and all of us.'

'How many know we're here?' said Garún harshly.

'No one but me, I swear,' the marbendill replied, flustered. 'But many of us are waiting. Waiting and praying. That everything will change.'

'Garún, relax,' said Diljá. 'We can trust him. How often are these tunnels used?'

'Rarely. Old and obsolete. You are safe here.'

With that he bade them farewell and dived back in.

Garún felt the weight of the earth above them, the city pushing down, wishing to crush her beneath its weight.

ᚢ

Katrín regained consciousness a few hours later. She didn't know where she was or what had happened. Her entire body was trembling uncontrollably, her skin cold and clammy. The cool air of the cave wasn't helping.

'What happened?' asked Garún, when Katrín had somewhat

gained her senses and gulped down way too much of their limited fresh water supply. 'Why did it take you such a long time to get to Rökkurvík? Why didn't they capture you?'

She tried to hold her hostile tone in check, but she couldn't help herself.

Katrín's eyes widened. 'My family, they...'

She couldn't bring herself to finish the sentence.

Garún nodded and ignored the looks Diljá and Hrólfur were sending her. They'd long moved past the point of pleasantries.

'The house was empty,' Garún said. 'Ransacked and some signs of struggle. We don't know what happened to them.'

'I wasn't at home when they came.'

'Then where were you?'

'Garún, relax,' said Hrólfur. 'She's obviously sick from... whatever that thing was that attacked you.'

Garún got up and sat down on one of the barrels. She was dying for a smoke.

'I'm fine,' she said. 'I was also in the mire with the thing.'

'What was that?' asked Katrín. Garún didn't like how she diverted the conversation elsewhere. 'It looked like a nightmare.'

Garún shrugged. 'No idea. But I think it was using or creating the hrævareldar to hunt.' She leaned back on her hands. 'I stabbed it in the face, if you could call that a face. I hope it's alive and kills a few of those fucking pigs.'

They told Katrín what had happened. How the Crown had raided Rökkurvík. They could only guess what had happened to the people caught in there.

'They'd have no rights,' said Hrólfur. 'It's a serious violation of the law, crossing a transdimensional border like that. They've most likely been categorised as non-citizens.'

Diljá snorted in annoyance. 'More like non-persons. How on

earth did they get clearance to mobilise into Rökkurvík, anyway? I thought the place didn't exist to them.'

'It doesn't, legally speaking,' said Katrín. 'They've been trying to find ways to isolate it since the Crown took over. But two new gateways open up when the seiðskrattar close one. They can't send the army over in an official sense, either, not without a royal decree.'

'Maybe they have that,' said Diljá.

'I doubt it,' Hrólfur said. 'It would almost be considered an act of war. I don't think that was the Crown that moved in. Not in a political sense, anyway.'

'Then who?'

'Those weren't soldiers, they were heavily armed police officers. It could have been a special operations task force set up by Trampe, or maybe it's some other government agency, but you can bet Trampe was behind it. There's no way that this would happen without him knowing and approving of it. But as far as Kalmar knows, it never happened. You'll never find any official reports about this. They'll bury the cost through some bureaucratic trappings. No reports, no trouble. The place doesn't exist, after all.'

'How the hell do you know all that?' asked Garún.

Hrólfur's brow furrowed with concern. Garún didn't care much for his mock offence. Let him be offended.

'I used to work for the city,' he said. 'As I'm sure I've mentioned to you. Urban planning. You'd be surprised how much we had to confer with Trampe's office, directly or indirectly. The stiftamtmaður has to personally approve almost anything that has to do with governing Reykjavík and the entire country. You'd think that he mostly dealt with legislation and so forth in Lögrétta, but no – his authority has a much greater reach. He's the cornerstone of Kalmar's rule. There's just no way he didn't plan this, logically speaking.'

'Logically. Right, so logically speaking...' Garún leaned forwards and started cracking her knuckles idly. 'How did the Crown know that we were hiding in Rökkurvík?'

Diljá stood up, fed up with her.

'Didn't some officer almost arrest you coming out of Rökkurvík in a fucking bar?' she shouted at her.

Garún grimaced. She hadn't told them about her encounter with Sæmundur, how they had been ambushed by that same officer. But they were all dead now. Probably.

'So why now?' Garún replied, raising her voice as well. 'Why do they move in at the *exact fucking moment* that Katrín comes back?'

Katrín was covering her face in her hands, crying quietly. Garún didn't care. She was furious. She remembered for a moment that she still had the delýsíð sheet up against her, underneath her clothes – the delýsíð sheet she had infused with seething, relentless rage, without compromise or compassion. It wasn't doing her any good at this moment, but she didn't know how much it was affecting her. Probably better to remain on her toes.

'You're hiding something,' Garún pressed. 'What aren't you telling us?'

Katrín held a hand up against her temple, her eyes closed. She couldn't look them in the eyes.

'I haven't been home for a few days. I think. I sometimes go to a... friend of mine. In Hlíðar.'

'Why? Who is this friend?'

'Garún! Can you shut up for a second?' Diljá spat. 'Let her talk.'

Katrín swallowed and forced herself to open her eyes.

'I was ...'

Her voice broke. She looked down, frantic hands playing with the hem of her skirt. She looked like a little girl. She steeled herself again and forced herself through the words.

'I was smoking sorti.'

The confession charged the air between them. Katrín kept talking, slowly.

'I was smoking sorti when they came ... when they came to my house. And now they're all ... My family is ...'

Something gave inside her. The crying was bitter and raw, pain that had to be released. Diljá sat next to Katrín, but hesitated in comforting her, unsure how to act even though she knew exactly what she was going through.

Garún let her grieve for her father and mother, her sisters, thinking of the feather-covered pool of blood in their house. She felt no compassion. They'd all known what risks their insurrection demanded. Perhaps Katrín had not fully realised it until this point, but there was nothing to be done about that now.

After Katrín had settled down she told them about how she'd woken in some drug den after someone shook her awake, telling her something she couldn't quite understand but knew was serious and important. Sorti was one of the strongest drugs you could find in Hrímland, a highly addictive substance made from thaumaturgical materials. People differed on what the components were in sorti, which was like a thick, dark ichor, but its users found a complete sense of numbness, apathy laced with ominous visions that faded from their memory as soon as the high did. But something else remained. Sorti ruined people, weathered them down into nothing. It was for the broken and desperate, people who were utterly devoid of hope. Katrín was the last person Garún thought would be using it.

'You've been lying to us,' Garún said in a flat voice. 'How can I trust anything you have to say?'

'I know!' Katrín's outrage gave her the strength she needed to calm down and speak. 'And I understand that. But don't act like you don't have any secrets. Didn't we keep on trusting you after we found out you were tagging everywhere in Reykjavík without us knowing?'

'You've got some fucking nerve!' said Garún, standing up, clenching her fists. The others tensed up. 'I'm fighting for something that matters! I'm trying to actually change things! Meanwhile you live your comfortable little life, hiding behind words posted by a pseudonym, wasting your time and your abundant money smoking drugs. Like a fucking idiot! Nobody forced you to go and play rebellion against your father! It's not my fault the Crown took your family – that's on you.'

'Garún!' Diljá got up into Garún's face, matching her aggressiveness with a sudden ferocity that had Garún reeling back. 'Can you shut the fuck up! Haven't we had enough? Just shut the fuck up and let her talk!'

They fell quiet for a while. Hrólfur eyed them cautiously, almost as if he was more curious about this whole affair than worried about it. Diljá went back to Katrín and placed a comforting hand on her back. Garún paced around the cave. It was too small. No way out. What a goddamn mess.

Katrín nodded slowly as Diljá encouraged her to go on.

'Like I said, I was in Hlíðar. Someone told me something about the police and my house. I didn't quite understand, I was … I was out of it. But I knew I had to go. So I swapped clothes with another girl and went outside.' She played with the hem of her skirt while she spoke. 'They were everywhere. The police. Soldiers. Seiðskrattar. The streets were barricaded. I didn't know where to go. None of my friends would help me, they are—'

Filth, Garún thought to herself. *Stuck-up filth.*

'—not quite ready to stand up against the Commonwealth. There are so many cops and soldiers in the city now. They have checkpoints set up everywhere. So I went and met the only person who I knew would be able to help me.'

'Who was that?' asked Hrólfur.

'Hræeygður. My dealer.'

Tuttugu og þrjú

Before

Katrín Melsteð was not her own person. To every person she met, she was first and foremost Valtýr Melsteð's daughter. A specimen of a fine pedigree. Everywhere she went she dragged the chains of her great lineage with her. Attached to it were the ancestral ghosts of her famous relatives: goðar, poets, bishops, scholars, merchants, not to mention her own father's overbearing presence. It was incredible how the long grasp of deceased men of wealth and power managed to claim her at every turn. She belonged to them. To others she was nothing but a reflection. A by-product of the achievements of great men.

When Katrín was a child she fantasised about going to the Royal University in Hafnía. The mainland seemed like a dream made manifest in the waking world, a beacon of everything cultured and refined: literature, architecture, philosophy, art. It was everything this island was not. She devoured travel journals of Hrímlanders visiting Kalmar's capital and travelling its great empire. She wanted to study archaeology in Hafnía. She was going to become an explorer. There were so many secrets hidden in the earth, waiting to be rediscovered: ancient sorcery; ruins of vast, forgotten empires. She'd find relics that would change the course of history. She would decipher hieroglyphs and runes that had riddled scholars for decades. She'd make a name for herself – her own legacy.

Katrín knew she was destined for something greater. So when she applied for Hafnía in secret, knowing her parents disapproved, she knew she would get in. What she didn't foresee was that her father did not suffer the dramatic change of heart she had hoped for when he saw her accomplishment of being accepted into one of the finest universities in the world. Instead he lashed out at her, submitting her to a relentless tirade in front of the whole family. He said that he would not be sponsoring her studies abroad and forbade her from going. Katrín had never felt more ashamed in her life, to be lectured like a naughty child in front of everyone. Only her anger managed to overpower the shame. This was an injustice. She was the oldest daughter. They had no sons. It was by no means unheard of that Hrímlandic women attended the university. They should be proud to have a prestigious daughter with her own ambitions. But none of that mattered. This was not where they intended her aspirations to take her.

There were no expeditions for Katrín, save for heading into the uncharted social territory of weekly cocktail parties, the only mysteries to unearth there being whatever inane local gossip was circling this week. She would not swat away flies, only would-be suitors, nor parley with natives of a newly discovered humanoid species. Instead she would have to play out her role in circles of vain, callous girls, to avoid becoming a social pariah. Which, after only a few months of this nonsense, became her inevitable fate.

It started with the first article she submitted to the newspapers under a male pseudonym. Housing had been a long-standing problem in Reykjavík since the city's population boomed after

Kalmar took over. Increasing urban density was the popular solution, but it was one plagued with difficulties of affordability, urban planning, priorities. The city walls held back further outward expansion, which was considered a dangerous move due to higher amounts of seiðmagn. Regardless of that fact, this was still the favoured stance of the Citizens' Party, who felt it was only fair that people who wanted affordable housing should find it in a more dangerous part of the city. Safe land, free of malicious seiðmagn, should not be available for everyone but sold at a premium. Housing was a popular topic of discussion among the men who visited her father every week. Her nights were too frequently occupied with social matters she found increasingly frivolous, but as her social status plummeted she had a chance to make the time to eavesdrop on their conversations by tangling yarn in the adjacent drawing room under the pretence of knitting.

In her article Katrín suggested a novel solution: build a new suburb in the village of Akranes, across the Bay of Faxaflói, and run a ferry service several times a day to Seltjarnarnes in Reykjavík. Akranes was quite low in seiðmagn compared to the outskirts of the city and an ideal place for further expansion. With a viable commute to the city centre it would prove a great relief to the housing issue, with too many young families unable to afford apartments of their own.

The responses over the next few days were staggering. Many of the people who wrote in were names and faces she recalled having visited her house, to discuss politics with her father over imported booze and cigars. She replied quickly and concisely, and when she overheard them talking about the exchange the next time they met she couldn't help but smile for the next few days. Her heart pounded with excitement. Her mother erroneously believed she had fallen in love, so rose-tinted had her daily life become. She finally felt as if she was doing something that was important. That she was someone who mattered.

She kept writing in, engaging with powerful men on the battlefields of the newspaper columns. Her contribution made a difference, she knew that – but she still knew that she could do so much more.

The initial feeling which had taken her over started to fade. The person under whose name she wrote didn't exist. It made her feel as if she herself did not exist. She moved like a zombie during the dances and parties, refusing to bother keeping up with whatever inane gossip the others were occupying themselves with.

It was at one of those parties where she had been offered her first pipe. She was wandering the back rooms of a large house, intentionally trying to get lost and find a quiet place to spend the evening in solitude. Her mother scolded her if she came back home too early. It was easier to just pretend.

She'd entered a study, decorated with exquisite leather sofas, tables made from dark, polished mahogany, delicate lamps made from glass so beautiful and refined it was hard to believe it had been made by hand, not through some thaumaturgic method. A man and a woman sat on one of the sofas. The man had straw-coloured hair and a neatly trimmed moustache; he was dressed in an evening jacket made from peculiar emerald fabric. He looked up, startled at her entrance, distracting her with a dazzling smile as he stood up to greet her, trying to steer her gaze and attention from the items laid out on the desk that he had been fiddling with.

'Elskan, you must be lost. Come, I will show you to the powder room...'

She ignored him grasping her upper arm, firmly but gently. The woman on the sofa was leaning back in an almost indecent manner, her eyes half-closed and fluttering, her breathing deep and heavy as if asleep. To Katrín she seemed both vulgar and enticing. Taking in the sight made her heartbeat pick up, her cheeks flushing warm with an embarrassment she didn't quite comprehend.

'Is she all right?'

Katrín didn't feel it was right to leave this woman alone with the man in this state.

'I'm fine,' the woman mumbled, her voice distant and heavy with lethargy.

Katrín took in the instruments laid out on the table: a long ivory pipe, a small wooden box, an oil lamp. The pipe seemed to be carved in an intricate pattern.

'What is that?' she said and pointed to the desk. 'Do you need help?' she asked the woman again.

'Leave me be.'

She sounded annoyed at the insistent interruption, dragged out of the viscous dreamscape she found herself stuck in.

'Elka is fine,' the man said. To Katrín's relief, he released his grip on her arm. He bowed slightly, apologetically. 'She's just a bit lost in the fog.'

'You're smoking drugs?'

Katrín immediately bit her tongue for sounding a bit too much like a goddamn schoolgirl.

'Yes, I suppose we are. You're free to join us, if you want.' He sat back down on the sofa and started messing around with the pipe and the wooden box on the table. 'It's quite harmless, really.'

This was the most exciting thing that had happened to Katrín in a long time. The monotonous parties, the lack of prospects, her stifled aspiration. She wanted to run away from everything. But she had nowhere to run to. She stared at the woman, Elka, on the sofa. She was smiling. Despite her dazed state, to Katrín she looked full of life and indulgence. The dreams in her mind were coming to life. She wanted that. She wanted to let go.

She sat down in a chair next to the man.

'What is it?' she asked.

The woman's hand reached out and found hers. Elka started stroking Katrín's hand, gently, affectionately. She felt herself blushing and was embarrassed for how her face must be glowing red.

The man remained impassive, tactfully ignoring Katrín's visible embarrassment. He handed her the pipe. It was made from bone, carved in a pattern of faces of demons and vættir, connected with vines and malevolent flowers in full bloom. It was a femur. It almost looked human.

'It's sorti,' he said, and smiled. 'It will show you how much beauty there is in the world. It will transform your pain into a wonderful dream.'

Katrín wasn't an idiot. She had known what it was. She'd heard rumours about Elka and this man, so she had gone look-ing for them. Still, she had enjoyed acting out this little play. She put the pipe to her mouth and leaned in towards the flame.

'You've got to be kidding me, Katrín! *Náskárar?* Are you insane?'

Hrólfur jumped to his feet as soon as she'd mentioned the name and started pacing. They had resumed the discussion of Katrín's situation now that she had rested properly. Garún felt an anxious knot when she thought of her short meeting with Rotsvelgur. Owing a náskári wasn't good.

'What else was I supposed to do, Hrólfur? Go to the police? Drop in for a visit at the Nine and see if Mother and Father could help? I did what I needed to, like the rest of you. I knew he could get me safely to the portal to Rökkurvík. The náskárar would never betray me to the Crown. Unlike what Viður did to Garún.'

That last sentence visibly stung Diljá. She clearly felt guilty about that. Garún filed that away for later.

'She's right,' said Garún. 'A náskári would rather die than aid the Commonwealth. They have a very strict code of honour. Well' – she hesitated – 'unless he didn't belong to a tribe.'

She looked at Katrín expectantly.

'I ... I'm not sure. Aren't all náskárar in a tribe?'

'No. Not all of them. A few have been excommunicated. Usually traitors or law-breakers. They're called korpar.'

'Korpar? How can I tell if Hræeygður was one of them?'

'If he's a korpur he won't be decorated with significant colours or adornments. Weapons, sure, but nothing much besides that. Did Hræeygður carry something on himself – dyed feathers, cloth or bone?'

Katrín thought for a while.

'He had all kinds of bones and junk on himself. Hooks or fish hooks? Femurs and all kinds of bones dangling everywhere. Does that mean anything?'

'A náskári never carries decorations without meaning. I'm not sure what the hooks mean and the bones are too generic. Do you remember any clear details about his decorations?'

'He had some kind of straps on, where all of this was hanging from. I remember he had a skull.'

'They call it hertygi. What kind of skull was it? Was it any specific colour?'

'I think it was a ram's skull. It had horns at least, but maybe it was a goat. I don't remember, I never really thought much about it. But it was all covered in red splotches. Like blood.'

Garún nodded. She had seen that before, during the meeting in Skeifan.

'He belongs to a tribe, so that's good. But I'm not sure if it's good company.'

'What do you mean?' asked Hrólfur.

'A ram's skull is the symbol of Those-who-pluck-the-eyes-of-the-ram,' said Garún. 'The Ram Eaters. They are one of the largest and most powerful tribes in Reykjavík. They roost in Hræfuglaey and consider most of the city to be their territory.'

'Were they the ones who showed up at the protest?' asked Diljá, hopefully.

Garún shrugged. 'I think so. Maybe they've decided to ally themselves with us?'

'No, he …'

Katrín had to gather herself for a while. Spilling out all her secrets in such a short time must be taking its toll on her. Things she'd kept secret for years. Begrudgingly, Garún found herself respecting her more for it. It was as if she was burning away the weaknesses that had been burdening her for so long. It was ruthless. It was kind of beautiful.

'I had to pay him,' Katrín finally managed to say. 'He wouldn't help me for free.'

'How much did you pay him for the trip into the Forgotten Downtown?' Hrólfur interjected.

Katrín didn't reply and looked away in shame.

'You didn't pay him, did you?' he said wearily. 'You owe him even more.'

'How much do you owe him?' asked Diljá.

'Fifteen,' answered Katrín, so faintly it was barely audible.

'Hundred?'

Katrín shook her head. 'Thousand.'

They took a collective breath. That was a small fortune.

'What else was I supposed to do?' said Katrín, growing more agitated. 'And so what if I owe him? I've owed him before!'

'Yes, but then you had the money to pay, didn't you?' said Garún. 'You went to dear Father and begged or stole a few krónur from him.' Katrín looked both angry and hurt. Garún felt a pang of conscience, but she couldn't help herself. 'Yeah. That's what I thought. But how are you going to pay him now? Nobody owes a náskári for long.'

'We don't need this on top of everything else,' said Hrólfur. 'We need more allies. Not enemies.'

'I know someone who can parley with them,' Garún said.

She didn't know where she was going with this. Why was she so certain that Sæmundur could clear the debt? But it was the only chance she could think of.

'We can't have the Commonwealth and the náskárar up against us at once. This person has dealt with the Ram Eaters many times before. I'll figure this out, don't worry.'

'All right, then.'

'Thank you,' said Katrín in a soft voice. 'And I'm sorry. For everything. For this whole mess.'

Garún nodded. 'It will be fine. You don't have to worry.'

But she was worried. Not that Sæmundur might find himself in harm's way, but because he could mess everything up and make things worse. She felt around in her backpack for what he had handed her after they crossed together into Rökkurvík. When he had done whatever he did to those police officers.

It was a black, bulbous square, with two thin tendrils going out from each corner. The egg case of a skate. They were believed to cause luck, and if you found an unruptured one on the beach you were supposed to hold it between your hands and whisper your wish to it. She remembered going out by herself on early summer mornings, looking for the egg cases among the seaweed-covered rocks. Hoping to wish herself to a new and better life. When the others weren't looking, she took the egg case in her hands and crushed it. Dissonant whispers escaped from it, fading rapidly away.

ᚠ

The pain shot through her arm, the sheer intensity of it shocking her even though she had now been expecting it. She jerked her hand away from the key rune, the delýsíð symbol barely dry on the smooth cavern wall. The pain lingered, a long needle threaded through the bones of her upper arm. She inspected the symbol again, scrutinising its form and trying to intuit the seiðmagn flowing from it. What was wrong? It looked right, felt right – it should have given her free access to the hidden network they had tagged across the city. She steeled herself and sprayed her palm quickly with blue delýsíð paint, placing it on the heart of the symbol.

A barrage of visions. Rapid fire, too quick to process, a ceaseless cacophony of sound and sight that was over before it truly began. Her vision cleared and vertigo set in. She was looking down a city street filled with carriages laden with goods. Traffic was at a standstill due to a barricade set up at one end of the street. A squad of police officers, armed with heavy skorrifles, went through each carriage thoroughly, opening crates and barrels filled with goods with absolute disregard of the tradesman or farmer standing by, yelling at them. She recognised the street – Hverfisgata, the traffic heading out of the city. A lot of people were shouting. Police raised their rifles to a group of older men, who were screaming in outrage and only became further incensed by looking down the barrels.

A crack, and she was pulled elsewhere. An empty alley. Two cats faced each other, swooping their tails back and forth in annoyance. Static, and she was inside a room, a mattress on the floor where a tangle of two bodies lay interwoven between sheets.

What the fuck? Who tagged this?

Then, an outlook of Austurvöllur, high up from the surrounding buildings. It was empty and desolate, the grave building of Lögrétta visible just to the right of her field of vision. It looked miserable, all grey stone laden with gravity. Funnily enough, the leftover materials from Lögrétta's construction had gone into making Hegningarhúsið – better known as the Nine.

Only too fitting, she thought.

She tried to push her vision back towards the city street, which looked as if it was about to erupt into a full-on riot, but she felt as if her efforts didn't accomplish anything. She was wrestling against some stronger, unseen current, which hadn't been there before. Then her vision cut to a street-level symbol, looking through a wired net out into the street, where a different checkpoint was set up. Two officers were calmly talking to a man and a woman, their two children standing behind them. The woman was arguing loudly. Something was wrong with the paperwork.

'They're my children,' the woman said. 'They've been with us to the city dozens of times.'

A snap, and she saw the street again. A crowd had gathered at the barricade, pushing against the police. Behind the front lines were officers with skorrifles readied. They still hadn't fired – these were ordinary folk, after all. Honest, working human men and women. Then, an unnatural crack in the air, screaming – her vision snapped elsewhere.

A mossy field, stretching out into the distant rocky terrain, undulating hills of jagged black lava. A line of carriages went out into the fields and Garún realised she was looking outside the city walls, near one of the gates. The line was at a standstill and people were agitated.

Then, the great rivers of Elliðaár entering the city, the flat barges of the marbendlar, pulled by the nykrar below the surface, lined up at the customs gate. They needed to get to the docks to trade with the outgoing ships.

Then, a room lit by a crimson light shining through tattered drapes, a room she was intimately familiar with but had only seen illuminated by flickering lights of oil lamps or tallow candles. Before her stood a creature clad in robes of dark sanguine, their black leather gloved hands poised in an odd gesture, frozen, the long-beaked ivory mask now familiar to her. The mask and beak were decorated with red sigils drawn by hand in what looked like blood, but she recognised it as the red paint she'd used to ruin the first key rune. This close she could see the faint traces of galdrastafir inlaid in the leather of the mask, and through the red lenses she saw the vague hints of human-looking eyes.

Ah, the voice in her mind said. *There you are. Our little deviant from the protest.*

A pain started blooming in her, a freezing kind of pain, shocking her body from the chest out, spreading into her limbs, a current of ceaseless phantom suffering rising to a crescendo.

Your network is quite ingenious, despite how hacked together and rudimentary it is. An improvement of your crude signs controlling your comrades. You might perhaps have made a decent seiðskratti in a different life.

The pain arose in her, but she could not scream, could not move her arm, could only suffer.

Perhaps. The network will be a great asset to us. To think we haven't considered the potential of delýsíð before.

They leaned in, filling Garún's entire field of vision. The edges of existence were becoming dark.

Where are you hiding, you little rat? A tunnel? A cave? We will find you. We will find you and—

Garún snapped back to herself and fell backwards on the rough cavern floor. Diljá stood shocked, perplexed, having just forcibly pushed her away from the symbol. She was now leaning over her, repeating over and over, what happened, what's wrong, reaching out to her in hope of establishing an unspoken connection, but Garún could not answer, only scream from the relentless pain.

ᚠ

They ruined the sign with delýsíð paint as thoroughly as they could and abandoned the cave pocket Garún had used to set up the key rune in. It was for the best that she'd had the good sense to paint it elsewhere than their regular base. After a while the pain had faded, and as her body felt fine they gathered it had been a psychological attack.

'It was careless of you to make a new symbol,' Diljá said, gesturing towards the stack of newspapers Kryik'traak had brought them. 'It's already clear that Reykjavík is at boiling point. Why would you risk that?'

'I had to see,' was the only thing Garún could say for herself. 'I had to know that it was true.'

'Right.'

Diljá sounded unconvinced. Garún reached out to her, wanting to communicate herself better, but Diljá didn't open herself to it. Garún felt slightly troubled.

I guess my standoffishness has finally worn her down, she thought to herself. *Figures.*

'Listen, every single newspaper out there is printing what practically constitutes anti-Kalmar propaganda,' Hrólfur said. 'Trampe has gone too far. They've fully armed the police, ground the traffic in and out of the city to a standstill, they're harassing regular people for documentation and detaining them if anything is off. They've arrested several families because their kids aren't properly documented.' He shook his head. 'I'm not sure why the hell they're so excessive, but it's working to our benefit. People are outraged – regular people. This is our chance.' He started pacing. 'Did you see that the Citizens' Party has split up? They've formed a new party, the Home Rule Party. They're pushing for more autonomy within the Commonwealth. This is huge news, although not entirely unforeseeable. It's the first step towards independence.'

Katrín sat up on her bed. She looked slightly better, being able to hold food down now.

'What? Where was this?'

Hrólfur shuffled the stack of newspapers and fetched one for her.

'I'm afraid they don't mention your father in there. Maybe he stayed with the old party,' he offered. 'Or, well...'

Or he's in the Nine with the rest of your family, was what none of them wanted to say. Katrín started poring over the newspaper.

'This is our chance,' Hrólfur continued. 'Call for a mass protest. Annexation Day is coming up. People normally gather for festivities in the city. It's the perfect opportunity.'

'How?' Diljá asked.

'Kryik'traak will spread the word. We can send couriers to certain people at the newspapers, get them to print bulletins, post ads. Reykjavík isn't that big. Everybody knows everybody.'

'I still haven't reached my contact with the náskárar,' said Garún. 'So Katrín should stay here and hide. She also could use the rest, maybe.'

Katrín nodded her agreement, still devouring every word of the newspaper. She looked better, healthier now. She looked concerned as she read. She didn't look that happy about the party split, which surprised Garún. Wasn't this what she had been hoping for?

'They might even show up,' said Hrólfur. 'Like at the last protest.'

Diljá looked hesitant. 'But why is Trampe cracking down so hard on the city gates? What is Kalmar looking for?'

'Us?' Hrólfur suggested. 'They raided Rökkurvík, after all.'

Diljá didn't look convinced.

Garún knew who they were looking for. A rogue galdramaður. One considered to be allied with their cause. But she kept quiet. Who cared why the Crown was showing its true nature now? All that mattered was that they strike while the iron was hot.

'Let's do it,' Garún said. 'We need to put the word out. Get the people to rise up, together. It's time to reclaim what is rightfully ours.'

Tuttugu og fjögur

The Stone Giant. Towering over all of creation. Wielding incomprehensible power and limitless wisdom. It was boundless, eternal, a ruling god over this timeless, unending landscape. When Sæmundur had conjured up the vision he'd shared with the crowd at the concert, he hadn't really known what was going to happen. All he knew was that he wanted to impart something of what Kölski had shown him, and that he couldn't do it with simple words. He had to show them, and so tried to emulate Kölski. He had failed, or at least only partially succeeded. But what he hadn't expected was in that trying to teach others, he had chanced upon a completely new understanding himself.

The memory of meeting Garún on the night of the concert stabbed him deeper than he'd expected. At the time, everything had seemed possible. Garún being there had set off a chain reaction. He'd wanted to show her a part of what he had learned, show her that all of this was for something greater. But there was also something he wanted to communicate, something he couldn't find the words for. An apology; a confession of love – he didn't know what it was. It had affected the music and galdur in an unforeseeable way. He had managed on some level to cast galdur instinctively. He'd used instruments before to assist in galdur, to give him rhythm, a foundation. But at that moment there had been no words, no form or set path before him. Just pure galdur.

None of that mattered now. Because now Sæmundur understood the truth of the matter: he hadn't learned a single worthwhile thing. He was just as weak, just as limited, as he had been before. The leaps he had made were microscopic, leaving him just as distant from the true, boundless potential of galdur. An untamable force that could make everything from nothing. Sure, he had grown competent enough at making cheap parlour tricks, which was all that the mortal tradition of galdur amounted to in the end. Small tricks and fleeting illusions. To understand time and the cosmos, to reshape these elements according to your will, to firmly grasp the reins of reality itself and stand outside the causal stream – that was the true, raw might of galdur. That was enlightenment. Divinity.

And the Stone Giant was the key.

He had also realised that all his new-found power stemmed completely from Kölski. When the demon was bound into shadow he found himself much weaker than before. Manifesting the demon had taken some toll on him he did not yet quite comprehend. He had paid a price that remained elusive to him, lost an intangible part of himself that was more than mere shadow. Even binding the demon into shadow was pushing his limitations. It took every ounce of focus he could muster to keep the galdur reinforced. When he had been cornered by the Crown, he had been effectively powerless facing them. Kölski had done all the work.

He was the problem. His human body and his human mind. That was the nature of the chains of life, the constraints holding him back. But to simply discard his corporeal form would only turn him into fodder for transmundane possession. No, he would have to find a way forward. He had to find a way to transform himself into something different – something *more*. Something beyond humanity.

He had to take certain steps before he could seek out the Stone Giant. He had an idea of what he had to do. But first he needed some answers.

After Garún kicked him out, Sæmundur had headed towards the edge of the Forgotten Downtown, to the limits where the mind couldn't clearly interpret what lay ahead and led you time and time again back into the same street. He kept an eye out in case anyone was shadowing him and made sure to take a long-winded detour towards the shack where the portal was. Everything seemed fine. It was slightly easier to keep Kölski bound into shadow when it was dark and he was alone. The presence of light and other people placed a significantly greater strain on him. Still, he found himself completely exhausted just being by himself. He didn't quite understand the fundamental, arcane nature of this galdur, as with so much else that Kölski had taught him. Claiming power alone wasn't enough. He had to claim true understanding as well. He was certain that if he only pushed a bit further, he would attain that state he craved above anything else: true power, and a higher understanding of the capabilities of galdur.

Miracles were within his grasp. All he needed was to make a small sacrifice. And he had so much still to give.

He stepped into Reykjavík in the temple cemetery of Landakotshof. He collapsed into the tall grass, lying there like one of the moss-grown gravestones, camouflaged with the collapsed obelisks half sunken into the earth. He stared up into the grey sky. It was cold and the grass had turned yellow.

He wanted to disappear, to petrify and become forgotten like an illegible gravestone. Let his face slowly erode, like all these faded runes and inscriptions. It would be so much easier to give up. To let go.

Landakotshof was an old wooden temple, built on ancient stone foundations that predated the building itself by centuries. It was roughly round in shape, its domed roof low. Four great sculptures of the landvættir were placed around the building, each facing the cardinal point they were associated with. The sculptures were great monoliths decorated with countless vættir and ancient beings long forgotten, with the landvættur itself at the top, lording it over the lesser beings. The Great Eagle was made from skrumnisiron, crass and uninviting, its enormous talons gnarled and sharp. The Wyrm was cast in thaumaturgical meteoric iron, the seiðmagn lending its scales an unnatural sheen, making it seem as fluid as liquid water. The Stone Giant was made from seemingly naturally formed lava rocks and obsidian. The Bull was carved into a single basalt column in sharp, brutally clear lines, an uncompromising force of destruction.

Technically it was illegal to hold any other faith than that of the royal church, which preached of the royal family's divine power and their godly right to rule, granted by the king's ancestral connection to the divine and the ancestors themselves, made manifest through the Machine of the Almighty. Still the Crown had let the temple stand, out of respect for the land and the old ways. The old faith could not be practised officially, but it was possible to worship in secret. On certain days of the year small groups of people would gather in abandoned temples and places of power to offer the land their sacrifices. After the wall had risen around Reykjavík, these secret rituals had diminished rapidly. The thaumaturgical, untamed nature was now out of sight, something that belonged to the highlands and not to the city. Sæmundur was not raised heathen, but he still found himself missing it. If it was possible to miss something one has never experienced or known, that is.

'You are deep in thought, master.'

A raw voice spoke and Sæmundur jumped. He'd almost fallen asleep. For a moment he'd let his mind wander and immediately Kölski had broken free from the shadow. The demon sat on top of a gravestone, a gargoyle brought to life. Now that Sæmundur had stopped ceaselessly muttering incantations, he fully felt how absolutely exhausted he was. He couldn't do this any longer.

'Do not despair,' said Kölski. 'Redemption is within your grasp.'

Did I say that out loud? Sæmundur thought to himself. *Or can he hear my thoughts?*

If Kölski was capable of it, he showed no sign. Sæmundur waited until the demon continued.

'As I've said before, you are at your limit. You are merely human. Creatures of my ilk are far removed from yours.' Kölski smiled. 'But ... there is *another* which could speak on your behalf. Which could give you the control, the liberty, which is rightfully yours. You could become something far more powerful than you are now. Take a step towards claiming true control over galdur. If you have the courage to call upon him.'

Sæmundur knew of what the demon spoke. He had been considering it himself. The answer to his problems. The only thing holding him back was his own fear.

Before sacrificing Mæja, he had briefly considered manifesting the demon in his own flesh, but hadn't had the guts to do it at the time. Which was perhaps for the best, it likely would have caused him to lose control of the ritual. Of the demon itself. But now ... Now he had changed. He had attained the right mindset to advance further. He craved to feel that fire consume his mind again, to feel himself burn up from the blinding light of pure enlightenment. That unsullied primal force he had barely touched before.

He was well beyond second-guessing himself. The only way forward was through the crucible. From which he would emerge transformed. A shining beacon of enlightenment. Someone worthy of seeking out the Stone Giant.

The temple smelled of earth and burned birch. It was in complete ruins. Benches had been thrown over, broken effigies lay scattered around. Shards of glass crunched under Sæmundur's feet. The walls were covered with graffiti, hearts and initials carved and sprayed over each other through the years. Clearly the temple was a popular place with the youth, somewhere they could let loose away from prying, judging eyes. Sæmundur doubted that the vættir minded. Clearly they were still being worshipped, although the sacrifices were wild debauchery instead of spilled blood. But he knew that wasn't important. There were many ways to make a sacrifice, as he knew himself. In the middle of the room was a large sacrificial stone. Its bowl was naturally formed, the glimmering black lava rock like frozen winter darkness.

Sæmundur righted one of the benches with some effort and sat down. Every bone in his body ached. He felt weak. All these incantations he had spoken. New power brought into the world from his lips. He'd been reckless. He couldn't be sure that a demon hadn't broken through, inhabited his bones without him knowing.

Kölski clawed its way up an oblong stone, a sculpture of some vættur or the other. It had three eyes but no mouth.

'You are at a crossroads. Something you should be used to by now. You have to make a choice, master – because after this there is no turning back.'

He grunted. 'That happened long ago, demon.'

'No, master. I've been standing guard over you, although you have not always been aware of it, holding back forces that would have devoured you instantly and filled your heart with the immeasurable hungering void. You've been dancing on the precipice, a lunatic only one false step from complete ruin. But now you can't go further on your own. That is why I tell you that there will be no turning back. If you perform the ritual you will let that which is and that which has never been into your body and soul. You will cease to completely belong to yourself.'

He wasn't sure how to respond. It was strange to hear these words of warning from the devil himself.

'Perhaps I've never really belonged to myself.'

The threat of possession had been hammered into Sæmundur's mind from the first day of his studies. Unlike almost every-thing else that teachers and others had tried to indoctrinate into students, Sæmundur had never seen any reason to doubt this universal truth. There were too many stories of galdramenn who went too far, became too careless, lazy, clumsy, ambitious. Every incantation, every syllable in a word of power, was a possible portal for the transmundane fiends to break through and possess the galdramaður. No master was safe from their corrupting force. The demon could overwhelm the galdramaður immediately or wait, hiding possibly for decades, before it struck at a prime moment. Sæmundur wasn't certain if Kölski had been shielding him or whether his own power was sufficient, but he had always remained on guard. So to invite the beyond intentionally, meaning to tame it... It had been unimaginable up to this point. Impossible.

Which was exactly what his teachers had said when he pitched to them his research studies on the fundamental nature of galdur, in which he meant to gain a higher understanding by experimenting on galdur by developing a method that relied more on insight and feeling, rather than precise rotes from memory.

Impossible. Unimaginable. Disastrous.

A childish idea, a sign of his lack of maturity and patience. No one became a galdramaður by removing themselves from the tradition that came before them. That was for superstitious kuklarar, amateurs who never gained a deeper understanding of the lore. Galdur was not supposed to be alive and free, it was to be chained down in immovable traditions and rituals. Any deviation from that was to invite danger and a fate worse than death.

Sæmundur gnashed his teeth, clenching his fists so his knuckles whitened. His former teachers at Svartiskóli had been wrong about so many things. Their ignorance was limitless. He had sacrificed so much for just the taste of true power – he would be a fool to stop here.

'Again you stand at the threshold, master. The choice is yours.'

'I abide no limits. I will call upon him.'

Kölski smiled. 'As you wish.'

For the first time for years, a pale column of smoke rose from the chimney of the temple at Landakot. It slithered up, merging with the grey clouds. Sæmundur sat inside the smoke-filled temple, his face shining with sweat. The smoke stung his eyes and made them well up with tears. Carved idols of vættir burned in the fire. On the other side of the flames stood Kölski, nearly obfuscated by the smoke, chanting galdur with him. Sæmundur chanted long and deep rhythmic tones, drawing forth every syllable for as long as his lungs could in all the smoke. Kölski was at the opposite end of the spectrum, spitting out forbidden names and incomprehensible invocations. The demon's pitch-black chitinous shell seemed to move in the flickering light, to become liquid.

Calling forth a demon was not easy. Any hack could lose his guard and attract malevolent entities that spread like mould through the bone marrow, but to summon forth a certain being from the abyss and bind it was a heresy known to few and rarely mastered. That is why Sæmundur had been so surprised to read the page he'd stolen from *Rauðskinna*. It had been way too simple for its intended purpose, and that was the source of its true power and danger. Almost any fisherman could have performed it, given that they knew the foundations of a few common fishing charms and invocations of fortune. But this was entirely different. This was like bleeding into the ocean to attract a specific shark. Sæmundur would have had no chance of attracting the demon he needed by himself. But he had Kölski. A guiding lighthouse in the void. Now he had to place his trust entirely in him.

He felt a distant pull on the edge of his consciousness. A sound, a scattering of dissonant whispers on the wind. He ignored it. His attention could not waver at this moment.

Sæmundur pulled out a razor-sharp knife and warmed the blade in the fire. His invocations became faster, weaving his galdur tighter in with Kölski's chanting.

Gögll'mín err þat vera, keyrrtrak vit óberðk, heyrit funakraðak, ódreyil að vittk.

They chanted in unison. Suddenly their rhythm was off, then brought back together, their words the anvil and the rhythm a hammer, fluctuating in an endless improvised struggle. With these tools they shaped the knife into a key. A key to flesh and blood and the internal void. Sæmundur raised the red-glowing knife from the fire and held it in front of himself.

Vomgeifl lýs drunheima, rák mót blótrauna, vit mín sker at þurrð, bit mitt sker at kumlum!

Then – silence.

Sæmundur turned the knife to himself, let the point touch his chest. It burned.

And he carved a portal into his flesh.

As soon as the blood touched the knife's edge, Kölski started to mumble, keeping away the forces that desired to break in. Those carrion feeders which swarmed around the bloody trail.

There are many other aspects to galdur besides words. Symbols. Movement. Intent. Supporting instruments, helping to manifest something unimaginable. His eyes were closed as he carved, letting the burning pain guide him onwards, rather than relying on sight. Sæmundur carved into himself a roughly elliptical symbol. He focused all his energy into this symbol, a gate which he retraced circle after circle, again and again, carving it into his mind as well as his flesh. He couldn't focus on guarding himself – that was entirely up to Kölski now. He couldn't even permit himself to worry about the imp at this moment – it would all be for nothing. He carved and carved and when the symbol was complete, when the portal stood fully open in a bloody, shredded wound, he filled his lungs with smoke and shadow and called out into the beyond.

'*Bektalpher!*'

He turned the knife's edge down, placed it at the top of the elliptical wound. Slowly he flayed the bloody skin back, cutting down, revealing red and shiny meat. The wound was like an open eye on his chest.

'*Bektalpher!*'

Again he turned the knife's point to himself and with a single, quick movement, he cut a horizontal, deep cut into the meat.

Blood poured down his chest, his stomach, but it was not warm – it was glacial.

'*Bektalpher!*'

The red flesh on his chest twitched and Sæmundur gasped as he felt something moving, a cavity forming inside himself. The meat spread apart and formed gruesome lips. A voice that belonged to neither Sæmundur nor Kölski spoke.

'*Sæmundur.*'

Tuttugu og fimm

The sky was a clear azure, in the south a spread of tattered clouds. The low winter sun was out, casting its thin light over the crowds of people swarming from train stations, down streets, flocking towards the centre of the city. Garún tugged on the collar of her jacket and tried to blend in with the crowd. Kryik'traak had kindly supplied them with fresh clothes. Garún had snagged an imported denim jacket, so new it was still stiff. It was designed for labourers, but had recently become a fashionable item with teenagers, who were commonly seen wearing them while out drinking at Ingólfstorg Square every weekend. She'd decided against tagging it with delýsíð. The seiðmagn would make her stand out to any possible seiðskrattar, marking her as an obvious target.

She walked with Hrólfur down Hverfisgata, two random people in the middle of a crowd. The stream of people was a river filling out the entire road, flowing on towards Austurvöllur. The air was thick with promise and excitement. It reminded her almost of the celebration on the king's birthday.

'Look.' Hrólfur pointed up to the eaves of the surrounding houses, where náskárar sat and surveyed the crowd. 'The raven-folk.'

In the sky the enormous náskárar flew in small groups, their blue-black feathers shimmering in the sunlight. On a few náskárar the light cast off the coarse and threatening iron fused to their beaks and claws.

'They're out in numbers.' Garún permitted herself some hope. 'Maybe last time wasn't a fluke. If they decide to fully show solidarity then you know that something has to change.'

She stretched to see over the crowd. It seemed as if there was an unusually high number of huldufólk, or so it seemed to her – it was hard to see the difference between them and humans in such a large crowd. She even saw groups of mar-bendlar, decorated in garments made from shimmering scales, inlaid with luminous pearls. People were smiling and laughing. It was intoxicating.

The Crown had set up roadblocks, but it hadn't been enough to hold back the sheer number of people going to the protest. Since it was Annexation Day, the gathering of massive crowds was technically legal. Garún couldn't help but beam at the sheer number of people. They were here. Together. They were going to change the course of history.

They crossed the bridges at Lækjargata, over the stream and into the heart of the central city. There were fewer smiles and less laughter now. People unfolded signs and banners, raising them before entering Austurvöllur. A few pulled up scarves to cover their faces. Mostly the younger people, but she saw a couple of elderly ladies do it as well. Was it because of shame? Or good sense? She was uncertain. The grandiose buildings in Austurstræti towered over the pedestrians, severe and imposing, built in the Hafnían style. A reminder of who truly controlled the city.

A large crowd had gathered at Austurvöllur, pushing up against the defensive wall the police had formed around Lögrétta. Garún felt her stomach sink when it looked as if the Crown's soldiers were among them, but as she got closer she saw they were just regular citizens wearing army helmets and armbands in the colours of the Royal Commonwealth. Occasionally they grabbed someone who they thought was getting too excited and dragged them behind their defence lines, disappearing them. Behind the front lines were rows of police officers, readily armed with the muzzle-loaded skorrifles. Just like last time. It sent a chill down her spine.

Garún felt the adrenaline rush as they merged with the protesters. A euphoric optimism was in the air, a certainty that new and brighter times were ahead.

No more Crown! No more Crown!

Garún quickly lost sight of Hrólfur. Most of the people arriving at the same time as her had charged to the front, signs in their hands – or else something they wanted to throw at the parliament building and lines of police. Their shouts shook Austurvöllur, their fists were raised in the air in sync with the chanting. Garún shouted, screamed, celebrated, and when she looked back a while later she saw the protesters had completely filled Austurvöllur. Signs were raised everywhere, like an angry rash. A symptom of the oppression that was smothering them. The house of Lögrétta faced the crowd, unshakable in its grey silence. Biplanes patrolled the skies above.

Rocks, skyr, rotten eggs and balloons filled with paint were let loose on the house of Lögrétta and the police. Whenever the curtains moved, ever so slightly, a rain of garbage came crashing down on the source of the movement. Windows shattered and the grey stone house was coloured with bright paint and filth, looking like a cliff roosted by seagulls, stained with decades of their droppings. Up on the surrounding roofs sat the náskárar, their massive, iron-beaked forms completely encircling Austurvöllur. Black-winged shapes circled the air above. They crowed with the protesters in their own language. To her surprise she recognised one of them. Clad in that unique breastplate, the leader of the tribe himself: Rotsvelgur. The náskárar bristled their feathers and cawed towards a group of police officers down on the street, who pointed their weapons up at the náskárar, ready to fire at the slightest hint of provocation. The náskárar nearest Rotsvelgur seemed tense, leaning away from him, looking tense and ready to fly off, almost as if they were more afraid of their leader than of the armed police below. Rotsvelgur did not agitate the police, instead occasionally cawing out a command, constantly scanning the crowd, an apex predator surveying his domain.

Hrímland out of Kalmar, no more Crown! Hrímland out of Kalmar, no more Crown!

She wasn't aware how long she'd been standing there, her voice raw from fighting chants, when she almost accidentally hit Styrhildur in the face with her outstretched fist.

'Styrhildur! I'm so sorry, I didn't see you!'

'I'm so glad I found you!' she shouted over the noise. Her brother Hraki stood next to her, a black handkerchief tied around his mouth and nose. 'Where have you been? Are you all right?'

She told her about their refuge in Elliðaárdalur. Styrhildur and Hraki had been hiding on the city streets. Garún told them where to meet, so they wouldn't have to resort to scavenging or stealing to be able to eat. Styrhildur went a bit pale when she told them about the jellyfish and diving into the deep caves, but still promised they would meet up with her.

The crowd suddenly pushed against them, threatening to separate them. The shouts were more agitated, rougher, angrier. The conflict at the front had got more intense.

Free Hrímland! Free Hrímland!

No more Crown! No more Crown! Hrímland out of Kalmar, no more Crown!

They grabbed hold of each other, afraid to drown in the ocean of people. Clubs were raised and brought down at the front. Stones rained over the police and an explosion came from the western side of Austurvöllur. Smoke rose and náskárar took to the sky. A volley of fire came from the skorriffles, seemingly from all directions. A few náskárar fell from the roofs. The rest took immediately to the air, diving in to the rows of police officers scrambling to reload, tearing into them mercilessly. She saw people rushing towards Lögrétta, knives and bludgeons in their hands.

A low hum that had just barely been audible kept steadily increasing. A growing shadow appeared in the eastern sky. Chimneys spewed out thick strokes of steam, which trailed in the behemoth's wake. The sun gleamed on towering walls of iron. Cannons jutted out of the fortress at irregular intervals, covering all directions, some of them so large that they looked as if they could fire an automobile. Rotors and jet engines spun by the dozen, steering the machine forwards. Biplanes flew in swarms around the fortress, protecting their great hive of war and destruction.

Loftkastalinn.

The flying fortress. A gargantuan, sluggish monster made from iron and smoke. A miracle of modern engineering, remaking the very laws of nature to suit its needs. The future of warfare and the ultimate weapon, a symbol of unity, safety, power.

Loftkastalinn crept on closer until it was floating right above Austurvöllur. The dark iron mass blotted out the sky, massive cannons and turrets pointing down at the people gathered below. The deafening noise from the engines drowned out the crowd.

A metallic voice came from the loudspeakers and megaphones, overpowering the engine drone.

'This is an illegal protest! Leave the square immediately!'

The voice repeated those lines like an incantation, but had the opposite effect from its stated intention. The crowd grew even more agitated, the shouts of protest turning into a steady, wordless cacophony. Hrólfur came charging through the crowd to find them.

'We have to get out of here!' he yelled over the noise. 'People are going to get killed!'

Garún stared at him, shocked. 'You want to give up?'

'No!' He looked offended. 'But this is all about to go south. Stick around and you'll end up dead or on your way to the Nine!'

'So what?' she yelled at him.

'So we've got to stay alive to fight another day!'

'It's not about you or me!' she shouted over the noise. 'Now is the chance to really make a difference! If we leave then nothing will ever change – and every non-human will always be a second-class citizen! And I won't even be that.'

Hrólfur refused to budge.

'It's futile! Do you think that the stiftamtmaður is sitting inside Lögrétta? Do you think that one goði is still in there? That house is empty – this is just a performance!'

'A performance that matters!' A calm, seething rage boiled up in her. 'Just fucking leave, then, if you are too scared to pay the price of real change! You fucking coward!'

She got up in his face and pushed him.

He stumbled backwards, barely catching himself on another person's coat. A dark look came over his face. He glared at Styrhildur and Hraki, who stood next to Garún, readied as if to fight. And he did what she told him. He left.

Her rage had no bounds. The mob had lost control and

everywhere she looked she could see brutal fighting. Supporters of the Commonwealth were now openly beating the protesters without hesitation, armed with batons from the police. She let anger guide her forward. A group of young people with bandanas over their faces were throwing stones at the police. She grabbed one stone, then another, and threw them until her shoulder hurt.

A red lightning struck, blinding her, and she stumbled forwards. Something had hit her in the head, hard. As she was falling, Hraki grabbed her and raised her to her feet. If she'd hit the ground she might not have managed to get back up from the stampeding crowd. Garún looked back and saw a young man holding a raised police baton, wearing an armband in the Kalmar colours on his right arm. He had an army helmet on his head. His woollen coat was thick and well tailored, his shoes with no visible wear. His face looked as if he didn't believe what had just happened. As if he was dumbstruck over this new power he found himself possessing. A slight smile crept over his face, the dawning satisfaction of the power he'd found at the end of the baton.

She still had a stone in her hand. She charged. He was so surprised that he didn't react, still holding his baton in the air like a statue. She hit him right in the face with the stone, sounding a loud crack, and followed through with a kick to the groin, bringing him to his knees. The helmet flew off his head when she bashed him once, twice, in the head with the stone, now stained a sickening crimson. The other protesters surged in and stomped him into the ground.

The metallic voice from the fortress above went quiet. There were no more protesting chants, only the sounds of fighting. There was a war raging around them. The roofs were empty of dark-feathered náskárar, who now circled above, diving in groups of three, shredding men, grabbing them with the strong krummafótur and flying off with them, flinging police and civilians alike through the air, arms flailing helplessly. Another volley of rifle fire was let loose, the air crackling with unnatural energy, bringing down several náskárar. The roar of the crowd shifted and Garún saw the Crown's regiments marching in. They appeared along the streets at Kirkjustræti, Pósthússtræti, and the alleyway leading to Ingólfstorg. In a moment they had completely sealed off Austurvöllur. The soldiers were clad in dark leather armour, fortified with steel, the iron masks over their faces making their appearance machine-like and inhuman. Many of them carried skorrifles, others had army-grade seizure-bludgeons charged with seiður and spiked tower shields. An occasional seiðskratti stood in their lines. There must have been at least a dozen. Garún found herself panicking. This was just like the last protest. Worse. So much worse. She was trapped. Hrólfur was right. They were going to fucking die here. They were going to massacre all of them.

Styrhildur grabbed her by the shoulders and shook her.

'Garún! Snap out of it! Stay close to us – we're going to m—'

A loud shot sounded over the noise. On the roof balcony of Landsímahúsið, the head offices of the National Telephone Company, were soldiers with a mortar. They had fired something over the crowd, going up in an arch of trailing smoke. People panicked, trying to get as far away from the shell as they could, but it was futile. There was nowhere to run now. The canister exploded almost ten metres above the centre of the crowd. Garún tried fleeing away, covering her mouth and nose with her sleeve, expecting toxic gas or something worse. But gas hadn't come out of the canister. It was something else.

A being floated in the air above Austurvöllur. It was formless, colourless – but simultaneously not. It was an uncolour that didn't match anything found in the spectrum of this world. Initially it was only a small, floating orb. It looked harmless.

Then it started to grow.

The uncolour spread through the air like oil over water. It grew, unwinding itself like an octopus uncoiling its tentacles. It reached out and down towards the crowd. Garún fought trying to stay upright, to keep the mob from trampling her into the ground in the panic. This was like nothing she had ever seen before, but it had to have some sort of explanation. A source. She suddenly remembered her goggles and hurriedly put them on.

The air was bursting with vibrant colour – an unnaturally high condensation of seiðmagn in the air. A supercharged stream of raw seiðmagn flowed down from Landsímahúsið towards the uncolour. The uncolour was a void of colour, the seiðmagn hyper-coloured – the former unnatural, the latter supernatural. Some of the hues in the seiðmagn reminded her of delýsíð colours, others were more akin to other-worldly colours that reminded her of the ruined world of the huldufólk.

Garún fought for a better look at the top of Landsímahúsið and then realised what was happening. Three royal seiðskrattar stood up on the roof, soldiers filed behind them, skorrifles trained up at the sky, shooting down any approaching náskárar. The seiðskrattar wore dark and heavy robes, covered with crimson symbols of seiður. Black leather covered their heads, with dark red lenses set in the beaked ivory masks. Mysterious materials and herbs were placed inside the beaks, a mixture infused with seiður that boosted their powers. She recognised one of the masks, decorated with red, hand-drawn sigils, and gritted her teeth in hateful frustration. The seiðskrattar amplified and contained the seiðmagn and cast it towards the uncolour, manipulating it. She saw that some kind of faint energy eman-ated from the uncolour itself, a force that was strikingly different from what the seiðskrattar used. As if it were from another world entirely.

The thing spread out like an umbrella, sending out slow-moving tendrils. Its furthest reaching feelers reached the panicked crowd. The tendrils, not exactly liquid or gaseous, grabbed hold of their first victims and pulled them into the air. They struggled, trying to resist, grabbing hold of their friends, but their efforts were futile against the creature's unnatural strength.

Garún watched in horror as people lifted into the air were drained of life in a matter of minutes, from the moment the first feeler hooked itself into the flesh of its victim. First, the vision went, the eyes swelling up as dark clots of coagulated blood, sometimes bursting. Delirious from pain and fear, the people fought against the overwhelming strength of the feelers, but more constantly grew out of the uncolour's mass, further hooking themselves into the victim's body. They shook and trembled. Eventually they stopped resisting. Their skin turned taut and grey. Their cheeks became hollow and their lips shrunk into nothing. When the tentacles dropped their prey to the ground all life had been drained from the bodies, leaving only withered and dried-out corpses behind.

Then the tendrils moved towards fresh prey.

All thoughts of fighting back had been abandoned. Escaping was the only option. The army and the police held the line at all fronts, trapping them in the square. A wave of people crashed on Garún as they rushed away from the floating uncolour, hitting her so hard that she lost her footing. She was only spared from being trampled into the ground because she was crushed so tightly up against others, somehow managing to keep herself upright. She'd lost sight of Styrhildur and Hraki. More people rose into the sky, hooked on the uncoloured tendrils, dropped moments later as lifeless husks. Garún could barely move her limbs. She struggled to breathe, pressed in between people. Suddenly she found her footing and pushed forwards, fighting for some room. Before she knew it the crowd had violently pushed her back, shoving her to the edge of the no man's land in the middle of the field.

The ground was already scattered with grey corpses: humans, huldufólk, marbendlar. A náskári had been trapped in the sky and crashed down in the middle of the field, its muted feathers falling from its body like autumn leaves. The uncolour kept on growing, hooking itself into anyone who found themselves at the edge of the crowd. The unnatural feelers danced above her, feeling blindly like lethargic lightning. She tried to squeeze herself back into the mass, into the safety of the crowd, but she might as well have been running into a brick wall. The feelers came closer, splitting into more, ravenous tendrils.

She didn't think. She ran.

Shrivelled flesh and brittle bones cracked under her feet. She kicked up grey ash with each hurried footstep. She tried not to look up at the monstrosity, did not look down at the massacre below, cleared her mind of everything except a single command: run.

She slipped and fell flat on her stomach. She was looking right into a mummified face, petrified in a look of absolute terror. She pushed the body away from her in dismay, kicking herself to her feet and sprinting back into the opposite side of the crowd, slamming into the wall of people so fast she managed to force her way through.

Suddenly something gave way and the crowd started to move. The military had opened a gap in their ranks, letting people through. They ran from Austurvöllur like a stampeding herd. Outliers were caught by rifle fire or seizure-bludgeons; people were tackled and handcuffed, black bags thrown over their heads.

The marbendlar proved slow in their escape, and she feared none of them would make it out. She wanted to help them. But she didn't know how. She ran from the merciless slaughter without looking back.

She ran until she couldn't take another step. The buildings were constricting, hostile. She felt as if Reykjavík wanted her dead. The streets were empty and quiet. Numb and exhausted, she started towards the only nearby place she thought could resemble a safe haven. Maybe it was a foolish thing to do, but she had to rest and find some semblance of comfort.

Sæmundur's apartment was unlocked. She walked in on trembling legs, flicking the light switches back and forth. None of them worked. The living room was a wreck – upturned furniture, broken items all over the floor. Except for a circle in the middle, white chalk in a sickening geometric shape, surrounded by birch branches. And in the middle of it, something she at first refused to recognise, refused to process – the dried blood and torn fur of what used to be her darling Mæja.

She fell to her knees, defeated. And she finally gave herself permission to break down and cry.

III

Sound

An artist's rendering of a náskári, based on traveller's descriptions of their warriors, called blóðgögl. Few have lived to tell the tale of close encounters with the fierce and ruthless warriors of the ravenfolk.

Tuttugu og sex

Before

'Here, put this somewhere,' said Lilja.

She handed Garún a convex stone, ocean-polished and soft. On one side an esoteric symbol had been carved into it.

'What is it?'

They purposely lagged behind the group, which sauntered onwards, cheerfully laughing, spilling beer.

'Huliðshjálmur. Or so I was told. Quick, put it in your pocket or something.'

'You have got to be kidding. Why? So I'll be invisible?'

She laughed. 'Come on, you won't turn invisible, you can't do that!'

She fell quiet for a moment and took a sip from the bottle of wine she was carrying. Almost as if she regretted Garún couldn't vanish completely.

'It will just make you blend in, so there won't be any trouble.'

A familiar, heavy weight settled over Garún's chest.

'Fuck. You.'

She threw the stone at the nearest house and shattered a window. The group looked back, shouting in shock and amusement.

Garún! Are you kidding me?
Did you break the window, are you insane?
You are so fucking crazy!

Someone shouted angrily into the street, presumably the window's owner. They ran away laughing, like naughty children. Lilja seethed, even though she tried to pretend that nothing had happened, but Garún didn't give a shit. Lilja was just like the rest of them, deceitful and false. She regretted not throwing the stone in her face. Garún went regularly enough to Karnivalið and even though they didn't know each other that well, Lilja knew as much. It was one of the few places that let blendingar in without much trouble. Most of the time. It still didn't mean that trouble wouldn't find her indoors, but she didn't intend to lie low and slink along the walls. She would not hide who she was.

Jón made himself fall behind the group and walked alongside Garún.

'Are you all right?' he asked in a quiet voice.

'Yeah. Just Lilja being a bitch.'

'There's no use in getting upset over that. You might as well get angry at the sun for setting.'

Garún looked up into the bright sky.

'The sun doesn't set. It's the summer solstice, you idiot. Shouldn't you, of all people, know that?'

He took a contemplative sip of his beer.

'What? Why?'

'It's Jónsmessa. The first priest of the first king apparently was born today and his name was Jón. Just like you. Don't they teach you anything at school here in Reykjavík?'

The question was laced with more than a hint of resentment. So much of what she knew of the world, how it worked and its history, she'd had to unearth herself. Nothing had been freely handed to her.

'Nothing and nothing. Nothing but bullshit.'

'Tonight all foul spirits are supposed to become unchained,' she said. 'And here we are. A fun coincidence, huh?'

'Poetic! he exclaimed. 'You should get into poetry, I'm telling you.'

'Ha – ha.' She pushed him jokingly. 'Paint me a picture and I'll write you a poem. Then we can compete in which is more dreadful.'

'I'll win, with no contest. The vættir have seen fit to bless me with consistently awful artistic talent.'

Outside the bar people stood smoking and talking, finishing their beers before they went inside. Some people had brought along entire six-packs and were trying their best to pound them down before the bouncers had enough and ran them off. It was bright out and relatively warm, as good as it got on a summertime northern island. It was just past midnight, but the place was absolutely packed. Gísli, whom Garún was on familiar enough terms with, was working the doors and he let her through without accepting the crumpled bill she tried to slide to him. That made her feel good. Even though no one else had to bribe the bouncers.

She made her way through the crowd towards the bar. Jón and the others were already there and called out to her.

'Garún! Brennivín shots!'

It was dark and humid inside, smoke mixed with stale beer and sweat. They ordered a line of shots, then another. Garún got a beer and the third shot along with it. She'd had some liquor earlier that night, home brew that she'd made herself from discarded fruit found in the colonial stores' trash bins. It was drinkable but dreadful, and wasn't strong enough to get her over the edge. After the third shot she felt a familiar numbness come over her. This was what she needed.

The bar was completely packed. Up in the corner an electronic musician stood on a minuscule stage consisting of a couple of pallets, jamming cassette reels into a massive home-made synthesiser precariously placed on top of a stack of speakers. She was constantly switching out reels, running them through the clunky device. With a simple keyboard she produced pounding electronic music. The music was loud and the tempo rapid. People danced in a ceaseless throng, writhing like a pile of worms. She danced along with them, song after song seamlessly blending together. She felt alive and free. Something came loose inside her and she loved to feel like a part of the crowd, felt as if she connected with everyone else in there through the music.

Suddenly someone pushed her. A few young huldukonur were shouting something at her she couldn't make out. She tried to reach out and find any common ground, but they rejected her attempt with disdain. People were looking at her, suspicious. Garún suddenly felt sick. She was squashed between humans and huldufólk who pushed her back and forth in waves, trapping her so that she felt as if the crowd was threatening to swallow her up, that she'd sink to the floor and be trampled to death. The music sounded like a relentless drone. The huldukonur were still yelling something aggressively at her. The only thought in her mind was to get out.

She saw a hint of daylight through an open door. The back alley. She tried to move towards it, squeeze herself through the crowd, but for every step she took she was pulled back by two.

She got hit in the back and lost her footing. The rest of her beer spilled on the floor and she was about to follow it when someone grabbed her hand and pulled her up.

He was tall and hefty, not fat and not muscular, just big. Even inside in the heat and the crowd he wore a thick coat; still, she didn't see a hint of sweat on his brow.

'I'm sorry! Are you okay?' he yelled over the noise.

'I'm going out!'

She turned away and kept moving towards the exit.

The light cut into her eyes and nothing made sense. The world was a collection of shards that by themselves had no meaning and that she couldn't put together. She managed to find a chair and sit down at a table. Everything spun around her. The man who had bumped into her suddenly sat next to her. He had two beers and put one on the table and pushed it towards her.

'Here. I'm sorry about being so clumsy before.'

'Ew,' she managed to say. She felt nauseous just looking at the beer. 'I'm too drunk. You'll have to drink it.' She leaned forwards on to the table. 'Eugh, I'm going to be so hung-over tomorrow!'

He laughed and started to roll himself a cigarette.

'I'll still take a cigarette if you can spare one,' she said.

'Of course. Do you smoke moss?'

'What?'

Her mind felt slow and groggy. Everything was crashing down around her. She felt like throwing up.

'Yeah, highland moss.'

She'd tried it once and didn't care for it. She didn't like those thaumaturgical drugs, like sorti and delýsíð.

'No, nothing like that, just tobacco. Lowland tobacco,' she said, drawing out the last words.

He laughed and handed her the cigarette.

'All right then. You should still have that beer. I'm not about to drink two at a time. If you want I can help with the hangover, sober you up a little.'

She lit her cigarette, but had a hard time doing it. She realised she was trying to light it in the middle. She adjusted her hand and lit it.

'What the hell are you talking about?'

He leaned in. 'I happen to know a thing or two. I'm a galdramaður.' He started to roll another cigarette for himself. 'I know a short incantation, a common household cantrip that I picked up out in the countryside. Carried me through all my student years. It's more like a kind of seiður, really, but there's some elements of galdur in it that technically...' He caught himself and shook his head. 'I'm sorry, never mind. That doesn't matter. It makes you sober up quickly, no hangover.'

'Aha. You don't say. Galdramaður.'

She mulled the word over, pronounced it slowly. She'd never met anyone who practised such a thing before. Not seriously, although lots of people knew simple chants or rituals. Herself included. Kukl had been a regular part of working life in Huldufjörður.

'So you're in Svartiskóli?'

He nodded.

'All right, then!' she said, throwing all caution to the wind. 'I don't want to be hung-over as shit tomorrow, I don't want to vomit, and I'd like that beer. So sing me one magic solution, please.'

He finished rolling the cigarette and lit it. The smell of moss was potent. He inhaled the smoke deeply. For a moment, she felt a distant sense of panic. Fear that she was doing something way too dangerous and reckless. Then he looked into her eyes and she saw nothing but kindness.

He started to talk. His voice sounded all around her. She closed her eyes and felt like a child in a cradle, in the arms of a mother who sang to her a comforting, incomprehensible poem.

Then she came back to herself. Her mouth was parched and the feeling of nausea was still as strong as before. She felt a pain gather behind her forehead.

'Aah!' She grabbed her head. 'You said there would be no hangover!'

'Yes, I'm sorry! That wasn't really accurate. It should only last for a moment.'

He was right. Suddenly the pain vanished and she felt as if she hadn't tasted a drop all night. She felt as if she had cheated in a test. She caught herself smiling. He beamed at her in return.

'You don't say. This is quite something.' She reached for the beer. 'I think I'll take this now.'

Her cigarette had gone out. She lit it again and tasted the drink. It tasted fresh, crisp. Like the first beer of the night. He sat there looking at her, suddenly kind of awkward. She found herself blushing. There was something different about him. There was something there she hadn't seen before. She didn't know what to call it. This was uncharted territory for her. A human stranger had rarely lent her a helping hand, except for that farmer who had smuggled her in through the wall years before. But even then it had mostly happened because of her own effort and determination.

'Skál,' she said and raised her beer.

He raised his drink and toasted with her, smiling.

'Skál to you.'

She smiled with him. 'My name is Garún.'

'Sæmundur.'

Tuttugu og sjö

Garún threw the waterproof sack tied around her waist on top of the decaying pier before she pulled herself up. Kryik'traak stayed behind in the river and stood watch. The jellyfish slid easily off her face. She spat out the blue mucus without retching or coughing, but still couldn't help an involuntary shiver. It became easier with practice, but was still always as repulsive.

The pier was about to fall apart, having been out of use for years. They were at a branch of the Elliðaár rivers that had once seen a lot of traffic, but had fallen into disrepair after the Crown came and a large part of the industry moved out to Grandi. Abandoned fisheries and machine workshops lined the docks, the crumbled coral buildings sticking out of the river on the verge of collapse. In the moonlight they looked like coarse porcelain, lined with cracks.

Sæmundur stood by a stack of fish tubs, almost invisible in the gloom. She wouldn't have noticed him except for the glow of a cigarette in his mouth. When Garún came closer she could smell the highland moss.

'So you finally showed up,' she said. 'I suppose the charm you gave me was just useless junk? Not like I'd tell the difference. Or did you spend your days in a stupor smoking moss?'

He shook his head. 'Stop it. I'm sorry I let you down. I was ...

in the middle of something difficult. But I'm here now. I want to help, if I can.'

'And you're going to do that by getting stoned?' It seemed as if he was about to protest, but she didn't give him the chance. 'No, you know what – I don't care. It's your business.'

He didn't let go. 'The thaumaturgical effect of the moss can affect galdur, Garún. I'm not—'

'A drug addict? Like I said – I don't give a shit. And I mean it.' She shuffled her feet. 'I need you to talk to the Ram Eaters. Katrín owes them money, a considerable amount. We need them on our side and we can't have them interfering with us because of Katrín, if we're going to pull this off.'

'Do what, exactly? And why does Katrín owe them money?'

'She smokes sorti. Smoked. She's clean now.'

'Right. I'll talk to him.'

'His people suffered greatly at the protest. He must be furious. We can offer him retaliation in the name of the Ram Eaters. Tell him we'll be striking against the Crown soon. We'd appreciate their help in the aftermath, if possible. You'll also be helping us with that – if you're up for the task.'

'Anything,' he said.

She winced from the sycophantic offering of help, the eagerness of it. Thought of the quagmire of guilt and cowardice it spawned from. Sickening.

'At a certain time, we need you to use galdur to disable Loftkastalinn. Permanently, if possible. That can be Rotsvelgur's revenge.'

It was an impossible request. A gargantuan undertaking, worthy of an army. But as she suspected, he instead tilted his head, considering it, weighing his options, probably already conceiving an insane method of making this suicidal request actually work. And that pleased her. She told him when, and where. Told him what they planned to do, and why. About the protests, the raid. He had no idea what had been happening.

'Níðstöng,' he said, after her summary. 'Raising a níðstöng might do the trick. Rotsvelgur has suffered great dishonour at the hands of the Crown. We could offer to take out Loftkastalinn as retribution for the Ram Eaters.'

Fucking bastard.

'I just said that, before. I literally just suggested that you do that.'

Sæmundur looked embarrassed.

'Oh, well, I...'

'Listen, I don't care. Whatever.' She refocused on what really mattered. 'Take it out? Do you think you can actually do that?'

'I can do wondrous things now, Garún.' He sounded gleeful, excited at the prospect. 'Unimaginable things. I'll do anything I can to help you.'

She looked out over the Elliðaár, away from him, taking in the city lights glistening like earthbound stars underneath the moon. Tried to calm herself, soothe the rage that threatened to burst at any moment. The moon was out, bathing the river in light, except the spot where Sæmundur stood.

'Why are you standing there in the shadows?'

'Because. It's safer.'

She squinted, trying to see him better than as a black outline. Her eyes hurt from the strain, despite her seeing just fine in the gloom. The darkness was stronger around Sæmundur. Just like she'd seen around the police officers who had tried to arrest him.

'What have you been doing these last days? How did you not know about the protest? About the crisis this society is facing? What are you hiding with you in the dark?'

She moved closer to him, starting to feel the restraints of her rage come undone. What kind of mental condition was he in if he really intended to risk raising a níðstöng? She wished she cared enough about him to tell him not to do it, but any semblance of sympathy towards him had been incinerated when she found Mæja's remains.

She'd buried her dead cat in the backyard. It was dangerous to linger, having found two decomposing corpses of soldiers in the living room. The sight made her sick to her stomach, the entire vile scene of horrors, but she felt that if she hadn't given herself that moment to say goodbye to Mæja she would have lost something integral to herself.

Sæmundur tossed away the cigarette and crushed it underneath his heel. He blew thick smoke and stepped out of the darkness.

Garún had been shocked when she last saw him in the Forgotten Downtown. She hadn't been prepared for the changes that had taken place. He had been skinny and pale, his eyes empty. But she'd told herself that it was temporary, that he was under pressure.

But now there was no question about it. He was like a walking corpse, a shade that was neither alive nor dead. His skin was waxy and stretched, his hair like dead weeds. But his eyes were the worst. He was like a thing out of a nightmare. His clothes were filthy, caked with dried blood and mud. His presence itself was uncomfortable, as if someone else was present with him, constantly whispering something just beyond hearing, so that it was driving her mad. It was as clear as day that he was walking a road to damnation, an irreversible path that he'd chosen for himself long before she had realised it.

'Sæmundur...'

She couldn't say anything else. She'd taken an involuntary step back, her hand brought up to her face in shock and revulsion.

He looked at her, broken, but in some depraved way stronger than she had ever seen him before.

'What did you do to yourself?'

'I'm close, Garún, so close,' he said in a trembling voice. 'All my theories have been accurate, about frequency, syllables, about *sound*, but I've learned so much more, and I've still got so much to learn.'

As he spoke his voice became more intense and the whispering that Garún felt she could almost hear became more agitated, still in this surreal place between hearing and imagining. For every step he took forwards, she took one back, until she was close to the end of the pier. She cursed herself for not bringing the goggles with her.

'You're sick, Sæmundur,' she said calmly. 'You're very sick. What would I see if I looked at you with thaumaturgical goggles?'

Sæmundur hesitated, looking shamefaced.

'I saw something, when you found me in the alley,' Garún continued, 'and I saw you through the goggles. The darkness around you was glowing with... some kind of force. But you seemed untouched. Would I still see that? Or is the darkness now a part of you, every bone in your body tinted blue, glowing with fiends and demons?'

'You know *nothing!*' he spat. '*Nothing!* You are as small-minded as the sheep in Svartiskóli! How can you say that, after the concert, after seeing that vision? You cannot begin to realise what sort of phases of existence have opened themselves to me, the thresholds I have crossed!' He ran his thin hand through his grimy hair and slowly breathed out, forcing himself to calm down. 'Don't give me this fake concern now, Garún,' he said in a defeated tone. 'Cut the bullshit. I'm about to raise a níðstöng for you, for your cause.' He snorted. 'Please. You're the same,

346

you'd sacrifice anything to further your own goals. Hypocrisy doesn't suit you.'

'I am also risking my life, and everyone else around me.'

It took everything she had to say these words with calm conviction. She felt as if she owed it to herself, to nail these points in his head with cold precision.

'But there's the difference between us, Sæmundur. I do what I do because I hope that something will change for the better. But you only want things to change for yourself. You're walking down a path that only ends in despair and darkness.'

'Darkness to you,' he said quietly, with zealous fervour. 'Enlightenment to me.'

She shook her head, filled with both disgust and an incredible rage against this idiotic stubbornness, this insufferable arrogance. He was worse than a child playing with fire.

'I don't know why I tried reasoning with you,' she said through clenched teeth. 'I do not give a fuck. Do what you will, Sæmundur, but for fuck's sake, don't mess this up. Try not to let others down for once in your life.'

She walked to the end of the dock, throwing her sack over her shoulders.

'There's another thing. After this is done I don't want to hear from you again – do you understand me?'

He had the nerve to look hurt.

'What? Why?'

'I went to your place. To hide, after the protest. I found Mæja. I buried her in your yard. Or what was left of her.'

He said nothing. Which was just as well. Reasoning, justifications, apologies, would have sent her over the edge. She was burning with anger, with resentment, hurt and betrayal. It felt good. It gave her something to hold on to.

She dived into the river. She didn't say goodbye.

ᚠ

'You've lost your fucking mind!'

Hrólfur was yelling, pacing back and forth in the plant-lit cave. Styrhildur and Hraki had joined the group, having safely made it to Elliðaár after the protest. They had called Kryik'traak in for the meeting as well. It was cramped down there, but that wouldn't matter much longer. Some of them would be moving locations soon.

'Kidnap Trampe? For what purpose? Parliament has already negotiated with Kalmar! We won!'

'Oh, cut the shit, Hrólfur!' Katrín spat out viciously. She'd recovered her strength now, and regained much of her fervour after seeing the news develop these last few days. 'You know that's a bullshit excuse of a settlement.'

'It's a start! They've cleared the gates for traffic,' Hrólfur continued, 'and they're limiting the roadblocks.'

'Roadblocks that shouldn't be there in the first place!'

'And there are still hundreds of huldufólk and huldumanneskjur inside the city, without any civil rights. Do you think that's fair?'

Hrólfur furrowed his brow and looked at Diljá. She shrugged. 'Huldumanneskjur?'

Garún was glad he'd caught that.

'I'm sick of this word – blendingur. Me, Styrhildur and Hraki have been talking. It's a word we've grown to despise. Blendingur. Hybrid. It's disgusting.'

'It's just a word,' said Diljá, sounding agitated about this change for some reason. 'It doesn't mean anything bad.'

Garún shook her head. 'Maybe devoid of all social context, of actually having to live carrying that around with you. Maybe in some detached, clinical meaning. But it's none of those things when it's used. It's hateful, divisive.'

'People spit it out like a curse,' said Hraki. 'It's not a nice word.'

'We're more than just a mix of two species,' said Styrhildur. 'It's a word of conflict and we're not conflicted – we know who we are. And we deserve an identity that's more than just focusing on being a mixture of something.'

Huldumanneskja was the word they'd landed on after some discussion: 'hulda' referencing the huldufólk, 'manneskja' meaning human person. A word they felt was free of conflict and ugly implications of tainted purity, that united rather than divided. When they'd found the word it was incredible how much lighter and freer Garún felt. It was a new beginning. And it was exhilarating.

'Whatever,' said Hrólfur, infuriatingly dismissive. 'This is all beside the point—'

'No, it's not,' said Styrhildur coolly.

'Lögrétta are negotiating with Kalmar,' he continued. 'They've even started discussions about giving us more control of Perlan, which is a huge step in gaining autonomy.'

'Who exactly is "us" here?' Katrín interjected. 'It's fantastic news for the Hrímlandic government, yes, many of whom are on the board of Innréttingarnar. Do you really believe they'll use this chance to improve the lives of regular people? It will only result in the Kalmar military paying a premium to Innréttingarnar for use of Perlan, flushing the board members' pockets. The Crown uses the power plant to fuel Loftkastalinn – a machine of war that they say is to protect us, but is used to keep us in our place! They'll never let it go.'

'Further drastic action at this point will only make things worse!' Hrólfur persisted.

'Worse?' Garún couldn't believe this. First his cowardice at the protest, now this. 'They're fucking killing us, Hrólfur! They massacre us in public like it's nothing, and then print news articles about how a wild mob attacked "innocent" people and police officers, who were just doing their honest duty defending Lögrétta! They kill us for demanding basic rights and rewrite history to make us sound like hooligans. Like the people who died deserved it.'

'So we fight back, the right way.' Diljá looked miserable as she saw the fracture forming in the group. 'We get a new printing press, we print the true side of—'

'Oh, please,' said Garún. 'Spare me. Just how long do you think you can fight a fucking war with only words? Do you really think that some well-worded articles will grant us basic rights?'

Hrólfur threw his arms up in an exaggerated gesture.

'What on earth do you hope to achieve with this? You kidnap the stiftamtmaður, and then what? Hmm? What then? They'll find you, and they'll kill you. More innocent people will suffer until they do. That's the only thing you'll accomplish. The slaughter at the protest will become a daily event.'

'You're talking about starting a war, Garún,' said Diljá. 'I can't condone that. I can't be a part of that.'

'We're already at war,' Garún responded. 'And we'll lose something much more important than our lives if we don't fight. I can't believe you're against us on this. After all the suffering they've made huldufólk endure.'

'Things are changing,' said Diljá. 'For the last few years, more and more huldufólk are getting proper citizenship. Blendingar—'

'Huldumanneskjur.'

'I didn't … I'm sorry … Huldumanneskjur will get more rights as society changes.'

Garún pretended to think this over, nodding to herself.

'Right. We just have to sit and wait for Kalmar to deem us worthy of receiving basic rights. Sit down and shut up. And for what? To have the right to fully belong to their sick, warmongering empire? Fuck that.'

Styrhildur, Katrín and Hraki showed their agreement with Garún, raising their fists in support as if they were at a meeting.

'Nothing really changes without direct action. You know that's true. But maybe you don't want things to really change.'

Diljá looked at them in turn, hurt and desperate. She reached out. Her face changed when she made the connection with Garún. Styrhildur and Hraki reached out as well, further twisting Diljá's face into some form of fear or despair. Garún felt her emotions: her uncertainty of being against doing this; the mortal fear of possibly following through with it; her nascent love for Hrólfur, and how it was pulling her in the opposite direction.

You're a coward, Garún couldn't help but think to herself.

She saw from Diljá's surprise, as if she had been stung, that she'd noticed some form of her emotional response through their connection.

'There is another way,' said Diljá as Garún cut her off. 'There always is.'

'No. This time there isn't.'

Hrólfur turned to Kryik'traak, who had been sitting silently in the small pool that provided the only exit from the cave.

'What do you make of this? I can't believe that the Coral Spires would be on board with a full-on act of terrorism.'

Kryik'traak took long moments to contemplate his words, his piscine face still unreadable to Garún. She'd already approached him and garnered his support, but she had only a vague idea of how reliable that was.

'There is a divide in the great lakes,' he said, measuring his words precisely. 'The general consensus is that Kalmar does ultimately – and inevitably – more harm to all marbendlar off the shores of Hrímland, especially those dwelling in lakes. Reykjavík has become a noose around our neck. We would not rely on the kindness of an empire such as Kalmar for the right to breathe.'

'Wait – do the Coral Spires of Þingvallavatn know about this?' asked Hrólfur.

Kryik'traak shook his head. 'There can be no outside communication. It is our consensus here, in Elliðavatn, that it would do us better to support further action against Kalmar.'

'Kalmar is your main source of trade!'

Kryik'traak pointed an accusatory finger at Hrólfur. *Mind yourself.*

'It is our *only* source of trade. My people have roamed the northern seas freely for centuries. Now, we cannot move unless it is with the blessing of their warships and accountants. They have developed underwater ships. Land, sky, ocean – they will soon move into the heart of our homeland. The deep sea. We must act.'

'And you think any of that will change by seceding?'

'It will grant us autonomy,' said Kryik'traak, a trace of annoyance seeping into his voice. 'It will grant us freedom to sail on our own terms, under our own banners.'

'You're starting to sound like a royalist,' said Styrhildur, glaring at Hrólfur.

'He does,' said Garún, disappointedly. 'But he's just afraid. Which is somehow worse.'

'I can't believe this,' said Hrólfur. 'I can't fucking believe this. And what's the plan? The stiftamtmaður is your hostage – let's just give us that fucking outrageous outcome – and then what? Declare independence? Put actions in motion that will end with Reykjavík being bombarded by Loftkastalinn, as Kalmar is forced to declare war on its own colony?'

'Loftkastalinn will—'

Hraki fell quickly silent as his sister grabbed his arm. Garún felt them reaching out to each other, communicating in an unseen whirlwind, then reaching a consensus.

'That's not your concern any more,' he said.

'You say that Lögrétta sold us out for Perlan,' said Diljá. 'What makes you think they'll use Trampe's kidnapping to further citizens' rights?'

'We'll demand that they do, publicly,' Katrín replied. 'And I think people will support us. The royalists still have a significant part of the seats in Lögrétta, but even they will know it's political suicide to stand firmly with Kalmar after what's happened. Most of them must be doubting their overlords by now. The Citizens' Party split into the Home Rule Party because of the events of the last few weeks. The political landscape is all set for a final push. They'll use Trampe's absence to push for further independence, I'm sure of it. They'd have the legal grounds to do so. And with home rule at least, we'll better be able to make our own laws for all our peoples.'

'The Coral Spires will want to use the opportunity as well,' said Kryik'traak. 'It is our hope to renew the old treaties from before the Commonwealth.'

'A unified nation,' said Katrín.

'That will happen with time.' Diljá sounded almost pleading. 'Please. Even if all this happens, Kalmar will just retaliate with even more force. No more violence. Haven't enough people died?'

The silence that followed smothered the question, still hovering in the air around them.

'I think it's best we go.'

Hrólfur reached for Diljá's hand. She hesitantly took it, not willing to believe that this was happening.

'The Crown will still be looking for you,' said Garún. 'They won't stop just because a temporary political ceasefire is in order.'

'I have other places to hide,' said Hrólfur sternly. 'Focus on worrying about yourselves.'

With that, they left. The people remaining – Garún, Katrín, Styrhildur, Hraki and Kryik'traak – started planning out how they would do the impossible.

Commit an act of treason and possibly war.

Disable Loftkastalinn.

Ambush Trampe.

Spark the revolution.

Tuttugu og átta

The train shook along the rails and Sæmundur suppressed a moan. The wound had stopped bleeding as soon as the ritual was completed, but the pulsing pain was steady and the flesh was weak and incredibly sensitive. He was unsure how long had passed since he'd performed the ritual. Days? Weeks? It still hurt as badly as the moments after the ceremony, before he had blacked out. He felt Bektalpher's lips move inside his shirt, a non-stop torrent of powerful incantations, whispers dancing just beyond the limits of human hearing. Kölski was bound into shadow, which frequently was cast in the wrong direction compared to how the light fell, sometimes moving out of sync with Sæmundur himself. There was nothing to be done about that. All he could hope was that no one would notice.

The ritual had taken a lot more out of him than he had imagined. After he regained consciousness he had just lain there in the temple for the longest time, discarded in the dust and broken rubbish like another forgotten idol. He shook from the blood loss, too weak to move from hunger and thirst. But also from something else. A loss, a sacrifice he didn't quite yet comprehend. When he found the strength to stand up he wasn't thirsty or hungry any more. He'd possibly been lying there for three or four days, maybe a week – he wasn't certain. And that was only the time he was conscious. The entire ordeal ran together into one, ceaseless moment. At some point he had realised that Garún had called out to him, that the charm he'd given her had been broken. It was effortless to place her in the city, hidden deep in the earth by the Elliðaár rivers. A pang of guilt stung him, all the more deep and hurtful because it was as if other emotions had become something more resembling a distant memory. She had been his last tether. Now, it seemed even that had been severed.

He sat on the train, heading towards Elliðabær and then north to the last stop at Gufunes. Nobody would sit near him. Probably he reeked of sweat and dried blood. He'd been sensible enough to try to clean the blood off his face and his clothes, but it didn't do much good. He still felt how it had dried in the nooks and crannies of his body and clothes. He could constantly smell iron in his nostrils. It felt somehow right to him. This is who he was now.

All logic went against taking the train. There were more seiðskrattar around than usual, and they'd see Sæmundur stand out like a wolf in a sheep shed, glowing from the demonic possession that had taken root in him. He should be moving through the city in secret, on foot, in the cover of night. But somehow he didn't care. He moved through the checkpoints like a ghost. He hadn't come across any seiðskrattar, but what would it matter? A seiðskratti stood no chance against him at this point. Sæmundur wondered idly which bone exactly Bektalpher had possessed in him. Was it the sternum? Or perhaps in a completely different place – his femur, perhaps? He didn't feel any different, except for the pain and the weird feeling coming from the newly grown orifice on his chest. He didn't feel Bektalpher's presence in a spiritual sense; he still very much felt like himself. How long could one walk around with a demon in one's bones without realising it?

The train came to a halt at Gufunes and Sæmundur got out. Police officers were standing watch inside the station, but didn't spare him a second glance. To them he was just another hobo, and as long as he got out of there they didn't want to turn him into their problem. The station was crowded with workers from the harbour or the factories. Sæmundur limped against the flow of workers heading home, getting out without trouble.

The city walls had three main gates: Grafarhlið to the east, Rauðavatnshlið to the south-east and the main gate to the south, simply called Suðurhlið. Officially those were the only ways in and out of the city – at least they were the only roads leading in or out. But dotted around the walls were smaller gates, not intended for heavy traffic, mostly used by the Crown or the authorities. One such entrance was at the north side of the wall in Gufunes. Sæmundur had a clear view of the exit straight down an empty street. The large, heavy iron doors were broad enough for a horse, but too small for a carriage. Two soldiers stood watch. There were no seiðskrattar nearby and neither of them seemed to have thaumaturgical googles, as far as Sæmundur could see. Behind them towered the city wall. Soldiers marched back and forth on top of its battlements, their helmets shining in the sunlight. The outer side of the wall was mounted with iron-grey cannons, like spears set against whatever threat the cursed nature could send their way.

Usually Sæmundur would have strolled up to the guards, calm as you can be, stealthily palming them a small bundle of bills without any suspicion. These types of men were not above accepting bribes – especially if they were guarding the gate leading to Hræfuglaey. But Sæmundur was filthy and bloody, and – what was worse – broke. The guards would perhaps let a hobo through, but only if he could pay them. He couldn't make himself literally invisible, and getting through with force could have some unfortunate consequences later on. He wanted to do this without any trouble. He considered if he could weave an illusion to appear like a ranking officer, but decided against it. Too complicated, too risky. Not every problem was a nail to be hammered down with galdur. He needed a natural, effortless solution.

He monitored them, contemplating his next step. What was it like to guard the way to the most powerful tribe of náskárar in the greater Reykjavík region? Whose scorn incited greater fear – the Crown or Those-who-pluck-the-eyes-of-the-ram? Sæmundur stumbled away from the gate, into the nearby industrial area.

Tall chimneys stood black and still like ancient obelisks. Steelworks, quarries, repair shops for decrepit train wagons. Small rusted fishing boats slowly weathered down to ruins on an open gravel field, everything useful reclaimed from the wrecks a long time before. Nearby were a few restaurants, clustered close together. Messy workers' fare, soured and smoked meats served in dining halls lined with grimy tables where people sat, snuffing tobacco and drinking oily, tar-coloured coffee. Sæmundur went behind one of the diners, to the alleyway where they took out the trash. A gust of blue-black wings swirled up at his arrival as ravens jumped up from open trash containers and rolled-over bins, which they had cleverly pushed over and opened. They sat up on the eaves and stared at him sideways and down their long beaks, so similar to their cousins that Sæmundur was made uncomfortable.

He rooted around in the open container until he found what he was looking for. Svið. The singed sheep's head was dried and half-eaten, likely around a week old. He shut the lid on the container and placed the leftovers on top of it. Then he waited.

ᚠ

A short while later Sæmundur walked up to the gate where the two soldiers stood guard. They saw him coming, but didn't show any reaction.

Good so far, Sæmundur thought to himself.

'Halt,' one of them said in a thick continental accent when Sæmundur was close enough. 'This gate is closed to general traffic.'

'My apologies, my lord, my apologies.' Sæmundur bowed reverently and repeatedly, making himself as low as he possibly could in front of these great lords in their polished armour, each wielding a skorrifle. 'I do not mean to interrupt, but ...' He hesitated, glancing behind him, as if he was afraid of being followed. 'I have an important message. Very important.'

'Get lost!' the soldier spat.

The other one tightened his grip on his rifle. They wouldn't hesitate to shoot him and no one would mind. It was fully within their rights.

'No, my lord, I beg your forgiveness, I am sorry, please, I am only a messenger.'

'What do you mean?'

Sæmundur hesitated again. The soldier lost his patience.

'What the fuck do you mean, man? Spit it out!'

At that moment Sæmundur pulled out the carcass he had been hiding under his coat. The raven's feathers were shredded, its eye sockets empty and its intestines hanging out.

'I have a message, my lord. I am but a messenger. A message to Those-who-pluck-the-eyes-of-the-ram, from Bare-bones-in-an-empty-ravine.'

The soldiers exchanged an uneasy glance. A tribal feud was a bloody and ruthless matter. Those-who-pluck-the-eyes-of-the-ram and Bare-bones-in-an-empty-ravine were two of the largest tribes in the south-west corner of the country. Other species rarely got involved in these feuds, so tribal politics weren't always clear to those outside náskárar society. But if they interfered with the message being relayed, they might have to pay for it. Nobody wanted a dishonoured or shamed náskári after them.

'Go on,' the soldier hissed.

Sæmundur limped towards them. They opened the iron doors just wide enough for him to get through, and as soon as he did they locked it behind him.

The fresh ocean breeze greeted Sæmundur on the other side of the wall. He breathed easier. Nature lay spread out before him, sea and snowy mountains, great and barren and immortal. To think that all of this ruthless, overwhelming nature was locked out of sight behind the walls, so people could forget that something greater and infinitely more powerful than them lurked at their threshold.

An overgrown path went down from the wall to the beach, where a thin stretch of land made of sand reached out towards the island of Hræfuglaey. The Crown had made a land bridge to it shortly after completing the wall, much to the chagrin of the náskárar. A black cloud of náskárar swarmed around the sheer cliffs of the island. He could hear the faint noise of their crowing and cawing, crude and ancient sounds.

Sæmundur tossed the raven's carcass as soon as he gained a proper amount of distance from the wall. A dead raven was one of the greatest insults there was, doubly so if mutilated, and if Bare-bones-in-an-empty-ravine had really sent Those-who-pluck-the-eyes-of-the-ram a dead raven, all hell would break loose in Reykjavík. The tribes regularly fought among themselves, but it was more tradition than real conflict. A mutilated and ravaged raven's carcass was a grave insult and equal to a declaration of war, having different meanings depending on what was done to the raven itself. Sæmundur had no idea what an eyeless raven with its intestines hanging out meant, but whatever it was it could not be anything good. He knew as much, as did the soldiers at the gate.

Two great shadows circled above him. He saw no glint of iron at this distance, but he was certain that they were blóðgögl. He kept on walking, not hesitating, trying not to consider if they'd notice that his shadow didn't fall according to the sunlight. Thankfully it was fairly overcast, but still the sun hung low in the sky at this time of year.

He looked up. The shadows were larger now, lower in the sky. He walked on to the beach. Black seaweed cracked under his feet, dried out from the sun and the frost. The waves fell in a droning murmur. The ocean was calm, unusual for Hrímland. Náskáraey loomed ahead of him. It wasn't a proper island, more like a cluster of cliffs jutting out of the ocean, close to each other. The rocks were sheer, so thin and tall that one could hardly deem them to be islands. But the cliffs had always been named as a single place, one of the oldest homes of náskárar in Hrímland. Their capital, so to speak.

The earth shook as two náskárar landed right in front of him, laden with iron. Blóðgögl, as he rightly suspected. They were considerably taller than him, despite stooping. One of them could barely keep his head aloft due to the sharp lump of iron that was fused to the upper side of his beak. The iron was dark, coarse and uneven, like lava that had only recently hardened.

'Away,' one of them cawed.

The náskárar strutted back and forth on the rocky beach, each step screeching from their iron talons. Their walk was uneven, mostly supporting themselves on the krummafótur, which was much larger than the other two legs, its claw big enough to carry grown sheep or men aloft.

'No humans. Away.'

Sæmundur raised his hands and showed that he was no threat. He wondered how different náskárar were from humans – if they could hear the demon fused in his flesh, whispering. It was too late to worry about that now. He felt Bektalpher's sensitive and bloated lips move, ceaselessly chanting the incantations that held Kölski back.

'I am Sæmundur. Rotsvelgur sent for me. This is regarding my debt to him.'

The one that had spoken regarded him inquisitively. As if he was considering if it was worth the trouble to devour this little vermin or not. Sæmundur stared down the long beak, not buckling under the heavy and crushing stare.

'He left me a rat king,' Sæmundur added.

The náskári tilted its head, turning to the one which was heavily ironed on his beak, spitting out a question in skramsl that Sæmundur didn't quite catch. The iron beak replied that Rotsvelgur would want to meet this one, in what Sæmundur felt was a harsh tone. He was too unfamiliar with the náskárar tongue. If he didn't focus completely every caw sounded like an ugly, warped sound that couldn't possibly have some sort of meaning behind it.

The iron beak turned to Sæmundur and spoke in a voice so rough it could hardly be deciphered as Hrímlandic.

'Go. You will pay.' This was not a question.

'I'm here to settle my debt, yes.'

The iron beak took a threatening step towards him, ruffling his wings.

'You – pay.'

He took flight with a powerful beat of his wings. The other

one followed, but not before also giving Sæmundur a threatening stare.

Sæmundur sighed and kept walking towards the island. He had never been to Hræfuglaey before; usually he met Rotsvelgur in Reykjavík. As he came closer he noticed sun-faded ropes hanging down the length of the cliff. Next to the ropes dangled a tattered rope ladder that went all the way to the top. The wooden steps were badly made and looked as if they would break under the smallest strain. Clearly the náskárar didn't care if their ground-dwelling visitors made it up or fell down to their deaths. Sæmundur was certain that they would have preferred to murder him where he stood and feed their hatchlings fresh meat. But he owed the hersir and that was more a matter of honour than money. To a náskári, Sæmundur as good as belonged to the hersir until his debt was paid. To murder him would be like killing livestock – restitution would be owed to its owner, should that occur. Sæmundur took hold of the rope ladder and slowly made his way up.

When Sæmundur moved to the city he'd quickly started smoking moss, which is what led to his connection to Rotsvelgur. They'd done a lot of business while Sæmundur attended the Learned School. He started selling to the students, who were mostly too afraid or prejudiced to deal directly with a náskári. The náskárar were prolific up north, where a clan ruled over each fjord, their power struggles constantly in motion but rarely interfering with human society. Mostly they left the farmers alone; the humans had picked up a few of their customs and knew how to approach the ravenfolk with honour and respect. Sæmundur used that to his advantage in Reykjavík, where the náskárar remained elusive and threatening. When Sæmundur graduated and moved abroad, Rotsvelgur had just made his way to power in Those-who-pluck-the-eyes-of-the-ram, after months of internal fighting. Rotsvelgur had slain his own father, a great bird of prey and hersir of many decades. To fall to your own offspring was not a disgrace among náskárar, it was a noble and good fate. It meant that the young were worth something, that the future was theirs to claim – not to suggest that the parents wouldn't fight for their lives with iron and claw. Many great tribal leaders killed their offspring in droves, but they never attacked them first. The initiative to murder and coup belonged to the youth.

After many years of study abroad, Sæmundur came back to Reykjavík and attended Svartiskóli. Rotsvelgur had stamped the other tribes down into the muck. Greater Reykjavík belonged to him, there was no denying it. Sæmundur had started selling for Rotsvelgur again, dealing directly with him as if nothing had changed, which was unique. Only his underlings dealt with humans and huldufólk directly, like Hræeygður, who had apparently sold Katrín sorti. Sæmundur didn't know why he'd been deserving of this exception and hadn't given it a great deal of thought. Until Rotsvelgur had demanded galdur of him. Now, as he clambered up the unforgiving cliffs of Hræfuglaey, blowing in the unpredictable wind, he wished he'd asked himself that sooner.

A gust of wind grabbed hold of his coat and he almost lost his footing. Despite appearances the ladder was sturdy, although in bad condition and rarely used.

He hoisted himself to the top of the cliff and lay there for a moment, exhausted. Pale yellow grass sprouted between the rocks, spattered with moss and bird droppings. The two náskárar were waiting for him, silent and motionless. Their feathers ruffled in the wind. Sæmundur started to get up, but started coughing so badly that he collapsed back into the grass. The coughing fit tore at his lungs deeply and he tasted blood. He thought of Bektalpher, of the wound on his chest which was even now whispering curses with a voice from a world other than this one. He wondered if they shared lungs or if the demon had grown its own. It didn't matter. All that mattered was that it worked.

Finally he got a hold on himself and breathed normally. He looked into his hand and expected to see blood. Instead there was a thick, black ichor, which he quickly wiped into the earth. He didn't know if it was caused by the demon in him or the amount of highland moss he had smoked, and he didn't care to know.

The náskárar led him to the centre of the island, toward a gaping cavern. At first it looked to be naturally formed, but when Sæmundur looked closer he saw that its edges were too curved, its form too regular. A circular staircase went down into the darkness. One náskári started walking down the stone stairs with loud clunks. Sparks flew with each step. Sæmundur looked up at the swarm of náskárar in the sky, over to the other island cliffs where they hung in droves like black soot. He wondered if any man had made it back alive from these catacombs.

'Move!' the iron beak spat.

When Sæmundur didn't move immediately the náskári jabbed him with his beak, causing him to stumble and almost fall down the steep staircase, where he would definitely have broken his neck. The other náskári was already out of sight, around the corner.

The tunnels were just wide enough for two náskárar to meet and pass each other. Small holes were carved into the walls where tallow candles burned. The tunnels were perfectly round, seeming rather to have been shaped like clay than carved out. Dense rows of incomprehensible hrafnaspark were etched into its surface, covering the entire circumference of the tunnel. Sæmundur had intended to learn the náskárar script but had given up when he realised how alien their method of writing was. Every letter was a sound, but also a specific word, which could be read from right to left, left to right, up, down, diagonally, however you wanted, constantly and consistently revealing new meanings its author had intended. He was surrounded by a woven tapestry of words, a dense net he neither felt nor understood.

The air carried with it the potent stench of rotten meat and wet animals. The tunnels split several times, but each path looked the same, dark and empty, every inch of surface covered with writing. Sæmundur could not keep count of how often they turned, one náskári ahead of him and the other just behind him. All he knew was that they were heading down.

The tunnels suddenly ended in a sheer drop. He was faced with grey daylight and the sound of crashing waves and the shouts of the ravenfolk. A weathered rope bridge danced in the wind, reaching out to the next cliff island. The drop to the ocean was significant. He must be higher up than Haraldskirkja, despite making his way down from the top. The náskári ahead of him had taken a step aside and was hanging off the side of the cliff like a gargoyle. Náskárar filled the air like swarms of enormous flies, crowing and shouting.

'Forward,' the iron beak crowed behind him.

Sæmundur didn't wait to be pushed a second time and walked out onto the bridge.

The bridge was in absolute disrepair, looking even worse than the rope ladder. He focused on not looking down, but then he did and the vertigo hit him so hard he almost lost his balance.

'The flesh is weak,' he mumbled to himself. 'The spirit is willing though the flesh is weak.'

The wind rushed around him as náskárar flew over and under him, shouting and cawing. Posturing or curious at the sight of the stranger, or perhaps only passing by, indifferent to his being there. The fear of heights was unfamiliar to them.

This island was much older than the other one. Its cavern walls were rougher and the hrafnaspark covering it was more weathered. The faded carvings were like ripples on water. The feeling filled him with dread. Nobody better knows the power of language than a galdramaður.

They entered a hall, the ceiling shrouded with darkness. Sæmundur was beset by náskárar everywhere. They were hanging from the cavern walls, filling up the alcoves that lined each side. They sat in nests made from shining metals, coloured glass and corrugated plates of iron, or stood like statues on their krummafótur, the claws on the other legs free to carve bone, sharpen tools, pick meat off bones. A menacing chatter erupted as he entered and every náskári turned to get a look at him. This was where the greatest warriors of the tribe resided. One such blóðgagl had an iron beak covered with long, sharp nails, another had a sawtoothed horn at the end of his beak. Every single náskári was heavily decorated with jewellery and bones. Sæmundur tried to spot the difference between male and female corvians, but could not see it. In the middle of the cavern was a roaring fire. The floor was covered with junk and carcasses picked clean. Cows, sheep and other things Sæmundur did not want to look too closely at. He and his guards headed straight to Rotsvelgur's throne at the end of the hall, where he waited alongside his closest court members and councillors.

Rotsvelgur loomed over the other náskárar, who all but cowered in his presence. The helskurn and infused beak and talons already made him look like a living weapon, coupled with the morbid trophies he displayed on his hertygi. As Sæmundur approached the hersir he felt the emanations of the galdur loaded in Rotsvelgur's armour radiate off him, a sickening wave of fear and awe.

Rotsvelgur's closest council was comprised of aged warriors, covered with scars and laden with symbols of victory, some of the oldest members with spots of rust in their iron. All of them were blóðgögl, except one, the náskári sitting closest to Rotsvelgur. The tribe's skrumnir was barely taller than Sæmundur, dressed in dark grey cloth, making him seem like a spectre or a monstrous creature out of legend.

Sæmundur halted at a respectable distance from Rotsvelgur. The hersir stood up when he saw who had arrived. The throne, if it could be called so, was a great nest made from scrap iron, fused together in the unique náskárar method. The iron beak who had escorted Sæmundur announced his arrival in skramsl and the chatter increased. Rotsvelgur let loose a single caw and the noise died out instantly.

'Sæmundrr,' Rotsvelgur said in rough Hrímlandic, 'arr þérr arriv'd to pay the skuld?'

'Hail and well met, Rotsvelgur. I received your message and have come to offer you a settlement. For my hand and for the hand of Katrín Melsteð, the debtor of Hræeygður.'

For a while the only sound came from the sparking of the fire.

'Skuld arr great,' Rotsvelgur said eventually. 'Higher after ... *faulty smithing* þérr ha't work'd.'

He especially enunciated those two words, glaring maliciously at Sæmundur. Something had gone wrong with the galdur he'd performed – or Rotsvelgur was bluffing. He was wearing the armour, so it had to be working in some regard. Sæmundur was not about to get hustled into even deeper debt.

'The skuld of other ...'

He nodded to a náskári hanging from the wall. A young, ironed blóðgagl. That must be Hræeygður. He crowed some kind of amount in skramsl. Sæmundur didn't quite catch it, but it sounded like a high number. Rotsvelgur feigned surprise at the amount of the debt.

'Arr-at small. But – þérr shall't settle?'

'Yes,' said Sæmundur, keeping his manner calm and natural. 'I have come on behalf of the people you have stood with against the Crown in the last two protests. The people who died with you on Austurvöllur, rising up against Kalmar.'

At this there was an eruption of noise around him, as outrage moved the náskárar. He must tread carefully. He had no idea of the political machinations which had led to the Ram Eaters showing up at the protests, nor of how he should speak of those who had died in them.

'For too long Kalmar has oppressed us. We intend to strike back.'

Rotsvelgur started strutting back and forth in front of Sæmundur, his claws hitting the nest of scrap iron.

'Ok hvat use shall't ek ha't of such weaklings? Reykjavík belong't to *Krxgraak'úrrtek!*'

At this the náskárar roared, crowing and shouting and slamming their talons against the rock.

'It is true that Those-who-pluck-the-eyes-of-the-ram are the most powerful tribe,' said Sæmundur, once they had settled down. 'Those-who-pluck-the-eyes-of-the-ram justly call the city of Reykjavík their territory. But one soars above every náskári. Kalmar now rules the skies, which once were your sole dominion! With Loftkastalinn and their biplanes!'

The náskárar went berserk. No one insults a náskári, let alone in his own hall. Rocks, scrap iron and gnawed bones rained over him. Rotsvelgur stood still, quiet. Silently waiting, like a raven waits for a lamb to get separated from its flock.

'Do I speak falsehoods?' Sæmundur shouted, and defended

himself against the junk that rained over him, tried to overpower the noise. 'Have they not, with biplanes and the flying fortress itself, ruled over the skies since they arrived?'

He wanted to keep going, but held back. He was dangerously close to being eviscerated, gouged with a beak or a claw and turned into a trophy to be hung from someone's hertygi.

'Did they not ruthlessly kill brave blóðgögl without retribution? Well, I offer you the ultimate retribution!' Sæmundur shouted in a grave voice. 'I will bring down Loftkastalinn – in the name of Those-who-pluck-the-eyes-of-the ram!'

The assembly laughed. A cascade of mocking, ugly sounds, horribly mimicking the human emotions behind it. Only Rotsvelgur did not caw at Sæmundur, staring heavily at him. The noise died down and the náskárar turned towards their hersir for an answer. Rotsvelgur remained silent, which Sæmundur took as a sign he could continue.

'Loftkastalinn is an abomination. A machine of war and destruction, drawing its power from the sorcerous energies in the land itself. Violence must be met with violence, fire with fire. This, every being knows – the náskárar doubly so. I will do what must be done to bring it down. I will make an abomination to bring down the abomination. For you I will raise a *níðstöng*, Rotsvelgur.' The word slithered through the air like a malevolent spirit. 'A svartigaldur so potent it will remove the flying fortress from the face of the earth.'

'Þérr err-at with honour,' said Rotsvelgur, his words echoing through the hall, 'to come hérr, to vor hall, deman't to pay't skuld wit' forneskju ok ruin the honour of *Krxgraak'úrrtek*.'

Sæmundur bowed deeply before the hersir.

'I did not intend to disparage your honour or the honour of Those-who-pluck-the-eyes-of-the-ram. You are without denial the strongest tribe in the greater Reykjavík area. But that doesn't change the fact that the Crown makes a mockery of you. It is obvious how great a thorn they are in your side. The truth does not belittle anyone. But I can change that. I can help you reclaim the sky.'

Rotsvelgur remained elusive to Sæmundur. He was hard to read. Still, years of camaraderie had something to show. He knew Rotsvelgur was intrigued. He only had to find a way to get him to accept without losing face.

'I know that galdur is an affront to your ways. But I am not suggesting that Those-who-pluck-the-eyes-of-the ram sully their talons with it. It is a low, dishonourable weapon – a human weapon. One human weapon to be used against another. That seems just to me.'

'Þérr lie't,' he said. 'Þérr megn-at that galdr.'

'I am not lying.'

Rotsvelgur ignored his claim.

'Hví shoul't þérr raise forneskja against Kalmar?' asked Rotsvelgur. 'Ok hví on vor behalf?'

'The debts I seek to pay are great, which calls for a great offering. The people who fought with you also need your help in the battle to come against Kalmar. Ensuring your supremacy over the skies will be in their benefit for the long term. Besides, we have a long history of mutual, beneficial trading.' Sæmundur tried not to sound as if he was attempting flattery. 'I must uphold my honour – and yours. It is clear to me that Kalmar is now the only thing standing in your way. Which means that Loftkastalinn was the only target that could ever be considered. That is why I offer my chosen profession – galdur.'

'Lies!' one náskári screeched in skramsl.

He was an ancient blóðgagl with such a great and heavy lump of iron on his beak that he could barely keep his head up. His feathers were faded and tattered, spots of rust in his iron claws and beak.

'If this *human* is telling the truth, if he can raise a níðstöng and contain' – Sæmundur didn't quite catch what he said – 'then it is for nothing!'

The corvian jumped down from his rock sill, stumbled towards Sæmundur in his odd three-legged gait and stopped right in front of him. It took everything Sæmundur had to hold his ground and not retreat from the threatening charge.

'Nothing!' the náskári screamed in his face and turned to Rotsvelgur. 'Where do you think the Crown would look first? Where would they next point their spears?'

Sæmundur had a hard time keeping up with the skramsl. If only human vocal cords were capable of properly pronouncing the náskárar language; he would be able to connect with them so much better if he spoke their tongue.

What about Bektalpher? he thought to himself. Would he be able to? Surely he must be able to generate non-human vocal sounds. He had to experiment on this later, in private.

'That's enough, Græðgnir,' said Rotsvelgur, but the old warrior kept on.

'It is not our way, *krrxgkh-hraak*. The malevolent poetry has been forbidden for generations!'

'Hold back your tongue, as you only speak what every single one of us is thinking!'

'*Krrxgkh-hraak*, I only—'

'I said silence!'

For a moment it was as if Rotsvelgur himself had flared up in a roaring blaze. The entire assembly recoiled, some náskárar letting out involuntary caws. For a moment, Rotsvelgur's voice and posture had commanded such fear and dominance that the entire room had succumbed to it. Græðgnir ruffled his feathers and tensed, as if he was about to challenge Rotsvelgur, but then flew up to one of the alcoves. Sæmundur suspected why Rotsvelgur wasn't entirely satisfied with the galdur he'd bound into the helskurn. It seemed way too potent, and possibly volatile. Rotsvelgur tilted his head, weighing the matter.

'Sólsvertnir!'

The hunched skrumnir came hobbling from the shadows behind the hersir, a wretch dressed in tatters. He looked like a runt next to the other proud warriors, but Sæmundur noticed that they still gave way, avoiding confrontation at any cost. They were frightened. It was a rare occasion when a náskári was born different from the rest, with a special feathered cape and breast shield they could raise up in a large, elliptical form. The feathers were coloured a vibrant azure, laced with seiðmagn, allowing them to devour either the mind or memory of whoever gazed upon them. These deviations became nearly without exception the tribe's skrumnir, powerful seiðskrattar that acted as the hersir's closest advisors. The skrumnir was also the tribe's chief blacksmith, using their unique form of seiður to bind molten iron to the náskárar's bodies.

Sólsvertnir bowed before Rotsvelgur, spreading out his wings, and addressed him formally.

Krrxgkh–hraak. Lord-master. Hersir.

They whispered among themselves. Sæmundur felt dizzy from the skrumnir's presence, now that he was closer. He almost glowed from the seiðmagn. Sæmundur thought of the power loaded in the blue-black feathers and felt a shiver run down his spine. But he did not avert his eyes, did not show any signs of weakness.

'I have known you for a long time, Sæmundur,' said Rotsvelgur in skramsl, making sure to speak slowly and clearly enough that Sæmundur could understand him. 'And I have not found any reason to suspect you of malice. So far.' He spread out his wings, raised his head back. 'What you suggest might spell the end of *Krxgraak'úrrtek* – or our salvation. We will glean what the future holds. Sólsvertnir!' he crowed out over the hall. 'Exercise the judgement of bones!'

The skrumnir ruffled around in his tattered robes and threw a clawful of bones on the floor. Ribs, jaws, skulls and bones of various shapes and sizes. Sólsvertnir huddled over the bones, investigating their layout and the shadows they cast carefully. Another náskári handed him a writhing sack and from it the skrumnir pulled a raven, tied at its beak and claws. The raven fruitlessly batted its wings. Sólsvertnir held the bird upside down over the bones and with a perfunctory movement decapitated it with one claw. Dark blood rained over the pale bones.

Sæmundur was familiar with this type of prophecy, but did not know the náskárar method specifically. He could not start to imagine what Sólsvertnir saw. He held an incantation mentally readied, a loaded gun or a dormant volcano, transformative words ready to erupt from his tongue and reshape the world.

Sólsvertnir pushed an occasional bone around with a long claw, contemplatively. He looked up at Sæmundur, right into his eyes. Then back to the bones, as if to verify something. Hesitantly, almost fearfully, the skrumnir glanced at Rotsvelgur's chest – his helskurn – and down at Sæmundur's feet. Where his shadow was cast in the wrong direction, towards the fire instead of away from it.

The skrumnir let loose a deafening screech and threw off his tatters. His blue-black feathers scintillated with an uncanny light, with streaks of turquoise so wondrous and maddening that Sæmundur couldn't help staring. The skrumnir tensed up, his feathers ruffling, preparing to spread out his feathered cape and devour Sæmundur's mind and memory. He couldn't speak. He wanted to, but found himself completely frozen up.

Then a voice that was not entirely human spoke.

Everything came to a halt. Nothing moved. The only sound was that measured rhythm of an unseen voice, those sharp syllables that unravelled reality. A dark blast blinded Sæmundur and for a moment nothing existed except this inversion, this blinding void, and then the world was pulled again over his consciousness like a veil.

Two blóðgögl jumped off from the walls above Sæmundur, diving with their jagged claws extended. One was knocked away by an unseen force, thrown against the stone wall with a sickening crack. The other one dived into Sæmundur, but his claws found no purchase, as if he had attacked a stone pillar instead of a human being. With a sharp spoken word, the skin on the náskári's back fissured open, erupting with blood, and the blóðgagl fell on the ground, writhing and twitching as it died in a pool of its own blood. The third blóðgagl jumped down in front of Sæmundur, crouching and pouncing with the krummafótur, coming at him beak-first. A wall of darkness burst from the ground, tethered to Sæmundur in long black coils. He ducked, and the náskári missed, crashing to the floor and sliding limply forward, the vivid darkness pooling rapidly towards it like ravenous carrion-eaters.

Sólsvertnir was lying on the ground. His feathers had lost their lustre and Sæmundur no longer felt disoriented looking at them. In front of him stood Kölski, now manifested from the shadow. He wasn't sure who had spoken the incantation – himself, the demon in front of him or the demon inside him. Partly he felt that there was no distinction to be made. Not a single náskári moved. Everything was still. They were too terrified.

Rotsvelgur's feathers were agitated with rage. He stared down at the man, or what he thought was a man, and the grinning demon at his feet. For the first time in the years Sæmundur had known Rotsvelgur, he truly feared the náskári and what he might do to enact his vengeance.

'Sólsvertnir,' Rotsvelgur said after a while. 'Rise.'

The skrumnir raised himself, shaking like a feeble elder. Sæmundur noticed that he had been mistaken before, Sólsvertnir's feathers were as dangerous and lustrous as before, the seiðmagn flowing from them like a fresh delýsíð painting Garún had made. But something was different. Something had changed.

Then he realised it. It was he himself who had changed. Not Sólsvertnir.

'What did the bones tell you?' Rotsvelgur asked, without taking his eyes off Sæmundur. 'What was the judgement?'

The skrumnir spoke in a weak voice. Not a soul stirred in the great hall.

'What has been bound in blood and locked in bone has spoken. The human carries' – he said a word Sæmundur couldn't quite understand – 'in himself. Will that be both curse and blessing to us. He stands blinded at the cave mouth, ruin is within his power and the foulest sorcery. He has shown his nature with shed blood, but no more will come of it. He means the tribe no ill. He will birth a horror into this world to end the iron fortress. Kalmar will not seek us because of his malevolence. But untold innocent lambs will pay with their blood. As is the nature of the world.'

'Very well.'

Rotsvelgur stepped forward and picked up a great spear that was lying hidden in the iron nest that was his throne. Sæmundur noticed something that, to his mind, didn't belong in this scrap metal heap. Hidden in the middle of the pile were a few speckled indigo eggs.

'Sæmundur, I name you a malefactor and harbinger of ruin,' said Rotsvelgur slowly in skramsl. 'I accept your galdur as payment of your debt and the one you call Melsteð, with the condition that you never set foot here and never consort with Those-who-pluck-the-eyes-of-the-ram again. Our association is at an end. Your debt shall be considered paid in full. Do you accept these terms, and that you shall pay its violation ninefold?'

'I accept.'

'Then go your way, *illvættur*.'

He spat out that last word in Hrímlandic. Naming him as a malevolent spirit.

Sæmundur turned around and walked back out. Kölski followed in his footsteps. As he exited the hall he heard the thud of a spear hitting the ground behind him. Outside the crowing of the náskárar had stopped and the sky was cleared of soaring dark shapes. Countless dark eyes glared at him as he crossed the bridge. The waves crashed on the rocks below.

Tuttugu og níu

They went over the plan daily. Every step had to be carefully planned – there could be no room for hesitation or doubt when the time came. Garún had been intentionally vague about Sæmundur's part in all this. All she told them was that he had a method to disable Loftkastalinn and cause an evacuation at Lögrétta, and that the less they knew, the better. She hadn't heard anything from him. She wasn't happy, but she had to trust that he would be able to deliver.

'All right, if Kryik'traak doesn't show, we'll make a run for the harbour here,' said Katrín as they went over the escape route yet again. The cave was damp and cold. They sat on rucksacks around a crate they used for a table. It was covered with roughly drawn maps. 'But likely that will end with us being captured within the hour. We need the náskárar for extraction.'

'I still haven't heard anything,' said Garún. 'I'm not sure if they'll get back to us in time. They did show up at the protests, both times, without any communication with our group. So they might keep an eye on us.'

'What do you mean?' asked Hraki. 'Do they know where we're setting up the ambush?'

'No,' said Garún, 'we'll just have to hope we can flag them down, that they'll help fight anyone in pursuit of us.'

'Right. Not exactly the best plan of action. But if we find ourselves surrounded by soldiers they might come to our aid.'

Styrhildur shuffled the maps around.

'Do you really think that with Loftkastalinn damaged and a captured stiftamtmaður, the people will rise up against the Commonwealth?' she asked.

The question sounded general, but was aimed at Katrín.

'There were a lot of people at the protest,' Katrín said. 'Regular humans. People died. Like I said before Diljá and Hrólfur left, Lögrétta will seize the opportunity. If they won't, the people will rally again and demand it for themselves.'

'And we'll force Trampe to sign a declaration of self-governance,' said Hraki.

Katrín snorted. 'Right. I somehow doubt that. Trampe is infamous for his stubbornness. He won't do a damn thing. And it won't hold up, anyway. It's just paper. Taking him hostage will mostly come in handy for negotiations when Kalmar wants to retaliate.'

'And what will we do then?'

Garún shrugged. 'Pray. Most of the military is stationed in Loftkastalinn, but they have barracks in Viðey and Seltjarnarnes. They've weaponised the police. If we can overpower them, we can claim their weapons. There are walls surrounding the city on all fronts. We could endure a siege, if it comes to it. Threaten to sabotage Perlan if they won't negotiate.'

Styrhildur shook her head. 'This is so fucking insane.'

'Right.'

A short while later Kryik'traak arrived and called out to them. It was time for today's firing drill. Without a word they took off everything except their undergarments, put on the jellyfish and swam after the marbendill.

The caves under the Elliðaár rivers were plentiful and most

of them abandoned. Kryik'traak led them to an elongated cave, almost a kind of tunnel, which suited them well for practising. They practised loading and firing the muzzle-loading guns.

The weapons were Kryik'traak's gift to them. The Crown occasionally shipped boatloads of ruined weapons down the Elliðaár, either for repairs or to sell for scrap iron or parts. It was all kinds of equipment, most of it so badly damaged that it couldn't be salvaged. From an entire heap of garbage the marbendlar had managed to scrounge together materials for a few usable pistols.

Kryik'traak's comrade, Aktarív'letar, taught them how to use the weapons. They would have been absolutely helpless without her aid. She knew how much gunpowder was supposed to be used for each shot, that you had to press it properly with the ramrod. She knew how the catch could be set to safety, and how they could fire quickly in case they encountered sudden combat. Garún hadn't even realised that the ramrod was kept in the gun itself, just below the barrel like a sheathed sword. To their surprise, Styrhildur showed some familiarity with handling the weapons. When they asked her how she knew so much about muzzle-loading guns, she replied that she had once had a job at a workshop that specialised in fixing up old stuff, including the Commonwealth's old equipment. That was all she would say on the matter, and that was good enough for them.

This firing drill was a test of resilience. One at a time they took turns in firing at sacks filled with sand. Garún did all right, but Katrín was clearly the best of the group. Her shots rarely missed, only excepting the longest range. After the training Garún started covering herself in a special type of fat that was kept in one of the sacks in their cave. It was whale blubber, processed by marbendlar for sale to humans. It reeked, but it was infused with crushed herbs, which Garún suspected were thaumaturgical in nature. The blubber insulated her completely, allowing her to swim in the freezing water without feeling it. When she'd covered every part of herself she tied a waterproof skin around her waist and dived in.

She could find her way in and out from memory now. She'd started following Kryik'traak out to train herself, and had gone back and forth until she knew the way by heart. Each night she headed out for a short excursion. In the skin she kept the audioskull and spray cans filled with clear delýsíð.

She enjoyed swimming by the dark river bottom. At times she saw marbendlar swimming in the distance, but they never approached her. She suspected that their presence there was a well-kept secret and she liked the thought that someone was on their side. Underwater was a new world, filled with tranquillity and peace. Sometimes she could see the bright moon through the rough river surface.

That night Kryik'traak found her swimming in the river depths. He motioned for her to follow him to the surface. He told her that a man had approached him that night, the same man she had met a few days earlier. His negotiations had been successful.

Loftkastalinn would fall in two days' time.

Þrjátíu

Sæmundur drove the last post down into the shallow hole and righted it by piling rocks around its base. The wind was sharp and relentless. The third horse's head was larger than the others and difficult to lift up to the stake. His breath was short and his hands trembled from the weight. He almost dropped the head, but eventually he managed to lift it on top of the stake so that it was securely in place.

A níðstöng was simply a gateway, a guiding post that directed forces from beyond into this world. It was up to the galdramaður to raise the post correctly and recite his incantations well enough that the weapons would not turn in his hands. Níðstangir had rarely been successfully used, as far as human knowledge went. The ritual was incredibly difficult and known to few people. Only the most vile users of svartigaldur in Hrímland would dare to cast this galdur, as more often than not the ritual failed in a catastrophic manner. No matter who was on the receiving end of a níðstöng's power, the result would be complete disaster, without exception. Even now, not a single blade of grass would grow on the land of Skálholt's former temple, due to the níðstöng that had been raised there in ancient times.

He took a step back and considered the three posts. Bloody and empty-eyed horses' heads were impaled on top of each one, their mouths hanging half-open as if they were trying to say something. It had taken him a considerable time to cut the ritual circle into the turf around the níðstangir. Still harder had it been to dig for the posts, as the earth was half-frozen. Eventually he had managed to dig deep enough that they would be stable. He had grown weak and would have preferred to use galdur or what little he knew of seiður to make the work easier. But every apprentice knew that the portal into this world had to be firmly connected to reality, a solid anchor that would hold the galdramaður steady in the raging tempest to come, which he could neither sense nor understand. Sæmundur knew that his perception of galdur was by now considerably clearer than with most other galdramenn, alive or dead, but he still saw no reason to take any unnecessary risks.

Sæmundur started the ritual by carving the lips, tongues and eyes off the heads while he hummed ancient verses to himself. Kölski was standing nearby, intently watching in silence. They were in Öskjuhlíð, away from plain sight but still far enough from the trees to have a clear view from the hilltop over the city. Spread out before them was Reykjavík, the city that cowered underneath the tower of Haraldskirkja, and above all of it – Loftkastalinn.

Öskjuhlíð was covered with a dense forest that few dared to explore. The trees were twisted and gnarled, constantly moving, even when the weather was completely still. The forest was home to countless creatures. Some of them had perhaps once been foxes, skoffín or small birds, but the seiðmagn had long since turned them into something unrecognisable. Even after Perlan was built and the thing under the hill had been harnessed, its influence could still be seen in the forest. The creatures kept to the hill, addicted to the faint residue of seiðmagn the thing radiated. Every year corpses were found on the outskirts of the forest, usually teenagers or hobos. This was a cursed place.

Sæmundur hadn't detected anything as he walked up the overgrown hill a short while before, a heavy and bloody sack over his shoulder. As he cut down three trees and carved them into sharp stakes the forest kept quiet, holding its breath. Now that he had finished the opening ceremony of the ritual he felt how the power in the earth amassed at his back. He was no seiðskratti, but he knew well the power of seiðmagn. An overwhelming presence came over him and he knew that the unearthly thing in Öskjuhlíð, trapped in the technological slavery of Perlan, wished nothing more than to assist him, to take revenge upon the city that had numbed and killed the land since colonisation. But even if he heeded its call and unleashed its power, it would not help him. Seiður was of this world. The power he was summoning was beyond the material, beyond all definition.

The preparation was complete; the ritual could start in earnest. He chanted the forbidden names of the void.

Svöl. Gunnþrá.

The knife's edge ran smoothly down his hand.

Fjörm.

With a bloodied finger he drew symbols on the disfigured horses' heads.

Fimbulþul. Slíður. Hríð. Sylgur. Ylgur. Víð. Leiftur. Gjöll.

Eleven names, eleven keys.

A gust of wind ran through the forest. Everything became still. The sky was grey and flat, the clouds were too close and too large. The circle had been sealed.

He took off his coat and neatly folded it. The stinking, worn shirt he wore had once almost been too small. Now it was draped on him as if on a hanger. When had he last eaten? It didn't matter. He'd left worldly sensations behind. He placed the shirt next to the coat and took his place in front of the níðstangir. It was cold enough that he could see his breath steaming in the air, but he felt nothing against his bare flesh.

Bektalpher's gaping maw was dark and swollen. Useless, jagged teeth jutted out of dark red gums and a three-forked tongue moved around them. The flesh around the mouth reeked, as if infested with rot. The veins were black and visibly pulsated. The demon was a growing tumour. Bektalpher breathed loudly, idle now that Kölski could roam free.

He closed his eyes and listened. Silence. Total silence. The forest, the city, the land held their breaths. He did the same. Then he filled his lungs with air and started to sing – að gala.

Tone. Steady and reliable. Deep. Up a minor second. Down a minor third. Then, up an augmented fourth. The tritone, *diabolus in musica*. The key to the ritual. Down a major seventh. Hold the tone. No words, no incantations, only sound – hljóð.

All his life Sæmundur had been taught that galdur was incomprehensible, but still rigidly bound into incantations and rituals, ceremonies where the most minute deviation could end the galdramaður. Doctrine and ideas set in stone were a hindrance; they were as limiting as the academics' refusal to let galdramenn experiment or their fear of demons. But he now understood that they were partially right in Svartiskóli. Mastering the fundamentals, holding every detail in your mind simultaneously, was critical. Sæmundur hadn't learned from Kölski how to raise a níðstöng, but he also didn't need to. The tools were already in his hands, ready to be used with the right knowledge behind them. So he did what he had been indoctrinated never to do – he improvised the galdur. He had been experimenting with improvising, that night he played in the Forgotten Downtown, when he met Garún. But that was nothing like this. Then, the galdur had no purpose except to cause ecstasy and hallucinations, a form of metapsychosis, a rather simple and unremarkable effect. Now, he meant to bridge the void between the real and the unreal.

Bektalpher chanted rapidly. The demon spoke in tongues like a holy man touched by spirits. But the sounds the abomination made were not words, they had no meaning aside from their rhythm, frequency and volume. Sæmundur's steady and deep tone provided the foundation Bektalpher built upon. Sæmundur stretched his last tone as far as he could, let it lethargically drop by a semitone. The sound waves reverberated through him entirely, growing stronger and stretching with the dropping tone.

Dissonance.

An enormous pressure overcame him as he felt the galdur open up to something else, a new source. Bektalpher tuned in with him so that he could no longer feel if he or the demon were chanting, or if another energy had taken over. Sæmundur felt odd, like when his consciousness had been split twice, thrice, when stealing the page from *Rauðskinna*. He both spoke in his own voice and controlled Bektalpher simultaneously. But he could not overthink what he was doing, could not structure the spell too much. The galdur had to be raw, untamed chaos. True to its nature.

Muscular spasms shook the horses' heads. Black, coagulated blood ran out of their eye sockets. Their rigid jaws stretched open, audibly cracking. The eye sockets were filled with clots of blood, making it seem as if new, black eyes had grown. The air was thin, as if Sæmundur was on top of a mountain. He had to draw his breath deeper and deeper in order to fill his lungs with air.

The left níðstöng screamed. The shriek cut through bone and marrow, stabbing into the frontal lobe like a cold needle. The horse's head on the right twitched and emitted a long, anguished wail that caused a lump in Sæmundur's throat, grabbed his heart like a freezing claw. The bloody symbols he had drawn on them moved and became disfigured, connected into new forms that he had not seen in any manuscript. The head at the centre reached up and opened its mouth as wide as it could. It made a noise, so loud that Sæmundur felt the sound waves crashing upon him, shaking through his entire body. Yet he heard nothing. His heartbeat slowed down and soon enough he didn't have to breathe in or out any more. There was nothing but the tone, the sounds he emitted. Now his own multitude of voices, Bektalpher and the horses' heads, sounded as one.

He closed his eyes in order to better focus. He was somehow still able to see the níðstangir and the ritual circle, which was rapidly changing. But outside it everything was a haze, distant, meaningless. He reached back his head and saw that above him was an incision in the world, like an infected wound, and beyond it ...

Nothing.

From the void stretched a shadow, reaching down to earth. The lower it went, the more material it became, until it ended up in an overpowering dark of night around Kölski. The silvery eyes stared at Sæmundur. The demon smiled when Sæmundur noticed that cords of shadow lay between himself and the imp.

He opened his eyes. The shadow was no longer there, but still he felt it. His vision had split, on the threshold between worlds as on the night that he exorcised Kölski, his self about to be torn apart by the monumental force flowing through him. As if in a trance, he turned around and looked over Reykjavík. The city was insignificant, an empty shell for faded souls. The steel fortress dominated the sky, moving lethargically towards Perlan's shining dome. High-tech engines powered by seiðmagn worked relentlessly to defy the laws of nature and keep the fortress afloat. Gigantic towers of heavy artillery were like rashes, the largest ones big enough to fire rounds the size of a carriage. Above the violent chaos of steel, chimneys spouted white-grey smoke.

The fortress drew ever closer, growing larger and larger. Thick cables hung out beneath it, like dangling entrails. When Loftkastalinn was right above Perlan, the cables would be connected to the thaumaturgical heart of the power plant and suck out of it enough power for a few days' worth of seiðmagn. An iron monstrosity that defied nature. One flying fortress was enough to break a siege, to wipe out an entire fleet. Loftkastalinn was only a prototype, an experiment. The next versions would have more economical engines, a more practical design. But despite its limited range, the destructive power was enough to cause fear in the hearts of the neighbouring nations of the Kalmar Commonwealth.

The gateway stood wide open. The environment was saturated with sound, polluting it, transforming it. He felt his bones glowing with energy, as if they wanted to burn off their flesh until nothing remained but the shining skeleton. He took a deep breath, and with a single syllable he shattered the wall between reality and unbeing and directed the ravenous forces from beyond towards Loftkastalinn.

Garún tightened the strap on the mask and checked if air seeped in anywhere. The mask was so tight over her mouth and nose that her face hurt, but she didn't mind. Anything was better than accidentally breathing in the thaumaturgical fumes. The effects were strong enough without making it worse.

She sat on a building rooftop and looked down at a vacant courtyard. The audioskull hung at her waist, the noisefiend emitting a calm beat. Rooftops were spread out like tussocks on a heath. Just out of sight was southern Hverfisgata. To the east she saw Loftkastalinn lazily moving towards Perlan, to Öskjuhlíð where Sæmundur should be preparing whatever arcane vileness was needed to raise a níðstöng. It hadn't been easy to get here unseen from Elliðaárdalur, but the noisefiend made it doable.

The bullet had dried. The others didn't know, but she'd been saving her last drops of delýsíð to coat her bullets. She wasn't sure exactly what kind of effect it would have, but she thought it couldn't hurt to try. Garún picked up a small paper square, rolled it up, and twisted one end closed. She dropped the round bullet in and poured the last measure of gunpowder behind it. The powder was loose, so she pressed it carefully with a small steel bit. She twisted the other end closed and tore off the extra paper with her teeth before packing the paper bullet case into her case, where the other nine shots were prepared and readied. The ammunition case was a wooden block cased in leather, with a strap so it could be carried over the shoulder. Nine holes had been drilled into it, just big enough to carry the paper ammunition.

She'd made good use of the delýsíð, now it was completely used up. Most of the last of it had gone into spraying cursed staves and symbols of destruction down by the alley leading out of the courtyard. Whoever came close to the clear delýsíð paintings would feel the repercussions. That was where the stiftamtmaður would escape when Sæmundur attacked Loftkastalinn. If Katrín's intelligence was correct.

She wrapped the blue bone into the delýsíð-coated sheet and tied its ends together, making a kind of sack which she carried over her shoulder underneath her clothes. The hate-filled delýsíð merged with the forbidden power of the bone, so she felt a burning cold up against her chest. It felt good. Her last resort.

If there was a large-scale attack on the nation it would be the top priority of Lögrétta to get the stiftamtmaður from the parliament building to shelter. According to Katrín there was a single set of underground tunnels still standing from the house of Lögrétta. The others had either collapsed or were unusable. She'd heard about this because her father was a goði. At first the tunnels had been well maintained, but as the war had ended decades earlier the maintenance had become a liability and they had suffered years of neglect. The tunnels exited here, their intention being to safely head to the stiftamtmaður's fortress in Viðey.

Although Katrín had no solid evidence for this, Garún had no choice but to trust her. This was their chance to hit the Crown so hard they couldn't easily recover. It was either this, or spending their lives in hiding and waiting to one day get dragged to the Nine. She'd rather die here today.

She checked the two pistols were prepared: loaded with powder and bullets, both half-cocked and ready to fire. They were in bad shape, eroded by sulphuric acid residue left behind by old gunpowder. But they'd do the job, she hoped. The pistol grip was decorated with the king's emblem, cast in silver. Garún smiled each time she saw it.

She gathered her things and swung down an open skylight. She landed softly in a hallway, where Katrín jumped and aimed her pistol before realising who it was.

'Fuck, Garún! Use the stairs, what are you thinking? I could have shot you!'

'Sorry. Don't freak out.'

Katrín was even paler in the daylight now, after spending several days underground. She'd changed during their time down in the cavern. After getting through the detox she was like a different person. A hard and resilient determination took her over and she finally looked like the person who had written all those scathing articles. When they'd gone out to practise firing their weapons she'd quickly exceeded both Garún and Hraki. Only Styrhildur outmatched her. She was still nervous and suffering from withdrawal symptoms, but when it came to loading, aiming and firing she moved quickly and with certainty. Before, Garún had been unsure of her. Now she didn't doubt that Katrín would pull the trigger without hesitation and bring death to the men who had ruined her family.

'Where are Styrhildur and Hraki?' asked Garún.

'They're downstairs, going over the weapons.'

'I'm going to check up on them. Keep an eye on Loftkastalinn and call us if you see something.'

The hallway was old but still unfinished. The cemented staircase was dusty and the walls coarse and bare. The windows and doors leading into the hallway had been bricked over. She heard a faint sound of conversation when she got to the bottom of the stairs. Hraki and Styrhildur. She stopped and listened. They kept going, seeming not to have heard her.

'...unsure about her.' A small voice, but determined. Hraki.

The echo of the empty house made Styrhildur's voice deeper and stronger.

'It has been a tough few days for... We can't expect her to...'

Katrín? Or were they talking about her?

'...like a psychopath. Screaming in her sleep and then... Can't trust her. Is she using...'

Garún had had enough – she wasn't going to listen to more of this – and stomped down the stairs. Hraki instantly fell quiet as he heard her approach. Their pistols and knives were laid out on a table in front of them, alongside two fully prepared cases of ammunition.

'Garún. Hi. We were just going over everything. Just to be

sure.' Styrhildur avoided looking straight at Garún, pointed out the weapons to her. 'Are you set?'

'I'm good.' She picked up one of the knives. The steel was spotted with rust, but it would do. Like anything else. Had to do. She slid it into a sheath on her belt. 'This is an unnecessary amount of ammunition, though. If it comes to it that we have to reload more than once, we are as good as dead.'

'Better safe than sorry,' said Hraki and attempted a smile. 'It could come in handy later on.'

Garún nodded. She tried to remain calm and composed. They could have been talking about Katrín. Or herself. She knew that her sleep had been restless these last few days. It was the delýsíð sheet she wrapped around her body, every day. Infused with relentless rage. It kept her going, like oil to a fire. But it was also burning her out.

'I don't know how much you heard,' said Styrhildur suddenly, 'but I just wanted to—'

A shout from above stopped her.

'Now! It's happening!'

Garún immediately sprinted up the stairs, the other two following closely behind her.

ᚠ

When lightning strikes it only lasts for a fraction of a second. One single moment where the destructive forces of nature break out in an almighty blaze. Mankind wasn't intended to suffer more than this brief contact with violent energy. Most people couldn't even handle that.

Sæmundur was like a lightning rod in a never-ending thunderstorm. An uncontrollable force flowed through him; his bones were aflame with power, burning him from the inside like glowing coals. There was no mercy to be found, no hope of a moment's respite. The pain was unbearable. He was a man stretched on a rack, about to be torn apart. His mouth spouted incomprehensible sounds, merging with the damned wails that Bektalpher and the níðstangir emitted. A wind blew through the trees and carried with it the unearthly sound, making the dire beasts inhabiting the forest howl and shiver. The sky was oppressive, the heavy clouds grey with malice. About them moved flares and sparks in uncanny colours. The earth shook, like a dormant primordial þurs being awakened with a heart kindled with burning hatred.

A rift in reality formed near Loftkastalinn.

The naked eye could not properly detect what it was, but the mind sensed that something had been torn and given way. Dark, unwordly tendrils reached out towards the flying fortress, like inquisitive tentacles. Where they stroked the iron it deformed, never twice in the same way. It melted and burned, poured over the soldiers that ran around in disarray. Disfigured limbs grew out of it and tore people apart without hesitation. Where the tendrils touched humans they fell down dead, or they shook and trembled, their flesh mutating and their eyes glowing with a starless void. Every single bone in their body turned dark blue with demons. The possessed chanted galdur in a frantic tongue, both out of their own mouths and whatever monstrous maw or orifice that had formed on their body. From the bodies of the living, dead and possessed creatures burst out, some of them a chitinous black like Kölski, others unimaginable horrors that were not shaped by any laws of nature. Soldiers loaded their rifles and fired, reloaded, fired, sometimes so rapidly that the powder burst too soon in the barrel due to embers that still glowed there from the last shot. The barrage had no effect. The creatures were unstoppable. Sæmundur saw the sweat beading on their brow, heard their last words, smelled the gunpowder and blood. He saw, he heard, he felt – *everything*.

Air-raid sirens sounded throughout the city. Beyond the rift *something* could almost be seen moving, something that was watching and waiting for a chance to fully break through. Loftkastalinn's heavy artillery turned slowly and fired at the dark tendrils. The shots that hit their targets were instantly transformed, some becoming like molten lava or crimson lightning, others a demonic life form that fell to the city, bursting with toxic fumes or soaring into the air on twisted wings. Most of the rounds missed their mark and hit the ground. Houses were blown apart by the barrage. Black columns of smoke rose throughout Reykjavík. A squadron of biplanes took off from the flying fortress, trying to fight the forces from beyond with impotent gunfire. The biplanes crashed or exploded in the air, or turned into something very, very different: living chimera of flesh, machine and violence that dived down to the city or attacked the soldiers still fighting on the fortress. Loftkastalinn had been heading towards Perlan when Sæmundur started the ritual, but now it wandered aimlessly over the city.

Sæmundur's voice was raw, rattling on like a broken engine. It was only a matter of time until he lost his voice. His throat was raw and shredded, every lungful of air like breathing in soot. He just about managed to maintain control of the rift and hold back the forces that were trying to break through. Only a fraction of a controlled flow of energy was intended to break through. Wetness streamed down his face and he tasted iron. He realised that he was bleeding, from his eyes, nose and ears. Blisters formed and burst on his flesh, but it was nothing compared to the pressure on his mind to keep control of the rift.

Loftkastalinn had started to slowly sag, tilting like a sinking ship. Fires burned and the turbines had stopped. Iron moaned and cracked. One of the chimneys collapsed and fell to the earth. An explosion flared up and the fortress tilted even further. The tendrils from beyond had become more solid, despite having no colour or a set form, a blank void in the world's image. Somewhere deep in the recesses of Sæmundur's mind he recalled Garún pouring turpentine over a painting. How the colours had eroded, vanished, as if they had never existed.

He was at his limit. The fire that roared inside him and used him as fuel was devouring him completely. If he didn't stop then little else besides ash would remain, if he was fortunate. When you deal with demons there are many things worse than death. It had gone far enough – way too far. Loftkastalinn was dangerously close to crashing. The city would be completely ruined and that was not a part of his plans. There were limits to what Sæmundur could place on his conscience.

In a regular galdur, the kvaðning was a short and simple part of the incantation. The preparation was what mattered the most, and with a strong foundation ending the spell should be easy enough. But now he wasn't sure how to start. Alongside him rapidly chanted voices that were his own, but still not. Demons manifested into flesh, unruly marionettes. He turned towards the níðstangir.

The red meat shone, almost writhing. Grey ooze dripped off the heads, puddles of ichor on the earth beneath them. The skin had been burned off them, melted. They chanted relentlessly over each other, and he saw that their tongues had split or multiplied. The air simmered with galdur and he felt the same intoxicating power radiate from himself. He started the kvaðning. Minute changes that slowly piled up, changes in rhythm and key. Normally, firmly established incantations and words of power would be recited, but he was far beyond them.

The struggle was like making a river flow upstream. The galdur resisted, refused to move back towards its source. Sæmundur's bones burned with pain. His teeth vibrated in his skull, which sounded rhythmically in his head like a cathedral bell. He was about to give in, to stop, but he started to feel that slowly the galdur was turning around with great resistance. In his mind he saw the demonic tendrils fading around Loftkastalinn, how reality seemed to start rearranging itself like a stitched wound.

No...

White. Pain.

He felt his body drop and fall limply to the ground. He felt his lips move, his lungs breathe in air, but he heard nothing except a constant, flat tone. When he tried to stop, tried to no longer feed the galdur, his body would not obey. The area over his chest, where Bektalpher regurgitated vile noises, impaled him like a spear.

No.

His vision slowly became clearer. He stood up, but it wasn't him doing it. His voice, Bektalpher's and the níðstangir were joined together in one ceaseless and revolting tone. Against his will he turned back around towards Loftkastalinn.

He saw. He saw beyond the gate, beyond the membrane that separated that which was and that which was not. He stared down into the unrecognisable, endless abyss that awaited beyond. He stared like a blind man staring into the sun, into the bright, burning core of the deep. He fell, lost himself in the void. It drained him and flowed back into his veins.

Þrjátíu og eitt

The door flew open and two soldiers rushed out. Garún leaned away from the broken window but still tried to keep them in sight. Katrín was near her, guns readied and loaded. Styrhildur and Hraki waited at the other side of the courtyard. After the soldiers came a man dressed in a suit. She couldn't catch a glimpse of his face, but it had to be him.

Count Trampe.

Garún drew a deep breath through the gas mask. The soldiers were almost at the end of the courtyard, where clear delýsíð patterns covered the earth and up the walls. Only a few more steps, and the seiður would be unleashed.

Another pair of soldiers followed behind Trampe. Garún gripped the pistol, ready to aim and fire. Her heart pounded rapidly in her chest, but not from fear. From hatred. From many weeks of accumulated rage, tormenting her awake and asleep. Something else exited the tunnels behind the soldiers. Something they hadn't accounted for. A dreadfully familiar sight that sent her heart sinking to her stomach.

The seiðskratti was dressed in a heavy and unshapely robe. They were covered in dark red symbols from head to toe, causing the mind to reel and become disoriented, drawing power as roots absorb water. The mask was fitted with thaumaturgical

397

glass, making it seem red-eyed from pure malice, the ivory beak curved and sharp. Distant and cold, like a vulture.

The mask was covered in sigils, hand-drawn in red paint. She recognised them; it was the visage that had appeared when she had tried to regain access to the delýsíð network. They had been the one who killed Jón and the others at the City Hall protest. They had stood up on the roof above the crowd, manipulating the uncolour.

Katrín gasped and moved away from the window. The beak turned in the direction of the sound. That was when the soldiers came to the end of the courtyard, where the staves of destruction were hiding. For a moment the air buzzed with energy. Garún saw the seiðskratti look in confusion at the energy about to be unleashed. She couldn't help but relish their surprise.

The courtyard exploded. Lightning ran over the ground, into the door they had exited, and another explosion sounded. Dust and shards of rock were blasted out. The soldiers shouted something at each other.

She aimed and pulled the trigger. The gun fired, the click and following gunfire like when a heart skips a beat. She barely saw anything for the smoke from the explosion, only vague forms. There was no time to wait for the dust to settle. She aimed the other pistol and fired again before throwing herself away from the window just as she felt a bullet rush past her head, hitting the wall behind her. The concrete shattered and she got dust in her eyes. She cursed herself for not wearing the thaumaturgical goggles. She pulled them down from her forehead, grabbed the weapons and the ammunition case and ran up the stairs. The air simmered behind her and the wall she had been standing at imploded with a deafening sound. She didn't look back, just kept running. Why hadn't they accounted for a seiðskratti in all their planning? Katrín was still down there, but she couldn't turn back now. Not while they could still escape. Katrín had to take care of herself now.

Upstairs, she loaded the guns as quickly as she could and got into position by another window. Two soldiers were lying still on the ground. One of them had been torn in half, his intestines dragged out of his body like an unspooled thread. The other two had taken shelter behind a dumpster. The stiftamtmaður was nowhere to be seen, so he had to be hiding with them. The soldiers fired at the windows on the other side of the courtyard, where Hraki and Styrhildur were located. The seiðskratti hadn't moved a single step. They slowly turned towards the window where Katrín had last been lying in ambush.

The seiðmagn moved around the seiðskratti like a torrent of colour and visual hallucinations. Small flares popped into being, in sync with the gunshots from Hraki and Styrhildur. Some kind of protective shield was in place around them. It was a waste of bullets to fire at the seiðskratti; they should have realised that and focused on the soldiers instead. But her delýsíð shots had a chance of harming them. They manipulated every shred of seiðmagn in the environment around themselves, but the delýsíð Garún had laced the trap with had confused them. They were surrounded by seiður hostile to them; the seiðmagn in the environment refused to come properly under their control.

Explosions sounded in the distance. Loftkastalinn. The buildings were too tall to see the fortress, but it didn't matter. It had worked, no matter how Sæmundur did after the fact. The seiðskratti was absorbing too much seiðmagn, too fast. Garún couldn't believe they were withstanding it, controlling the vicious current of seiðmagn raging around them. There was only so much the human body could take, no matter what thaumaturgical measures had been taken to strengthen it. Garún had been lucky at first, surprising them with the trap. There wouldn't be a next time. They were aflame with energy. Except in one place. Where the red runes didn't properly reach, the neckline where the mask met the stiff collar.

Garún slowly took a deep breath and aimed. She emptied her mind and slowly let her breath out.

She was a silent battlefield, drenched in blood. She was a wasteland. She was still and cold hatred.

The gunshot sounded. The sour smell of smoke filled her senses. Something around the seiðskratti cracked, some inner shield she hadn't seen despite the goggles.

They stumbled backwards and dropped to one knee. Sparks flew off them and the air shimmered with heat. Blood flowed from their neck and they pressed their hand weakly against the wound. The earth rose up around them. Dirt and rock flew up and rained back down on the seiðskratti. The blood flowing from their neck was moving around them, in unpredictable strings and half-formed symbols, a serpent of blood. Garún aimed the other pistol. Exhaled. Fired.

The flash of sorcerous light blinded her. She stumbled back and tore off the glasses. A quake shook the building and she fell down on the floor.

Then – a deathly silence, so complete that Garún thought she had lost her hearing. For a moment everything was still before a deafening roar shook everything. The building rumbled and pieces of concrete cracked and fell from the ceiling. Garún was lying in a huddle, hands over her head, as if that would help if a slab of concrete fell and crushed her.

As soon as the earthquake was over Garún scrambled to her feet and stumbled down the stairs. She was dizzy and she felt her head for a wound, but found no blood. Downstairs a thick cloud of dust covered everything.

'Katrín?'

She made her way through the debris that covered the entire floor, making sure not to stumble where fissures had formed in the floor.

'Katrín!'

'I'm here,' she heard down the hallway.

Katrín's face was bloody, but it looked as if it wasn't a major wound. Her right hand was lying limp down her side, in the other she had her pistol in a death grip.

'Are you okay?'

Katrín frowned. 'I think my arm is broken,' she said in a slightly slurred voice.

'Keep behind me. Is your gun loaded?' Katrín nodded. 'Good. Only shoot if they are close enough that you don't have to aim.'

Garún started reloading her pistols with hands that, despite everything, moved quickly and calmly.

The courtyard was completely wrecked. Shards of glass and pieces of rock covered the ground. A huge fissure had opened in the earth and a pale yellow gas burst from it in great torrents. The crack went right across the courtyard and crawled up the building, which seemed to be on the verge of collapse. There was not a trace to be seen of the seiðskratti. Garún was glad she had the gas mask on, unsure if the fumes were toxic or not. Through the goggles she saw seiðmagn moving in angry tatters, like distorted black smoke in the wake of an explosion. She checked the noisefiend, but it emitted nothing but a long, relentless screech. She frowned and tore off the headphones.

They moved together towards the hole the seiðskratti had blasted in the wall. There was no movement visible. Styrhildur and Hraki appeared in a doorway on the other side. They seemed relatively unharmed. She signalled to them, nodding towards the dumpster.

She moved outside quickly and kept tight to the wall. There

was no cover in the courtyard except for the dumpster, but the thick fumes would lower their visibility and give her some cover as long as she kept down. Hraki and Styrhildur moved towards the dumpster, their guns readied.

Styrhildur signalled Hraki to move on the left side of the dumpster. She moved to the right. Garún tried to get into a better position for visibility, but had a hard time due to the gas and smoke in the air. Styrhildur moved rapidly towards the dumpster. A soldier, covered in blood and grey with dust, leaped forward and charged Styrhildur with his skorriffle in the air.

Garún froze. She didn't dare take a shot – she could accidentally hit Styrhildur instead. Styrhildur fired her gun, but the soldier dodged and the shot missed. With a savage scream he stabbed her with his bayonet. The soldier jerked the gun rapidly to the sides, right-left, right-left, so Styrhildur's entire body shook with the movement.

This couldn't be happening. She heard Hraki scream. She felt everything sink and fade away. Just a moment earlier she had thought she had things under control. The plan was working. She ran towards Styrhildur without thinking. She fired, the soldier fell and she shot him again with her other pistol. Blood gushed out of his wounds and a red growth sprouted from his chest, like frozen lightning. The barbed weed bloomed with leaves in thaumaturgical colours, the delýsíð bullet a seed deep in the flesh.

Styrhildur slowly fell to her knees. Her entrails slithered out of the open wound, slipping through her fingers. Hraki ran to Styrhildur, tore off his jacket and tried to press it against the wound, to keep her intestines in. Garún threw away the pistols and pulled out her knife. There was one soldier remaining. If it came to it, she would use the blue jawbone tucked away in her belt, but not until she had no other choice. Trampe was hiding behind the dumpster, crouching in the foetal position, covered in blood like the soldier next to him, or what remained of him. The ground was covered in body parts, fragments of bone and guts glued to the wall. The other soldier had clearly exploded alongside the seiðskratti from the rampant seiðmagn saturating the air.

Hraki kneeled next to Styrhildur, his jacket drenched in blood. She was pale as a sheet, her chin shaking like a whimpering child's. He was crying but Styrhildur's face was completely blank. She tried to say something, but nothing except blood came out of her.

'It's going to be all right, it's going to be all right,' Hraki kept repeating, and he held her close.

Katrín came running, despite her limp.

'Keep an eye on him, behind the dumpster,' Garún told her.

Katrín hesitated and looked from Garún to Hraki in confusion. He paid her no attention, still speaking to Styrhildur in his futile effort to keep her alive.

'Now! Or it was all for nothing!'

Katrín jumped and went to stand guard over the stiftamt-maður.

Garún kneeled next to Hraki. He held Styrhildur close against himself and was silently crying.

'Hraki.' She placed a hand on his shoulder. 'She won't make it.'

Air-raid sirens sounded in the distance. Explosions burst out in random staccato. Sounds of war. Hraki didn't look likely to move. Styrhildur's breathing was shallow. Slimy entrails were leaking out from under Hraki's jacket.

'We have to go.'

He acted as if he hadn't heard her, still mumbling something to Styrhildur.

'Hraki!' She pushed him, perhaps too hard. He fell back and

was so startled that he dropped Styrhildur from his arms. 'Before it's too late! Then she will have died for nothing!'

Suddenly Hraki jumped up with his fists clenched white and punched her right in the face. He made ready to attack her again, but hesitated when he saw that her knife was ready in her hand.

'She's not fucking dead yet, Garún! We're not leaving her! If we bring her to Sálnanes, then she can make it!'

There was no time for arguing. They had to get the hell out of there. She had known that this could have happened, that they all could have died, but perhaps she hadn't really believed it. She felt the deep pain of sorrow come pouring over her. The feeling was so overwhelming that she almost broke completely into tears.

No. She buried the feeling. Not now. She couldn't face this. It was simply too much, too difficult. She buried her grief beneath her rage.

'All right,' she said. 'But Katrín's injured and we have a hostage. So you're carrying her.'

He seemed to accept that.

Garún went behind the dumpster, where Katrín was aiming her gun at the stiftamtmaður. Something about her made Garún hesitate. She almost looked ashamed.

'We fucked up,' Katrín blurted out. 'This isn't Trampe.'

Of course she had never seen him with her own eyes, much like the majority of Hrímlanders, but there was a statue of him somewhere downtown and low-quality images of him were regularly printed in the newspapers. He was unsightly, but carried a stern look, with strong wrinkles from worry. He seemed the type of man who only smiled on special days of celebration. When he sat in Lögrétta the balconies were closed for security reasons, but usually his seat stood vacant, a clear message of what he thought of Hrímland's little parliament. He was a representative of the king, his powers were beyond reproach.

Count Trampe. Frederik Ditlev Trampe.

When she took a closer look at the man, she saw that he looked nothing like Trampe. He was huddled as far away from Katrín as he possibly could, like a terrified mouse. A thin face and a delicate, weak chin beneath large, teary eyes. His shoulders were square and bent, his chest seemed almost caved in. He looked like a common scribe or a petty criminal, not a nobleman. He clenched his eyes shut when Garún came into his view, quietly trembling. In all the excitement she hadn't got a proper look at him. Had barely spared him a second glance. She'd only seen what she wanted to see.

He wasn't the stiftamtmaður. But he was someone. He had to be.

'It's his assistant,' said Katrín. 'He's inner circle, at least.'

Good enough.

Garún gagged him, dragged a black cloth sack over his head and pushed him down to the ground. She forced his hands behind his back and quickly tied them.

'Get up.'

The man didn't move, just kept lying on the ground. She grabbed under his armpits and yanked him up.

'Get on your fucking feet!'

They pushed him back up the stairs and to the rooftop. The portal to the Forgotten Downtown wasn't far. Explosions sounded in the distance and the air stank of acrid smoke.

'Garún.' Katrín stopped and looked at something in the distance. She pointed forward with her good hand. 'Look.'

In the sky floated a horror from another world. An unthinkable nightmare, forged from malevolence and dread. Its very existence was a crass violation of the natural order. Loftkastalinn squirmed with detestable life. Its cannons were gaping maws with hanging tongues, its chimneys spouted bile and blood, inhuman abominations crawled on its every surface like insects. Around the fortress swarmed a cloud of demons, some like bloated beetles, others slithering through the air like serpents. Every part of its surface squirmed, covered in eyes and mouths, hands and claws. An enormous fissure cut across the fortress and Garún realised that these were lips, which separated and showed a glint of enormous, terrifyingly human-looking teeth.

Loftkastalinn flickered like candlelight. Garún blinked, feeling as if her eyelid was twitching. She couldn't tear her eyes away from it, even though every second of looking at it burned into her some irreversible, unseen wound. Writhing, unworldly tentacles took hold of the unrecognisable fortress, a warped nightmare of what it used to be. The flying fortress now belonged to other masters.

It flickered more rapidly, faster and faster. Garún's eyes hurt but she couldn't look away.

Then it disappeared. Erased. Nothing remained but the grey sky.

ᛦ

The Forgotten Downtown had changed.

They ran a risk going through it, but they still figured that it would be safer than going through the chaotic city streets. It was likelier that the patrolling officers in Rökkurvík would be caught unawares, and if they encountered trouble they could jump back and forth as they needed.

That part of the plan quickly changed as Garún realised that the number of portals connecting Reykjavík and Rökkurvík had significantly decreased. It was a lot harder than she recalled to listen for a potential gate, and she quickly started to worry that she might not make it back so easily.

They ran down muddy paths, past decrepit houses, some of them practically ruins. Those houses which had been usable had been reduced to charred remains or broken, miserable wrecks. The sky was lit by a swarm of red lights, bathing everything in crimson. The hrævareldar were nowhere to be seen, and the streets were completely empty as well. Rökkurvík had regressed into a literal ghost town.

Katrín and Garún held the man upright between themselves, so he wouldn't fall when he lost his footing. The black sack over his head decreased his humanity, making it easier to treat him like an object. Katrín carried a stiff look of pain, but she didn't complain. Garún hoped that the arm was merely broken, not infected with the unleashed seiðmagn. She knew well what fate would await Katrín if it was. It would be better to go like Styrhildur, who remained motionless in Hraki's arms. She might already be dead.

To wander at the limits of the Forgotten Downtown is like being lost in a fog. You're uncertain where the town ends until you cross the boundaries, and the change is sometimes quick and abrupt, at other times slow and gradual. Garún had spent considerable time mapping out the Forgotten Downtown in her mind, as much as she possibly could, since nothing at the edge appeared to be exactly the same two times in a row.

They had started to run in the opposite direction without realising it. Garún was the first to notice and stopped.

'We're heading back the way we came. We won't get much further than this.'

Katrín was out of breath, and coughed nastily. She tried to hide it, but Garún noticed her teeth were stained with blood. If she was coughing blood because of her injuries or from smoking sorti, she didn't know, but it hardly mattered. She held the prisoner while Garún looked for a nearby portal.

The path they were on could hardly be considered a road – a muddy trail that crossed the mire, almost undetectable. The houses were more spread out, without roofs or windows, sometimes only crumbling walls that stood over a pile of rocks. Garún went out into the mire towards a nearby abandoned ruin, the others followed. The audioskull buzzed in her ears and she looked for that unique static that indicated that a path into Reykjavík was nearby. It was hard to make it out. Something was deeply wrong with this place.

One of the concrete walls had been split in two. The crack was tight, but enough for a person to squeeze through. This was it.

Her foot touched the ground on the other side of the wall and the unforgiving red glow of the Forgotten Downtown gave way to the fading winter light of Reykjavík. It was afternoon and the sun was low in the sky. She wasn't squeezing herself through a crack in a concrete wall, but a tall wooden fence where one of the boards had fallen off. She was surrounded by apartment buildings. She was disoriented, confused as always after having gone so quickly between places and worlds. Was this the right place? Yes, those were the student apartments. And there, in between houses, she saw a glimpse of the city walls. She was in Seljamýri, a bit further north than she had hoped for, but close enough.

Katrín stumbled through the portal in the fence. Garún caught her, supported her.

'Are you all right? How is your arm?'

'It stings, in a strange way, but more like pins and needles. I hope it's only bruised, or broken.'

Katrín looked to Garún for some form of comfort or

reassurance that everything was going to be fine, but when Garún didn't respond she looked away.

'Worst case scenario, it comes off,' she said in a cold voice.

The man fell through next, right on his face. Garún yanked him to his feet. He didn't make a sound, didn't even moan, and it worried her. Why was he so calm when faced with terrifying circumstances such as these? Styrhildur and Hraki went through last. Hraki was fortunate that the portal had been simple enough to carry an unconscious person through.

Garún took off her backpack and got the white masks, handing them to Katrín and Hraki. They were rough but fitted them well enough. She'd spent some time down in the cavern making them out of pulped paper and glue. Kryik'traak hadn't asked her anything when she requested him to provide the materials she needed. She'd mixed a considerable amount of delýsíð into the white paint she coated the masks with. One layer with a heavily diluted delýsíð mix, another with regular paint, again and again. The masks could only be worn for a short amount of time, since the delýsíð fumes could potentially prove lethal. This in itself was cutting it close enough.

She put on her own mask and pulled another over the prisoner's covered head. It surprised her how close it was to the effect she had been hoping for. The assistant now looked more like a form rather than an individual, ill-defined and out of focus, like a single person lost in a mob of people. The masks themselves made their faces distorted and strange, completely forgettable. The eye couldn't capture any details, not the length of their hair, the colours or cut of clothing, barely anything besides roughly the shape of them. She could only tell the difference between Katrín and Hraki because he was tending to Styrhildur, putting on her mask, and Katrín was clearly wounded. The assistant was quite similar to Katrín, and if his hands hadn't been bound she wouldn't have been able to spot the difference. The only uncertainty was how noticeable this would be in a group of people. Would it make them disappear into the crowd or stand out?

The air-raid sirens were still sounding. Smoke rose from nearby houses, numerous black columns rose in the distance. Garún stood in cover by the fence, waiting for a chance to sprint towards the ocean. She held her pistol tight against the assistant's back, making it clear in no uncertain terms what would happen if he tried to run. The street was crowded with people, most of them human students at the university. Some were carrying buckets filled with water, others dragged injured people between themselves or on makeshift stretchers; panicked horses drew wagons filled with trunks and valuables. She wondered how many of them had been at the protests, if they'd lost someone to the uncolour or if they'd been wearing white armbands. Many were injured or covered in the blood of others, their faces filthy with soot.

There was no time to waste. Sæmundur's galdur had been greater and more dreadful than they had ever imagined. All they could now hope for was that the chaos would conceal them. Garún sprinted. The prisoner almost fell over, but Katrín held him under her other arm, keeping him up. They only had three guns up and ready. Three shots. Not much, but enough to get to the shoreline. Hopefully.

People stopped in their tracks and stared. At first they hesitated, frozen from fear and surprise. The masks, the prisoner, the pistols in the air. It was clear that the people saw that they had something to do with the attack on the city, but how? There was no way of knowing if they were agents of the Crown or someone else. After that fretful moment of initial hesitation, people ran out of their way or ducked into hiding, letting go of whatever they had been carrying. Tried to hide until this unprecedented pandemonium had passed.

They ran down the street. Screams and sirens filled the air, gunfire and explosions in the distance. Houses were on the verge of collapse, with gaping, open wounds after Loftkastalinn's crazed bombardment. Smoke flowed out of them as fires roared. The roads were blasted to pieces in this area, which had been heavily hit. The tram that went between the residential student district and Svartiskóli was lying on its side in a deep crater. It had been going along the tracks and had gone right off the rails as they abruptly came to an end at the crater's edge. People were standing on top of the tram, helping to drag passengers out, dead or alive. At the edge of the crater was a line of bodies. Only a few of them stirred, holding on to life, fighting their severe injuries.

There was not a soldier in sight. They were presumably all in defensive positions in the garrison on Seltjarnarnes or the Viðey fortress. Defending against the attack on *them*, not on Reykjavík. A storm of conflicting emotions raged inside Garún. Their not being there worked to their advantage, but Hrímland was supposed to be under Kalmar's protection. Their city had faced demonic invasion and the denizens were left to fend for themselves. A demonic invasion caused by her. Garún's anger was transformed into a deep self-loathing that welled up in her like black, sour bile, and no matter how hard she tried she could not swallow it back down.

They heard a volley of gunfire as they crossed an intersection. In all the chaos they had not noticed a police squadron down the road. The officers all had their backs turned to them, facing a monstrosity from another world. It was the size of a small building, its flesh a molten horror of iron and broken bodies. It gave a blood-curdling roar, sounding like a cross between a furnace and a dying man, and the officers let loose a volley from the skorrifles. It hissed and spat as the wounds transformed into new orifices in its flesh, spewing out greenish smoke at the riflemen, who filled the air with their screams as the gas made contact with their bodies. Náskárar dived out of nowhere, attacking the horror from all sides at once, using their massive wingspan to blow the lethal gas away. Garún sprinted as the demon grew new, sharp limbs and impaled several of the blóðgögl at once on spikes of bone fused with iron. The others followed her, running as fast as they could, not stopping for anything or anyone.

Kryik'traak was waiting on the beach, just like he had promised. He was visibly agitated. It was almost impossible for Garún to read his piscine face, but she thought she saw a mixture of horror and profound betrayal.

They waded into the ocean to the marbendill. The prisoner started to wail and squirm, but Katrín hit him and spat at him that they did not intend to drown him. Without speaking a word Kryik'traak handed them a watertight skin, into which they tossed their weapons along with Garún's backpack and the remaining ammunition. Kryik'traak had also brought the whale blubber, which they spread on themselves as quickly as they could.

Garún tore the black hood off the prisoner. Hraki had started to tie a rope to his bound hands. The man saw the marbendill and the jellyfish, swimming lazily in a nearby net. Now was the first time that a true sense of fear showed in his eyes.

'This is going to be very simple,' said Garún. 'You're going to get one of those things on your face and our friend here' – she nodded towards the marbendill – 'is going to tow you through the deep. If you resist or somehow remove the jellyfish, you will drown. And we will not try to save you. Do you understand what I'm saying?'

He nodded. She removed his gag and, before he could get a word in, she pushed a jellyfish on to his face and submerged him.

Kryik'traak took the leash from Garún and coiled it tightly around his hand.

'This is not the stiftamtmaður,' he said when he handed her the rope.

'I know,' she said. 'Things went wrong.'

'Wrong. You could say that.'

The marbendill looked towards Reykjavík. In the distant glow of the city lights, columns of smoke could be seen rising into the twilight sky, all over the city.

'You've committed an atrocity. There was nothing said of demons.'

'It wasn't supposed to happen like this. We never intended for the people to suffer.'

'But still you did. With nothing to show for it but a grásleppa instead of a rauðmagi.'

Garún's temper flared. She didn't need this, not now, not from this fish-faced son of a bitch.

'Loftkastalinn disappeared, do you understand that? It vanished and it's never coming back! The only one in the world! Do you think that the Crown won't feel that?'

The marbendill grunted. 'They will build another. Better. Their warships will be here in great numbers.' He turned away from her, walking into the open sea. 'It's over. Our collaboration is terminated. Do not look to us again for help.'

He dived into the deep.

The deep was freezing and dark, but after the chaos and the horrors on the surface it was a welcome change. All sounds were muted and distant, the light from the surface quiet and calming. Kryik'traak swam ahead of them with the prisoner under one arm. Hraki and Garún pulled Styrhildur together, while Katrín braved through the pain. They had tied the glowing anemones to their waists, giving them some small light in the rapidly darkening ocean. The marbendill's tail, so useless and cumbersome on the surface, sent him flying through the water with effortless elegance. The small feet that lay along its side acted as fins, providing better and quicker manoeuvring.

The city walls went right over Fossvogur, sealing the bay off. A tall iron grate shut off a massive tunnel that let ship traffic through, similar to the one in Kópavogur.

The wall appeared from the deep, a murky, dark form that slowly came into view. The weight was supported by great black pillars, between them a gigantic iron grating. Between the bars was a net of reinforced barbed wire, made so the sea could flow through, but little else. Seaweed and a green film of algae covered the net, as if the ocean was trying to dull the sharp bite of the barbed wire.

They dived deeper and deeper, until the wall ended on the rough ocean floor. The whale blubber only reduced the cold – without it they would have gone into shock already. The stones on the bottom were sharp and coarse. Kryik'traak dived down and disappeared into the ocean floor. Hraki and Garún followed and saw a deep crack hidden behind the rock. The opening was surrounded by green algae. They followed him into the freezing darkness.

Þrjátíu og tvö

Once the earth was alive. In ceaseless permutation. The entire world was charged with seiðmagn, pregnant with energy and possibility. But now there are only a handful of places left in the world where more than the dregs of this power can be found. Some say it's because life itself has manifested this energy and bound it into a different form. Others theorise that millennia ago a sorcerous war raged, completely changing the world and using up all thaumaturgical stores of power.

Some say it is because the earth is dying.

Sæmundur came to in creaking, salty darkness. A weight was on his chest. He couldn't breathe or move. It took all the willpower he could muster to force his eyelids open. Kölski sat on his chest and stared at him.

'Master,' the demon said. 'Your humble servant welcomes you back to the world of the material.'

'What?'

He spat out the word but didn't have the energy for anything else.

Kölski quietly shushed him. 'You must rest, master, rest and gather strength. You have gone further than any human before you. You must regain your foothold in this world, or else become lost for all eternity.'

Sæmundur refused to listen. His mind flooded with memories, of Loftkastalinn and the níðstangir, the shocking force that had roiled within him. After that: nothing. A dreamlike void that was just out of reach, a fleeting dream that can't be explained but still remains for a long time, deep within the soul.

'Where … are we?'

His voice was dry, altered. He almost didn't recognise it.

'All according to your plan, master. You are on a ship heading to the channel of Suðurnes, where you will disembark at Bæjarháls. From there you will seek that which can lead you onwards, the Stone Giant that awaits in the living lava fields. As I promised, master, I will show you the way.'

His vision darkened as Kölski spoke to him. A nightmare woven together with waking. He felt as if he was dreaming, that living was a fleeting hallucination, a thin film he could now see and tear through, if only he could find the strength to move. There were so many things burning on his lips. The darkness overwhelmed him and he faded back into the nothingness.

The waves crashed on the unsightly cliffs that towered on both sides. The ship rose and fell smoothly, rhythmically, moving slowly but surely through the channel. Waterfalls poured down the cliffs, waterfalls that had perhaps been rivers or lakes before Suðurnes split from Hrímland hundreds of years earlier. He stood in the prow, looking out into the gloom. The wind stung and carried the promise of frost. Salty spray washed over him as the ship cut through the waves. Even though he sensed the cold and the wetness, he didn't feel it. Not truly. He didn't feel much else besides thirst. An unworldly thirst for knowledge, power and understanding of galdur. In his cabin he had tried to scribble down in his notebook the beginning of his theory of the nature of galdur, language and sound, but found that he couldn't possibly put his experience and knowledge into words. He was beyond words and incantations, beyond organised systems of knowledge. There was no way to communicate this with teaching and academic terms. The only way was to experience it and seek ever further.

The crew kept to themselves and didn't speak a word to him. Sæmundur had no idea how Kölski had got him on board, or what had really happened in Öskjuhlíð after he'd blacked out. It didn't matter, it was all petty details. His sole focus was the Stone Giant, sitting and waiting for him somewhere in the volcanic fields of Reykjanes, a stoic transcendent in the wastes. This was what he'd been preparing for from the beginning – he understood this now. It had always been his goal, even though he had perhaps not fully understood it until now. This wasn't about Svartiskóli or theories or something so insignificant. It was about an absolute connection to the outside.

Kölski had advised him to cover his head with a scarf or some cloth, which he had done. There was no mirror on board but he suspected that something had happened to him – something had changed, similar to when Bektalpher had manifested in his bones and flesh. When he put on his shoes he noticed that one of his feet was as black as obsidian and hard, completely numb and without any sensation, but the skin on the other foot seemed to be peeling off in big flakes, giving way to some sort of scales. Interesting changes, whose purpose was still not clear to him. He wished that there was a mirror on board so that he could see what was so interesting about his face, if anything. The terror he had experienced when manifesting Kölski, and especially Bektalpher, was so insignificant to him now. This was not an invasion or infestation, but symbiosis, without which he would have been insane or dead a long time ago. Humans cannot breathe in water, so if they intend to explore the depths they dress themselves in isolating protective clothing, heavy boots, a helmet connected to an oxygen hose, or they use creatures such as the marbendlar's jellyfish. Was he not in that exact same position, using the helpful tools he needed to explore that which was beyond the limits of human nature?

In the distance faint lights came into sight on top of the eastern cliff edge, on the Suðurnes side. Dots of light went from the top down to the ocean where the docks were located, steps cut into the cliff itself. The dock was the only one operational in Suðurnes, a short stop on the way to Vestmannaeyjar or out along the southern shore. Few ships bothered to dock at all.

A large crowd of people waited by the pier. They were competing in assisting the ship to tether itself to the dock and put out the plank. The captain commanded the crew not to let anyone on board; they did not intend to trade.

'Are you heading to Eyjar?' asked a gawky man, with bad teeth and covered in grime. 'I'm a capable sailor, work faster than anyone and never tire. I could work my way to Eyjar and then some.'

Two women competed in showing off torn sheepskin and poorly made clothing.

'Good wool, fine skin, and the best sailor's coat you can find.'

Someone had dragged barrels of salted fish up to the pier and opened them. Flies swarmed around the reeking fish.

'Do you have any meal or wheat to trade? Or soured meats?'

'We're not here to trade, but to unload a passenger!' the captain shouted. 'Step away from the plank!'

The villagers retreated slightly, but didn't stop trying to peddle their wares to the crew. The captain glanced at Sæmundur for the first time. He was visibly uncomfortable.

'Grákufl – isn't this where you disembark? What are you waiting for?'

Sæmundur nodded. Grákufl. The name he'd told Kölski to call him. How had the demon arranged this?

'I thank you for my passage.'

'Right.'

The captain stared straight ahead, down towards the prow.

Sæmundur stepped out on to the gangplank. The gathering went quiet, like a smell of rot that slowly spreads. People jumped out of his way. Bektalpher's whispers were clearly audible, and Sæmundur was glad that he had covered his face, so people would think it was him doing the whispering. He didn't want to deal with any trouble if these fine people became upset for no good reason. He started to walk up the stone stairway cut into the cliff. The crew rapidly pulled away the gangplank and cast off from the dock so they could get away from this wretched place as soon as possible. People stood and stared, or tried not to stare at Sæmundur. The men were gaunt and dressed in rags or torn sailors' clothing. The women wore determined looks, in fishery workers' uniforms, their aprons filthy and shadows under their eyes. There were stories of outlaws that hid in the rough and rocky lava wastes of Suðurnes. Sæmundur now realised that it was the people themselves who were all outlawed, cut away from the land centuries before like a malignant tumour. He smiled. It was appropriate for him to end up here. The ship went on its way along the narrow channel and Sæmundur walked with heavy steps up to Suðurnes.

If anything was comparable to the miserable hovels in Bæjarháls, it was the cursed timelessness of the Forgotten Downtown. The same feeling dominated the air in this place, the uncomfortable notion that time and the world itself had forgotten this place, that it had slid through the cracks and left nothing behind to be remembered by. Only two houses came close to being something that could be called buildings, ugly and grey houses of concrete with crumbling walls and slumping roofs. Everything else was unshapely shacks made from rotten wood and rusty corrugated iron, badly constructed turf houses, lava rocks and dead grass. One of the concrete buildings appeared to be some type of gathering hall, the other was completely dark.

He had intended to head straight into the lava fields, to start his search without any delay, but there was something calling out to him. How long had it been since he had been a man among men? Drunk beer and laughed, told stories and listened, enjoyed the heat and companionship that comes with belonging to a society? Neither thirst nor hunger, cold nor heat, were still tangible concepts to him. He knew that, just as he knew that the moon waxes and wanes, the sun rises and sets. Still he headed slowly towards the light.

The conversation hadn't been lively before he went inside. What little there was died down immediately as the door shut behind his back.

Behind an old and crooked counter stood a teenager holding a large clay pitcher. Sæmundur walked up to him in complete silence. Bektalpher's whispers surrounded him like the rustle of autumn leaves in the wind.

'What have you got there?' asked Sæmundur.

The boy looked away, as if looking for help. Sæmundur turned around but everyone averted their gaze, acting as if nothing was amiss.

'L-landi,' the boy finally stuttered.

'I will have one glass, with thanks.'

Sæmundur's voice was muffled underneath the scarf wrapped over his mouth. He pulled the scarf away.

The boy froze. He stared at Sæmundur as if he'd seen a ghost. Something worse than a ghost. With shaking hands he poured liquid into a grimy glass. Sæmundur picked it up and sniffed it. A potent smell of unfiltered moonshine. The landi was murky, probably borderline toxic. What the hell, all these fine people drank it. He downed the glass of alcohol.

Something was different. He didn't feel any heat from the liquor; the taste of pure spirits wasn't disgusting to him, as was usual when he had strong stuff like this. Instead the liquid felt cold and thin, tasted like muddy water. He was about to ask for another glass when he saw that the boy was standing and whimpering in front of him, his entire body shaking.

'Ah, I'm sorry,' he said, and searched his coat pockets. 'I have a few krónur hiding somewhere.'

'No!' the boy shouted. 'It's free, do you want some more?' He poured Sæmundur another glass. 'There's more than enough, also fish and some soured meat.'

Sæmundur felt someone sneaking up behind him. He turned around and a bent old woman handed him a tray full of blood sausage and jellied meat, dried fish, herbs and hard rye bread.

'My apologies, my lord,' she said in a quavering voice. 'We are poor workers and do not have much. But all we have to offer is yours, only if you—'

Another woman stepped forth and placed a hand on her arm, softly but determinedly, slightly shaking her head. The old woman put down the tray and walked away, ashamed.

Sæmundur's knowledge, and the entirety of his senses, had undergone such tremendous and rapid changes these last few days that regular, everyday happenings went completely un-noticed by him. He now felt the morbid fear that was lying in the air – fear of him, as if he was a butcher in a sheep shed. He now noticed children, hiding behind chairs and benches, underneath tables. Everyone stared at him but looked down in submission as soon as he glanced towards them. And there! In between them, the most awful monstrosity he had ever seen. That was the reason they were acting in this manner, not because of him.

Except that he was staring into a mirror. A filthy mirror hanging on the wall. He saw what the Suðurnesjamenn feared.

The hair and beard that remained hung in uneven patches. The cheeks were sunken, the flesh pale and stretched across the skull. The lips were gone, completely eroded, along with a great part of the flesh around the cheeks and mouth. The bare bone and teeth were shades of blue. An ugly hole was where his nose had been. But the worst part was the eyes. They were sunken and deep. The right one was crimson and the iris glowed dark blue. The left eye was worse. It was a void. Nothing. Not an empty socket, not the black of the pupil, but a void. Nothing. Blank. An abyss. A negative space the eye could not capture, the brain could not comprehend.

He was the king of the huldufólk on New Year's Eve, who repaid lack of hospitality with cruelty. He was the horror in the darkness, who carried the promise of warm murder on its voice. He was the ancient creature who stole children and people into the night.

Without a word he picked up a piece of dried fish and some slices of rye bread, in the hope that the people would see that their offering had been accepted, that they had no reason to fear.

'I give you my thanks,' he said, but his mouth did not move in the reflection.

In surprised delight, mixed with a distant and elusive sense of horror, he realised it was not him doing the talking, but

Bektalpher, or something else, a new growth upon his flesh. Of course. How could he speak, looking like a withered corpse?

'Your hospitality is to your great credit,' he managed to say, his thoughts in disarray. 'I will now continue my journey.'

It had started to rain. Drops played on the iron roof. When he shut the door behind him he felt how the entire town breathed lighter. In harsh wind and rain, Sæmundur walked out into the dark lava fields.

Þrjátíu og þrjú

The moon was out and strokes of clouds few and far between. Garún stood on the ruined battlements of Hrímland's only medieval castle. There was not much left standing. The towers had collapsed long before, the wounds like badly healed bone fractures. Half-sunken stones littered the earth. Time and weather were ill custodians; to add to that, the earth shuddered and shook every few years. It was as if this land didn't want to host anything at all. Or perhaps it knew that this place was cursed and best kept buried and forgotten.

She looked over abandoned farmsteads, bathed in the moonlit night. Low, grassy ruins of turf houses marked the landscape like ancient etchings. More recent concrete foundations stood silently, sometimes accompanied by a lone, crumbling wall, solemn like abandoned monuments, tombstones. Garún felt as if someone was watching them, but every time she looked towards the ruins she saw nothing except the dark.

Sálnanes was a landscape dotted with ruins, some ancient, others merely a few decades old. Every once in a while someone got the bright idea to start farming on Sálnanes, regardless of what folk tales and superstition said on the matter. It had rich soil, some of the best farmland in the country, and it should be used.

A few months later the farms would be abandoned. Every single one. No one knew exactly how it happened. The details were of no consequence. Everyone knew why.

To the north the city cast a faint yellow light towards the sky, its source mostly covered by the city walls. Black columns of smoke were still rising from Loftkastalinn's chaotic attack, but they had grown fewer in number. Over Starholt a thicker and darker smoke was rising. Fresh fires. Perhaps retaliation from Kalmar. Or demonic mayhem.

They had rested through the night, in a castle chamber the siblings had sworn was safe. Garún was certain that the stories surrounding Sálnanes were nothing but folklore, but she was still not about to challenge them. They had sworn that it was a safe haven, and that they had stayed there before when times got tough. Back when they were young, presumably after Garún had left Huldufjörður. The village was only a short distance away to the south.

She had gone up there to clear her mind and smoke a cigarette, but she was nowhere closer to collecting herself. Her thoughts were static, a haze of fear, anxiety and regret. She felt exhausted. As if she wanted to sleep for ever and forget everything. The only thing that was any real source of energy to her was the delýsíð sheet, still up against her, burning with resentment, cradling the blue bone.

She went down the stairs into the courtyard. The open entrances to the castle stood black and empty, the doors ruined ages before. A rusty iron portcullis blocked off the main gate, but the walls had crumbled. She lit an oil lamp hidden behind a pile of rocks. Inside was a steep spiral staircase.

'Garún. Can I talk to you for a second?'

She jumped and turned around to see Katrín, who had sneaked up on her. Her arm was resting in a makeshift sling.

'What the fuck was that?' said Katrín quietly.

'What?'

'Artillery fire on Reykjavík? That was never in the picture.' Her voice was trembling with rage. 'And whatever this… this *Sæmundur* did – it was supposed to be a nuisance to Loftkastalinn, not open a fucking demonic portal in the sky above the city!'

'Do you think I foresaw any of this? That I asked for this? He said he could handle the galdur! Nothing about this was a part of the plan!'

'Who the fuck is this guy? How did he do that?'

'It doesn't matter. He was the only one who could give us what we needed.'

'What we needed. Right. Those… things. Demons that murdered and possessed innocent people. Was that what we needed? It vanished, Garún. It was there and suddenly, *not*. Where the fuck did it go?'

'I don't know. And for what it's worth, I don't care.'

'Right. Because who cares about soldiers? Or pilots? Or engineers, chefs, electricians, janitors? They didn't deserve this. Many of them were regular Hrímlanders, such as you.'

'They were nothing like me,' she said through gritted teeth.

'No. I don't expect so. They were *human*.'

Garún punched Katrín as hard as she could. Katrín reeled back, blood flowing from her lip. She stared at her, bewildered, as if she couldn't believe Garún had laid hands on her. Garún stared her down, dared her to repay the favour.

'Right,' she said. 'I'm not *human*. I'm not proud of what happened today, but if this is what it took, then so be it.'

'So be it? To kidnap this piece of shit? Did I perhaps lose my arm all for him? For a fucking nobody?'

There was a dangerous hint of panic in her voice. She was

near breaking point. Garún couldn't afford to lose her as well. She needed help.

'You know who he is,' said Garún. 'Trampe's right hand. That's what you said. He was escorted by a royal seiðskratti. He's someone.'

'So what? What does it matter? He won't tell us shit. And even though we're hiding here, where only fucking insane people think to hide, they will find us. They have seiðskrattar. And now that Loftkastalinn is gone, they'll call for backup. An armada of warships. We're all fucking dead in the water.'

The wind wailed over the fortress walls.

'Unless we do something drastic.'

Katrín spat blood on the ground and walked inside.

Garún let loose a breath she hadn't realised she had been holding in. One argument and she had resorted to violence. Ready to ruin everything and completely lose sight of what mattered. Katrín had seemed likely to do the same. They were exhausted, she told herself. Exhausted and under pressure. Maybe this had happened because of the bone up against her heart, cold and still, wrapped in the hate-filled delýsíð sheet, pushing her towards acting on her relentless anger. Or perhaps it had been inevitable.

The sky had begun to grow brighter. Late winter morning was upon them. The light stung her eyes. She headed inside the castle. In the weak dawn gleamed faint outlines of humanoid forms, crowding hungrily around the entrance like maggots on carrion.

ᚠ

The walls leaned inwards, the shoddy construction giving way after centuries of weathering. The stone floor was muddy and wet. Where the ceiling or walls had collapsed, their path was sometimes blocked by large piles of stone. She managed to squeeze her way past or climb over the stones. There were few windows in the castle and the only light came from her lamp.

The others were resting in a long chamber with a high ceiling. A glimpse of sun made its way through a hole in the roof. At the end of the room was a raised floor, a dais carved into the natural rock in the ground. In its middle was a massive and unshapely stone; in it was a deep bowl, naturally formed. The walls were covered in faded and incomprehensible runes and symbols, all the way up to the roof where the scribbles met. A holy silence lay heavy upon this place.

In one corner were filthy blankets and an assortment of items and junk. Empty wooden bowls, rotten fish skins, piles of discarded bones. Garbage left by whoever had been desperate enough to make this their home for a while.

A vagrant's bed, Garún thought to herself. *That's my life now.*

She threw off her backpack and sat down on the ground. She was exhausted.

Katrín had taken over watching the prisoner for Hraki. He checked on Styrhildur, who was resting, the wraps around her wound stained dark red. She would likely die in the next days unless they got her to a doctor who knew seiður.

'You could take her to Huldufjörður,' Garún said, and sat down next to him.

He shook his head. 'They're probably already there looking for us. We're fine here.'

'You said this place might save her,' Katrín said. 'Earlier.'

'I was upset.'

They left it at that. He was keeping something from them. Garún looked into her backpack and got out a bundle of dried fish. She handed Hraki a piece, and went over to Katrín to offer her some as well. She took it, begrudgingly.

'So this temple keeps ... them away?' asked Katrín, after they had eaten quietly for a while.

'Yes,' said Hraki. 'We've stayed here before. Years ago. At least we've never noticed anything in here. But sometimes going in or out we can see them.'

'Who?' asked Katrín.

'Ghosts. Afturgöngur. They're angry but we always manage to get away,' he said between mouthfuls. 'It's only if you move here for good that they take you. Or if you spend too much time outside the temple, in the castle. This room is the only place they avoid.'

'How do you know?' asked Garún.

Hraki shrugged. 'Fæðey told us, years ago. Back in Huldu-fjörður. She wanted us to have a safe place to hide if the worst came to the worst.' He tore a bite out of the dried fish. 'I guess it's come to that.'

ᚤ

Garún pushed the prisoner up against the wall. He was like a piece of meat, a sack of potatoes. He remained completely silent and detached. Removed from emotion, like a monk. For the first time she wondered if he knew any seiður.

'We're not giving up,' she said. Katrín and Hraki stared at her, confused. 'Trampe's still managing things. Holding the fort until reinforcements arrive. We can't let him do that. We can't have brought all this upon people and not have anything to show for it.'

'So what are we going to do?'

'We're going to complete our mission. No matter the cost. We're going to capture Trampe and follow through with the plan.'

Katrín looked uncertain, so Garún reached out to Hraki. He

accepted her and she felt the pain he was going through. The anger at the injustice, at his sister dying for a cause which could flicker out into nothing. The horror at the things he had seen. And she felt something else – an emotion almost resembling hope. A malformed, unrecognisable form of hope, tainted with despair and lunacy. He was certain his sister would come back to life.

She, in turn, shared her intentions with him. She saw the conflict on his face, no connection needed. Then she felt his acceptance.

'Wait,' said Katrín, looking between them uncertainly. 'What's going on?'

She'd never tried using this dark heritage – this gift she'd received at birth, which had followed her mother's clan like an ancient curse. Garún sensed that the ability was there, just as she could reach out to other huldufólk and huldumanneskjur. She had felt it stir in the terrifying, overwhelming moment she'd experienced in the darkness of the Forgotten Downtown when the huldumaður had moved over her, had felt it resist and desire to fight, because it wanted to feed as he did, not be fodder for someone else.

She pulled the hood off the prisoner. The man refused to open his eyes. As if he knew what she was about to do. She grabbed his head and kept it still, forcing his eyelids up with her fingers. For only a moment his dark pupils met hers. That was enough.

Viscous. Warm. Soft. Like a mother's womb. Like sex. Only better. More intimate. More obscene. More dangerous. Trapped in the intense moment just before the crash of orgasm.

His name was Hálfdán Þorsteinsson. He was forty-six years old. He had a wife named Ingigerður Barkardóttir. She was beautiful, but tired, her eyes cold and distant. Garún felt their first kiss, their wedding night, the first time they held hands, all those moments pour over her in one continuous chain where one event merged with another.

He had cared for Ingigerður, but didn't love her. He'd loved her before, but a decade and three children later the feeling had eroded and faded into a numb sense of caring. Every time he went to Hafnía for his work he cheated on her at the same brothel. They knew him there and he always booked the same girls in advance. His two daughters, Drífa and Sæunn, were the same age as the whores working there and he found it uncomfortable. The desire, the guilty conscience, the self-loathing, all ran together into a thick ooze that drowned and clouded Garún's mind.

The stiftamtmaður. Stern, grave, strict. He prepared documents which the stiftamtmaður stamped and signed in what he felt was a complete and thoughtless autonomy, every official stamp like a death sentence. Hálfdán feared Trampe, but still considerably less than others. He stood closest to him, almost acting as official counsel, and was often made to be the bringer of bad news because whatever official was assigned to the task felt he didn't have the courage to do so.

He's small. His father is whipping him. This was the only memory he had of his father. He didn't remember his face, how he smelled, how his voice sounded. Only pain. He drowned out at sea. Hálfdán is terrified of sailing and hates the trips to and from Hrímland.

Jörundur the Ninth is sitting on his throne, the divine engine that advises him. Controls him, according to some. Hálfdán is kneeling along with the rest, but still dares to cautiously look up and gaze upon the king. His face is gaunt and his eyes dull, his hair thin and dirty, the crown too small on his large head. With jagged teeth and an open mouth, he carries all the signs of the endogamy the royal line is known for. Behind him the obsidian throne towers. Through thick, greenish windows ancient organs can be seen floating, the brains of deceased kings that still rule through their descendant. Black cables pour from the throne into the crown. Suddenly the king meets Hálfdán's gaze and he looks down, feels himself blush from shame and foolishness. He trembles and is about to wet himself. But the gaping fool says nothing.

He is in Viðey, escorting officials. Noblemen. Tries to smile and participate in the conversation without being too forward. It does not become a Hrímlandic commoner. Trampe points out the defensive fortress, the tower, various precautions. His pride. His home. The eagle's nest. Garún drowns in information. Pantries, rooms, servants, soldiers, cannons, powder. The layout of corridors and connections to rooms, parlours, the library and the basement. The basement that goes down to the docks. The ferry comes twice a day, mostly with supplies. The stiftamtmaður usually makes use of his private vessel, which is a modern piece of equipment powered by oil, even though the ferry is heading back to the city at the same time. This squandering and arrogance was a great source of annoyance to Hálfdán. Trampe never took a carriage, he only travelled in that obscenely expensive machine that spewed black smoke like a mobile factory.

Viðey was the key. She sank herself into his mind, devoured knowledge in great gulps. She knew how to get into Viðey. How you could sail by the rocks, enter the cavern, go up the tunnels and from there move into Trampe's bedroom. She had everything she needed. This insignificant, disgusting man and his life repulsed her. But she couldn't stop.

The next memory was of him at school, when he intentionally poured his inkwell over his writing exercise so he had to do detention, because he didn't want to go home. Drífa was a baby and threw up over his polished dress shoes before he was going to a celebratory dinner. Ingigerður crying at the kitchen table.

When he found his first grey hair. When he woke up in an alley in Hafnía and didn't know where he was, penniless, his clothes torn.

She devoured and devoured. Her hunger was insatiable, a bottomless pit she dived into. Joy, sorrow, regret, lies – regular details of everyday life were transformed into magnificent delicacies in front of her and she ate without inhibition.

She wasn't satiated until she swallowed the sweet memory of a newly formed human being, cradled in the dark warmth of its mother's womb.

They could not risk digging a grave in the rocky fields, so they dragged the corpse out into the lava fields under cover of night. The scribe had choked when he had forgotten how to breathe, after Garún had finished. Katrín and Hraki had not spoken a word to her. They knew this was the quickest and safest way they had to extract the information they needed, and that there was no chance they could release the scribe or leave him alive. But what Garún had done was so repugnant, so absolutely immoral, that their feelings of revulsion could not be masked.

Garún pushed the corpse with her foot and it rolled into a deep crevice. She and Hraki collected large stones and threw them after him. With luck the snow would soon fall and no one would find the corpse until the spring, if ever.

Later that night Garún woke up to the sound of quiet crying. Katrín was lying on her side and cradling her numb hand. It must have been deep into the morning, but it was still dark out. Garún wanted to reach over and comfort her, but she couldn't bring herself to do it. Katrín's arm was worsening. It had become grey and dead, the skin like a clump of hardened lava. She could hardly move her fingers. She thought of Fæðey and her fate, and she had known Hraki was thinking of it as well. Neither of them said anything to Katrín.

Garún slept with the delýsíð sheet bundled up as a pillow. Fuel to the fire burning inside her. Her dreams were a confused mess of her own self and the scribe's memories. She felt as if she had another person living inside her. The delýsíð-induced rage was roaring in the background of these dreams, stitching together these different minds like a seam closing a wound.

'Why are you doing this to yourself?' Hraki asked her one night, when Garún had woken up in the pitch dark, drenched in sweat, her teeth aching from grinding them together.

'It keeps me on edge,' said Garún. 'It helps me stay focused.'

'It has changed you,' he said. 'It's going to break you.'

'You don't know what you're talking about.'

'That bone you're hiding ... there's a demon in there. But different from the skull you've got.'

'It's a last resort, Hraki, in case I'm cornered. Nothing else.'

'It's for him, isn't it? Trampe. It always has been.'

'You don't know what the fuck you're talking about. Go back to sleep. And mind your own fucking business.'

He turned back to his sister, wiping the sweat off her brow. Her breathing was shallow and rapid.

After having devoured the scribe's memories, Garún had clearly seen how ill-prepared and flawed their former plan had been. It was really a miracle that they had lived and managed to capture anyone at all. There was a response plan for almost every scenario. Invasion, rebellion, assassination, economic crisis, war, world war, a thaumaturgical catastrophe. Anything. In this case they had put into action the emergency response plan for a demonic invasion of manifestation grade 3-A, where an important military target was completely taken over by trans-mundane possession and transformation.

The flaw was that most plans assumed to utilise Loftkastalinn's power in some degree, and if Loftkastalinn was about to fall a self-destruct sequence was to be initiated, which obviously had not happened. If the fortress hadn't vanished the Crown would have been forced to completely annihilate the fortress – and possibly the entire city – by forcing the thaumaturgical power plant in Öskjuhlíð to go into limited meltdown. Experiments with this type of overcharging were very limited and most likely they would have ended up with a complete meltdown, causing absolute destruction over a radius of several kilometres. It was still a better option than letting a demonic manifestation of this degree roam free. Unavoidable collateral damage that would pay off in the end. The thought made her sick. Not that they were ready to take such desperate measures, but how easily they could execute these plans. How thoughtlessly they converted lives into statistics. But this methodical planning for every possible event would be the cause of their downfall.

After an event like this security would be so strict that it would be almost impossible to get to the stiftamtmaður, but Garún knew exactly how they would react. She saw the cracks, where she could get in and collapse this house of cards that they had built around themselves, like a small stream of water that freezes and shatters a boulder from the inside.

Þrjátíu og fjögur

Reykjanes. The living lava fields. Black and rough, rocky and hostile. Blades of yellow grass jutted out of black sand, moss locked its claws into the unweathered rock. The land was flat, but uneven, letting winds play recklessly. It was never the same any two days in a row, as if the lava had never stopped flowing even though it had hardened centuries earlier. Sæmundur stopped on top of a hill. Daylight came late in the day and it was grey and pale through the thick clouds. The black waste spread itself out before him. He took a deep breath of fresh air and smiled. It was good to be free of the city, the fear of being captured, other people in general. He sensed the flow of seiðmagn all around him. This would have remained invisible to him before, he couldn't have felt or seen it without using Garún's thaumaturgical goggles. In a way he did not actually see the seiðmagn, but this was still completely different from before. He felt it moving, almost breathing.

They walked in silence, he and Kölski. It was pointless to bind the demon into shadow here in the wasteland. They crossed rocky hills and crevices, chasing some feeling, a presence that was so powerful all around that it was hard to discern where it was stronger and where it was weaker. It was like the wind, the sky over the earth, thin sunlight on a winter's morning. The presence was the lava fields themselves, the conscious land.

The Stone Giant. The southern landvættur.

All Hrímlanders knew of the four landvættir, even though it was now forbidden to hold blót in their honour. Just as every person knew the cycles of high and low tide, or how the pitch black of winter is turned into the bright nights of summer, the vættir were known to all. The primal beings had not been seen for centuries, but that had never been considered to be reason to consider them mere myth or folklore. Sæmundur himself had never given them much thought before. He considered them a consequence of seiðmagn rather than being remotely related to galdur. Besides, how should he possibly communicate with these primordial beings? But that was before. Galdur was a force that could alter reality itself, but that was not all. Galdur was also a language that transcended the boundaries of time and causality. He felt that now he would be able to connect to this ancient, esoteric consciousness.

If he could ever find it. Only a single feeling reached him, saturating his entire being. An insatiable thirst for more – for understanding, for transcendence. He had plenty of time, but he'd waited long enough.

On the second day he came upon a battlefield. Corpses lay over rough stones, the thick moss absorbing the blood. Ravens sat and picked at the carrion. He made his way through the silent battleground. Dismembered limbs, bodies still with the weapons stuck in the killing wounds, men split in twain. Here no quarter had been given. The men were dressed in rags, armed with rusty swords and knifes, decaying shields of wood and leather. An unstable vortex of seiðmagn surrounded a particular spot, where shards of bone and body parts were scattered all around in a bloody mess. An unlearned kuklari had lost control of the seiðmagn he had tried to tame. Instead of being able to use it to cause harm, it had literally torn him to pieces.

Sæmundur stopped in the middle of the bloodied field. With a raw voice he started the galdur. His voice carried on the wind, an arcane whisper that moved silently around. The world reverberated with hljóð – a word that could mean both sound and silence. Just as Kölski had said about darkness having an essence, so did the silence. He now understood that galdur was also in the silence. As a composer breaks up his work with the absence of sound, he used the silences as well to draw in the power from beyond, lying behind the entirety of creation.

Faint shadows appeared like frost roses on glass, unclear and dark lights that indicated human forms, but not much more than that. He called to them, wove into the galdur a request of knowledge, of the battle and of the landvættur of the south. One by one they stepped forward, and he listened to their stories in the quiet stillness of the field.

Their fates had been decided generations before. They could not recall their names, but they recalled their clans. Grindvíkingar, Keflvíkingar, Vogamenn, Njarðvíkingar, mercenaries and opportunists from Sandgerði, Garður and Hafnir. Generation after generation fought and avenged, spilled blood for the sake of blood. Alliances were formed and broken according to the way the winds blew.

This time it was Grindvíkingar and Vogamenn who met Keflvíkingar and Njarðvíkingar, both parties with mercenaries on their side. Full of betrayal and counter-betrayal, their voices crashed over Sæmundur in a contradictory flood of words, where every revenant was inconsistent with the next. With a high tone and a few choice words, which he had used years before when he put down Hóla-Skotta, he calmed the ghosts and made them listen. Where was the Stone Giant? Where was the vættur of the south?

The answers were vague. Poetic riddles, instructions from those who were no longer constrained by human fetters. Despite all the transformations that he had undergone, all the mysteries that had revealed themselves to him, he was still shackled to this mortal coil. The reality of these souls was completely unfamiliar to him.

He is where the shell cracks and the wolves howl.
You find him in the worm's entrails, the wave's foam, the poisoned
  edge of the sun.
He is here. He is here and has never been here.
You do not seek him. He seeks you. But you have vanished.
He is the living lava! He lives!
He lives! He lives! The chained giant still lives!

Every answer struck some truthful chord, but it was only a fraction of the complete picture, which he could neither identify nor place. With a weary tone he put the spirits to rest, let them fade again into forgetful nothingness.

The sacrificial stone was filled with blood. It poured down on the floor in a steady stream. It was hot, and its stench was foul. The stone bowl was big enough for both of them. Styrhildur looked up at Garún, who cradled her in her arms.

'You killed me.'

Garún held her tight and tried to push Styrhildur's intestines back in.

'No! It wasn't me. It was those pigs. Those fucking pigs.' Hot tears stung her eyes. She had a terrible pain over her chest, so she could barely breathe. There was a foul taste in her mouth. 'I'm sorry, Styrhildur. I'm so sorry.'

Seething hatred twisted Styrhildur's face.

'It was you. All along.'

Garún couldn't hold back. For the first time in so long she let herself cry.

'It hurts at first, but then you get used to it.' Hálfdán was standing in front of them. 'Before you know it you can't stop.'

Garún held Styrhildur tighter. He was here for her. She'd never let that happen.

'You're dead! I killed you!'

He smiled mockingly, as if she'd unwittingly said something funny.

'You're me.'

'No! Shut up! You're dead, you're nothing!'

Styrhildur was cold and still. She was dying. Garún shook off her jacket and pushed it against her wound. The intestines writhed out of her body like an angry pit of snakes. The foul taste in her mouth was stronger and she almost retched.

'The first time is always difficult. It takes a lot. But still, somehow less that you would have thought. It's in all of us, I suppose. Then comes the thirst.'

He smiled and she noticed his teeth were stained red.

She held Styrhildur even closer.

'Shut up, you fucking pig!'

'Please, Garún, don't. Stop. I can't any more. Please.'

Garún loosened her hold. Styrhildur was weakly trying to push her away. New wounds had opened on her neck and by her collarbone. Dark red blood flowed out of her, into the bowl.

The bad taste was different in Garún's mouth. She didn't feel it any more. On the contrary, there was a sweet and salty taste on her tongue. She was so thirsty. So incredibly thirsty.

'Don't ...'

Styrhildur fell quiet when Garún leaned over her yet again.

ᚤ

Sæmundur wandered through the lava fields, purposeful but aimless, following a vague but strong feeling that guided him like a compass following the magnetic poles. It was fleeting, uncertain, wandering, but still guiding him somewhere. Every day was shorter than the next. The sun rose and set rapidly, so exhausted that it barely managed to peek above the horizon. Winter was here. The cold didn't affect Sæmundur, but he was still relieved it didn't snow. He didn't have the time to waste energy in melting snow or chanting at the land to avoid pitfalls and other dangerous traps of the lava.

He didn't feel tired so he didn't rest. Occasionally he stopped to mutter a few incantations and words to try to sharpen his wits, try to locate the presence which was everywhere but nowhere. Usually it accomplished nothing, but sometimes he felt he was on the verge of uncovering something, locating the centre, but the knowledge slipped out of his grasp without exception.

The Reykjanes peninsula-turned-island was a hostile and life-threatening place. The seiðmagn polluted the landscape and saturated everything. Simple beasts like foxes or sheep were transformed into other, uncanny creatures, if they survived the contamination. The endless fields of barren rocks were in constant flux, never giving reliable shelter from malevolent beings or fierce weather.

It was on the third night after Sæmundur invoked the spirits that the land began to tremble. Heavy impacts shook the earth with a steady rhythm, as if a thunderstorm was moving through the ground itself. He didn't seek shelter, but he reinforced the spell of hiding he had clouded himself in and was constantly – almost involuntarily – chanting. Two voices or more participated in the incantation. He didn't know how many organs of speech he had sprouted underneath his robes, and he didn't care. As long as it was useful to him, it didn't matter.

Kölski climbed on top of a split stone and looked towards the source of the impact.

'You should cover your face, master.' The heavy sounds grew gradually louder. Whatever was moving was getting closer. 'Stop reciting the incantations. Do not breathe in.'

'Why?'

Something moved in the dark. Something huge and ancient. The demon flashed a malevolent smile.

'You of all people should know that.'

Dark outlines, which Sæmundur had thought to be a rocky hill, moved and trembled. The form grew larger, closer, and he saw what was coming. It was gigantic, like a hill which had one day decided to get up and start trudging along. Coarse and stone-faced skin, covered in craters and cracks. The cavernous maw hanging slack so the jagged fangs were clearly visible. A faint glow from the eye sockets, like a glint in a cat's eye. It walked on its knuckles like a beast, with a great and tall hunched back, but where the back should have ended in a sharp peak was an ugly, open wound and from it stood an evil growth. A thick cloud surrounded the creature, like a swarm of flies.

Sæmundur pulled in his coat and held his sleeve up to his nasal cavity and bared teeth. He hoped that whatever new organs that had possibly manifested on his body were able to close themselves off, or at least would manage not to breathe for a while – if they needed to at all.

The cloud surrounded him completely. For the first time in a very long while a real sense of fear came crashing over him. His heart pounded in his chest, in an irregular and sporadic beat. As if it were at its end. He wanted nothing more than to breathe, which was odd, because when he thought of it he didn't quite remember having to do so recently.

The back of the night-troll was broken, like the shell of an egg. Mushrooms sprouted from the wound, large and thick like trees, their roots a thick mess of tiny, glowing fungal growths. They had burst out from the inside, pushed until the stony skin had cracked. With every step, every resounding impact, the mushrooms shook so that a thick cloud of spores came pouring out of them.

An enormous fist hit the earth. Shards of stone flew up at the impact and rained over Sæmundur. He retreated in a panic – the spores had hidden just how close the troll was. He tripped over a rock and fell onto the jagged, barren ground. The impact knocked the breath out of him and it took every ounce of willpower he had not to gasp for air. The spell of hiding would not help him now – he'd stopped reciting it as soon as he'd realised what was coming. The troll might have already seen him.

He lay still, in an odd and uncomfortable position, his face against earth and black sand. He was helpless, completely vulnerable. He was nothing without sound. Silence would be the end of him.

Another impact, so close that Sæmundur would have been crushed had he been just a few metres closer. So this is how he would die. Infected by the gandreið fungi in the wilderness. Killed by the plant which had made it possible for him to start all this madness.

The troll took another step. Further away this time. Then another. Sæmundur sat up. The night-troll had its back turned to him, moving on in its mindless march. It didn't notice him.

Didn't notice anything. It didn't need to. Everything that came upon its path became infected and died.

Sæmundur rushed to his feet. Water. He had to get to water. He was covered in spores, which stuck to him. He couldn't shake all of them off and could not use galdur to remove them. One breath and he was doomed. The shore was too far off. He didn't know the lie of the land, if there was a lake or a pond nearby. He hadn't noticed anything like it on his travels. There was nothing here but fucking rocks.

Kölski was standing in the same place, still smiling. Sæmundur had turned a deathly blue from the lack of oxygen.

'Despite everything you are still just a man. Chained in flesh. Regardless of what path you choose, only doom awaits you in the end. You fear the fungus, to become its slave. To dance according to its invisible strings, like a grotesque puppet.'

Sæmundur collapsed into the dirt. His ears were ringing.

'Why?' Kölski kept on. 'Is that not all you know? Is that not the foundation of the illusion you call reality?'

Sæmundur's vision darkened. He didn't have much left. It couldn't end like this.

Galdur transforms reality – can turn it upside down. It reaches out to something larger and greater than that which makes the world and pulls it back into itself.

Sæmundur had sensed how it was not the words themselves that affected the world, but the frequency, the rhythm. The sound waves. However, they had always come from him. A vibration from his throat, a sound sung out into the world. That was how he learned to use galdur; the galdur began and ended with the voice and will of the galdramaður.

He closed his eyes.

And he listened.

Kölski's voice, mocking and cold, saturated with hate which

welled up to the surface, an overflowing river. In the distance, the rumble of the night-troll, the rumble of rocks as they moved and shattered under its knuckles and feet. The delicate sprinkling sound of spores falling from the mushrooms, landing on the ground, brushing against each other on the way down before they sat on moss and stone. The wind howling over bare rocks, blowing earth and gravel, alternating between absolute stillness and fierce gusts. Chattering birds in the sky, hissing predators in their burrows and in the distance, the roar of the ocean, eternal and ceaseless. He listened and he heard everything. Everything he had learned to ignore, for how can you hear that which is never silenced?

He heard the moonlight shining on the ground. He heard the clouds gliding through the sky. He heard fine droplets of moisture condense inside them.

He looked up at Kölski, who fell silent in the middle of his speech. Sæmundur smiled his bare grin even wider. He exerted his will to the heavens.

And it started to rain.

Þrjátíu og fimm

The fortress in Viðey was laid out in detail in her mind. She knew every nook and cranny as if she'd grown up there. The living room where Hálfdán's son had taken his first step. The garden where he'd walk around with the Crown's most powerful consultants. The hollow where Trampe would sit by himself and smoke. Hálfdán had mimicked him in this and sometimes stood there by himself, with his pipe and his thoughts. The pantry where he'd sometimes meet the maid and take her.

The fortress was designed as the Crown's last line of defence. Viðey could stand a siege for months, as long as their food supplies were ready for it. But if everything went sour the stiftamtmaður would still have to make his escape. In a few well-hidden places were invisible portals, crafted with seiður, hidden behind slabs of stone and secret trapdoors. Most of the routes were well monitored. The soldiers might not know they were there, but there was always a guard patrolling close by.

Garún started to draw up the rough outlines of the fortress by lining up rocks and drawing lines in the mud. There was an entrance here, guards here, change of guards here and here at these times. Katrín and Hraki listened with complete concentration. They'd need a boat to get to the fortress. Hraki thought he could sneak away to Huldufjörður to find a usable boat,

446

preferably a regular rowing boat. There was a natural harbour just outside Huldufjörður, where rowing boats could probably be found. It sounded familiar to Garún. Most likely they belonged to fishermen from the village, or smugglers, perhaps. One of them should do, at least.

The deep blue sheep's jaw was freezing cold against Garún's chest, where it was tied with the delýsíð sheet. She ached from the cold and the seething heat of the hatred, but in a good way. The bone hungered, and that hunger sharpened her mind. She would satiate it.

It was time for a reckoning.

The rain ran down his filthy hair, streaming down his neckline and soaking the rags he wore. Sæmundur was drenched. He hadn't felt so good for a long time.

A fog had lifted from his mind. The Stone Giant was shining clearly, like a bright beacon. The power of the giant was all around him, but now its centre was clear, obvious. Kölski followed behind Sæmundur. The demon hadn't spoken another word since Sæmundur had made it rain. If he didn't know any better, he could have sworn the abomination was sulking.

Every living thing ran from his path, like animals fleeing a fire. Outlaws lay still in hiding, frantically whispering prayers and kukl, incantations of protection against the malevolent being. Him. He was death itself made flesh.

He heard them long before he saw them. They tore through the land like an avalanche. Without any regard, an unstoppable force of destruction. They were supercharged with seiður, drawing in the untamed force from the land and conducting it through themselves so they burned with almighty supernatural force.

Seiðskrattar. Sent after him. They were so mercilessly driving themselves that there was no chance they'd survive. The human body wasn't intended to handle these amounts of seiðmagn flowing through it in such a short period of time, regardless of how powerful the seiðskratti was. But it didn't matter. The demon-worshipper should be destroyed, no matter the cost.

The landscape started to writhe as they gained on him. Undulating. Clumps of rock melted again, shining amber-red with heat. Boiling water erupted from freshly formed geysers, steam roaring like a lamenting choir. The earth shook. Trembled from joy or revulsion at the destruction which was being unleashed.

They shone like two suns in the sky. Sparks of lightning flew from the floating human shapes. Their robes were tattered, the black masks like melted wax.

With their seiður came the most wonderful cacophony Sæmundur had ever heard. Like a child hammering a piano but still managing to produce sounds one could call music. Something undisciplined and ugly, but undeniably music.

They stopped at a distance from him. He felt them draw in power, bloat themselves even more with the unending flow of seiðmagn from the land. It looked as if they intended to unleash it all at once. The thaumaturgical explosion would vaporise all of them. The crater would span kilometres. Their plan was to obliterate Sæmundur into molecules, leaving nothing of the demonic infection behind. He felt around them and found the edges of runes of fate and protective incantations which held up a shield against galdur and demonic possession. It would be hard for an average galdramaður to break through these defences in time.

But Sæmundur was no longer an average galdramaður.

He listened to the frequency of their bodies. Of the vibrations of the bones, which resounded with sound and life.

And there he opened a gate.

ᚠ

Garún jumped up. Again she had been awoken by a sound. Some terrible sound. The oil lamp was lying on the floor next to her. In the fading light she saw Hraki standing by the exit. Away from her, like she was a wild beast.

The sound suddenly stopped. It was her. Her own screams. She felt hot tears on her face. Katrín was kneeling next to her, as if she was about to wake her up, but had hesitated for some reason.

'Are you all right?' said Katrín in a weak voice.

Garún nodded. 'Just a nightmare.'

'I got the boat,' said Hraki. 'But it was close. There are houses burning in Huldufjörður. Soldiers. We should get moving.'

The sacrificial stone was a sombre, vague form in the darkness at the end of the hall. She wanted to take a closer look, make sure that it was not filled with blood. But she didn't have the courage to. Nothing was as terrifying to her as the thought of taking one step towards that stone.

She checked on Styrhildur. Her skin was feverishly hot, sweat beading on her forehead. She hadn't regained consciousness since they got here. Her breathing was rapid and shallow.

'You'll stay with her?' Garún asked. Hraki nodded. 'Good.'

'I'll wait for you,' he said. 'Styrhildur will be awake when you come back.'

She nodded, unwilling to shatter his delirious hope.

ᚠ

The smell of the ocean was a welcome feeling. The waves tumbled up to the beach and made soothing sounds as they drew back the small stones. Garún took a deep breath. She felt a little bit better already. She couldn't understand how Styrhildur and

449

Hraki had stayed in those ruins for days, perhaps weeks at a time, as children.

'There's no sense in waiting.' Garún started to push the boat out. 'I do not want to spend another minute in this place.'

'Agreed,' said Katrín.

Garún pushed the boat out to sea. Katrín jumped in first, then she followed. Garún rowed, as Katrín's arm was all but dead weight. Hraki stood still on the shore, alone and helpless with the looming castle ruins behind him. He didn't move. Garún tried to keep an eye on him, to make sure he went back, but it was dark and cloudy and he quickly melded with the night.

The pillar was unshapely, a crooked and jagged monument in the wasteland. It stuck from the earth like a dagger in a wound. At a distance it seemed a part of the rough and barren landscape, but as it drew closer it was more apparent that even here in the sorcerous lava fields this rock did not belong. Every day the rocky terrain changed, but the rock's shape always adhered to the original form that it had taken when it had erupted from the heart of the earth. It was a rock pillar that would have belonged at the shoreline, a lone column left alone, chipped and polished by waves and time. It had a hole going all the way through at ground level, making it seem as if it stood on two solid feet.

Sæmundur stopped at the roots of the Stone Giant. The overwhelming vortex that came pouring over him made his mind reel, swirling around him in powerful waves.

This was the eye of the storm. The epicentre.

Sæmundur walked around the rock. There was nothing unusual about it, except for the lack of geological explanation for its place there. But there was something there. Something so potent that its presence covered the entire land. A sleeping giant who, if disturbed from his sleep, could tear the land apart. Kölski waited while he walked, silent and grave.

The seiðskrattar were hanging in thin air like carcasses hung on meat hooks. The demons infesting their bones had deformed them completely and the long-lasting effects of the seiðmagn in their bodies had started to devour them. It was barely perceptible that the creatures had once been human. He considered sending them back to Reykjavík, to let the Crown taste their own medicine, but he couldn't bring himself to do it. He remembered how the cannons had let destruction rain over the city. The demons that must have manifested and torn through the streets. Reykjavík had suffered enough by his hand.

Nothing worked, no matter how he tried. The energy that raged here was too chaotic, too disturbing for him to grasp. He made one of the seiðskrattar float down and reached up to the half-melted mask that was still hanging on their face, tearing out a red lens. Through the gap he saw a crazed eye flickering back and forth, the pupil split in three and dilated. The skin was pale and the veins a patchwork of inky darkness.

He didn't really need the lens, but it was a matter of concentration rather than utilising the filter in the thaumaturgical lens. He looked through the crimson glass and tried to concentrate. Let everything tune out of focus, so he could glimpse the bigger picture. In the thaumaturgical storm that raged all around him, the rock was shining like a crashed sun. The brightness was overwhelming. But somewhere there, deep within the chaos, was a shape. Glowing blue with arcane power.

Þrjátíu og sex

The fortress of Viðey rose from the horizon. A fortified wall covered the entire island. Over them the towers of the main fortress could be seen. The residence of the stiftamtmaður, one of the oldest buildings of the Crown in Hrímland. The fort had grown and prospered as the years passed. Inside the walls were upscale houses of high-ranking officials and military officers, army barracks, a botanical garden and a small village, where the servants and lower-ranking bureaucrats lived.

Garún knew that Viðey was by now crawling with soldiers and without a doubt more than a handful of seiðskrattar. The fall of Loftkastalinn was an impossible shock, which called for the highest possible state of emergency. It made things harder for them, but they couldn't afford to wait. With each day that passed the Commonwealth's net tightened around them.

The approach to the island was the most dangerous part. Everything depended on them getting to the walls unseen. It was impossible to see in the dark, but Garún knew that up there soldiers would be on guard, even more alert than usual. But if there was a seiðskratti up there, gazing out over the battlements to the sea, they might just as well have sailed up on a fine summer day in clear weather. She had her headphones over one ear and listened to the noisefiend. It was more to calm her

452

nerves than to ensure that they approached unseen. It was a long way still to the fortress and the audioskull didn't have that kind of range.

Her arms burned from exertion. Rowing was difficult, but twice as difficult when trying to be as quiet as possible. The boat creaked with every pull of the oars. The sound merged with the waves, but Garún felt it must be so deafeningly loud that it was impossible to think it would not carry right to the top of the island walls.

'We're here,' Katrín whispered. 'Quick, before we hit the shore.'

The walls towered overhead. They jumped ship and carried the boat up the shore. The beach was rocky, but Garún knew where it would be the sandiest, making the least noise. They carried the boat all the way to the wall, minimising the chance that it would be spotted from above. It slowed down their escape, but if they were outed before having a chance to strike, then it would all be for nothing.

The entrance was a few minutes on foot along the wall. Garún went over her weapons, felt the spot where the bone was cradled up close to her. Everything was in place.

'Ready?' Katrín asked. Garún nodded.

They started to make their way along the bottom of the wall.

The Stone Giant was human.

Or at least, a humanoid being. Sæmundur couldn't be certain. The torrents of galdur that raged around it and aggravated the seiðmagn in the land still disturbed him, despite hours of sitting still in calm, focused contemplation. He hummed multi-voiced tones with Bektalpher's mouths, letting them reverberate around him so he became like a vibrating tuning fork. Synchronised. Focused. Nothing.

The landvættur did not react to any of his experiments. No matter how he called out – with a ritual, incantation or pure tones – the being showed no reaction. It was deaf and dumb, bound in some cursed sleep. He started to chant a spell of awakening, trying to rouse the giant from its coma.

It was after some considerable time that Kölski said, unprovoked, 'You cannot wake him, for he is already awake.'

Sæmundur ceased his chanting. So, the demon had dropped his formal tone, no longer addressing him as master. He didn't know if it was an improvement or to his detriment.

'If he is awake, why does he not respond?'

'Because he cannot find the strength to.'

'What do you mean?'

The demon ignored his question.

'You cannot converse with him,' Kölski said after a while. 'Even if you could, it would accomplish nothing. You will only comprehend his power by wielding it yourself. This much, you already know.'

He knew where Kölski was heading. But he did not want to believe it.

'You must take over his burden.'

Sæmundur looked down at himself. Looked into himself. Every bone in his body was cerulean blue. Saturated with raw galdur. Demons. It was still nothing when compared to the forces bound within the Stone Giant.

'Impossible. I've already absorbed all the power I can wield – there is no room for more. You might as well ask me to drink the oceans away, or pull the moon down to the earth.'

'All those things are possible, and even more. You are still thinking like a man.' Kölski grimaced. 'Rigid. Limited. Bound in flesh and clay.' Sæmundur did not respond. The demon snorted. 'No space is as infinite as the gulf between the mind of a living being and the reality outside it. Infinity is the most common size in the universe, and eternity is the only temporal unit.'

An arm fell off one of the seiðskrattar. They were floating in the air behind him and Kölski. Their bodies were decomposing. The wind suddenly picked up. There was no shelter from the wind on Suðurnes. He found himself staring at a straw, bending in the wind. Its roots were shallow, barely gripping the volcanic earth. But still it held fast. Still it did not break.

'What do I have to do?'

'You only need to ask.'

ᚠ

Biðja.

A word that could mean to pray or to ask for something. Two meanings in the same word, both acts humble in their nature.

Sæmundur had never been freely handed anything when it came to galdur. In Svartiskóli secrets were hoarded, like a dragon hoarded gold, guarded with envy and greed. Every grain of truth he had acquired was something he'd had to fight for – something he'd had to take, with cunning, trickery, or brute force.

The possibility had not even come to his mind.

In the distance a buzzing sound grew in volume. Dark dots moved in the sky. Biplanes. He could not afford any further distractions. The two seiðskrattar floated up to meet them, crackling with seiðmagn. Two birds with one stone.

Sæmundur cleared his mind. Shut off the noise, the vibration in everything. Focused on the being inside the stone.

A calm fell over his consciousness. A stillness of the like he had never experienced before.

He reached out his hand. Without words, without galdur or anything at all. Just him, alone out in the lava fields.

Gravel crumbled down the pillar. The earth trembled. With a colossal effort the Stone Giant tore its foot from the ground, breaking it away. First one, then the other. It turned towards Sæmundur. The giant was like an ancient statue, a vague human form without hands. Two legs, an unshapely body, a roughly shaped head. The land made flesh.

The giant bent down until its head was right in front of Sæmundur. He saw the creature glowing inside the rock. It twitched like a child in the womb.

A crack erupted down from the top of the head, opening the stone. There, in the middle of the wound, like a flower found on the highland heath, was an ivory hand. It seemed human, but in an artificial manner. Shaped, like a marble statue. It listlessly reached out its fingers.

Sæmundur reached out towards it.

Their fingertips met.

And he became inflamed with might.

The stone wall was completely smooth. The stones were so closely fitted that only faint lines remained where they interlocked. It was as if the wall had been slightly melted. Garún felt around the wall, trying to find the right spot. Hálfdán's memories were vague when it came to the exact location. He had only tried the pathway once.

'What is it?' Katrín asked in a low voice.

'Nothing, hold on.'

Her fingertips threaded delicate lines, diagonal and vertical, crooked and straight, feeling for the symbol of release. They didn't have much time – too many errors or too much time spent trying to open it and the defensive seiður of the portal would be unleashed.

Something clicked and a hexagonal shape sank into the wall. On it was carved an esoteric symbol. Garún leaned up against it.

'*Rögnezkjar máttreilíf rekmírum.*'

The hexagon twisted and disappeared into the wall. The stones slid back and to the sides, silently forming a pathway wide enough for two people. Inside was a steep spiral stairway leading up into the darkness.

Katrín lit a small oil lamp. They moved as quickly and quietly as they could. Inside the spiral tower the pitch blackness was absolute, oppressing the tiny light. Garún counted the floors in her mind.

Armoury. Soldiers' barracks. Servants' quarters. Pantry and kitchen. The main hall. The large banquet hall. Drawing room. Bedrooms.

Here.

They were out of breath once they reached the right place, but there was no time to rest. With every minute that passed it was more likely that some soldier would look down and notice the boat. Garún headed right towards the wall and mumbled the chant, drew on it three runes of power: the secret emblems of the king, the state and the royal family.

The wall opened with a low click. Katrín hurriedly turned off the lamp.

Ever so slightly, Garún pushed the false wall and took a look inside. A dark living room, richly decorated. So neat and tidy that it seemed completely untouched, as if no one had ever been in there. In the air was a faint fragrance of summer flowers mixed with cigars. In stark contrast, Garún found herself to stink. Like a vagrant.

Her heart was pounding in her chest. Beating up against the

bone, which pushed back with an unworldly chill. The audioskull was set low, so she could barely hear it. She held one end of the headphones up against her ear. The electronic music was soft and calm.

She moved quietly inside. Katrín stood behind, keeping the wall open, making sure that their exit remained accessible.

She leaned up against a door at the end of the room, leading into the stiftamtmaður's private office, and listened. Two sitting rooms for one man, on a floor which was completely set aside for him alone. The excess was despicable.

Everything was quiet. She carefully grabbed the doorknob and risked taking a look inside. The private office was considerably more lived-in. Papers and documents covered the tables, the ashtrays were full, filthy glasses and an unclean plate were left to the side. By the doors was a dirty pair of boots. The golden baroque grandfather clock showed a quarter past four. She was dying to go through the papers. Without a doubt they were about Loftkastalinn and all of them, every detail of their lives. She unplugged the audioskull to better take in the stillness.

The door to the bedroom was halfway shut. The room was fit for a king, after all housing the holder of his power, but it was so excessively decorated that it would normally have driven Garún to a rage. But she did not pay it any attention. The only thing she saw was the man lying at the end of a wide bed, large enough for five people. He was fully dressed, but his chest fell and rose with the calming rhythm of deep sleep.

Not a sound was heard as she walked up to the lying man. Stood over him. Watched him sleeping.

Frederik Ditlev Trampe. Hrímland's appointed stiftamtmaður. Count Trampe. Appointed by King Jörundur and the wielder of his earthly powers.

The jawbone was like frozen steel in her hand. This was the

moment. This was the spark which would bring down the Crown colonial government.

She held the bone over him like a sacrificial dagger. She wanted to wake him up. Drag him out of there. Change history. She wanted to scream at him. She wanted to make him understand what he and those like him had done to her.

But he did not deserve understanding.

Only suffering.

She stabbed him in the chest with the bone, using all the force she could muster. The bone slid effortlessly through flesh and bone, like a sharp dagger. He jumped awake, opening his eyes with a startled look – but he did not scream.

They stared into each other's eyes.

She smiled and broke the bone in the wound.

That was when the screaming started.

She was supposed to be escaping. The guards would be here in a moment. But she could not move. She could not stop watching. She'd never felt so good. About herself, about life, about the order of the world in its entirety.

Everything was just as it was supposed to be. Justice could be attained, or at least, the only justice that truly mattered. Justice which demanded blood, which required hatred to fuel it. Which boiled and seethed and burned. Justice with a blood sacrifice, with a baptism in fire.

Trampe rolled down to the floor. He was on all fours, like a beast. She'd never heard a man scream like that. As if he never needed to draw in breath. Or – he did not draw in breath. He wasn't truly screaming.

Not with his lungs.

Unnatural waves moved through his flesh. Up the back, down

his thighs, the calves. Dark blotches of blood grew on his clothes. Like a photograph slowly coming to light.

Church bells sounded in the distance. Rapid, as if a lunatic was ringing in the Mass.

He arched and twisted, then turned and slammed himself down on his back. Twitched and slammed himself down again and again, as if he had something on his back and was trying to kill it.

No, those weren't church bells. Something else. Alarms.

A geyser of blood erupted from his bowels. Frantic tendrils sprouted rapidly, swinging back and forth. Smelling. Sensing.

He arched his head unnaturally far back. His face was locked in a silent scream, the jaw open as far as it could go. She saw something crawl from his mouth. Something with eyes and teeth. He kept on flailing his arms the entire time, battling invisible spirits. It was rather funny, in fact. The flesh ran off him like overcooked meat off a bone.

He was dead. Worse than dead. It was over. She had to go – now.

But she could not bring herself to look away.

She was so happy.

ᚠ

It was seconds, minutes or hours later that the trance broke. She was hit in the temple with the stock of a rifle and fell limp to the ground. More beating followed, in her stomach, back, head. Iron locked itself around her hands and muddy boots pushed her head against the carpet. Drops of blood were leaking into it. From her. She thought.

Trampe would not stop screaming. No matter how completely ruined and unrecognisable his body became. He screamed after the jaw fell off him, after the skull collapsed into itself and was sucked into the torso.

A black sack covered her vision and she was pulled to her feet.

She could not stop smiling. They dragged her down, outside. The screams of Trampe could be heard just as clearly as inside the bedroom. Resounding in her head, along with the bells. And some other sound, which she could not quite recognise.

It sounded like laughter.

Þrjátíu og sjö

Darkness is the only constant in the world. The only thing which is not fleeting. It was before everything else, and will remain after everything vanishes. Darkness is eternal.

Even in bright daylight, in a well-lit home, darkness is there. You simply cannot see it for all the light. It is misleading, interfering. But it's there, behind everything.

Waiting.

ᛁ

It was not pain which awoke her. Not the swelling and the wounds. But her guilt. Guilt reaches deeper than any cut. It pierces your soul. Dissects you alive.

She told herself Katrín might have got away. There was a chance. Katrín had not come inside after the screaming started. That was good. That was according to plan. She might have escaped. How long had she stood there? Hypnotised by the horror she had manifested. She had no way of knowing.

A part of her felt as if she was still standing there. Frozen in the same tracks. Felt as he was still screaming, forever and relentless. That she was still laughing hysterically.

It was pitch black. Completely and absolutely dark. It did not matter if she opened or closed her eyes. A dreamless sleep came and left, but she was never certain if she'd fallen asleep at all. What was the difference? The nightmare and the guilt never left her side.

The cell was around a metre and a half on each side. It was made from stone. There was no door, at least none that Garún could find with her searching fingers. No bed, no chair, no toilet, no bucket, or anything else. Just her and the darkness.

She was not confused. She knew exactly where she was.

She was in the Nine.

There was no end to the gossip about Hegningarhúsið on Skólavörðustígur. That its dungeons went hundreds of metres down into the ground. Kept on going until they encountered lava, and that was where the worst criminals ended up. In a man-made hell. Others said that those who ended up in the Nine were brainwashed and turned into the agents of the Crown. That was why no one ever returned. They were serving the Commonwealth somewhere else entirely. One story went that criminals were sentenced to carry demons in their bones. They were then slaughtered and harvested, the blue bones weaponised and sent to the front lines, to hidden arcane armouries. Others said that there was nothing in there. The house was completely empty. Except for one cell, which held nothing but a chair and a noose hanging from a ceiling beam.

None of this mattered. They were only rumours. The only thing that mattered was the truth:

No one returns from the Nine.

The darkness shuts you off. Pushes up against you, into every nook and cranny. Locks you inside your own body. You sense nothing but your own heartbeat, the buzz in your ears, your own foul breath.

She never heard them coming. The pain was not the worst part. The worst part was how absolutely shut off inside herself she was, which made every single blow that much heavier.

The guilt gnawed at her like a worm on the root of a tree. Nothing but hatred and poison. She should be trying to get herself out of there. She'd failed them.

Sometimes she let herself hope. That Katrín and Hraki were safe and, if not, that the people had risen up against their oppressors. Diljá and Hrólfur would still be in Reykjavík, working towards that goal. Regardless of everything that had happened. They might not understand why, but they would still keep fighting for what they believed. They'd accomplished their task, after all, and so much more than that. They'd brought down Loftkastalinn. She'd executed the stiftamtmaður.

Reykjavík was like a powder keg. And she was the spark. She had to believe that someone had taken her torch from her.

The light was like an electric shock. It paralysed her. She could not move. Had she been asleep? Was she still in her cell? She closed her eyes, tried to adjust to the light, but she just saw a blinding whiteness.

Slowly her eyes adjusted to the light.

On the table in front of her was an electric lamp shining directly into her face. She was tied to a chair. She could only see out of one of her eyes. The other was too swollen. She was only realising this now.

Someone was sitting at the other end of the table. It was

impossible to see his face, but she saw his neat suit, the sheen of his polished cufflinks.

'I'm not talking,' she said eventually. 'Not a word.'

She was surprised by how weak and raw her voice had become.

'You won't have to speak at all,' the man said.

There was something familiar about his voice. She heard a door close behind her. Someone walked up to them. She tensed up. Prepared herself for the coming pain.

But it never came. The person who'd walked in dragged a chair along the floor and sat at the table. A thin huldumaður. Viður.

She had no words. There was too much she wanted to say, so much that the weapons turned in her hands and fell to the ground.

'How much do you want, Þráinn? All of it?' asked Viður in a casual voice. He did not look directly at Garún.

'Not all of it,' the man named Þráinn responded. 'Not yet, anyway. The commissioner was quite clear on that. Let's start with the bone, then the galdramaður. This Sæmundur.'

He nodded his approval.

She realised who the man behind the light was. That same, repugnant voice. It was the man who'd caught her after she bought delýsíð in the Forgotten Downtown. The officer she thought Sæmundur had killed.

She tried to free herself. Screamed. Viður moved closer, now staring at her intently. She refused to look at him, clenched her eyes shut.

But it was for nothing.

ᚠ

Hljóð.

A single word encompassing both silence and sound. One and the same.

For everything is sound.

His heart was no longer beating. Instead a thunderstorm raged inside him. His bones sang with reverberation.

Everything trembled. Everything quaked. Everything resounded.

The world was a stage. This was something he had been absolutely certain of. Every world and every dimension there was. Deceptions and illusions. But he now saw that was only a fraction of the truth.

Every world is a frequency. A sound wave. Only existing as long as the movement does, as the frequency rises and falls. In the beginning, there was nothing. Then, there was the word. The sound. The wave rises and the vibration, the reverberation, births existence. The frequency reaches its limit, and falls back down into nothingness. The world ends, only to dive and rise again and birth a new universe. The sound wave vibrates up and down, up and down. Every peak and valley only a fraction of a single note, which itself only lasts for a moment in a long and majestic work of music which his mind could barely fathom. Everything was sound, birthed from the same source.

That was the fountain galdur drew its power from. When galdur worked, it was only because a minor harmonisation occurred with that original sound, the tone of creation which was the source of everything. Planets, dimensions, life and darkness itself. Everything. Only a side effect of whatever end the greater score was working towards.

He could hear them. All the worlds, together, sounding. Nothing but echo that is thrown back and forth until it fades away.

But behind that was the beginning and the end. That which Kölski had talked about. That which is and is not. Was never and has always been.

The almighty overwhelmed him completely.

Life is chaos. An incomprehensible pandemonium. We try to place events in context, understand cause and effect, but behind each incident is a meeting of endless threads into one possibility, which then multiply. How can the infinite multiply itself? It is impossible. The human mind cannot fathom infinity. Not in a real sense.

But time had unwound itself in Sæmundur's mind, spread out and poured over him in its true image. That which had been a linear and comprehensible form, stretched out and mutated. Became incomprehensible. Time did not exist. Had always existed.

There was no cause and effect. No past or future. That which living beings experienced as fundamental change – every death and every birth, revolutions, supernovas burning out, galaxies colliding, entire dimensions collapsing – all of this was drowned out in the background and blended into one constant.

She couldn't move.

Katrín, Styrhildur and Hraki were standing in front of her and shaking their heads in disappointment. They were covered in terrible wounds.

'We should never have trusted her.'

'I am so glad she's dead.'

'She deserves worse.'

'Selfish bitch. Stupid, selfish bitch.'

'You deserve this.'

Then they set her on fire. But she couldn't die. She was alive and she felt the flames cover her, the fat crackling and the eyes bursting.

ᛣ

He could send planets off their orbits. Make suns pull his chariot. Let ocean and sky change their place. Remove the force of gravity. Rewrite the laws of nature.

But none of that mattered. The entire work of creation was an insignificant detail, a speck in a microscope, completely without significance. So many things moved before his eyes, in his mind. Greater and more important than anything he had ever imagined.

ᛣ

In the beginning was the word.

Tone.

Sound.

But before the tone of creation sounded, the same which still resounded and created reality itself, there had been silence. And after the tone would fade, silence would still remain.

Emptiness. Nothing.

Silence. Sound.

Hljóð.

Galdur.

ᛣ

They were robbing her of herself. It was not enough for them to simply execute her – no, they had to reach back in time and kill her there as well. Murder her memories and her along with them.

The same thing she had done to Hálfdán. She felt as if he now took up more room in her head that she herself did. They'd mostly let him be once they realised what had taken place. What would happen if it kept on like this? When would Garún disappear and this other element take over?

She held on dearly to those good memories she had left. They had no reason to take them away from her, but she was certain that Viður was sneaking into them and feeding upon them like delicacies. But she could not be certain. She could not know what she had lost. She only knew that it happened, had to have happened, because she remembered the interrogation. But there were also some things in her life that didn't fit together any more. She couldn't remember how she'd met Sæmundur. Why they'd broken up. Where he was. What she'd asked him to do.

But she remembered when she was painting in the living room one summer evening, and he was playing some ditty on his guitar and singing along with it. Just making something up. She had been so happy. She held on to this memory with all her might, reliving it again and again in her mind.

She tried killing herself by beating her head against the rock. There was nothing else in the cell. The only things she accomplished were new wounds and being unconscious for a vague amount of time.

The beatings had stopped. She didn't know how long she'd been kept here. Time had no meaning to her any more. But she wished that they'd kept on. Perhaps they would have accidentally killed her.

It didn't add up. The same man she'd seen overpowered by living darkness. Þráinn Meinholt. Sæmundur had killed him. At first she thought she had gone insane. Had imagined it all along. But the next interrogation happened in the same bright room, and he was always there. Him and Viður. She screamed at him, demanded answers, said it wasn't him, she would not fall for this trick, but he never did anything except to smile in return. Then, when Viður drew closer her words of hate immediately evaporated. She begged for mercy. She would tell them everything. Anything they wanted to know. So long as they did not take anything further from her.

She hated herself for breaking down like this. Being turned into this wreck. After every interrogation, she decided to never beg them again, but she broke down each time. It kept on happening faster and faster.

ᚠ

She was tied to the chair when she came to. She was alone in the interrogation room. No officer, no Viður, not even the table was there. Perhaps it was a different room. Opposite her was an empty chair.

The sound of steps, behind her. Someone walking down the hall outside. The sound of keys jingling and then the door being unlocked. Someone entered. The door slammed shut.

She didn't look up. Her head hung limply forward.

A man in an expensive suit sat in the chair opposite her. Well-polished shoes, trousers neatly pressed.

'Hello, Garún.'

She looked up. She had assumed it to be the officer, Þráinn. But the voice had been too familiar.

Hrólfur leaned back in the seat against her.

No words. No words would do for her. They were all ruined, meaningless.

'I'm not quite sure what I'm doing here.' He reached into his pocket for a pack of cigarettes and shook one out. 'They told me to leave it be. That it was pointless. But I felt like you deserved something. Some explanation. So I asked them to ensure that you would remember enough for the purposes of this conversation.'

She watched him light his cigarette and inhale the blue-grey smoke. Factory-rolled cigarettes. With no character. Her ears buzzed.

'You...'

She swallowed. It was hard to speak. Every word she tried to speak out loud only came forth as involuntary twitching as they all simultaneously fought for purchase. She felt nauseous.

'All this time?'

He nodded, brushed ash off his trousers.

'All this time.'

'Also Diljá? Katrín?'

She could hardly form sentences. Her mind reeled as she went through their time together, or what she had remaining of it, re-examining every single word, every moment, every decision.

'No. Just me.'

'Where is Katrín?' Garún struggled to keep her voice level. 'What did you do to her?'

'She's here. In the Nine.'

'And Diljá?

Some shadow of pain had moved across his face when she said Diljá's name. As if it hurt him to be reminded of her. As if he had loved her. Garún felt heat flow into her. Her heart pounding. Screaming.

'That's none of your concern.'

She spat in his face. There was blood in the saliva.

'You've killed them! You've killed them! You disgusting fucking pig!'

She struggled against her restraints and screamed, not aware of what she was saying. The chair rocked and she fell to the floor.

But she still kept on going. The doors opened and guards came in, but Hrólfur said it was fine, they could go.

She pushed, fought and screamed until she became completely numb. Sore and empty. Hrólfur lifted up her chair and sat back down opposite her. He'd wiped the spit off himself.

'Finished?'

She said nothing.

'I cared for Diljá. I really did. But she was always trouble. These huldufólk are always groping your emotions when you least expect it. It just won't do. So when the pressure became considerable, I decided to develop some feelings towards her. Only let her sense love and affection. I wished it hadn't had to come to this. But I was always prepared for it. As you said yourself, she was completely aware of what she was signing up for.'

'Knew what she was signing up for?' Garún screamed. 'Are you completely fucking insane? You betrayed us! You killed her!'

He shook his head. 'I knew you wouldn't understand. I don't know why I thought you would, after you went so completely off the rails.'

'Understand what? That you are an inhuman piece of shit?' She shook her head and laughed. 'It doesn't matter. You didn't manage to stop us. The stiftamtmaður is dead. Loftkastalinn is gone. The Crown is not invincible. The people will rise up against their oppressors and tear down all the despicable walls you have built around yourselves.'

He stared at her, dumbfounded. 'Stop you? But that was exactly the purpose. To remove Trampe.'

She could not speak. This was the last thing she'd thought he would say.

'Well, all right. The goal wasn't exactly to kill the stiftamt-maður,' Hrólfur went on, twirling the cigarette in his hands.

'It was to destabilise Trampe and get some leverage on him. Removing him was a long-term *political* plan, if you can wrap your head around something like that. That was always the agenda, long before that crappy little newsletter was founded. This course of events was set in motion before you needed more delýsíð and went to Viður to buy more. The trap he set you up with. Everything.'

He took a drag of smoke and studied her as he blew it out.

'The only thing I did not expect was that fucking Sæmundur. And you going so absolutely off the goddamn rails. Never expected him to be the lunatic he turned out to be. But it was fine, we will have Sæmundur neutralised soon enough. And it turned out well for us that Loftkastalinn vanished.'

'Well for you? You work for the fucking Crown!'

He sighed and leaned forward in his seat.

'Garún, think. Who benefits the most from getting the stiftamtmaður out of the way? Do you have any idea of the political landscape in this country? Or are you so completely absorbed in your own revolutionary rage and sense of self-righteousness that you are absolutely out of sync with reality?'

He threw his cigarette to the ground and crushed it under his heel.

'I work for Innréttingarnar. For Sheriff Skúli. For the party. Trampe was trouble from the get-go, and he had to be managed. That was why we let your little rebellion operate for as long as it did, printing *Black Wings* without repercussion. It worked, for a while – Skúli thought he could slowly undermine Trampe. But then Katrín got *that* fucking article in the paper and sabotaged the deal for Perlan. Goddamn, how you bitches went behind my back. You ruined everything, Trampe went berserk when he heard about it. The entitled moron . . . He never compromised!'

Hrólfur leaned back and crossed his legs.

'I guess you two had that in common. Trampe never understood how everyone could profit. How everyone's interests could be ensured, so that everyone could come out of a deal having gained something. He never knew how to compromise. So we had to put some pressure on him. That's why the protests were allowed to happen. You weakened Trampe's hold on Hrímland and gave us the chance to form the Home Rule Party. Everything you did, everything you fought for, was for our benefit.'

'He's dead,' said Garún. 'So your little plan, to use the protests to manipulate him, fucking exploded in your hands. No matter what the reason for it was. He's dead and the people will rise up against you.'

'Why should one dead nobleman ensure a nation's independence? Even if he was assassinated. Even if Loftkastalinn, their little science experiment, has disappeared. People still know their place, as always. The Crown still controls the army, their warships and biplanes. And now they have those fucking alien things that suck the life out of people – as you've seen first-hand.'

She did not know what he meant by that.

'So, Trampe is dead. Maybe not exactly what we were planning for, but we knew the possibility was there. A political failure removing Trampe from office would have been preferable – but beggars can't be choosers. So, Hrímland needs a new stiftamt-maður. It just so happens that the most suitable candidate is the king's close nephew, Loretz Engel Gyldenlöve. Respected in the court, an educated person of great pedigree, but at heart a simple man who likes to drink and thinks more about fucking than politics. He is a man who will do as he's told and like it, unlike Trampe. A man who sees that it's to everyone's benefit to, for example, properly privatise Perlan and put some real industry on the map here. Put all this fucking unnature around us to some use and let the cogs of the economy work freely, so cash can flow in the right place. Everyone benefits, and we won't have to destabilise the country just to get the stiftamtmaður to do as he's told.'

He leaned in towards her. 'The only thing we needed was a credible reason behind the dissent. A buffer between us and the protests. Along came the spirit of the revolution: you.'

'You're lying! I'm in the Nine, a prisoner of the Crown! That officer, Þráinn, works for them! They would have realised this long ago!'

'Hegningarhúsið at Skólavörðustígur 9 is not run by the Crown, although many people think it is. It's run by the Ministry of Justice – specifically, the Directorate of Immigration. The Hrímlandic government. Lögrétta. This house was built by Innréttingar, one of their first ventures, along with the parliament building. And that officer, Meinholt, he's just like me, and his boss, the commissioner. On the party's payroll.'

Hrólfur stood up. 'The revolution isn't coming. I just wanted you to know that. I always found your pretentious righteousness to be completely insufferable.'

He walked behind her and knocked on the door. Her heart was beating so fast that she thought she might die. She wished she could die. There were so many things she wanted to say, she wanted to do. She wished she had said, or done.

'They will execute you in a few days,' he went on in the same, casual tone. 'I convinced them to leave some memories behind.' She could hear the guard opening the door for him. 'You won't simply die. You know that, right? You haven't earned death in some blissful ignorance. The seiðskrattar will ensure you get a traitor's death. You'll be tortured for an eternity.'

She leaned back in the chair, stretching to see him. She could not hold back the tears that now flooded unhindered from her eyes.

'What about Katrín and Diljá? Hraki? Is Styrhildur alive?'

'Styrhildur and Hraki will find themselves here soon enough. Katrín will be executed along with you, but in a more humane way. Her father managed to get that through, although he could not convince Skúli to completely spare her. Diljá is none of your concern.'

The door slammed shut.

ᚠ

A sorrowful scream woke Sæmundur from his torpor, the overwhelming ennui which had overtaken him. He brought his tiny fragment of the world back into focus. The sound came from Reykjavík.

He turned towards the city. His limbs were so heavy that he barely managed to find the strength to move them. Turning his torso was like weathering down a mountain with nothing but the wind. An impossibly long and exhausting effort.

He listened closely. It was a terrible wail, which never needed to draw breath. It cut him to his deepest core. He knew that voice.

Garún.

She was in a bottomless pit, imprisoned deep within the ground, bound with sorrow and regret. Tortured. Memories ripped out, bloody, and devoured raw. Blasphemy.

Her suffering and despair came pouring over him in full force. Touched something deep within him, a sensitive core which had still not hardened and become numb to emotion.

He had abandoned her so many times before. He'd lied to himself that he wasn't ashamed of bringing her to the party at Svartiskóli. But it wasn't true. He'd sacrificed a creature Garún loved dearly, just to further his own selfish desires. He had betrayed her over and over again.

In those moments he had only cared about himself. Himself and his perceived destiny. It was all about his journey, about what he had still to learn, still to discover. He had to show the stuck-up academics at Svartiskóli what was what. Everything revolved around him and his own ego. Nothing else mattered.

The scream came to him again, like the sound of instruments carried with the wind.

Garún.

She called out to him, like frenzied church bells in the distance. Woke him up from the dead.

Garún.

I am coming.

ᛉ

The land shook with his every step. Sharp volcanic stones were torn from the ground and attached themselves to his feet, layer after layer. The seiðmagn in the land erupted and boiled from his coming. The rock piled up on his back, hands and feet, enveloped him entirely. He was about to give up after each step he took. He was completely exhausted. Nothing was as tempting as to give up and let the comforting apathy overwhelm him again. Lose himself in the cacophony, in the sounds of the abyss.

But from the city came a terrifying scream which cut at the very roots of his soul. Struck at one of the few nerves of humanity that still remained.

And he took another step.

Garún.

ᛉ

The sun shone in the sky with an odd, flickering light. It was dark but still bright. An everlasting dusk followed him. Time eluded his grasp. Everything had already happened, was still to happen. He had reached Reykjavík. He was heading there. He was taking Mæja from Garún on his doorstep. Sounds of the cascading rain. He was meeting her for the first time at Karnivalið. Heart racing. Smiling. Laughing.

He focused on placing one foot in front of the other. It took every ounce of grit he possessed to keep on going. He knew he was well on his way when he crossed the Suðurnes channel in one, gigantic step. There was not much left.

ᚠ

Reykjavík was hiding behind her city walls. He had once thought them tall, but now he towered over them. The city was nothing but a sandcastle waiting to be swept away by the waves. And how easily he could be that wave, if only he mustered the will to do so. The city's – the entire island's – unavoidable end seemed so close at hand that he couldn't be bothered to lay it all waste prematurely.

Garún's suffering was maddening. He ached from her pain. She was there, in the city. There was so little distance between them now. He would not abandon her. Not again.

Biplanes buzzed around his head like flies. Men writhed on the walls like insects. Something hit him. Hail. No. Gunfire.

Garún.

He stopped just outside of the city walls. He had to think – to concentrate. Cannons at the walls pelted him with distracting explosive volleys. They were too insignificant to act on. There was so much noise coming from all the life and death piled up there behind the walls. She was drowned out in the sound, blended in to it.

She was all over the city. In Starholt, drunk and happy, sharing her bed with him. Painting the first work she sold, for ten krónur. Spraying delýsíð graffiti in secret spots, piling up the bonfire she wanted to ignite. Stabbing a man in the chest with a blue bone, laughing as he was transformed into a beautiful flower. Suffering in a dark hole downtown, buried and forgotten, losing fragments of herself with each day that passed. Smuggling herself into the city, hidden under furs of skuggabaldur...

But now... Now she was...

He had almost located her when a powerful seiður disturbed his concentration. Down at his feet, seiðskrattar had gathered on the fortifications of the main city gate. They worked together in weaving seiður against him. The air crackled with raw power.

He raised his arm, laden thick with moss-grown stone and broken rock, and he brought it down upon them.

The air erupted with a sorcerous storm, as the seiðskrattar attempted to fight back, but their power was nothing when faced with the landvættur itself at their gates. With a deafening explosion the southern gate collapsed under his fist. He took a step forward, then another. He tore through the city wall like paper.

People swarmed around his feet like ants. Past, present, future lives, all melding into one relentless flow of life. Sorrow, regret, joy, hope. He moved through the city, crushing buildings beneath his feet, sweeping away entire city blocks, trying to pinpoint Garún's voice. He saw her laughing with him in a bar, meeting for the first time. Them sleeping together in her apartment, the summer sun shining through her curtains. The first time they kissed, hesitant, their hearts racing in sync with one another.

Then he felt the source. Hegningarhúsið. He turned towards the city's central area, the top of the hill of Skólavörðuholt where the split tower of Haraldskirkja loomed. And with determined, lethargic steps, the Stone Giant moved towards it.

Soldiers blasted him with mortars; squadrons of biplanes took to the air and bombarded him. The biplanes circled him, firing at will, and he distractedly blasted them out of the sky with piercing rays of black light. Seiðskrattar ambushed him on rooftops, channelling dreadful energies towards this leviathan of stone. None managed to break his stride. They all fell to the crashing wave of his footsteps, crushed under his fist, or erupted in blood as he seized hold of the torrents of seiðmagn around them and drove that energy back against their limited minds and bodies, melting iron and brick and concrete into glowing slabs in a deafening explosion.

With heavy steps he ascended Skólavörðuholt. He swung his arm carelessly, breaking through the tower of Haraldskirkja as he neared Hegningarhúsið. The tower collapsed upon the church, instantly reducing the Crown's monument to rubble, a cloud of dust and detritus rising up from its ruins, crawling along the streets. He stood in front of Hegningarhúsið on Skólavörðustræti. People trampled each other, automobiles and carriages running down other people on the roads, crashing into each other. He tuned out the hectic drone of their pointless suffering. Garún was there, in the earth underneath the Nine. He was about to reach down for her when he found what he was looking for.

On top of the building were three tall stakes. A torso was impaled on each one, without head or limbs. Intestines, organs, limbs and heads were impaled on other, smaller stakes, all around them. Like saplings spread around three, bloody trees.

Garún.

That was the source of the scream. Right at his feet. The echo of her life and death, which still sounded and called out to him. Screamed out into the world. The desecrated remains of her soul, trapped in a torturous limbo. She had been given a traitor's execution. A seiðskratti working with a galdramaður, her spirit unwound and threaded through her bones, trapping her soul in an inescapable cycle of torture. A ceaseless nightmare. On the other stakes were her friend, Katrín, and an innocent homeless man who was killed in the place of another woman, for the crime of being in the wrong place at the wrong time. They had not suffered as she did. They had already vanished from this world. She alone was forced to endure this hell.

He was too late. He had been too late before he started on his way, he now realised. These events had been set in motion long before he headed towards Reykjavík, long before they met. He had always been too late.

He looked over Reykjavík. The death and destruction he had left in his wake. He could create continents, drain oceans, re-arrange the orbit of the stars, but he could not save Garún. But that had never been his purpose.

Time had unfolded before him. And he saw the threads of Garún's fate, laid out before him. With a gleeful smile, he pulled at the seam of the seiður which had brought her to the end of her life, the galdur which trapped her spirit. He undid the curses, the malevolent seiðmagn, the brutal incantations which had bound her spirit to her bones, nails through the essence of her very being. He unwound the crude, ugly sorcery in an instant and to his surprise, Garún chose to remain, even though she was free. But then he remembered – she had always chosen to remain.

He lifted a hand and brought it crashing down upon the Nine. The stone fist broke through the roof effortlessly, crushing floors, digging into the earth and towards the chambers in the dark. Where so many souls were locked and imprisoned. With a small effort of his will, the prison doors burst open, shattered into pieces, and the prisoners came flooding out of the ruined building like a swarm of ants. One of them, a woman trans-formed by a cruel seiðskratti under the orders of a loathsome man, found Garún's bones in the rubble. They were calling to her. She heeded the call and picked them up. The bones told her where to take them. Then, she found the person she had been looking for. Her lover, who still recognised her, despite all the terrible harm they had done to her body with seiðmagn. The soldier who had abandoned his post for her love. He took her hand and they ran for safety.

Numbness crashed over him like an ocean, drowning his consciousness and smothering him completely. It had been so inconceivably hard to find the strength to make this slight interference. It felt so good to finally let go. He raised his head and looked towards the endless sky, seeing the universe stretch out before him.

The cacophony of suffering merged with the noise of the city, blending in with the rhythm which rose and fell like waves crashing on the shore. Reykjavík faded into the background, disappearing into the painful scream which was all this harmful world.

Epilogue

The demon waited by the stone, silent and patient. The sun gleamed on its black chitinous shell. Time did not exist to it, only eternity. The stone was stooped and long, like a chrysalis made from lava rock. From its end hung a limp, pale hand.

Something gave. The hand twitched. From the stone slid an arm, a head, shoulders, a torso following it. The creature hit the earth like a stillborn lamb. It was hairless and gaunt. Human-shaped, but not quite.

Kölski started the incantation.

Þykkt blóð, þreytast rekkar.	*Thick blood, fighters grow weary.*
Þjóð mörg vos öld bjóða,	*The nation endures centuries of hardship,*
grand heitt, gumar andast,	*great destruction, men die,*
glatast auður, firrast snauðir.	*wealth is lost, the destitute are shunned.*
Hætt grand hræðast dróttir	*Perilous ruin the people dread,*
hríð mörg, vesöld viða,	*storm upon storm, plagued by misery,*
angur vænt, ærnar skærur.	*heavy remorse, relentless warfare.*
Illur sveimur nú er í heimi.	*An evil stir haunts the world.*

The creature twitched and opened its eyes. There was nothing behind the eyelids. The eyes were not obsidian black, nor the void of the night sky. They were nothing. The creature stood up on unstable feet. Its bare head was crowned with a tangle of black horns, gnarled and sharp like the cold of winter.

'*Illur sveimur nú er í heimi,*' the creature responded in a low voice.

Kölski took a deep bow and addressed the being.

'*My Lord, what is your command?*'

Glossary

Amma ['amːa] – Grandmother.

Blendingur ['plɛntin,kʏr] – A person with human and huldufólk parents. *Word refers to a being which is a mixture of two species.*

Blóðgagl ['plouð,kakl̩] / **Blóðgögl** ['plouð,kœkl̩] – Clan warriors of the náskárar tribes. *Old poetical kenning for raven. Blóð = blood; gagl = bird (young goose).*

Blót [plouːt] – A ritualistic worship or sacrifice to the gods. *From old Norse paganism.*

Brennivín ['prɛnːɪ,vin] – A type of strong liquor. *Literally means burning wine.*

Delýsið ['tɛːlisɪð] – A sorcerous narcotic, can be fluid or solid. Most often snorted in powder. Frequent use erodes the nasal septum. *Approximate pronunciation: de ('e' as in 'bed') – lee – seeth.*

Draugur ['trœiːɣʏr] – A ghost, resentful, hateful and dangerous. *In Icelandic folklore, draugar are physical unliving beings, not ethereal spirits.*

Elskan ['ɛlskan] – Word of affection; darling, dear.

Galdramaður ['kaltra,maːðʏr] / **Galdramenn** ['kaltra,mɛnː] – Practitioners of galdur. *Galdur = magic; maður/menn = man/men.*

487

Galdrastafur [ˈkaltraˌstaːvʏr] / **Galdrastafir** [ˈkaltraˌstaːvɪɽ] – Arcane symbols, runes, staves. *Galdur = magic; stafur/stafir = stave/staves.*

Galdur [ˈkaltʏr] – Type of spoken magic. *From old Norse paganism. Word derived from the verb gala, meaning to yell or sing, deriving its power from poetry chanted in a particular way.*

Gandreið [ˈkantˌrɛið] – A vile, arcane method of control or possession. *In Icelandic folklore, witches used gandreið to control an object to fly through the air. The worst method of gandreið used a man as a mount to fly.*

Goði [ˈkɔːðɪ] / **Goðar** [ˈkɔːðar] – A parliament member of Lögrétta. *In the Icelandic Age of Settlement, around AD 930, goðar were ruling chieftains who sat in Alþingi.*

Haugbúi [ˈhœiːɣˌpuɪ] / **Haugbúar** [ˈhœiːɣˌpuaɽ] – A type of undead creature, a corporeal ghost, a draugur.

Hegningarhúsið [ˈhɛkniŋkarˌhuːsið] – Translated means 'the Penalty House'. Also called *Steinninn* (the Rock) and *Nían* (the Nine). *Located on Skólavörðustígur 9, it was Iceland's first prison, built from the same stone as the house of parliament, Alþingi.*

Helskurn [ˈhɛːlˌskʏrtn̩] – A renowned armour of a hersir. *Literal translation is death's shell.*

Hersir [ˈhɛɽsɪr] – The leader of a tribe of náskárar. *Old poetical kenning for king.*

Hertygi [ˈhɛɽtʰijɪ] – A harness the náskárar wear around their torsos, displaying trophies and important status symbols. *Old word for military equipment: her = army; tygi = clothes.*

Hljóð [l̥jouːð] – Can mean sound or silence, depending on the context.

Hrafnaspark [ˈr̥apnaˌspaɽk] – The script of the náskárar language, called skramsl. *Word used to describe bad handwriting, ugly scrawls, in Icelandic. Hrafna = raven's; spark = kick.*

Hrímland ['r̥im‚lant] – An island far in the north, almost un-inhabitable with wild, sorcerous energies infesting the country.

Hrævareldur ['r̥aivar‚ɛltʏr] / **Hrævareldar** ['r̥aivar‚ɛltar] – A flame, floating in the air, luring people to their death. They seem to frequent forgotten or cursed places.

Huldufólk ['hʏltʏ‚foul̥k] / **Huldukona** ['hʏltʏ‚kɔːna] / **Huldumaður** ['hʏltʏ‚maːðʏr] – Extradimensional exiles in the world of Hrímland. *Hulda/huldu is a prefix meaning 'hidden'. Can also be a female name. Maður = man; kona = woman; fólk = people.*

Hulduheimar ['hʏltʏ‚hɛiːmar] – The original dimension of the huldufólk. *Huldu = hidden; heimar = worlds.*

Huldumanneskja ['hʏltʏ‚manːɛsca] / **Huldumanneskjur** ['hʏltʏ‚manːɛscʏr] – A word for people with huldufólk and human parents which better accepts and fully encompasses who they are: not a mixture of two beings, but a unified, whole being. *Hulda = hidden; manneskja = human being.*

Korpur ['kʰɔr̥pʏr] / **Korpar** ['kʰɔr̥par] – Náskárar warriors without a tribe. *Old Icelandic word for raven.*

Kukl [kʰʏhkl̩] / **Kuklari** ['kʰʏhkları] / **Kuklarar** ['kʰʏhklarar] – Kukl is unlearned, ill-understood magic, meddling and tampering with the occult. A kuklari is a practitioner of such low, unlearned sorcery.

Króna ['kʰrouːna] / **Krónur** ['kʰrouːnʏr] – Currency. One króna consists of one hundred aurar.

Krummafótur ['kʰrʏmːa‚fouːtʏr] – The third foot of the náskárar, much stronger than the other two claws. Used for standing on for long periods and picking up heavy objects. *Also used to indicate a shoe put on the wrong foot, that's a krummafótur.*

Lögrétta ['lœɣ‚riɛhta] – The Hrímlandic parliament. Used for both the parliament and the parliament building itself. *Historically, a legislative institution of Iceland's parliament, Alþingi.*

Mamma [ˈmamːa] – Mother.

Marbendill [ˈmarˌpɛntɪtl̩] / **Marbendlar** [ˈmarˌpɛntlar] – Aquatic humanoids who live in both fresh waters and the sea. *Word from Icelandic folklore for aquatic beings.*

Náskári [ˈnauːˌskarɪ] / **Náskárar** [ˈnauːˌskarar] – The ravenfolk. *Word is an old poetical kenning for raven. Ná = corpse; skári = bird (young seagull).*

Níðstöng [ˈniðˌstœiŋk] / **Níðstangir** [ˈniðˌstauŋkɪr] – An incredibly dangerous type of svartigaldur, used to curse someone with awful magic, bringing complete ruination to them. *In Icelandic folklore, a níðstöng was often a raised pole with a horse's head impaled on it, facing the location it should curse. In modern times, níðstangir have been raised against authorities and people, usually with a cod's head on the pole.*

Nykur [ˈnɪːkʏr] / **Nykrar** [ˈnɪkrar] – An underwater creature, often towing barges for the marbendlar. *A terrible creature from Icelandic folklore in the guise of a horse. It lived in lakes, luring people into the waters.*

Seiðmagn [ˈseiːðˌmakn̩] – Sorcerous energy, found in nature. *Seiður = sorcery; magn = power. Compound word is similarly structured as rafmagn = electricity.*

Seiðskratti [ˈseiːðˌskrahtɪ] – A practitioner of seiður, highly skilled and learned in its application. *In Icelandic, used to refer to a malevolent sorcerer. Seið = sorcery; skratti = fiend.*

Seiður [ˈseiːðʏr] – Type of sorcery. *Type of magic from old Norse paganism.*

Skoffín [ˈskɔfːin] – A type of small, wild animal, terribly ugly and dangerous. *From Icelandic folklore: a spawn of a fox and a cat, with the cat being the mother.*

Skramsl [ˈskramstl̩] – The language of the náskárar. *Archaic word for cawing. The more common, modern word for cawing is krunk.*

Skrumnir ['skrʏmnɪɾ] – The sorcerer in a tribe of náskárar. *Old poetical kenning for raven.*

Skuggabaldur ['skʏkːaˌpaltʏr] – A type of small, vicious animal, similar to a fox or a mink. Very dangerous to livestock and hard to kill. *From Icelandic folklore: a spawn of a fox and a cat, with the fox being the mother.*

Sorti ['sɔɾtɪ] – Dangerous sorcerous narcotic. *Word for something pitch black; can also refer to thick, heavy fog or weather.*

Stiftamtmaður ['stɪftˌam̥tˌmaðʏr] – The governor of the colony of Hrímland; the stiftamtmaður acts out the will of the king and rules in his name. *Historical political title in Iceland, from when Denmark ruled the country. The stiftamtmaður served as the highest royal authority and representative of the king in Iceland. The country was separated into units of amt, which amtmenn governed, the stiftamtmenn governing the entire country.*

Svartigaldur ['svaɾtɪˌkaltʏr] – The vilest, most heinous kind of galdur.

Tilberi ['tʰɪːlˌpɛrɪ] – A simple creature made with galdur, usually to work simple repeated tasks. *In folklore, a tilberi was most often used to steal milk from nearby farms.*

Tröll ['tʰrœtl̥] – A troll.

Útburður ['uːtˌpʏrðʏr] – The word for a newborn infant which was carried out into the freezing wilderness shortly after being born. *In Iceland's history, famine and shortage has been very common, resulting in these kinds of practices. Many folklore stories deal with the guilt and horror caused by the spirits of these newborn children.*

Vættur ['vaihtʏr] / **Vættir** ['vaihtɪr] – A kind of nature being or spirit. *Illvættur ['itl̥ˌvaihtʏr] is malevolent. Landvættur ['lantˌvaihtʏr] is one of the four landvættir in Iceland, protecting the country from outside threats.*

A Traveller's Notes on
Hrímlandic Culture

Various sentient aquatic species can be found throughout the world, several within the vast reaches of the Commonwealth. Hrímland's marbendlar are known for their industry and trade – renowned for their cunning in negotiations.

History

Manuscripts reclaimed from Hrímland (where they were rotting away in terrible storage conditions, being used for shoe- or pattern-making – or worse, eaten) tell that human settlers arrived on the island approximately one thousand years ago, although scholars differ on the exact dates of migration. Some recent theories claim that settlement happened much earlier than previously thought, but they remain highly controversial. The human settlers were not alone in this endeavour, however, as the ravenlike *náskárar* and the aquatic *marbendlar* competed with them to claim the unpopulated land. A tentative alliance quickly formed with the *marbendlar*, who live in bodies of water and were quite amicable to trading and negotiating fishing rights (with only minor conflicts), but the *náskárar* proved to be a constant thorn in our human ancestors' sides.

It cannot be a mere coincidence that this migration happened in the same timeframe simultaneously between these very different peoples. Thaumaturgic geohistorians believe that an ebb in the torrent of sorcerous energies happened at around this time in Hrímland, making the land much safer for settlement than before. No sentient beings are native to the island, although some scholars speculate that some ancient race might have inhabited the island in prehistoric times. At this moment of writing there is only speculation on the origin of the sorcerous energies of Hrímland, but many scientists research the workings of this arcane natural force, so that future ebbs and flows in its generation can be accurately predicted or divined.

Since settlement the peoples of this desolate island have strived to survive in this harsh, sorcerous landscape. Centuries of shortage, famine, plague, along with geological and sorcerous calamities, combined with their isolation, have deprived the Hrímlanders of the uplifting spirit of cultural advances and rendered their national character opportunistic, short-sighted and hard-working.

Today, Hrímland enjoys a secure place as a colony of the Kalmar Commonwealth. The location of the island is most benefactory for naval domination of the North Atlantean Ocean, as well as harnessing the raw potential of the sorcerous energies so wildly rampant on the island. Thus, Hrímland contributes to the betterment and security of the Commonwealth, which in turn protects its citizens and spends considerable resources in improving its infrastructure.

Kalmar introduced modern railway systems to the capital of Reykjavík, as well as constructed fortified walls around the city, to protect it from both invader and malevolent beings from the sorcerous wilderness. Kalmar also assisted in establishing the company *Innréttingarnar*, led by fine local luminaries and entrepreneurs, to further build up and strengthen the country's infrastructure and industry.

The island is classified as one *stiftamt*, governed by a single *stiftamtmaður* who serves as the King's substitute in all matters pertaining to ruling and lawmaking. *Lögrétta* acts as the nation's parliament with the *stiftamtmaður* at its head, the *goðar* serving as elected parliament members. Local and mainland governance intersect often, such as with the police force and the Directorate of Immigration. Count Frederik Ditlev Trampe has been appointed as *stiftamtmaður* for more than a decade now, leading revolutionary projects such as building the thaumaturgical power plant and the miraculous flying fortress.

Culture

The Commonwealth in its vastness encompasses a seemingly endless variety of peoples and cultures. Remote Hrímland is not exempt from hosting a number of non-human peoples. We strive to bring the light of civilization and order to these wild, untamed lands, with varying results. It remains to be seen whether Hrímland can transform into a haven of civilization on the distant shores of the north.

When the Crown came to the shores of Hrímland, its people still were heathen, worshipping natural spirits and beings referred to as *vættir*. The four *landvættir*, each a lord of their own quadrant of the country, were revered above all other *vættir* in the country. This practice was quickly outlawed and many shrines and sites of worship were torn down or ruined, replaced with the magnificent churches of the Almighty. Now, Hrímlanders worship the divine lineage of King Haraldur I, through which the kings of old and the grace of the Almighty itself channel their holy powers. May their blessed rule be everlasting.

Huldufólk:

A traveller in Hrímland will be sure to encounter one of the *huldufólk*, a fallen people exiled from their once glorious world, a living reminder of the hubris of a once mighty civilization. Although largely forgotten on the mainland, one might still recall old folktales or nursery rhymes referring to these cruel people, who hunted and feasted upon unwary humans for untold centuries. Ancient sources indicate that they were clad in gold-woven robes and dresses, manifesting from thin air. They likely utilised a network of interdimensional tunnels to invade our world, since lost to time. They saw humans as a lesser species, game to be hunted for amusement, and lured them into their wicked realm to feast upon their memories until nothing remained but an empty husk. When their world ended, it was in a swift and ruthless manner. One only hopes that it was the divine work of the Almighty that saw fit to finally smite them down for their endless sin and depravity, but it is just as likely that their own hubris and lust for power became their unmaking.

The *huldufólk* fled their apocalypse to our world, where swift retribution awaited the fallen royalty – except in remote Hrímland, where they hid and endured, likely due to the low population being unable to overpower them, relatively unarmed and unprepared as they were. The calamity caused rifts in dimensional space, and is believed to be the source of many anomalies of that nature. Dimensional anomalies are more common in Hrímland than elsewhere, sometimes even spawning entire pocket dimensions, although sources on this are vague and unverified.

Since then, the *huldufólk* have become very much part of the Hrímlandic nation, although integration is sporadic through the country. In Reykjavík, the settlement of Huldufjörður was strategically placed outside the city walls, to ensure the safety of Kalmar's citizens.

Beware these manipulative beings, who can and will use their cursed gifts to read your emotions like an open book – and rumours say that some still keep to the old ways, indulging in their sacrilegious feasting on minds and memories.

Marbendlar:

Another commonly encountered species is the aquatic *marbendlar*, which have their cousins in the Atlantean Ocean and the great rivers and lakes of the mainland. The fish-folk might be hideous to the virtuous traveller, unaccustomed to their unblinking, piscine eyes – but worry not. The *marbendlar* are industrious craftsmen and merchants, and their abilities can be used for the betterment of the people of Kalmar. Using their tradition of sorcery, honed to perfection over untold millennia, the *marbendlar* craft their cities and underwater districts from coral. The coral spires emitting from the great lake of Þingvellir is a sight many a visitor travels to witness, whose lustruous, cultivated pearls and delicate crafts are plentiful and coveted throughout the world. One Traat'úrrk has led the High Council for years now, after having played an instrumental part in settling the fishing zone disputes known as the Cod Wars. Through his guidance, the Coral Spires have worked with the Kalmar government to ensure that trade between the lakes and Reykjavík flourishes, further boosting the trade and security of Kalmar and its peoples.

Náskárar:

Last but not least are the cruel raven-folk, called Corvians by some Kalmar academics, but known simply as *náskárar* in the untamed north. These violent predators have fought with human settlers for territory since the Age of Settlement. Most notable in the Hrímlandic Sagas is the story of Raven-Flóki Vilgerðarson's settlement, credited with finding the island after being led there by ravens. He battled famously with the merciless Grímuskelfir, leader of the tribe Entrails-swelling-from-a-bloated-carcass. Raven-Flóki eventually drove the *náskárar* away from his lands in a tragic, pyrrhic victory, now legendary amongst Hrímlanders as proof that wars against the *náskárar* never pay off.

With the Kalmar Commonwealth having taken this remote island under its protective wing, a tense stalemate with the many tribes of *náskárar* has finally secured peace for decades. Each tribe claims its own territory, regardless of the laws of other species inhabiting the area, and they frequently feud with each other over matters of honour (warped as their sense of good and evil might be) and dominance. Each tribe has a strict hierarchy, with many ironed warriors in their ranks.

The most infamous tribes of the Greater Reykjavík Area are 'Those-who-pluck-the-eyes-of-the-ram' and 'Bare-bones-in-an-empty-ravine' (the names in the original *skramsl*, tongue of the *náskárar*, are quite unpronounceable), commonly referred to as the Ram Eaters and Bare Bones. Throughout the country many tribes vie for dominance in a seemingly endless struggle, oftentimes catching ground-dwellers in the crossfire. Many facets of their culture remain obfuscated to outsiders (and good riddance in this scholar's opinion). The *náskárar* care naught for our laws and morality, often resorting to bloodshed and violence at the slightest provocation. Indeed, sources say (who survived such a close encounter) that human bones adorn their persons as trophies, among other sentient races. Beware these cruel folk, traveller, and stay well from their roosts, easily identified at a distance by the scores of dark shadows circling in the sky.

The Supernatural Sciences

Hrímland is a cursed land, made nearly uninhabitable by a corrupting torrent of sorcerous energies emitting from the land itself, like toxic smoke and melted lava. Called *seiðmagn* in the Hrímlandic, this sorcerous energy is immensely scarce in the entire Commonwealth, but here it is so condensed and unruly that it spells the bane of every living being in its proximity. Indeed, death might seem an acceptable option compared to surviving the corrupting forces of *seiðmagn*. A few places, notably by the coastline, are habitable, and it is here that the scientists of the Commonwealth seek to tame this arcane storm.

The scientific progress of these last few decades has given Kalmar the capacity to build a thaumaturgical power plant, called Perlan – the Pearl – in the heart of the capital city of Reykjavík. Royal magisters, called *seiðskrattar*, so rarely seen here on the mainland and considered nearly mythical, make their pilgrimage to this northern island to learn and practice their arcane craft of *seiður*. Many fall to the overbearing, corrupting forces of the *seiðmagn*, but others endure and work for the betterment of the Crown. Using the supernatural potential of this industrious marvel, the scientists of Kalmar, led by Dr Vésteinn Alrúnarson, have managed to create the means to power the greatest addition to the Kalmar military as of yet – an indomitable flying fortress, host to scores of artillery cannons and swarms of airborne state-of-the-art warmachines. Once this new technology is fully mastered nothing will be able to stand in the way of the Commonwealth to ensure stability and dominance over the entire Atlantean Ocean.

Due to Hrímland's remoteness and close proximity to sorcerous powers, there is a strong but dangerous tradition of practising the arcane. For centuries the Hrímlanders ran an institution of learning, named *Svartiskóli* – the Black School. Today, this relic of superstition and malevolent learning has been transformed to an institute of true higher learning, as part of the University of Hrímland.

Seiður is one of the two departments in the studies of Supernatural Sciences, a methodical and thoroughly modernised method of channeling *seiðmagn* to work wonders. These rigid studies demand a constant source of *seiðmagn*, and so the students mostly remain in Hrímland for the duration of their studies to attain practical mastery of their craft.

The other department is that of *galdur*, which is practiced to a lesser extent in the Commonwealth, although significantly more common in Hrímland. This dangerous practice of magic relies on spoken incantations and incredibly rigid and complex rituals. These practitioners, called *galdramenn*, are strictly forbidden to practice *galdur* without the appropriate education and permissions, and even so it is only ever done under strict and controlled circumstances, due to the risk of transmundane entities possessing the *galdramaður* in question.

The use of *galdur* is uncharacteristically common in this remote land, despite fervent efforts to eradicate centuries of reckless misuse. Indeed, this fell art is widely illegal in the known world. Unlearned and dangerous individuals who use dated, misinterpreted and reckless method of both *galdur* and *seiður* are commonly called *kuklarar* – *kukl* being a catch-all word for this method of unlearned meddling in the arcane and forbidden. It is usually only a matter of time until these short-sighted individuals find themselves falling victim to transmundance influence – a demonic possession. Most often, their raw channeling of *seiðmagn* overpowers them, quickly and ruthlessly undoing the *kuklari* before they can do even more harm to others. A well-suited fate for such malpracticioning, uneducated criminals.

Credits

Alexander Dan Vilhjálmsson and Gollancz would like to thank everyone at Orion who worked on the publication of *Shadows of the Short Days* in the UK.

Editorial
Craig Leyenaar
Brendan Durkin

Copy editor
Steve O'Gorman

Proof reader
Gabriella Nemeth

Audio
Paul Stark
Amber Bates

Contracts
Anne Goddard
Paul Bulos
Jake Alderson

Design
Lucie Stericker
Rabab Adams
Joanna Ridley
Nick May
Clare Sivell
Helen Ewing

Editorial Management
Charlie Panayiotou
Jane Hughes
Alice Davis

Finance
Jennifer Muchan
Jasdip Nandra
Afeera Ahmed
Elizabeth Beaumont
Sue Baker

Marketing
Brittany Sankey

Production
Paul Hussey

Publicity
Stevie Finegan

Sales
Jen Wilson
Esther Waters

Victoria Laws
Rachael Hum
Ellie Kyrke-Smith
Frances Doyle
Georgina Cutler

Operations
Jo Jacobs
Sharon Willis
Lisa Pryde
Lucy Brem